"What are you [...]

"I had to see you. [...]
Could we talk?"

Chase.

Mary felt heat rush to her center. The cowboy standing in front of her set off all kinds of desires with only a look. And yet after all this time, did she know this man?

"I got your letter," he said as he took off his Stetson, turning the brim nervously in his fingers.

"You didn't call or write back."

His gaze locked with hers. "What I wanted to say couldn't be said over the phone, let alone in a letter."

Her heart pounded. *Here it comes.*

There was pain in his gaze. "I've missed you so much. I had to go. Just as I had to come back. I'm so sorry I hurt you." His blue-eyed gaze locked with hers. "I love you. I never stopped loving you."

Wasn't this exactly what she'd dreamed of him saying to her before she'd gotten the call from his fiancée?

Except in the dream she would have been in his arms by now...

B.J. Daniels is a *New York Times* and *USA TODAY* bestselling author. She wrote her first book after a career as an award-winning newspaper journalist and author of thirty-seven published short stories. She lives in Montana with her husband, Parker, and three springer spaniels. When not writing, she quilts, boats and plays tennis. Contact her at bjdaniels.com, on Facebook or on Twitter, @bjdanielsauthor.

Books by B.J. Daniels

Harlequin Intrigue

Cardwell Ranch: Montana Legacy

Steel Resolve

Whitehorse, Montana: The Clementine Sisters

Hard Rustler
Rogue Gunslinger
Rugged Defender

The Montana Cahills

Cowboy's Redemption

Whitehorse, Montana: The McGraw Kidnapping

Dark Horse
Dead Ringer
Rough Rider

HQN Books

Sterling's Montana

Stroke of Luck
Luck of the Draw

Visit the Author Profile page at Harlequin.com.

B.J.
NEW YORK TIMES AND USA TODAY
BESTSELLING AUTHOR
DANIELS

STEEL RESOLVE
&
CRIME SCENE AT
CARDWELL RANCH

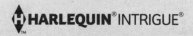

HARLEQUIN® INTRIGUE®

ISBN-13: 978-1-335-01669-0

Steel Resolve & Crime Scene at Cardwell Ranch

Copyright © 2019 by Harlequin Books S.A.

The publisher acknowledges the copyright holder of the individual works as follows:

Steel Resolve
Copyright © 2019 by Barbara Heinlein

Crime Scene at Cardwell Ranch
Copyright © 2006 by Barbara Heinlein

Recycling programs for this product may not exist in your area.

Printed in U.S.A.

www.Harlequin.com

CONTENTS

This one is for Terry Scones, who always brightens my day. I laugh when I recall a quilt shop hop we made across Montana. She was the navigator when my GPS system tried to send us through a barn.

STEEL RESOLVE

Chapter One

The moment Fiona found the letter in the bottom of Chase's sock drawer, she knew it was bad news. Fear squeezed the breath from her as her heart beat so hard against her rib cage that she thought she would pass out. Grabbing the bureau for support, she told herself it might not be what she thought it was.

But the envelope was a pale lavender, and the handwriting was distinctly female. Worse, Chase had kept the letter a secret. Why else would it be hidden under his socks? He hadn't wanted her to see it because it was from that other woman.

Now she wished she hadn't been snooping around. She'd let herself into his house with the extra key she'd had made. She'd felt him pulling away from her the past few weeks. Having been here so many times before, she was determined that this one wasn't going to break her heart. Nor was she going to let another woman take him from her. That's why she had to find out why he hadn't called, why he wasn't returning her messages, why he was avoiding her.

They'd had fun the night they were together. She'd felt as if they had something special, although she knew the next morning that he was feeling guilty. He'd said he didn't want to lead her on. He'd told her that there was some woman back home he was still in love with. He'd said their night together was a mistake. But he was wrong, and she was determined to convince him of it.

What made it so hard was that Chase was a genuinely nice guy. You didn't let a man like that get away. The other woman had. Fiona wasn't going to make that mistake even though he'd been trying to push her away since that night. But he had no idea how determined she could be, determined enough for both of them that this wasn't over by a long shot.

It wasn't the first time she'd let herself into his apartment when he was at work. The other time, he'd caught her and she'd had to make up some story about the building manager letting her in so she could look for her lost earring.

She'd snooped around his house the first night they'd met—the same night she'd found his extra apartment key and had taken it to have her own key made in case she ever needed to come back when Chase wasn't home.

The letter hadn't been in his sock drawer that time.

That meant he'd received it since then. Hadn't she known he was hiding something from her? Why else would he put this letter in a drawer instead of leaving it out along with the bills he'd casually dropped on the table by the front door?

Because the letter was important to him, which meant that she had no choice but to read it.

Her heart compressed into a hard knot as she carefully lifted out the envelope. The handwriting made her pulse begin to roar in her ears. The woman's handwriting was very neat, very precise. She hated her immediately. The return address confirmed it. The letter was from the woman back in Montana that Chase had told her he was still in love with.

Mary Cardwell Savage, the woman who'd broken Chase's heart and one of the reasons that the cowboy had ended up in Arizona. Her friend Patty told her all about him. Chase worked for her husband, Rick. That's how she and Chase had met, at a party at their house.

What struck her now was the date on the postmark. Her vision blurred for a moment. *Two weeks ago?* Anger flared inside her again. That was right after their night together. About the same time that he'd gotten busy and didn't have time, he said, to date or even talk. What had this woman said in her letter? Whatever it was, Fiona knew it was the cause of the problem with her and Chase.

Her fingers trembled as she carefully opened the envelope flap and slipped out the folded sheet of pale lavender paper. The color alone made her sick to her stomach. She sniffed it, half expecting to smell the woman's perfume.

There was only a faint scent, just enough to be disturbing. She listened for a moment, afraid Chase might come home early and catch her again. He'd been angry the last time. He would be even more furious if he caught her reading the letter he'd obviously hidden from her.

Unfolding the sheet of paper she tried to brace herself. She felt as if her entire future hung on what was inside this envelope.

Her throat closed as she read the words, devouring them as quickly as her gaze could take them in. After only a few sentences, she let her gaze drop to the bottom line, her heart dropping with it: *I'll always love you, Mary.*

This was the woman Chase said he was still in love with. She'd broken up with him and now she wanted him back? Who did this Mary Savage of Big Sky, Montana, think she was? Fury churned inside Fiona as she quickly read all the way through the letter, the words breaking her heart and filling her with an all-consuming rage.

Mary Savage had apparently pretended that she was only writing to Chase to let him know that some friend of his mother's had dropped by with a package for him. If he confirmed his address, she'd be happy to send the package if he was interested.

But after that, the letter had gotten personal. Fiona stared at the words, fury warring with heartbreaking pain. The package was clearly only a ruse for the rest of the letter, which was a sickening attempt to lure him back. This woman was still in love with Chase. It made her sick to read the words that were such an obvious effort to remind him of their love, first love, and all that included. This woman had history with Chase. She missed him and regretted the way they'd left things. The woman had even included her phone number. In case he'd forgotten it?

Had Chase called her? The thought sent a wave of nausea through her, followed quickly by growing vehemence. She couldn't believe this. *This woman was not taking Chase away from her!* She wouldn't allow it. She and Chase had only gotten started, but Fiona knew that he was perfect for her and she for him. If anyone could help him get over this other woman, it was her. Chase was hers now. She would just have to make him see that.

Fiona tried to calm herself. The worst thing she could do was to confront Chase and demand to know why he had kept this from her. She didn't need him to remind her that they didn't have "that kind" of relationship as he had the other times. Not to mention how strained things had been between them lately. She'd felt him pulling away and had called and stopped by at every opportunity, afraid she was losing him.

And now she knew why. If the woman had been in Arizona, she would have gone to her house and— Deep breaths, she told herself. She had to calm down. She had to remember what had happened the last time. She'd almost ended up in jail.

Taking deep breaths, she reminded herself that this woman was no threat. Mary Cardwell Savage wasn't in Arizona. She lived in Montana, hundreds of miles away.

But that argument did nothing to relieve her wrath or her growing apprehension. Chase hadn't just kept the letter. He'd *hidden* it. His little *secret*. And worse, he was avoiding her, trying to give her the brush-off. She felt herself hyperventilating.

She knew she had to stop this. She thought of how good things had been between her and Chase that first night. The cowboy was so incredibly sexy, and he'd remarked how lovely she looked in her tailored suit and heels. He'd complimented her long blond hair as he unpinned it and let it fall around her shoulders. When he'd looked into her green eyes, she hadn't needed him to tell her that he loved her. She had seen it.

The memory made her smile. And he'd enjoyed what she had waiting for him underneath that suit—just as she knew he would. They'd both been a little drunk that night. She'd had to make all the moves, but she hadn't minded.

Not that she would ever admit it to him, but she'd set her sights on him the moment she'd seen him at the party. There was something about him that had drawn her. A vulnerability she recognized. He'd been hurt before. So had she, too many times to count. She'd told herself that the handsome cowboy didn't know just how perfect he was, perfect for her.

Fiona hadn't exactly thrown herself at him. She'd just been determined to make him forget that other woman by making herself indispensable. She'd brought over dinner the next night. He'd been too polite to turn her away. She'd come up with things they could do together: baseball games, picnics, movies. But the harder she'd tried, the more he'd made excuses for why he couldn't go with her.

She stared down at the letter still in her hands, wanting to rip it to shreds, to tear this woman's eyes out, to—

Suddenly she froze. Was that the door of the apartment opening? It was. Just as she'd feared, Chase had come home early.

At the sound of the door closing and locking, she hurriedly refolded the letter, slipped it back into the envelope and shoved it under his socks. She was trapped. There was no way to get out of the apartment without him seeing her. He was going to be upset with her. But the one thing she couldn't let Chase know was that she'd found and read the letter. She couldn't give him an excuse to break things off indefinitely, even though she knew he'd been trying to do just that for the past couple of weeks—ever since he'd gotten that letter.

She hurried to the bedroom door, but hesitated.

Maybe she should get naked and let him find her lying on his bed. She wasn't sure she could pull that off right now. Standing there, she tried to swallow back the anger, the hurt, the fear. She couldn't let him know what she was feeling—let alone how desperate she felt. But as she heard him coming up the stairs, she had a terrifying thought.

What if she'd put the letter back in the drawer wrong? Had she seen the woman's handwriting on the envelope? Wasn't that why she'd felt such a jolt? Or was it just seeing the pale lavender paper of the envelope in his sock drawer that had made her realize what it was?

She couldn't remember.

But would Chase remember how he'd left it and know that she'd seen it? Know that if she'd found it, she would read it?

She glanced back and saw that she hadn't closed the top dresser drawer all the way. Hurrying back over to it, she shut the drawer as quietly as possible and was about to turn when she heard him in the doorway.

"Fiona? What the hell?" He looked startled at first when he saw her, and then shock quickly turned to anger.

She could see that she'd scared him. He'd scared her too. Her heart was a drum in her chest. She was clearly rattled. She could feel the fine mist of perspiration on her upper lip. With one look, he would know something was wrong.

But how could she not be upset? The man she'd planned to marry had kept a letter from his ex a secret from her. Worse, the woman he'd been pining over when Fiona had met him was still in love with him—and now he knew it. Hiding the letter proved that he was at least thinking about Mary Cardwell Savage.

"What are you doing here?" Chase demanded, glancing around as if the answer was in the room. "How the hell did you get in *this* time?"

She tried to cover, letting out an embarrassed laugh. "You startled me. I was looking for my favorite lipstick. I thought I might have left it here."

He shook his head, raking a hand through his hair. "You have to stop this. I told you last time. Fiona—" His blue gaze swept past her to light on the chest of drawers.

Any question as to how he felt about the letter was quickly answered by his protective glance toward the top bureau drawer and the letter from his first love, the young woman who'd broken his tender heart, the woman he was still in love with.

Her own heart broke, shattering like a glass thrown against a wall. She wanted to kill Mary Cardwell Savage.

"Your lipstick?" He shook his head. "Again, how did you get in here?"

"You forgot to lock your door. I came by hoping to catch your building manager so he could let me in again—"

"Fiona, stop lying. I talked to him after the last time. He didn't let you in." The big cowboy held out his hand. "Give it to me."

She pretended not to know what he was talking about, blinking her big green eyes at him in the best innocent look she could muster. She couldn't lose this man. She wouldn't. She did the only thing she could. She reached into her pocket and pulled out the key. "I can explain."

"No need," he said as he took the key.

She felt real tears of remorse fill her eyes. But she saw that he was no longer affected by her tears. She stepped to him to put her arms around his neck and pulled him down for a kiss. Maybe if she could draw him toward the bed…

"Fiona, stop." He grabbed her wrists and pulled them from around his neck. *"Stop!"*

She stared at him, feeling the happy life she'd planned crumbling under her feet.

He groaned and shook his head. "You need to leave."

"Sure," she said and, trying to get control of her emotions, started to step past him. "Just let me look in one more place for my lipstick. I know I had it—"

"No," he said, blocking her way. "Your lipstick isn't here and we both know it. Just like your phone wasn't here the last time you stopped by. This has to stop. I don't want to see you again."

"You don't mean that." Her voice broke. "Is this about the letter from that bitch who dumped you?"

His gaze shot to the bureau again. She watched his expression change from frustrated to furious. "You've been going through my things?"

"I told you, I was looking for my lipstick. I'm sorry I found the letter. You hadn't called, and I thought maybe it was because of the letter."

He sighed, and when he spoke it was as if he was talking to a small unruly child. "Fiona, I told you from the first night we met that I wasn't ready for another relationship. You caught me at a weak moment, otherwise nothing would have happened between the two of us. I'd had too much to drink, and my boss's wife insisted that I let you drive me back to my apartment."

He groaned. "I'm not trying to make excuses for what happened. We are both adults. But I was honest with you." He looked pained, his blue eyes dark. "I'm sorry if you thought that that night was more than it was. But now you have to leave and not come back."

"We can't be over! You have to give me another chance." She'd heard the words before from other men, more times than she wanted to remember. "I'm sorry. I was wrong to come here when you weren't home. I won't do anything like this again. I promise."

"Stop!" he snapped. "You're not listening. Look," he said, lowering his voice. "You might as well know that I'm leaving at the end of the week. My job here is over."

"Leaving?" This couldn't be happening. "Where are you going?" she cried, and felt her eyes widen in alarm. "You're going back to Montana. *Back to her.* Mary Cardwell Savage." She spit out the words as if they were stones that had been lodged in her throat.

He shook his head. "I told you the night we met that there was no chance of me falling for another woman because I was still in love with someone else."

She sneered at him. "She broke your heart. She'll do it again. Don't let her. She's nobody." She took a step toward him. "I can make you happy if you'll just give me a chance."

"Fiona, please go before either of us says something we'll regret," Chase said in a tone she'd never heard from him before. He was shutting her out. For good.

If he would only let her kiss him… She reached for him, thinking she could make him remember what they had together, but he pushed her back.

"Don't." He was shaking his head, looking at her as if horrified by her. There was anguish in his gaze. But there was also pity and disgust. That too she'd seen before. She felt a dark shell close around her heart.

"You'll be sorry," she said, feeling crushed but at the same time infused with a cold, murderous fury.

"I should have never have let this happen," Chase was saying. "This is all my fault. I'm so sorry."

Oh, he didn't know sorry, but he would soon enough. He would rue this day. And if he thought he'd seen the last of her, he was in for a surprise. That Montana hayseed would have Chase over her dead body.

Chapter Two

"I feel terrible that I didn't warn you about Fiona," his boss said on Chase's last day of work. Rick had insisted on buying him a beer after quitting time.

Now in the cool dark of the bar, Chase looked at the man and said, "So she's done this before?"

Rick sighed. "She gets attached if a man pays any attention to her in the least and can't let go, but don't worry, she'll meet some other guy and get crazy over him. It's a pattern with her. She and my wife went to high school together. Patty feels sorry for her and keeps hoping she'll meet someone and settle down."

Chase shook his head, remembering his first impression of the woman. Fiona had seemed so together, so...normal. She sold real estate, dressed like a polished professional and acted like one. She'd come up to him at a barbecue at Rick's house. Chase hadn't wanted to go, but his boss had insisted, saying it would do him good to get out more.

He'd just lost his mother. His mother, Muriel, had been sick for some time. It was one of the reasons he'd come to Arizona in the first place. The other was that he knew he could find work here as a carpenter. Muriel had made him promise that when she died, he would take her ashes back to Montana. He'd been with her at the end, hoping that she would finally tell him the one thing she'd kept from him all these years. But she hadn't. She'd taken her secret to the grave and left him with more questions than answers—and an urn full of her ashes.

"You need to get out occasionally," Rick had said when Chase left work to go pick up the urn from the mortuary. It was in a velvet bag. He'd stuffed it behind the seat of his pickup on the way to the barbecue.

"All you do is work, then hide out in your apartment not to be seen again until you do the same thing the next day," Rick had argued. "You might just have fun and I cook damned good barbecue. Come on, it's just a few friends."

He'd gone, planning not to stay longer than it took to drink a couple of beers and have some barbecued ribs. He'd been on his second beer when he'd seen her. Fiona stood out among the working-class men and women at the party because she'd come straight from her job at a local real estate company.

She wore high heels that made her long legs look even longer. Her curvaceous body was molded into a dark suit with a white blouse and gold jewelry. Her long blond hair was pulled up, accentuating her tanned throat against the white of her blouse.

He'd become intensely aware of how long it had been since he'd felt anything but anguish over his breakup with Mary and his mother's sickness, and the secret that she'd taken with her.

"Fiona Barkley," she'd said, extending her hand.

Her hand had been cool and dry, her grip strong. "Chase Steele."

She'd chuckled, her green eyes sparking with humor. "For real? A cowboy named Chase Steele?"

"My father was an extra in a bunch of Western movies," he lied since he had no idea who his father had been.

She cocked a brow at him. "Really?"

He shook his head. "I grew up on a ranch in Montana." He shrugged. "Cowboying is in my blood."

Fiona had taken his almost empty beer can from him and handed him her untouched drink. "Try that. I can tell that you need it." The drink had been strong and buzzed through his bloodstream.

Normally she wasn't the type of woman he gravitated toward. But she was so different from Mary, and it had been so long since he'd even thought about another woman. The party atmosphere, the urn behind his pickup seat and the drinks Fiona kept plying him with added to his what-the-hell attitude that night.

"How long have you two been dating?" Rick asked now in the cool dark of the bar.

"We never dated. I told her that first night that I was in love with someone else. But I made the mistake of sleeping with her. Sleeping with anyone given the way I feel about the woman back home was a mistake."

"So you told Fiona there was another woman." His boss groaned. "That explains a lot. Fiona now sees it as a competition between her and the other woman. She won't give up. She hates losing. It's what makes her such a great Realtor."

"Well, it's all moot now since I'm leaving for Montana."

Rick didn't look convinced that it would be that easy. "Does she know?"

He nodded.

"Well, hopefully you'll get out of town without any trouble."

"Thanks a lot."

"Sorry, but according to Patty, when Fiona feels the man pulling away… Well, it makes her a little…crazy."

Chase shook his head. "This just keeps getting better and better." He picked up his beer, drained it and got to his feet. "I'm going home to pack. The sooner I get out of town the better."

"I wish I could talk you out of leaving," Rick said. "You're one of the best finish carpenters I've had in a long time. I hope you're not leaving because of Fiona. Seriously, she'll latch on to someone else. I wouldn't worry about it. It's just Fiona being Fiona. Unless you're going back to this woman you're in love with?"

He laughed. "If only it were that easy. She's the one who broke it off with me." He liked Rick. But the man hadn't warned him about Fiona, and if Rick mentioned to Patty who mentioned to Fiona… He knew he was being overly cautious. Fiona wouldn't follow him all the way to Montana. She had a job, a condo, a life here. But still, he found himself saying, "Not sure what I'm doing. Might stop off in Colorado for a while."

"Well, good luck. And again, sorry about Fiona."

As he left the bar, he thought about Mary and the letter he'd hidden in his sock drawer with her phone number. He'd thought about calling her to let her know he was headed home. He was also curious about the package she'd said a friend of his mother had left for him.

Since getting the letter, he'd thought about calling dozens of times. But what he had to say, he couldn't in a phone call. He had to see Mary. Now that he was leaving, he couldn't wait to hit the road.

MARY CARDWELL SAVAGE reined in her horse to look out at the canyon below her. The Gallatin River wound through rugged cliffs and stands of pines, the water running clear over the colored rocks as pale green aspen leaves winked from the shore. Beyond the river and the trees, she could make out the resort town that had sprouted up across the canyon. She breathed in the cool air rich with the scent of pine and the crisp cool air rising off the water.

Big Sky, Montana, had changed so much in her lifetime and even more in her mother's. Dana Cardwell Savage had seen the real changes after the ski resort had been built at the foot of Lone Peak. Big Sky had gone from a ranching community to a resort area, and finally to a town with a whole lot of housing developments and businesses rising to the community's growing needs.

The growth had meant more work for her father, Marshal Hud Savage. He'd been threatening to retire since he said he no longer recognized the canyon community anymore. More deputies had to be hired each year because the area was experiencing more crime.

Just the thought of the newest deputy who'd been hired made her smile a little. Dillon Ramsey was the kind of man a woman noticed—even one who had given her heart away when she was fifteen and had never gotten it back.

Dillon, with his dark wavy hair and midnight black eyes, had asked her out, and she'd said she'd think about it. If her best friend Kara had been around, she would have thought Mary had lost her mind. Anyone who saw

Dillon knew two things about him. He was a hunk, and he was dangerous to the local female population.

Since telling him she'd think about it, she had been mentally kicking herself. Had she really been sitting around waiting to hear from Chase? What was wrong with her? It had been weeks. When she'd broken it off and sent him packing, she hadn't been sitting around moping over him. Not really. She'd been busy starting a career, making a life for herself. So what had made her write that stupid letter?

Wasn't it obvious that if he'd gotten her letter, he should have called by now? Since the letter hadn't come back, she had to assume that it had arrived just fine. The fact that he hadn't called or written her back meant that he wasn't interested. He also must not be interested in the package his mother's friend had left for him either. It was high time to forget about that cowboy, and why not do it with Dillon Ramsey?

Because she couldn't quit thinking about Chase and hadn't been able to since she'd first laid eyes on him when they were both fifteen. They'd been inseparable all through high school and college. Four years ago he'd told her he was going to have to leave. They'd both been twenty-four, too young to settle down, according to her father and Chase had agreed. He needed to go find himself since not knowing who his father was still haunted him.

It had broken her heart when he'd left her—and Montana. She'd dated little after he left town. Mostly because she'd found herself comparing the men she had dated to Chase. At least with Dillon, she sensed a wild, dangerousness in him that appealed to her right now.

Her father hadn't liked hearing that Dillon had asked

her out. "I wish you'd reconsider," he'd said when she'd stopped by Cardwell Ranch where she'd grown up. She'd bought her own place in Meadow Village closer to the center of town, and made the first floor into her office. On the third floor was her apartment where she lived. The second floor had been made into one-bed-room apartments that she rented.

But she still spent a lot of time on the ranch because that's where her heart was—her family, her horses and her love for the land. She hadn't even gone far away to college—just forty miles to Montana State University in Bozeman. She couldn't be far from Cardwell Ranch and couldn't imagine that she ever would. She was her mother's daughter, she thought. Cardwell Ranch was her legacy.

Dana Cardwell had fought for this ranch years ago when her brothers and sister had wanted to sell it and split the money after their mother died. Dana couldn't bear to part with the family ranch. Fortunately, her grandmother, Mary Cardwell, had left Dana the ranch in her last will, knowing Dana would keep the place in the family always.

Ranching had been in her grandmother's blood, the woman Mary had been named after. Just as it was in Dana's and now Mary's. Chase hadn't understood why she couldn't walk away from this legacy that the women in her family had fought so hard for.

But while her mother was a hands-on ranch woman, Mary liked working behind the scenes. She'd taken over the accounting part of running the ranch so her mother could enjoy what she loved—being on the back of a horse.

"What is wrong with Dillon Ramsey?" Dana Cardwell

Savage had asked her husband after Mary had told them that the deputy had asked her out.

"He's new and, if you must know, there's something troublesome about him that I haven't been able to put my finger on yet," Hud had said.

Mary had laughed. She knew exactly what bothered her father about Dillon—the same thing that attracted her to the young cocky deputy. If she couldn't have Chase, then why not take a walk on the wild side for once?

She had just finished unsaddling her horse and was headed for the main house when her cell phone rang, startling her. Her pulse jumped. She dug the phone out and looked at the screen, her heart in her throat. It was a long-distance number and not one she recognized. Chase?

Sure took him long enough to finally call, she thought, and instantly found herself making excuses for him. Maybe he was working away from cell phone coverage. It happened all the time in Montana. Why not in Arizona? Or maybe her letter had to chase him down, and he'd just now gotten it and called the moment he read it.

It rang a second time. She swallowed the lump in her throat. She couldn't believe how nervous she was. Silly goose, she thought. It's probably not Chase at all but some telemarketer calling to try to sell her something.

She answered on the third ring. "Hello?" Her voice cracked.

Silence, then a female voice. "Mary Cardwell Savage?" The voice was hard and crisp like a fall apple, the words bitten off.

"Yes?" she asked, disappointed. She'd gotten her

hopes up that it was Chase, with whatever excuse he had for not calling sooner. It wouldn't matter as long as he'd called to say that he felt the same way she did and always had. But she'd been right. It was just some telemarketer. "I'm sorry, but whatever you're selling, I'm not inter—"

"I read your letter you sent Chase."

Her breath caught as her heart missed a beat. She told herself that she'd heard wrong. "I beg your pardon?"

"Leave my fiancé alone. Don't write him. Don't call him. Just leave him the hell alone."

She tried to swallow around the bitter taste in her mouth. "Who is this?" Her voice sounded breathy with fear.

"The woman who's going to marry Chase Steele. If you ever contact him again—"

Mary disconnected, her fingers trembling as she dropped the phone into her jacket pocket as if it had scorched her skin. The woman's harsh low voice was still in her ears, furious and threatening. Whoever she was, she'd read the letter. No wonder Chase hadn't written or called. But why hadn't he? Had he shown the letter to his fiancée? Torn it up? Kept it so she found it? Did it matter? His fiancée had read the letter and was furious, and Mary couldn't blame her.

She buried her face in her hands. Chase had gone off to find himself. Apparently he'd succeeded in finding a fiancée as well. Tears burned her eyes. Chase was engaged and getting married. Could she be a bigger fool? Chase had moved on, and he hadn't even had the guts to call and tell her.

Angrily, Mary wiped at her tears as she recalled the woman's words and the anger she'd heard in them. She shuddered, regretting more than ever that stupid letter she'd written. The heat of humiliation and mortification burned her cheeks. If only she hadn't poured her heart out to him. If only she had just written him about the package and left it at that. If only...

Unfortunately, she'd been feeling nostalgic the night she wrote that letter. Her mare was about to give birth so she was staying the night at the ranch in her old room. She'd come in from the barn late that night, and had seen the package she'd promised to let Chase know about. Not far into the letter, she'd become sad and regretful. Filled with memories of the two of them growing up together on the ranch from the age of fifteen, she'd decide to call him only to find that his number was no longer in service. Then she'd tried to find him on social media. No luck. It was as if he'd dropped off the face of the earth. Had something happened to him?

Worried, she'd gone online and found an address for him but no phone number. In retrospect, she should never have written the letter—not in the mood she'd been in. What she hated most since he hadn't answered her letter or called, was that she had written how much she missed him and how she'd never gotten over him and how she regretted their breakup.

She'd stuffed the letter into the envelope addressed to him and, wiping her tears, had left it on her desk in her old room at the ranch as she climbed into bed. The next morning before daylight her mother had called up to her room to say that the mare had gone into labor. Forgetting all about the letter, she'd been so excited about the new foal that she'd put everything else out of her mind. By the time she remembered the letter, it was gone. Her aunt Stacy had seen it, put a stamp on the envelope and mailed it for her.

At first, Mary had been in a panic, expecting Chase to call as soon as he received the letter. She'd played the conversation in her head every way she thought possible, all but one of them humiliating. As days passed, she'd still held out hope. Now after more than two weeks and that horrible phone call, she knew it was really over and she had to accept it.

Still her heart ached. Chase had been her first love. Did anyone ever get over their first love? He had obviously moved on. Mary took another deep breath and tried to put it out of her mind. She loved summer here in the canyon. The temperature was perfect—never too cold or too hot. A warm breeze swayed the pine boughs and keeled over the tall grass in the pasture nearby. Closer a horse whinnied from the corral next to the barn as a hawk made a slow lazy circle in the clear blue overhead.

Days like this she couldn't imagine living anywhere else. She took another deep breath. She needed to get back to her office. She had work to do. Along with doing the ranch books for Cardwell Ranch, she had taken on work from other ranches in the canyon and built a lucrative business.

She would get over Chase or die trying, she told herself. As she straightened her back, her tears dried, and she walked toward her SUV. She'd give Deputy Dillon Ramsey a call. It was time she moved on. Like falling off a horse, she was ready to saddle up again. Forgetting Chase wouldn't be easy, but if anyone could help the process, she figured Dillon Ramsey was the man to do it.

Chapter Three

Chase was carrying the last of his things out to his pickup when he saw Fiona drive up. He swore under his breath. He'd hoped to leave without a scene. Actually, he'd been surprised that she hadn't come by sooner. As she was friends with Rick's wife, Patty, Chase was pretty sure she had intel into how the packing and leaving had been going.

He braced himself as he walked to his pickup and put the final box into the back. He heard Fiona get out of her car and walk toward him. He figured it could go several ways. She would try seduction or tears or raging fury, or a combination of all three.

Hands deep in the pockets of her jacket as she approached, she gave him a shy smile. It was that smile that had appealed to him that first night. He'd been vulnerable, and he suspected she'd known it. Did she think that smile would work again?

He felt guilty for even thinking that she was so calculating and yet he'd seen the way she'd worked him. "Fiona, I don't want any trouble."

"Trouble?" She chuckled. "I heard you were moving out today. I only wanted to come say goodbye."

Chase wished that was the extent of it, but he'd come

to know her better than that. "I think we covered good-bye the last time we saw each other."

She ignored that. "I know you're still angry with me—"

"Fiona—"

Tears welled in her green eyes as if she could call them up at a moment's notice. "Chase, at least give me a hug goodbye. Please." Before he could move, she closed the distance between them. As she did, her hands came out of her jacket pockets. The blade of the knife in her right hand caught the light as she started to put her arms around his neck.

As he jerked back, he grabbed her wrist. "What the—" He cursed as he tightened his grip on her wrist holding the knife. She was stronger than she looked. She struggled to stab him as she screamed obscenities at him.

The look in her eyes was almost more frightening than the knife clutched in her fist. He twisted her wrist until she cried out and dropped the weapon. The moment it hit the ground, he let go of her, realizing he was hurting her.

She dived for the knife, but he kicked it away, chasing after it before she could pick it up again. She leaped at him, pounding on his back as she tried to drag him to the ground.

He threw her off. She stumbled and fell to the grass and began to cry hysterically. He stared down at her. Had she really tried to kill him?

"Don't! Don't kill me!" she screamed, raising her hands as if she thought he was going to stab her. He'd forgotten that he'd picked up the knife, but he wasn't threatening her with it.

He didn't understand what was going on until he realized they were no longer alone. Fiona had an audience.

Some of the apartment tenants had come out. One of them, an elderly woman, was fumbling with her phone as if to call the cops.

"Everything is all right," he quickly told the woman.

The older woman looked from Fiona to him and back. Her gaze caught on the knife he was holding at his side.

"There is no reason to call the police," Chase said calmly as he walked to the trash cans lined up along the street, opened one and dropped the knife into the bottom.

"That's my best knife!" Fiona yelled. "You owe me for that."

He saw that the tenant was now staring at Fiona, who was brushing off her jeans as she got to her feet.

"What are you staring at, you old crone? Go back inside before I take that phone away from you and stick it up your—"

"Fiona," Chase said as the woman hurriedly turned and rushed back inside. He shook his head as he gave Fiona a wide berth as he headed toward his apartment to lock up. "Go home before the police come."

"She won't call. She knows I'll come back here if she does."

He hoped Fiona was right about the woman not making the call. Otherwise, he'd be held up making a statement to the police—that's if he didn't end up behind bars. He didn't doubt that Fiona would lie through her teeth about the incident.

"She won't make you happy," Fiona screamed after him as he opened the door to his apartment, keeping an eye on her the whole time. The last thing he wanted was her getting inside. If she didn't have another weapon, he had no doubt she'd find one.

Stopping in the doorway, he looked back at her. Her makeup had run along with her nose. She hadn't bothered to wipe either. She looked small, and for a moment his heart went out to her. What had happened to that professional, together woman he'd met at the party?

"You need to get help, Fi."

She scoffed at that. "You're the one who needs help, Chase."

He stepped inside, closed and locked the door, before sliding the dead bolt. Who's to say she didn't have a half dozen spare keys made. She'd lied about the building manager opening the door for her. She'd lied about a lot of things. He had no idea who Fiona Barkley was. But soon she would be nothing more than a bad memory, he told himself as he finished checking to make sure he hadn't left anything. When he looked out, he saw her drive away.

Only then did he pick up his duffel bag, lock the apartment door behind him and head for his truck, anxious to get on the road to Montana. But as he neared his pickup, he saw what Fiona had left him. On the driver's-side window scrawled crudely in lipstick were the words *You'll regret it*.

That was certainly true. He regretted it already. He wondered what would happen to her and feared for the next man who caught her eye. Maybe the next man would handle it better, he told himself.

Tossing his duffel bag onto the passenger seat, he pulled an old rag from under the seat and wiped off what he could of the lipstick. Then, climbing into this truck, he pointed it toward Montana and Mary, putting Fiona out of his mind.

THERE WERE DAYS when Dana felt all sixty-two of her years. Often when she looked at her twenty-eight-year-old daughter, Mary, she wondered where the years had gone. She felt as if she'd merely blinked and her baby girl had grown into a woman.

Being her first and only daughter, Mary had a special place in her heart. So when Mary hurt, Dana did too. Ever since Chase and Mary had broken up and he'd left town, her daughter had been heartsick, and Dana had had no idea how to help her.

She knew that kind of pain. Hud had broken her heart years ago when they'd disagreed and he'd taken off. But he'd come back, and their love had overcome all the obstacles that had been thrown at them since. She'd hoped that Mary throwing herself into her accounting business would help. But as successful as Mary now was with her business, the building she'd bought, the apartments she'd remodeled and rented, there was a hole in her life—and her heart. A mother could see it.

"Sis, have you heard a word I've said?"

Dana looked from the window where she'd been watching Mary unsaddling her horse to where her brother sat at the kitchen table across from her. "Sorry. Did you just say *cattle thieves*?"

Jordan shook his head at her and smiled. There'd been a time when she and her brother had been at odds over the ranch. Fortunately, those days were long behind them. He'd often said that the smartest thing he'd ever done was to come back here, make peace and help Dana run Cardwell Ranch. She couldn't agree more.

"We lost another three head. Hud blames paleo diets," Jordan said, and picked up one of the chocolate chip cookies Dana had baked that morning.

"How many does this make?" she asked.

"There's at least a dozen gone," her brother said.

She looked to her husband who sat at the head of the table and had also been watching Mary out the window. Hud reached for another cookie. He came home every day for lunch and had for years. Today she'd made sandwiches and baked his favorite cookies.

"They're hitting at night, opening a gate, cutting out only a few at a time and herding them to the road where they have a truck waiting," the marshal said. "They never hit in the same part of any ranch twice, so unless we can predict where they're going to show up next… We aren't the only ones who've had losses."

"We could hire men to ride the fences at night," Jordan said.

"I'll put a deputy or two on the back roads for a couple of nights and see what we come up with," Hud said and, pushing away his plate and getting to his feet, shot Dana a questioning look.

Jordan, apparently recognizing the gesture, also got to his feet and excused himself. As he left, Hud said, "I know something is bothering you, and it isn't rustlers."

She smiled up at him. He knew her so well, her lover, her husband, her best friend. "It's Mary. Stacy told me earlier that she mailed a letter from Mary to Chase a few weeks ago. Mary hasn't heard back."

Hud groaned. "You have any idea what was in the letter?"

"No, but since she's been moping around I'd say she is still obviously in love with him." She shrugged. "I don't think she's ever gotten over him."

Her husband shook his head. "Why didn't we have all boys?"

"Our sons will fall in love one day and will probably have their heartbreaks as well." She had the feeling that Hud hadn't heard the latest. "She's going out with Deputy Dillon Ramsey tonight."

Hud swore and raked a hand through his graying hair. "I shouldn't have mentioned that there was something about him that made me nervous."

She laughed. "If you're that worried about him, then why don't you talk to her?"

Her husband shot her a look that said he knew their stubborn daughter only too well. "Tell her not to do something and damned if she isn't even more bound and determined to do it."

Like he had to tell her that. Mary was just like her mother and grandmother. "It's just a date," Dana said, hoping there wasn't anything to worry about.

Hud grumbled under his breath as he reached for his Stetson. "I have to get back to work." His look softened. "You think she's all right?"

Dana wished she knew. "She will be, given time. I think she needs to get some closure from Chase. His not answering her letter could be what she needed to move on."

"I hope not with Dillon Ramsey."

"Seriously, what is it about him that worries you?" Dana asked.

He frowned. "I can't put my finger on it. I hired him as a favor to his uncle down in Wyoming. Dillon's cocky and opinionated."

Dana laughed. "I used to know a deputy like that."

Hud grinned. "Point taken. He's also still green."

"I don't think that's the part that caught Mary's attention."

Her husband groaned. "I'd like to see her with some-one with both feet firmly planted on the ground."

"You mean someone who isn't in law enforcement. Chase Steele wasn't."

"I liked him well enough," Hud said grudgingly. "But he hadn't sowed his wild oats yet. They were both too young, and he needed to get out of here and get some maturity under his belt, so to speak."

"She wanted him to stay and fight for her. Sound familiar?"

Hud's smile was sad. "Sometimes a man has to go out into the world, grow up, figure some things out." He reached for her hand. "That's what I did when I left. It made me realize what I wanted. You."

She stepped into his arms, leaning into his strength, thankful for the years they'd had together raising a fam-ily on this ranch. "Mary's strong."

"Like her mother."

"She'll be all right," Dana said, hoping it was true.

CHASE WAS DETERMINED to drive as far as he could the first day, needing to put miles behind him. He thought of Fiona and felt sick to his stomach. He kept going over it in his head, trying to understand if he'd done anything to lead her on beyond that one night. He was clear with her that he was not in the market for anything serious. His biggest mistake though was allowing himself a mo-ment of weakness when he'd let himself be seduced.

But before that he'd explained to her that he was in love with someone else. She said she didn't care. That she wasn't looking for a relationship. She'd said that she needed him that night because she'd had a bad day.

Had he really fallen for that? He had. And when she

became obsessed, he'd been shocked and felt sorry for her. Maybe he shouldn't have.

He felt awful, and not even the miles he put behind him made him feel better. He wished he'd never left Montana, but at the time, leaving seemed the only thing to do. He'd worked his way south, taking carpenter jobs, having no idea where he was headed.

When he'd gotten the call from his mother to say she was dying and that she'd needed to see him, he'd quit his job, packed up and headed for Quartsite, Arizona, in hopes that his mother would finally give him the name.

Chase had never known who his father was. It was a secret his mother refused to reveal for reasons of her own. Once in Arizona, though, he'd realized that she planned to take that secret to her grave. On her death bed, she'd begged him to do one thing for her. Would he take her ashes back to Montana and scatter them in the Gallatin Canyon near Big Sky?

"That's where I met your father," she said, her voice weak. "He was the love of my life."

She hadn't given him a name, but at least he knew now that the man had lived in Big Sky at the time of Chase's conception. It wasn't much, but it was better than nothing.

HE WAS IN the middle of nowhere just outside of Searchlight, Nevada, when smoke began to boil out from under the pickup's hood. He started to pull over when the engine made a loud sound and stopped dead. As he rolled to stop, his first thought was: could Fiona have done something to his pickup before he left?

Anger filled him to overflowing. But it was another emotion that scared him. He had a sudden awful feeling that something terrible was going to happen to Mary if he didn't get to Montana. Soon. The feeling was so strong that he thought about leaving his pickup beside the road and thumbing a ride the rest of the way.

Chase tried to tamp down the feeling, telling himself that it was because of Fiona and what she'd done before he'd left when she'd tried to kill him, not to mention what she'd done to his pickup. The engine was shot. He'd have to get a new one and that was going to take a while.

That bad feeling though wouldn't go away. After he called for a tow truck, he dialed the Jensen Ranch, the closest ranch to Mary's. He figured if anyone would know how Mary was doing, it would be Beth Anne Jensen. She answered on the third ring. "It's Chase." He heard the immediate change in her voice and realized she was probably the wrong person to call, but it was too late. Beth Anne had liked him a little too much when he'd worked for her family and it had caused a problem between him and Mary.

"Hey Chase. Are you back in town?"

"No, I was just calling to check on Mary. I was worried about her. I figured you'd know how she's doing. Is everything all right with her?"

Beth Anne's tone changed from sugar to vinegar. "As far as I know everything is just great with her. Is that all you wanted to know?"

This was definitely a mistake. "How are you?"

"I opened my own flower shop. I've been dating a rodeo cowboy. I'm just fine, as if you care." She sighed. "So if you're still hung up on Mary, why haven't you come back?"

Stubbornness. Stupidity. Pride. A combination of all

three. "I just had a sudden bad feeling that she might be in trouble."

Beth Anne laughed. "Could be, now that you mention it. My brother saw her earlier out with some young deputy. Apparently, she's dating him."

"Sounds like she's doing fine then. Thanks. You take care." He swore as he disconnected and put his worry about Mary out of his mind. She should be plenty safe dating a deputy, right? He gave his front tire a kick, then paced as he waited for the tow truck.

IT HAD TAKEN hours before the tow truck had arrived. By then the auto shop was closed. He'd registered at a motel, taken a hot shower and sprawled on the bed, furious with Fiona, but even more so with himself.

He'd known he had a serious problem when he'd seen the smoke roiling out from under the hood. When the engine seized up, he'd known it was blown before he'd climbed out and lifted the hood.

At first, he couldn't understand what had happened. The pickup wasn't brand-new, but it had been in good shape. The first thing he'd checked was the oil. That's when he'd smelled it. Bleach.

The realization had come in a flash. He'd thrown a container of bleach away in his garbage just that morning, along with some other household cleaners that he didn't want to carry all the way back to Montana. He'd seen the bleach bottle when he'd tossed Fiona's knife into one of the trash cans at the curb.

Now, lying on the bed in the motel, Chase swore. He'd left Fiona out there alone with his pickup. He'd thought the only mischief she'd gotten up to was writing on his pickup window with lipstick. He'd underestimated her, and now it was going to cost him dearly. He'd have to have a new engine put in the truck, and that was going to take both money and time.

THREE DAYS LATER, while waiting in Henderson, Nevada for his new engine to be installed, he called Rick.

"Hey, Chase, great to hear from you. How far did you make it? I thought you might have decided to drive straight through all night."

"I broke down near Searchlight."

"Really? Is it serious?"

"I'm afraid so. The engine blew. I suspect Fiona put bleach in the oil."

Rick let out a curse. "That would seize up the engine."

"That's exactly what it did."

"Oh, man I am so sorry. Listen, I am beginning to feel like this is all my fault. Is there anything I can do? Where are you now? I could drive up there, maybe bring one of the big trailers. We could haul your pickup back down here. I know a mechanic—"

"I appreciate it, but I'm getting it fixed here in Henderson. That's not why I called."

"It's funny you should call," Rick said. "I was about to call you, but I kept putting it off hoping to have better news."

His heart began to pound. "What's wrong?"

His former boss let out a dry chuckle. "We're still friends, right?"

"Right. I forgave you for Fiona if that's what you're worried about."

"You might change your mind after you hear what I have to tell you," Rick said. "I didn't want you to hear this on the news." He felt his stomach drop as he waited for the bad news. "Fiona apparently hasn't been at work since before you left. Patty went over to her place. Her car was gone and there was no sign of her. But she'd called Patty the night you left from a bar and was pretty wasted and incoherent. When Patty wasn't able to reach her in the days that followed, she finally went over to her condo. It appeared she hadn't been back for a few days." Chase swore. She wouldn't hurt herself, would she? She'd said he would regret it. He felt a sliver of fear race up his spine. As delusional as the woman was—

Rick cleared his voice. "This morning a fisherman found her car in the Colorado River."

His breath caught in his throat. "Is she…?"

"They're dragging the river for her body, but it's hard to say how far her body might have gone downstream. The river was running pretty high after the big thunderstorm they had up in the mountains a few days ago."

Chase raked a hand through his hair as he paced the floor of his motel room as he'd been doing for days now. "She threatened to do all kinds of things, but I never thought she'd do something like this."

"Before you jump to conclusions, the police think it could have been an accident. Fiona was caught on video leaving the club that night and appeared to be quite inebriated," Rick said. "Look, this isn't your fault. I debated even telling you. Fiona was irrational. My wife said she's feared that the woman's been headed for a violent end for a long time, you know?"

He nodded to himself as he stopped to look out the motel room window at the heat waves rising off desert floor and yearned for Montana. "Still I hate to think she might have done this on purpose because of me."

"She wasn't right in the head. Anyway, it was probably an accident. I'm sorry to call with this kind of news, but I thought you'd want to know. Once your pickup's fixed you'll be heading out and putting all of this behind you. Still thinking about going to Colorado? You know I'd love to have you back."

No reason not to tell him now. "I'm headed home as soon as the pickup's fixed, but thanks again for the offer."

"Home to Montana? You really never got over this woman, huh."

"No, I never did." He realized that when he thought of home, it was Mary he thought of. Her and the Gallatin Canyon. "It's where I grew up. Where I first fell in love."

"Well, I wish you luck. I hope it goes well."

"Thanks. If you hear anything else about Fiona—"

"I'll keep it to myself."

"No, call me. I really didn't know the woman. But I care about what happened to her." He thought of the first night he'd seen her, all dressed up in that dark suit and looking so strong and capable. And the other times when she'd stopped by his apartment looking as if she'd just come home from spring break and acting the part. "It was like she was always changing before my eyes. I never knew who she was. I'm not sure she did."

He and Rick said goodbye again. Disconnecting, he pocketed his phone. He couldn't help wondering about Fiona's last moments underwater inside her car. Did she know how to swim? He had no idea. Was it too deep for her to reach the surface? Or had she been swept away?

Chase felt sad, but he knew there was no way he could have helped her. She wanted a man committed to her, and she deserved it. But as he'd told her that first night, he wasn't that man.

If only he had known how broken and damaged she was. He would have given her a wide berth. He should have anyway, and now he blamed himself for his moment of weakness. That night he'd needed someone, but that someone had been Mary, not a woman he didn't know. Not Fiona.

"I'm so sorry," he whispered. "I'm so sorry." He hoped that maybe now Fiona would finally be at peace.

Looking toward the wide-open horizon, he turned his thoughts to Mary. He couldn't wait to look into her beautiful blue eyes and tell her that he'd never stopped loving her. That thought made him even more anxious. He couldn't wait to get home.

DILLON WALKED HER to her door and waited while Mary pulled out her keys.

"I had a wonderful time," he said as he leaned casually against the side of her building as if waiting to see if she was going to invite him up. Clouds scudded past the full moon to disappear over the mountaintops surrounding the canyon. The cool night air smelled of pine and clear blue trout stream water. This part of Montana was a little bit of Heaven, her mother was fond of saying. Mary agreed.

She'd left a light on in her apartment on the top floor. It glowed a warm inviting golden hue.

"I had fun too," she said, and considered asking him up to see the view from what she jokingly called her penthouse. The balcony off the back would be especially nice tonight. But her tongue seemed tied, and suddenly she felt tired and close to tears.

"I should go," Dillon said, his gaze locking with hers. He seemed about to take a step back, but changed his mind and leaned toward her. His hand cupped her jaw as he kissed her. Chastely at first, then with more ardor, gently drawing her to him. The kiss took her by surprise. Their first date he hadn't even tried.

His tongue probed her mouth for a moment before he ended the kiss as abruptly as it had begun. Stepping back, he seemed to study her in the moonlight for a moment before he said, "I really do have to go. Maybe we could do something this weekend if you aren't busy?"

She nodded dumbly. She and Dillon were close to the same age, both adults. She'd expected him to kiss her on their first date. So her surprise tonight had nothing to do with him kissing her, she thought as she entered her building, locking the door behind her and hurrying up to her apartment.

It had everything to do with the kiss.

Mary unlocked her apartment door with trembling fingers, stepped in and locked it behind her. She leaned against the door, hot tears filling her eyes as she told herself she shouldn't be disappointed. But she was.

The kiss had been fine, as far as kisses went. But even when Dillon had deepened the kiss, she had felt nothing but emptiness. The memory made her feel sick. Would she always compare every kiss with Chase's? Would every man she met come up lacking?

She didn't bother to turn on a lamp as she tossed her purse down and headed toward her bedroom, furious with herself. And even more furious with Chase. He'd left her and Montana as if what they had together meant nothing to him. Clearly it didn't. That's why he'd gotten engaged and wasn't man enough to call her himself and tell her.

Still mentally kicking herself for writing that letter to him, she changed into her favorite T-shirt and went into the bathroom to brush her teeth. Her image in the mirror startled her. She was no longer that young girl that Chase had fallen in love with. She was a woman in her own right. She dried her tears, the crying replaced with angry determination. If that was the way Chase wanted to be, then it was fine with her.

Her cell phone rang, startling her. She hurried to it, and for just a moment she thought it was going to be Chase. Her heart had soared, then come crashing down. Chase had moved on. When was she going to accept that?

"I couldn't quit thinking about you after I left," Dillon said. "I was wondering if you'd like to go to the movies tomorrow night?"

She didn't hesitate. "I'd love to." Maybe she just hadn't been ready for his kiss. Maybe next time...

"Great," Dillon said. "I'll pick you up at 5:30 if that's all right. We can grab something to eat before we go to the theater."

"Sounds perfect." If Chase could see her now, she thought as she hung up. Dillon was handsome, but less rugged looking than Chase. Taller though by a good inch or two, and he wanted to go out with her.

She disconnected, determined to put Chase Steele behind her. He had moved on and now she was too. Next time, she would invite Dillon up to her apartment. But even as she thought it, she imagined Chase and the woman he was engaged to. While she was busy comparing every man she met to him, he'd found someone and fallen in love. It made her question if what she and Chase once had was really that unique and special. Just because it had been for her...

Mary willed herself not to think about him. She touched her tongue to her lower lip. Dillon had made her laugh, and he'd certainly been attentive. While the kiss hadn't spurred a reaction in her, she was willing to give it another chance.

Her father didn't trust the man, so didn't that mean that there was more to Dillon than met the eye? Chase had always been a little wild growing up. Her father had been worried about her relationship with him. Maybe there was some wildness in Dillon that would make him more interesting.

As she fell asleep though, her thoughts returned to Chase until her heart was aching and tears were leaking onto her pillow.

Chapter Four

"How was your date?"

Mary looked up the next morning to find her mother standing in the doorway of her office holding two cups of coffee from the shop across the street. "Tell me that's an ultimate caramel frappaccino."

Dana laughed. "Do you mean layers of whipped cream infused with rich coffee, white chocolate and dark caramel? Each layer sitting on a dollop of dark caramel sauce?"

"Apparently I've mentioned why I love it," she said, smiling at her mother as Dana handed her the cup. She breathed in the sweet scent for a moment before she licked some of the whipped cream off the top. "I hope you got one of these for yourself."

"Not likely," her mother said as she sat down across the desk from her. "The calories alone scared me off. Anyway, you know I prefer my coffee to actually taste like coffee. That's why I drink it black."

Mary grimaced and shook her head, always amazed how much she looked like her mother but the similarities seemed to have stopped there. What they shared was their love of Montana and determination to keep Cardwell Ranch for future generations. At least for the ones who wanted to stay here. Her three brothers had left quickly enough, thrown to the far winds. She wondered about her own children—when she had them one day with the man she eventually married. Would they feel wanderlust like Chase had? She knew she wouldn't be able to make them stay nearby any more than she had him.

She took a sip of her coffee, hating that she'd let her thoughts wander down that particular path.

"I'm trying to tell if the date went well or not," her mother said, studying her openly. "When I walked in, I thought it had, but now you're frowning. Is your coffee all right?"

Mary replaced her frown with a smile as she turned her attention to her mother and away from Chase. "My coffee is amazing. Thank you so much. It was just what I needed. Normally I try to get over to Lone Peak Perk when it opens, but this morning I was anxious to get to work. I wish they delivered."

Her mother gave her a pointed look. "Are you purposely avoiding talking about your date, because I'm more interested in it than your coffee habit."

Laughing, she said, "The date was fine. Good. Fun, actually. We're going out again tonight."

Her mother raised a brow. "Again already? So he was a perfect gentleman?" Her mother took a sip of her coffee as if pretending she wasn't stepping over a line.

"You're welcome to tell Dad that he was," she said with a twinkle in her eye.

"Mary!" They both laughed. "So you like him?"

Mary nodded. *Like* was exactly the right word. She had hoped to feel more.

"You are impossible. You're determined to make me drag everything out of you, aren't you?"

"Not everything," she said coyly. Her mother seemed to like this game they played. Mostly Dana seemed relieved that Mary was moving on after Chase. She didn't like to see her daughter unhappy, Mary thought. It was time to quit moping over Chase, and they both knew it.

"So how did we do?" Deputy Dillon Ramsey asked his friend as he closed the cabin door and headed for the refrigerator for a beer as if he lived there.

"Picked up another three head of prime beef," Grady Birch said, and quickly added, "They were patrolling the fences last night just like you said they would be. Smart to hit a ranch on the other side of the river. We got in and out. No sweat."

"It's nice that I know where the deputies will be watching." Dillon grinned as he popped the top on his beer can and took a long swig.

"Trouble is, I heard around town that ranchers are going to start riding their fences. Word's out."

Dillon swore. "It was such easy pickings for a while." He plopped down in one of the worn chairs in Grady's cabin, feeling more at home in this ratty-ass place than in his nice apartment in Big Sky. "So we'll cool it until the heat dies down."

"Back to easy pickings, how did your date go?"

He grinned. "A couple more dates and I'll have her eating out of my hand."

Grady looked worried. "You're playing with fire, you know. The marshal's daughter?" His friend shook his head. "You sure this game you're playing is worth it?"

Dillon laughed. "To be able to drive out to the

Cardwell Ranch, sit on that big porch of theirs and drink the marshal's beer right under his nose? You damn betcha it's worth it."

"Maybe I don't understand the end game," Grady suggested.

"I need this job until I can get enough money together to go somewhere warm, sit in the shade and drink fancy drinks with umbrellas in them for the rest of my life. I have plans for my future and they don't include a woman, especially Mary Savage. But in the meantime…" He smiled and took a slug of his beer. "She ain't half bad to look at. For her age, I get the feeling that she hasn't had much experience. I'd be happy to teach her a few things."

"Well, it still seems dangerous dating his daughter," Grady said. "Unless you're not telling me the truth and you're serious about her."

"I'm only serious about keeping the marshal from being suspicious of me. I told you, he almost caught me that one night after we hit the Cardwell Ranch. I had to do some fast talking, but I think I convinced him that I was patrolling the area on my night off."

"And dating his daughter will make him less suspicious of you?"

"It will give him something else to worry about," Dillon said with a grin. He knew he'd gotten the job only because of his uncle. He'd gone into law enforcement at his uncle's encouragement. Also, he'd seen it as a get-out-of-jail-free card. No one would suspect a cop, right?

Unfortunately, his uncle had been more than suspicious about what Dillon had been doing to make some extra money. So it had come down to him leaving Wyoming to take the deputy job in the Gallatin Canyon of Montana.

"Mary Savage is a good-looking woman, no doubt about that," Grady said as he got up to get them more beer.

Dillon watched him with narrowed eyes. "Don't get any ideas. I've been priming this pump for a while now. And believe me, with your record, you wouldn't want Marshal Hud Savage looking too closely at *you*. That's one reason we can't be seen together. As far as anyone knows, you and I aren't even friends."

MARSHAL HUD SAVAGE had been waiting patiently for the call since Deputy Dillon Ramsey had gone off duty. Still, when his phone rang, it made him jump. It wasn't like him to be nervous. Then again, this was about his daughter. He had every right given his feelings about Dillon Ramsey.

He picked up the phone, glad to hear the voice of Hayes Cardwell, Dana's cousin, on the other end of the line. It was nice to have several private investigators in the family. "Well?"

"You were right. He headed out of town the moment he changed out of his uniform," Hayes said. "He went to a cabin back in the hills outside Gallatin Gateway. You're probably more interested in who is renting the cabin than who owns it. Ever heard of a man named Grady Birch?"

The name didn't ring any bells. "Who is he?"

"He has an interesting rap sheet that includes theft and assault. He's done his share of cattle rustling."

"And Dillon went straight there."

"He did. In fact, he's still inside. I'm watching the place from down the road with binoculars."

"So it's away from other houses," Hud said. "Any chance there's a truck around with a large horse trailer?"

"The kind that could be used to steal cattle?"

"Exactly," the marshal said.

"There's an old one parked out back. If they both leave, I might get a chance to have a look inside."

"I doubt they're going to leave together," Hud said. "Thanks for doing this but I can take it from here."

"No problem. What's family for?"

"I'll expect a bill for your time," the marshal said. "Or I'll tell Dana on you."

Hayes laughed. "Don't want *her* mad at me."

"No one does. Also," Hud added, "let's keep this just between the two of us for now." He disconnected and called up Grady Birch's rap sheet. Hayes was right. Grady was trouble. So why wasn't he surprised that his new deputy was hanging out with a man like that?

He'd known it the moment he laid eyes on the handsome lawman. Actually, he'd suspected there would be a problem when Dillon's uncle called, asking for the favor. He'd wanted to turn the man down, but the uncle was a good cop who Hud had worked with on a case down in Jackson, Wyoming.

Hud rubbed a hand over his face. Dillon was everything he'd suspected he was, and now he was dating Mary. He swore. What was he going to do about it? In the first place, he had no proof. Yet. So warning Mary about him would be a waste of breath even if she *didn't* find something romantic about dating an outlaw. Some people still saw cattle rustling as part of an Old West tradition. Also, his daughter was too old to demand that she stop seeing Dillon.

No, he was going to have to handle this very delicately, and delicate wasn't in his repertoire. That didn't leave him many options. Catching Dillon red-handed wouldn't be easy because the deputy wasn't stupid. Arresting him without enough evidence to put him away was also a bad move.

Hud knew he had to bide his time. He told himself that maybe he'd get lucky, and Dillon or Grady would make a mistake. He just hoped it was soon, before Mary got any more involved with the man.

CHASE FINALLY GOT the call. His pickup engine was in and he could come by this afternoon to pick it up. He hadn't talked to Rick in a few days and feeling at loose ends, pulled out his cell phone and made the call, dreading the news. Rick answered on the second ring.

"Has there been any word on Fiona?" The silence on the other end of the line stretched out long enough that Chase knew what was coming.

"They gave up the search. The general consensus is that her body washed downstream and will be found once the water goes down more."

"I'm sorry to hear that. I'm sure Patty is upset."

"She is," Rick said. "She felt sorry for Fiona. That's why she didn't cut ties with her after high school. Patty's over at Fiona's condo now cleaning it out since she has no next of kin. She found out from a bank statement that Fiona had drained her bank account almost a week ago. Took all of it in cash. Who knows what she did with that much money. Hell, it could be in the river with her. Patty's going to try to organize some kind of service for her."

"She doesn't have any family?"

"I guess I didn't tell you. Her whole family died in a fire when Fiona was eleven. She would have perished with her parents and three older stepbrothers, but she'd stayed over at a friend's house that night."

"Oh man. That could explain a lot," he said more to himself. "I wish I'd known all of this. Maybe I could have handled things better."

"Trust me, it would take a psychiatrist years to sort that woman out. So stop blaming yourself. I'm the one who should have warned you. But it's over now."

The fact that he felt relieved made him feel even more guilty as he promised to stay in touch and hung up.

Chapter Five

"Just fill out this application and leave it," the barista said as she dropped the form on the table in front of the dark-haired woman with the pixie haircut and the kind of cute Southern accent and lisp because of the gap between her front teeth.

She'd introduced herself as Lucy Carson, as if Christy was supposed to recognize the name.

"You're sure there's no chance of an opening soon?" Lucy Carson asked now before glancing at her name tag and adding, "Christy."

Christy shook her head. "Like I said. I just got hired, so I really doubt there will be anything for the rest of the season unless someone quits and that's unlikely. Jobs aren't that easy to find in Big Sky. Your application will be on file with dozens of others, so if I were you, I'd keep looking."

She didn't mean to sound cruel or dismissive, but she'd told the woman there weren't any openings. Still, the woman had insisted on filling out an application. If she wanted to waste her time, then Christy wasn't going to stop her. She just thought it was stupid.

From behind the counter, she watched how neatly Lucy Carson filled in each blank space. Was it stubbornness or arrogance? The lady acted as if she thought the manager would let someone go to hire *her*. That sounded like arrogance to Christy.

"What about a place to live nearby?" the woman asked, looking up from the application.

Christy laughed. "You'll have even worse luck finding an apartment. I've been waiting for months to get into the one across the street, and it's just a small bedroom."

Lucy glanced in the direction she pointed. "There's rentals over there?"

"There *was*. I got the last one. I'm moving in tomorrow." This Lucy was starting to get on her nerves. She found herself wishing that some customers would come in just so she had something to do. Usually she loved the slow afternoons when she could look at magazines and do absolutely nothing, even though she was supposed to be cleaning on her downtime.

The woman studied her for a moment, then smiled and resumed filling out the application.

"You should go down to Bozeman," Christy told her. "More opportunities in a college town than here in the canyon." Jobs weren't easy to get in Big Sky especially during the busy times, summer, and winter. Not just that, this job didn't even pay that well. Too many young people would work for nothing just to get to spend their free time up on the mountain biking and kayaking in the summer, skiing and snowboarding in the winter.

The woman finished and brought her application over to the counter. Christy glanced at the name. "Is Lucy short for something?" she asked.

"My mother was a huge fan of *I Love Lucy* reruns." She looked at the application, almost feeling sorry for the young woman. According to this, she had a lot of experience as a barista but then so did a whole lot of other people. "I see you didn't put down an address." She looked up at the woman who gave her a bright smile.

"Remember, I'm still looking for a place to stay, but once I start working I'm sure an apartment will open up."

Christy couldn't help but chuckle under her breath at the woman's naive optimism. "Most everyone who works in Big Sky ends up commuting at least forty miles a day. There just aren't any cheap rentals for minimum wage workers even if you should luck out and get a job."

Lucy smiled. "I'm not worried. Things just tend to work out for me. I'm lucky that way."

Whatever, Christy thought. "I'll give your application to Andrea but like I said, we don't have any openings."

"Not yet anyway," Lucy said. "So where do you go to have fun on a Saturday night?"

"Charley's if you like country. Otherwise—"

"I'm betting you like country music," Lucy said. "Your car with the George Strait bumper sticker gives you away."

"My car?" Christy frowned.

"Isn't that your SUV parked across the street?"

She looked out the window and laughed. "Not hardly. Mine is that little blue beat-up sedan with all the stuff in the back since I can't move into my apartment until tomorrow. I've been waiting for weeks, staying with my mother down in Bozeman and driving back and forth when I can't find someone to stay with here. Do you have any family you could stay with?"

Lucy shook her head. "No family. Just me. Maybe I'll check out Charley's tonight." She smiled her gap-toothed smile. "Hopefully I'll get lucky and some handsome cowboy will take me home with him. Or maybe it's not that kind of place."

"No, it is. There'll be cowboys and ski bums."

"I might see you there then?" Lucy said. "Don't worry. I won't intrude if you've found your own cowboy. I'm guessing there's one you're planning to meet tonight."

Christy felt herself flush. "Not exactly. I'm just hoping he'll be there."

Lucy laughed. "Hoping to get lucky, huh? Well, thanks again for your help." She left smiling, making Christy shake her head as she tossed Lucy's application on the desk in Andrea's office. She'd ended up almost liking the woman. Now if she could just get through the rest of the day. She was excited about tonight at Charley's. She did feel lucky. She had a job, an apartment to move into tomorrow and with even more luck, she would be going home with the man she had a crush on. Otherwise, she would be sleeping in her car on top of all her belongings.

Tomorrow though, she'd be moving into the apartment across the street that Mary Savage owned. How handy was that since she could sleep late and still get to work on time with her job just across the street?

LUCY CARSON WAS also looking at the small apartment house across the street from Lone Peak Perk as she walked to her car. She had her heart set on a job at the coffee shop and an apartment across the street in Mary Cardwell Savage's building. Not that she always got what she set her heart on, she thought bitterly, but she would make this happen, whatever she had to do.

As she climbed into her new car, she breathed in the scent of soft leather. She really did like the smell of a new car. Her other one was at the bottom of the Colorado River—or at least it had been until a few weeks ago when it was discovered.

Her disappearing act had gone awry when she'd tried to get out of the car and couldn't before it plummeted toward the river that night. By the time she reached the bank way downriver, she'd wished she'd come up with a better plan. She'd almost died and she wanted to live. More than wanted to live. She'd wanted to kill someone. Especially the person responsible for making her have to go to such extremes: Chase Steele. As she'd sat on that riverbank in the dark, she knew exactly what she had to do. Fortunately, when she'd tried to bail out of the car, she'd grabbed her purse. She'd almost forgotten the money. Her plan really would have gone badly if she'd lost all this money. With it, she could do anything she wanted.

But as close a call as it had been, everything had worked out better than even she'd planned. The authorities thought she was dead, her body rotting downriver. Fiona Barkley was dead. She was free of her. Now she could become anyone she chose.

Since then she'd had to make a few changes, including her name. But she'd never liked the name Fiona anyway. She much preferred Lucy Carson. Getting an ID in that name had been easier than she imagined. It had been harder to give up her long blond hair. But the pixie cut, the dark brown contacts and the brunette hair color transformed her into a woman not even she recognized. She thought she looked good—just not so good that Chase would recognize her.

Her resulting car wreck had pretty much taken care of her change in appearance as well. She had unsnapped her seat belt to make her leap from the car before it hit the water. Had she not been drunk and partway out of the car, she wouldn't have smashed her face, broken her nose and knocked out her front teeth.

As it turned out, that too proved to be a stroke of luck. She'd lost weight because it had hurt to eat. When she looked in the mirror now, she felt she was too skinny, but she knew once she was happy again, she'd put some pounds back on. She still had curves. She always had.

It was her face that had changed the most. Her nose had healed but it had a slight lean to it. She liked the imperfection. Just as she liked the gap between her two new front teeth. It had taken going to a dentist in Mexico to get a rush job. She liked the gap. It had even changed the way she talked giving her a little lisp. She'd been able to pick up her former Southern accent without any trouble since it was the way she'd talked before college. It was enough of a change in her appearance and voice that she knew she could get away with it—as long as she never got too close to Chase.

In the meantime, she couldn't wait to meet Mary Cardwell Savage.

MARY STOOD ACROSS the street from Lone Peak Perk thinking about her date last night with Dillon. She'd seen the slim, dark-haired woman come out of the coffee shop and get into a gray SUV, but her mind had been elsewhere. As the SUV pulled away, she turned from the window, angry with herself.

She was still holding out hope that Chase would contact her. The very thought made her want to shake herself. It had been weeks. If he was going to answer, he would have a long time ago. So why did she keep thinking she'd hear from him? Hadn't his fiancée told him that she'd called? Maybe he thought that was sufficient. Not the man she'd known, she thought.

And that was what kept nagging at her. She'd known Chase since he was fifteen. He'd come to work for the Jensen Ranch next door. Mary's mom had pretty much adopted him after finding out the reason he'd been sent to live in the canyon was because his mother couldn't take care of him. Muriel was going through cancer treatment. He'd been honorable even at a young age. He wasn't the kind of man not to call and tell her about a fiancée.

So his not calling or writing felt…wrong. And it left her with nagging questions.

That was only part of the problem and she knew it. She'd hoped that Dillon Ramsey would take her mind off Chase. They'd been dating regularly, and most of the time she enjoyed herself. They'd kissed a few times but that was all. He hadn't even made a pass at her. She couldn't imagine what it was about Dillon that had worried her father. At one point, she'd wondered if her father the marshal had warned him to behave with her.

The thought made her cringe. He wouldn't do that, would he?

She'd asked Dillon last night how he liked working for her dad.

"I like it. He's an okay dude," he'd answered.

She'd laughed. No one called her father a dude.

Now, she had to admit that Dillon was a disappointment. Which made her question what it was she was looking for in a man. A sense of adventure along with a sense of humor. Dillon didn't seem to have either.

Was that why she felt so restless? She looked around her apartment, which she'd furnished with things she loved from the turquoise couch to the weathered log end tables and bright flowered rug. But the spectacular view was the best part. The famous Lone Peak, often snow-capped, was framed in her living room window. The mountain looked especially beautiful in the moonlight.

Which made her think of Chase and how much she would have liked to stand on her back deck in the moonlight and kiss him—instead of Dillon. She groaned, remembering her hesitation again last night to invite Dillon up to her apartment. He'd been hinting that he really wanted to see it. She could tell last night that he'd been hurt and a little angry that she hadn't invited him up.

Standing here in the life she'd built, all she could think about was what Chase's opinion would be of it. Would he be proud of her accomplishments? Would he regret ever leaving her?

She shook him from her head and hurried back downstairs. She still had work to do, and all she was doing right now was giving herself a headache.

BY THE NEXT MORNING, news of the hit and run death of Christy Shores had spread through most of Big Sky and the canyon.

As Marshal Hud Savage walked into Charley's, the

last place Christy Shores had been seen alive, he saw the bartender from last night wasn't alone.

"Mike French, bartender, right?" Hud asked the younger of the two men standing nervously behind the bar. Twentysomething, Mike looked like a lot of the young people in Big Sky from his athletic build to the T-shirt and shorts over long underwear and sandals.

If Hud had to guess, he'd say Mike had at least one degree in something practical like engineering, but had gotten hooked on a lifestyle of snowboarding in the winter and mountain biking or kayaking in the summer. Which explained the bartending job.

He considered the handsome young man's deep tan from spending more hours outside than bartending. It made him wonder why a man like that had never appealed to his only daughter.

He suspected Mary was too much of a cowgirl to fall for a ski bum. Instead, she was now dating his deputy, Dillon Ramsey. That thought made his stomach roil, considering what he suspected about the man.

The bartender stepped forward to shake his hand. "Bill said you had some questions about Christy?"

Hud nodded and looked to the bar owner, Bill Benson, before he turned back to Mike. "I understand she was one of the last people to leave the bar last night?"

Mike nodded as Hud pulled out his notebook and pen. "I was just about to lock up when she came out of the women's bathroom. She looked like she'd been crying. I hadn't realized she was in there since I had already locked the front door." He shot a guilty look at his boss. "I usually check to make sure everyone was gone, but last night..."

"What was different about last night?" Hud asked.

Mike shifted on his feet. "A fight had broken out earlier between a couple of guys." He shot another look at Bill and added, "Christy had gotten into the middle of it. Not sure what it was about. After I broke it up, I didn't see her. I thought she'd left."

"Christy's blood alcohol was three times the legal limit," Hud said.

Again Mike shot a look at his boss before holding up his hands and quickly defending himself. "I cut her off before the fight because she'd been hitting the booze pretty hard. But that doesn't mean she quit drinking. The place was packed last night. All I know is that I didn't serve her after that."

Hud glanced toward the front door. "Her car is still parked outside. You didn't happen to take her keys, did you?"

The young man grimaced. "I asked for her keys, but she swore to me that she was walking home." He shrugged. "I guess that part was true."

Hud had Christy's car keys in a plastic evidence bag in his patrol SUV. The keys had been found near her body next to the road after she was apparently struck by a vehicle and knocked into the ditch.

"I'm going to need the names of the two men who were involved in the fight," he said. He wrote them down, hiding his surprise when he wrote Grady Birch, but Chet Jensen was no surprise. Chet seemed to think of the local jail as his home away from home. "What about friends, girlfriends, anyone Christy was close to."

Mike shook his head. "She hadn't been working at Lone Peak Perk very long. I'm not sure she'd made any friends yet. When she came into the bar, she was always alone. I think someone said that she was driving back and forth for work from Bozeman where she was living with her mom."

"Did she always leave alone?" he asked.

With a shake of his head, the bartender said, "No." He motioned toward the names he'd given the marshal. "It was usually with one or the other of those two."

Hud thanked Mike and went outside to the car. He'd already run the plates. The vehicle was registered to Christy Shores. Bill came out and drove off, followed by Mike who hopped on his mountain bike.

Christy's older model sedan wasn't locked Hud noted as he pulled on latex gloves and tried the driver's-side door. It swung open with a groan. He looked inside. Neatness apparently wasn't one of the young woman's traits. The back seat was stuffed full of clothing and boxes. He'd been told that she was planning to move into an apartment on the second floor of Mary's building today. The front floorboard on the passenger side was knee-deep in fast-food wrappers and Lone Peak Perk go cups.

He leaned in and took a whiff, picking up the stale scent of cigarettes and alcohol. All his instincts told him that after the apparent night Christy'd had, she would have driven home drunk rather than walk.

On impulse, he slid behind the wheel, inserted the key and turned it. There was only a click. He tried again. Same dull click. Reaching for the hood release, he pulled it and then climbed out to take a look at the engine, suspecting an old battery.

But he was in for a surprise. The battery appeared to be new. The reason the car hadn't started was because someone had purposely disabled it. He could see fresh screwdriver marks on the top of the battery.

Hud suspected that whoever had tampered with her battery was the same person who had wanted Christy to take off walking down this road late last night.

WHEN MARY WALKED across the street to the Lone Peak Perk the next morning, she was surprised to find her favorite coffee shop closed. There was a sign on the door announcing that there'd been a death.

She wondered who had died as she retraced her footsteps to climb into her pickup and head for the ranch. Cardwell Ranch was a half mile from Meadow Village on the opposite side of the Gallatin River. She always loved this drive because even though short, the landscape changed so drastically.

Mary left behind housing and business developments, traffic and noise. As she turned off Highway 191 onto the private bridge that crossed the river to the ranch the roar of the flowing river drowned out the busy resort town. Towering pines met her on the other side. She wound back into the mountains through them before the land opened again for her first glimpse that day of the ranch buildings.

Behind the huge barn and corrals, the mountains rose all the way to Montana's Big Sky. She breathed it all in, always a little awed each time she saw it, knowing what it took to hang on to a ranch through hard times. Behind the barn and corrals were a series of small guest cabins set back against the mountainside. Her aunt Stacy lived in the larger one, the roof barely visible behind the dark green of the pines.

At the Y in the road, she turned left instead of continuing back into the mountains to where her Uncle Jordan and his wife, Liza, lived. The two-story log and stone ranch house where she'd been raised came into view moments later, the brick-red metal roof gleaming in the morning sun.

There were several vehicles parked out front, her father's patrol SUV one of them. When she pushed open the front door, she could hear the roar of voices coming from the kitchen and smiled. This had been the sound she'd come downstairs to every morning for years growing up here.

Mary knew how much her mother loved a full house. It had been hard on her when all of her children had grown up and moved out. But there were still plenty of relatives around. Mary had seven uncles and as many aunts, along with a few cousins who still lived in the area.

As she entered the kitchen, she saw that there was the usual group of family, friends and ranch hands sitting around the huge kitchen table. This morning was no exception. Her uncle Jordan signaled that it was time to get to work, giving her a peck on her cheek as he rose and headed out the door, a half dozen ranch hands following him like baby ducks.

Mary said hello to her aunt Stacy and kissed her mother on the cheek before going to the cupboard to pull down a mug and fill it with coffee. There was always a pot going at Cardwell Ranch. The kitchen had quieted down with Jordan and the ranch hands gone. Leaning against the kitchen counter, she asked, "So what's going on?" She saw her mother glance down the table at the marshal.

"Some poor young woman was run down in Meadow Village last night," Dana said, getting up from the table as the timer went off on the oven. "It was a hit and run," she added, shaking her head as if in disbelief.

Mary moved out of the way as her mother grabbed a hot pad and pulled a second batch of homemade cinnamon rolls from the oven.

"You might have known her," her mother said. "She worked at that coffee shop you like."

"Lone Peak Perk?" she asked in surprise as she took a vacated seat. "I stopped by there this morning and it was closed. There was a note on the door saying there'd been a death, but I never dreamed it was anything like that. What was the woman's name?"

"Christy Shores," her father said from the head of the large kitchen table.

"Christy." She felt sick to her stomach as she called up an image of the small fair-haired young woman. Tears filled her eyes. "Oh, no. I knew her."

"Honey, are you all right?" her mother asked.

"Christy was going to move into the apartment I had available today. She'd only been working at the coffee shop for a few weeks. I can't believe she's dead. A hit and run?" she asked her father.

He nodded and glanced at his watch. "The coroner should have something more for me by now," he said, getting to his feet.

"Do you have any idea who did it?" she asked her father.

Hud shook his head. "Not yet. Unfortunately, it happened after the bars closed, and she was apparently alone walking along the side of the road dressed in all black. It's possible that the driver didn't see her."

"But whoever hit her would have known that he or she struck something," Dana said.

"Could have thought it was a deer, and that's why the person didn't stop," Hud said. "It's possible."

"And then the driver didn't stop to see what it was? Probably drunk and didn't want to deal with the marshal," Aunt Stacy mocked. "I've heard he's a real—"

"I'd watch yourself," her father said, but smiled as he took his Stetson off the hook on the wall, kissed his wife and left.

Mary took a sip of her coffee, her hands trembling as she brought the mug to her lips. It always shocked her, death and violence. She'd never understood how her father could handle his job the way he did. While there wasn't a lot of crime in the canyon, there was always something. She remembered growing up, overhearing about murders but only occasionally. Now there'd been a hit and run. Poor Christy. She'd been so excited about renting Mary's apartment, which was so close to her work. It would save her the commute from her mother's house in Bozeman, she'd said.

As the patrol SUV left, another vehicle pulled in. "Well, I wonder who that is?" she heard her mother say as she shifted in her seat to peer out the window.

Mary did the same thing, blinking in the bright morning sun at the pickup that had pulled up in front of the house almost before the dust had settled from her father leaving.

She stared as the driver's-side door opened and Chase Steele stepped out of the vehicle.

Chapter Six

"It's Chase," Mary said as if she couldn't believe it. For weeks she had dreamed of him suddenly showing up at her door. She shot a look at her mother.

"Do you need my help?" Dana asked. "If you aren't ready to talk to him, I could tell him this isn't a good time."

She shook her head and turned back to watch Chase stretch as if it had been a long drive. He looked around for a moment, his gaze softening as he took in the ranch as though, like her, he still had special memories of the place. He appeared taller, more solid, she thought as she watched him head for the front porch. Was he remembering how it was with the two of them before he left?

"I can't imagine what he's doing here," Mary said, voicing her surprise along with her worry.

Her mother gave her a pitying look. "He's here to see you."

"But why?"

"Maybe because of the letter you sent," Dana suggested.

She couldn't believe how nervous she was. This was Chase. She'd known him since they were teens. Her heart bumped against her ribs as she heard him knock. "He could have just called."

"Maybe what he has to say needs to be said in person."

That thought scared her more than she wanted to admit. She hadn't told her mother about the call from Chase's fiancée. She'd been too embarrassed. It was enough that her aunt Stacy had told her mother about the letter she'd sent him.

"Do you want me to get that?" her mother asked when he knocked. "Or maybe you would like to answer it and let him tell you why he's here."

Another knock at the door finally made her move. Mind racing, she hurried to the door. Chase. After all this time. She had no idea what she was going to say. Worse, what *he* would say.

As she opened the door, she glanced past him to his pickup. At least he was alone. He hadn't brought the woman who'd called her, his fiancée who could by now be his wife.

"Mary."

The sound of his voice made her shift her gaze back to the handsome cowboy standing in her doorway. Her heart did a roller-coaster loop in her chest, taking all her air with it. He'd only gotten more handsome. The sleeves on the Western shirt he wore were rolled up to expose muscled tanned arms. The shirt stretched over his broad shoulders. He looked as solid as one of the large pines that stood sentinel on the mountainside over-looking the ranch.

He was staring at her as well. He seemed to catch himself and quickly removed his Stetson and smiled. "Gosh dang, you look good."

She couldn't help but smile. He'd picked up the expression "gosh dang" from her father after Hud had caught Chase cussing a blue streak at fifteen out by their barn. The words went straight to her heart, but when she opened her mouth, she said, "What are you doing here?"

"I had to see you." He glanced past her. "I'm sorry it took me so long. My pickup broke down and… Could we talk?"

She was still standing in the doorway. She thought of her mother in the next room. "Why don't we walk down to the creek?"

"Sure," he said, and stepped back to let her lead the way.

Neither of them spoke until they reached the edge of the creek. Mary stopped in the shade of the pines. Sunlight fingered warmth through the boughs, making the rippling clear water sparkle. She breathed in the sweet familiar scents, and felt as if she needed to pinch herself. Chase.

She was struck with how different Chase looked. Stubble darkened his chiseled jawline. He was definitely taller, broader across the shoulders. There were faint lines around his blue eyes as he squinted toward the house before settling his gaze on her.

She felt heat rush to her center. The cowboy standing in front of her set off all kinds of desires with only a look. And yet after all this time, did she know this man? He'd come back. But that didn't mean that he'd come back to *her*.

"I got your letter," he said as he took off his Stetson to turn the brim nervously in his fingers.

"You didn't call or write back," she said, wondering when he was going to get to the news about the fiancée.

His gaze locked with hers. "I'm sorry but what I

wanted to say, I couldn't say over the phone let alone in a letter."

Her heart pounded as she thought, *Here it comes.*

There was pain in his gaze. "I've missed you so much. I know you never understood why I had to leave. I'm not sure I understood it myself. I had to go. Just as I had to come back. I'm so sorry I hurt you." His blue-eyed gaze locked with hers. "I love you. I never stopped loving you."

She stared at him. Wasn't this exactly what she'd dreamed of him saying to her before she'd gotten the call from his fiancée? Except in the dream she would have been in his arms by now.

"What about your fiancée, Chase?"

"*Fiancée?* What would make you think—"

"She called me after I sent the letter."

He stared at her for a moment before swearing under his breath. "You talked to a woman who said she was my fiancée?"

She nodded and crossed her arms protectively across her chest, her heart pounding like a drum beneath her ribs. "Wasn't she?"

He shook his head. "Look, I was never engaged, far from it. But there was this woman." He saw her expression. "It wasn't what you think."

"I think you were involved with her."

He closed his eyes and groaned again. When he opened them, he settled those blue eyes on her. "It was one night after a party at my boss's place. It was a barbecue that I didn't even want to go to and wish I hadn't. I'd had too much to drink." He shook his head. "After that she would break into my apartment and leave me presents, go through my things, ambush me when I came home. She found your letter, but I never dreamed that she'd call you." He raked a hand through his hair and looked down. "I'm so sorry. Fiona was…delusional. She was like this with anyone who showed her any attention, but I didn't know that. I told her that night I was in love with someone else." His gaze came up to meet hers. "You. But I didn't come here to talk about her."

Fiona? Of course he had dated while he was gone. So why did hearing him say the woman's name feel as if he'd ripped out another piece of her heart? She felt sick to her stomach. "Why *did* you come here?"

"That's what I've been trying to tell you. I hated the way we left things too," Chase said. "Mary, I love you. That's why I came back. Tell me that you'll give us another chance."

"Excuse me."

They both turned to see a man silhouetted against the skyline behind them. Mary blinked as she recognized the form. "Dillon?"

Chase's gaze sharpened. "Dillon?" he asked under his breath.

"What are you doing here?" she asked, and then realized that she'd agreed to a lunch date she'd completely forgotten about because of Chase's surprising return.

"Lunch. I know I'm early, but I thought we'd go on a hike and then have lunch at one of the cafés up at the mountain resort," he said as he came partway down the slope to the creek and into the shelter of the pines. "More fun than eating at a restaurant in the village." He shrugged. "When your pickup wasn't at your office, I figured you'd be here." Dillon's gaze narrowed. "Why do I feel like I'm interrupting something?"

"Because you are," Chase said, and looked to Mary. "A friend of yours?"

"Mary and I are dating," Dillon said before she could speak. "I'm Deputy Dillon Ramsey."

"The deputy, huh," Chase said, clearly unimpressed.

Dillon seemed to grind his teeth for a moment before saying, "And you are…"

"Chase Steele, Mary's…" His gaze shifted to her.

"Chase and I grew up together here in the canyon," she said quickly as she saw the two posturing as if this might end with them exchanging blows before thrashing in the mud next to the creek as they tried to kill each other. "I didn't know Chase was…in town."

"Passing through?" Dillon asked pointedly.

Chase grinned. "Sorry, but I'm here to stay. I'm not going anywhere." He said that last part to her.

His blue eyes held hers, making her squirm for no reason she could think of, which annoyed her. It wasn't like she was caught cheating on him. Far from it since he had apparently recently dated someone named Fiona.

"If you're through here," Dillon said to her, "we should get going before it gets too hot."

"Don't let me stop you," Chase said, his penetrating gaze on her. "But we aren't finished."

"You are now," Dillon said, reaching for Mary's hand as if to pull her back up the slope away from the creek.

Chase stepped between them. "Don't go grabbing her like you're going to drag her away. If she wants to go with you, she can go under her own steam."

Dillon took a step toward Chase. "Stop," Mary cried, sure that the two were going to get physical at any moment. She looked at Chase, still shocked by his return as well as his declaration of love. "I'll talk to you later."

He smiled again then, the smile that she'd fallen in love with at a very young age. "Count on it." He stepped back and tipped his Stetson to her, then to Dillon. "I'll be around." In a few long-legged strides, he climbed the slope away from the creek.

"You coming?" Dillon asked, sounding irritated.

She sighed and started up the slope away from the creek. As they topped the hill, she saw Chase had gone to the house and was now visiting with her mother on the front porch. She could hear laughter and felt Dillon's angry reaction to Chase and her mother appearing so friendly.

He seemed to be gritting his teeth as he asked, "What's his story, anyway? He's obviously more than a friend," Dillon said as he opened the passenger-side door of his pickup and glared in Chase and Dana's direction.

"I told you, we grew up together," she said as she slid in and he slammed the door.

Dillon joined her. He seemed out of breath. For a moment he just sat there before he turned toward her. "You were lovers." It wasn't a question.

"We were high school and college sweethearts," she said.

"He's still in love with you." He was looking at Chase and her mother on the porch.

She groaned inwardly and said nothing. Of course with Chase showing up it was only a matter of time before he and Dillon crossed paths in a place as small as Big Sky. But why today of all days?

"He acts like he owns you." Dillon still hadn't reached to start the truck. Nor did he look at her. "Did he think he could come back and take up where the two of you left off?"

She'd thought the same thing, but she found herself wanting to defend Chase. "We have a history—"

He swung his head toward her, his eyes narrow and hard. "Are you getting back together?"

For a moment she was too taken aback to speak. "I didn't even know he was back in town until a few minutes ago. I was as surprised as you were, but I don't like your tone. What I decide to do is really none of your business." Out of the corner of her eye, she saw Chase hug her mother, then head for his pickup.

"Is that right?" Dillon demanded. "Good to know where I stand."

"You know, I'm no longer in the mood for a hike or lunch," she said, and reached for the door handle as Chase headed out of the ranch.

Dillon grabbed her arm, his fingers biting into her tender flesh. "He comes back and you dump me?"

"Let go of me." She said it quietly, but firmly.

He quickly released her. "Sorry. I hope I didn't— It's just that I thought you and I... And then seeing him and hearing him tell you that he was still in love with you." He shook his head, the look on his face making her weaken.

"Look, I told you. It came as a shock for me too," she said. "I don't know what I'm going to do. I'm sorry if you feel—"

"Like I was just a stand-in until your old boyfriend got back?"

"That isn't what you were."

"No?" His voice softened. "Good, because I'm not ready to turn you over to him." As he said the words, he trailed his fingers from her bare shoulder slowly down to her wrist. Her skin rippled with goose bumps and she shivered. "I still want to see that penthouse view. Can I call you later?"

She felt confused. But she knew that she wasn't in any frame of mind to make a decision about Dillon right now. She felt herself nod. "We'll talk then," she said, and climbed out of the pickup, closing the door behind her. Still rattled by everything that had happened, she stood watching him drive away, as tears burned her eyes. Chase had come back. Chase still loved her.

But there was the threatening woman who'd called her saying she was his fiancée. Fiona. And no doubt others. And there was Dillon. Chase had no right to come back here and make any demands on her. He'd let her go for weeks without a word after he'd gotten the letter.

Chase and Dillon had immediately disliked each other, which Mary knew shouldn't have surprised her. Dillon's reaction threw her the most. Did he really have feelings for her? She felt as if it was too early. They barely knew each other. Was it just a male thing?

Still, it worried her. The two men were bound to run into each other again. Next time she might not be around to keep them from trying to kill each other.

CHASE MENTALLY KICKED HIMSELF. He should have called, should have written. But even as he thought it, he knew he'd had to do this in person. If it hadn't been for Fiona and her dirty tricks... He shook his head. He was to blame for that too and he knew it.

Well, he was here now and damned if he was going to let some deputy steal the woman he loved, had always loved.

He let out a long breath as he drove toward the ranch where he would be working until he started his carpenter job. All the way to Montana he'd been so sure that by now he'd be holding Mary in his arms.

He should have known better. He'd hurt her. Had he really thought she'd still be waiting around for him? He thought of all the things he'd planned to tell her—before that deputy had interrupted them.

Assuring himself that he'd get another chance and soon, he smiled to himself. Mary was even more beautiful than she'd been when he left. But now there was a confidence about her. She'd come into her own. He felt a swell of pride. He'd never doubted that the woman could do anything she set her mind to.

Now all he had to do was convince her that this cowboy was worth giving a second chance.

HUD READ THROUGH the coroner's report a second time, then set it aside. Prints were still being lifted from Christy Shore's car, but the area around the battery where someone had disabled the engine had been wiped clean. Fibers had been found from what appeared to be a paper towel on the battery.

There was no doubt in his mind that Christy's death had been premeditated. Someone had tampered with her battery, needing her to walk home that night so she could be run down. Which meant that the killer must have been waiting outside the bar. Just her luck that she had stayed so late that there was no one around to give her a ride somewhere.

The killer wanted him to believe the hit and run had been an accident. He'd already heard rumors that she'd been hit by a motor home of some tourist passing through. He knew better. This was a homicide, and he'd bet his tin star that the killer was local and not just passing through.

Picking up his notebook, he shoved back his chair and stood. It was time to talk to the two men who'd fought over Christy earlier in the night. Only one name had surprised him—Grady Birch, Deputy Dillon Ramsey's friend—because the name had just come up in his cattle rustling investigation.

He decided to start with Grady, pay him a surprise visit, see how that went before he talked to the other man, Chet Jensen, the son of a neighboring rancher who'd been in trouble most of his life.

But when he reached the rented cabin outside Gallatin Gateway, Grady was nowhere around. Hud glanced in the windows but it was hard to tell if the man had skipped town or not.

MARY JOINED HER mother in a rocking chair on the front porch after Chase and Dillon had left. Dana had joked about feeling old lately, and had said maybe she was ready for a rocking chair. Mary had laughed.

But as she sat down in a chair next to her, she felt as if it was the first time she'd looked at her mother in a very long time. Dana had aged. She had wrinkles around her eyes and mouth, her hair was now more salt than pepper and there was a tiredness she'd seldom seen in her mother's bearing.

"Are you all right?" her mother asked her, stealing the exact words Mary had been about to say to her. Dana perked up a little when she smiled and reached over to take her daughter's hand.

"I saw you visiting with Chase," Mary said.

Her mother nodded. "It was good to see him. He left you his phone number." With her free hand she reached into her pocket and brought out a folded piece of note-paper and gave it to her.

She glanced at the number written on it below Chase's name. Seeing that there was nothing else, she tucked it into her pocket. "What did he tell you?"

"We only talked about the ranch, how much the town has grown, just that sort of thing."

"He says he came back because he loves me, never stopped loving me. But I never told you this…" She hesitated. There was little she kept from her mother. "I got a call from a woman who claimed to be his fiancée. She warned me about contacting him again."

Dana's eyes widened. "This woman threatened you?"

"Chase says it was a delusional woman he made the mistake of spending one night with. Fiona." Even say-ing the name hurt.

"I see. Well, now you know the truth."

Did she? "I haven't forgotten why we broke up." She'd caught Chase kissing Beth Anne Jensen. He'd sworn it was the first and only time, and that he hadn't initiated it. That he'd been caught off guard. She'd known Beth Anne had had a crush on Chase for years.

But instinctively she'd also known that her parents were right. She and Chase had been too young to be as serious as they'd been, especially since they'd never dated anyone else but each other. "You try to lasso him and tie him down now, and you'll regret it," her father had said. "If this love of yours is real, he'll come back."

She'd heard her parents love story since she was a child. Her father had left and broken her mother's heart. He'd come back though and won her heart all over again. "But what if he isn't you, Dad? What if he doesn't come back?"

"Then it wasn't meant to be, sweetheart, and there is nothing you can do about that."

"Will you call him?" her mother asked now.

"I feel like I need a little space without seeing either Dillon or Chase," she said. "I still love Chase, but I'm not sure I still know him."

"It might take some time."

"I guess we'll see if he sticks around long enough to find out." She pushed to her feet. "I need to get to my office."

"I'm glad he came back," her mother said. "I always liked Chase."

Mary smiled. "Me too."

But as she drove back to her office, she knew she wouldn't be able to work, not with everything on her mind. As she pulled into her parking spot next to her building, she changed her mind and left again to drive up into the mountains. She parked at the trailhead for one of her favorite trails and got out. Maybe she'd take a walk.

Hours later, ending up high on a mountain where she could see both the Gallatin Canyon and Madison Valley on the other side, she had to smile. She was tired, sweaty and dusty, and it was the best she'd felt all day.

The hike had cleared her mind some. She turned back toward the trailhead as the sun dipped low, ignoring calls on her cell phone from both men.

Down the street from Mary's building, Lucy studied herself in the rearview mirror of her SUV, surprised that she now actually thought of herself as Lucy. It was her new look and her ability to become someone else. It had started in junior high when she'd been asked to audition for a part in a play.

She'd only done it for extra credit since she'd been failing science. Once she'd read the part though, she'd felt herself become that character, taking on the role, complete with the accent. She'd been good, so good that she'd hardly had to try out in high school to get the leading roles.

Now as she waited, she felt antsy. Mary had come home and then left again without even getting out of her car. Lucy had been so sure that Chase would have made it to Montana by now. Waiting for him, she'd had too much time to think. What if she was wrong? What if he hadn't been hightailing it back here to his sweet little cowgirl?

What if he'd left Arizona, then changed his mind, realizing that what he had with her was more powerful than some old feelings for Mary Cardwell Savage? What if he'd gone back for her only to find out that she'd drowned and that everyone was waiting for some poor soul to find her body along the edge of the river downstream?

The thought made her heart pound. Until she remembered what she'd done to his pickup engine. Who knew where he'd broken down and how long it would take for him to get the engine fixed. If it was fixable.

No, he'd made it clear that he didn't want her. Which meant he would show up here in Big Sky. She just had to be patient and not do anything stupid.

She'd realized that she should approach this the same way she'd gone after prospective buyers in real estate. The first step was to find out what she was up against.

Lucy smiled. She would get to know her enemy. She would find her weakness. She already had a plan to gain Mary's trust.

Not that she was getting overconfident. Just as important was anticipating any problems—including getting caught. With each step toward her goal, she needed to consider every contingency.

Some precautions were just common sense. She'd purchased a burner phone. She hadn't told anyone she'd known that she was alive, not even Patty. She hadn't left a paper trail. Taking all her money out of the bank before what the authorities thought was an attempted suicide had been brilliant. Just as was wearing gloves when she tampered with Christy Shores' battery.

It had been pure hell living with three older stepbrothers. But they'd taught her a lot about cars, getting even and never leaving any evidence behind. She'd used everything they'd taught her the night she burned down her stepfather's house—with her stepfather, mother and stepbrothers inside.

But sometimes she got overzealous. Maybe she'd gone too far when she'd put the bleach into Chase's engine oil. She'd considered loosening the nuts on his tires, but she hadn't wanted him to die. *Not yet.* And definitely not where she wouldn't be there.

But what if he couldn't make it to Montana now? Shouldn't he have been here by now? If he was coming. She was beginning to worry a little when she saw him. As if she'd conjured him up, he drove past where she was parked to stop in front of Mary's building. Lucy watched him park and jump out. Her heart began to pound as he strode purposely toward Mary's building to knock on the door.

Her stomach curdled as she watched him try to see into the windows before he stepped back to stare up at the top floor. "Sorry, your little cowgirl isn't home," she said under her breath. There were no lights on nor was Mary's pickup where she always parked it. But it was clear that Chase was looking for her. What would he do when he found her? Profess his undying love? As jealousy's sharp teeth took a bite out of her, she was tempted to end this now.

She'd picked up a weapon at a gun show on her way to Big Sky. All she had to do was reach under her seat, take out the loaded handgun, get out and walk over to him. He wouldn't recognize her. Not at first.

He would though when she showed him the gun she would have had hidden behind her back. "This is just a little something from Fiona." She smiled as she imagined the bullet sinking into his black heart.

But what fun would that be? Her plan was to make him suffer. The best way to do that was through his precious Mary. She'd promised herself she wouldn't deviate from the plan. No more acting on impulse. This time, she wouldn't make the same mistakes she'd made in the past.

As she watched Chase climb back into his pickup and drive away, she was trembling with anticipation at just the thought of what she had in store for the cowboy and his cowgirl.

Chapter Seven

The next morning, Mary saw that Lone Peak Perk was open again. Just the thought of one of her ultimate caramel frappaccinos made her realize it was exactly what she needed right now.

Stepping through the door, she breathed in the rich scent of coffee and felt at home. The thought made her smile. She would be in a fog all day if she didn't have her coffee and after the restless night she'd had...

As she moved to the counter, she saw that there was a new young woman working. Had they already replaced Christy? The woman's dark hair was styled in a pixie cut that seemed to accent her dark eyes. She wore a temporary name tag that had LUCY printed neatly on it.

"So what can I get you?" Lucy asked with a slight lisp and a Southern accent as she flashed Mary a wide gap-toothed smile.

"One of your ultimate caramel frappaccinos to go."

The young woman laughed. "That one's my favorite."

"I was so sorry to hear about Christy," Mary said.

"I didn't really know her." Lucy stopped what she was doing for a moment to look over her shoulder at her. "I was shocked when I realized that Christy was the one who took my application. She was nice. I couldn't believe it when I got the call. I hate that her bad luck led to my good luck. My application was on the top of the pile."

"What brought you to Big Sky?" Mary asked, seeing that she'd made the young woman uncomfortable.

"Wanderlust. I had a job waiting for me in Spokane, but I found exactly what I was looking for right here in Big Sky, Montana. Is this the most beautiful place you've ever seen?"

Mary had to smile. "I've always thought so. Where are you from? I detect an accent."

Lucy laughed. "Texas. I can't seem to overcome my roots."

"I'd keep it if I were you."

"You think?" the woman asked as she set down the go cup on the counter in front of her.

Mary nodded. "I do. I hope you enjoy it here."

"Thanks. I know I will."

CHASE WAS RELIEVED when he got the call from Mary. He'd had a lot of time to think, and he didn't want to spend any more time away from her. He'd gone over to her place last night in the hopes that they could talk. But she hadn't been home. Was she out with the deputy? The thought made him crazy.

But he had only himself to blame. He'd broken her heart when he'd left Montana. Even now though, he knew that he'd had to go. He was definitely too young for marriage back then.

But he'd grown up in the years he'd been gone. He'd learned a trade he loved. He'd seen some of the world. He wasn't the kid Mary used to hang out with. He'd known for some time what he wanted. It wasn't until he'd gotten her letter that he'd realized there was still hope. He'd been afraid that Mary had moved on a long time ago. But like him, she hadn't found anyone who tempted her into a relationship. That was until the deputy came along.

"I'm sorry about the other day, surprising you like that. You were right. I should have called."

"That's behind us," she said in a tone that let him know there was a lot more than a simple phone call to be overcome between them. He'd hurt her. Had he really thought she'd forgive him that quickly? "Just understand, I wrote that letter to tell you about the package that came for you. The rest of it was just me caught in a weak moment."

"I didn't think you had weak moments," he joked.

"Chase—"

"All I'm asking is for a chance to prove myself to you." Silence. "There's something I didn't tell you. My mother contacted me. She'd been sick off and on for years, in and out of remission. This time she was dying and wanted to see me. That's why I went to Arizona. She recently died."

"Oh, Chase, I'm so sorry. I hadn't heard."

"She asked me to bring her ashes back here. To Big Sky." He could almost hear Mary's hesitation.

"Did she…?"

"Tell me who my father was? No. I was with her the night she died. She took it to her grave."

"I'm so sorry." Mary knew how not knowing had haunted him his whole life. It was a mystery, one that had weighed him down. He wanted to know who he was, who he came from, why his mother refused to tell him. Was his father that bad? He'd known there was much more to the story, and it was a story he needed to hear.

"She did tell me one thing. She'd met the man who fathered me here in Big Sky. It's why she wanted her ashes brought back here."

"But that's all you know."

"For now. Listen—"

"I called about the package," Mary said quickly. "If your mother met your father here, well that would explain why a woman saying she was once your mother's friend left you the package. If you'd like to stop by my office to pick it up—"

"I can't come by before tomorrow. I'm working on the Jensen Ranch to earn some extra money. I had pickup trouble on the way back to town. But I was hoping we could go out—"

"I need time. Also I'm really busy."

"Is this about that deputy?" he asked, then mentally kicked himself.

"I'm not seeing Dillon right now either, not that it is any of your business. You don't get to just come back and—"

"Whoa, you're right. Sorry. I'll back off. Just know that I'm here and that I'm not going anywhere. I want you back, Mary. I've never stopped loving you and never will."

As if Mary could forget that Chase was back in town. After the phone call, she threw herself into her work, determined not to think about the handsome cowboy who'd stolen her heart years ago. Dillon kept leaving her messages. She texted him that she had a lot of work to do, and would get back to him in a day or two.

That night, she lay in bed, thinking about Chase, her heart aching. He'd hurt her, and angry, she'd broken up with him only to have him leave. She'd lost her friend and her lover. After all the years they'd spent growing up together, Mary had always thought nothing could keep them apart. She'd been wrong, and now she was terrified that she'd never really known Chase.

In the morning, she went down to work early, thankful for work to keep her mind off Chase even a little. Midmorning she looked up to see the new barista from the Lone Peak Perk standing in her doorway.

"Don't shoot me," Lucy said. "I just had a feeling you might need this." She held out the ultimate caramel frappaccino.

Mary could have hugged her. "You must be a mind reader," she said as she rose from her desk to take the container of coffee from her. "I got so busy, I actually forgot. I had no idea it was so late. I can't tell you how much I need this."

"I don't want to interrupt. I can see that you're busy," Lucy said, taking a step toward the door. "But when I realized you hadn't been in…"

"Just a minute, let me pay you."

Lucy waved her off. "My treat. My good deed for the day." She smiled her gap-toothed smile and pushed out the door.

"Thank you so much!" Mary called after her, smiling as she watched the young woman run back across the street to the coffee shop.

Hud found Chet Jensen in the barn at his father's place just down the canyon a few miles. The tall skinny cowboy was shoveling manure from the stalls. He heard him gag, and suspected the man was hungover even before he saw his face.

"Rough night?" he asked, startling the cowboy.

Chet jumped, looking sicker from the scare. "You can't just walk up on someone like that," he snapped.

"I need to talk to you," Hud said. "About Christy Shores."

"I figured." Chet leaned his pitchfork against the side of the stall. "I could use some fresh air." With that he stumbled out of the barn and into the morning sunshine.

Hud followed him to a spot behind the ranch house where a half dozen lawn chairs sat around a firepit. Chet dropped into one of the chairs. Hud took one opposite him, and pulled out his notebook and pen.

"You heard about the fight."

He nodded. "What was that about?"

"Christy." Chet scowled across at him. "You wouldn't be here unless you already knew that. Let's cut to the chase. I had nothing to do with her getting run over."

"Who did?"

He shrugged. "Not a clue. Beth Anne heard that a motor-home driver must have clipped her."

Hud shook his head. "I'm guessing it was someone local with a grudge. How long have you been involved with her?"

"It wasn't like that. I brought her back here a couple of times after we met a few weeks ago. I liked her."

"But?"

"But she liked Grady who was always throwing his money around, playing the big shot. I tried to warn her about him." He shook his head, then leaned over to take it in his hands.

"Are you saying you think Grady Birch might be responsible?"

"Beats me." Lifting his head, he said, "After we got thrown out of Charley's, I came home and went to bed."

"Did you see Grady leave?"

He nodded. "That doesn't mean he didn't come back."

"The same could be said about you."

Chet wagged his head. "Beth Anne was home. My sister knows I didn't leave. She was up until dawn making cookies for some special event she's throwing down at the flower shop. I couldn't have left without her seeing me."

"Christy have any enemies that you knew about?" he asked.

"I didn't think she'd been in town long enough to make enemies."

"But she'd been in town long enough to have the two of you fighting over her," he pointed out.

Chet met his gaze. "Grady and I would have been fighting over any woman we both thought the other wanted. It wasn't really even about her, you know what I mean?"

He did, he thought as he closed his notebook and got to his feet. "If you think of anyone who might have wanted her dead, call me."

Chapter Eight

Mary was just starting across the street the next morning to get her coffee when the delivery van from the local flower shop pulled up in front of her building. It had been three days since she'd seen Chase. Both men had finally gotten the message and given her space. Not that the space had helped much except that she'd gotten a lot of work done.

She groaned as she saw Beth Anne Jensen climb out of the flower shop van. "I have something for you," the buxom blonde called cheerily.

Mary couldn't remember the last time anyone had sent her flowers. Reluctantly, she went back across the street since she could already taste her ultimate caramel frappaccino. Also, the last person she wanted to see this morning was Beth Anne. The blonde had her head stuck in the back of the van as she approached.

As her former classmate came out, she shoved cellophone wrapped vase with a red rose in it at her. "I'm sure you've already heard. Chase is back."

"I know. He came by the ranch a couple of days ago." That took some of the glee out of Beth Anne's expression.

"He's gone to work for my daddy."

Mary tried not to groan at the old news or the woman's use of "daddy" at her age. Of course, Chase had gone to work for Sherman Jensen. The Jensen Ranch was just down the road from the Cardwell spread. No wonder Chase had said he would be seeing her soon. The Jensens would be rounding up their cattle from summer range—just like everyone on Cardwell Ranch.

"Chase looks like being gone didn't hurt him none," the blonde said.

She didn't want to talk about Chase with this woman. She hadn't forgotten catching Chase and Beth Anne liplocked before he left. Mary didn't know if she was supposed to tip the owner of the flower store or not. But if it would get Beth Anne to leave... She pulled out a five and shoved it at her. "Thanks," she said, and started to turn away.

"That's not all," the blonde said as she pocketed the five and handed her a wrapped bouquet of daisies in a white vase. "Appears you've got more than one admirer." Beth Anne raised a brow.

Mary assumed that the woman knew who had sent both sets of flowers—and had probably read the notes inside the small envelopes attached to each. But then again seeing the distinct handwriting of two men on the outside of the envelopes, maybe Beth Anne was as in the dark as Mary herself. The thought improved her day.

"Have a nice day," she sang out to Beth Anne as she headed for her office. Opening the door, she took the flowers inside, anxious to see whom they were from. She didn't want to get her hopes up. They both could be from one of the ranchers she worked for as a thank-you for the work she'd done for them.

She set down the vases on the edge of her desk and

pulled out the first small envelope. Opening it, she read: "I know how you like daisies. I'm not giving up on us. Chase."

It would take more than daisies, she told herself even as her heart did a little bump against her ribs.

Shaking her head, she pulled out the other small white envelope, opened it and read: "Just wanted you to know I'm thinking of you, Dillon."

"I don't believe this," she said, and heard the front door of her building opening behind her. Spinning around, she half expected to see one or both of the men.

"Lucy," she said on a relieved breath. As touched as she was by the flowers, she wasn't up to seeing either man right now.

"Did I catch you at a bad time?" the barista asked, stopping short.

"Not at all. Your timing is perfect."

"I saw you start across the street to get your coffee and then get called back, so I thought I'd run it over to you. Your usual." She held out the cup.

"Thank you so much. I do need this, but I insist on paying you." Mary looked around for her purse. "Let me get you—"

"I put it on your account."

She stopped digging for money to look at her. "Lucy, I don't have an account."

The woman smiled that gap-toothed smile of hers that was rather infectious. "You do now. I just thought it would be easier but if I've overstepped—"

"I don't know why I hadn't thought of it, as many of these as I drink," Mary said, and raised the cup.

"I hope you don't mind. But this way, if you get too

busy, just call and if we aren't busy, one of us can bring your coffee right over."

"Lucy, that's so thoughtful, but—"

"It really isn't an inconvenience. We haven't been that busy and I could use the exercise. Also it looks like you're celebrating something." She motioned to the flower delivery.

Mary laughed. "It's a long story."

"Well, I won't keep you. I better get back. It wasn't busy but it could be any minute. My shift ends soon, and I have to get back on my search for a place to live." She started to open the front door to leave.

"Lucy, wait. I have an apartment open. I haven't put up a notice that it's available. Christy was going to move in."

"The girl who died." She grimaced. "The one I replaced at Lone Peak Perk."

"Is that too weird for you?" Mary asked.

"Let me give it some thought. But could you hold on to it until later today? Thanks." And she was gone.

Mary sipped her coffee, thinking she probably shouldn't have offered the apartment without checking the young woman's references. But it was Lucy, who'd just bought her a coffee and run it across the street to her.

She turned to look at her flowers, forgetting for the moment about anything else. What was she going to do about Chase? And Dillon?

Sitting down at her desk, she picked up her phone and called her best friend, Kara, who had moved to New York after college. But they'd managed to stay in touch by phone and Facetime. It was the kind of friendship that they could go without talking for weeks and pick up right where they'd left off.

"Chase is back," she said when her friend answered.

"In Big Sky?"

"He says he loves me and that he won't give up."

Kara took a breath and let it out slowly. "How do you feel about that?"

She sighed. "I still love him, but I've been seeing someone else. A deputy here. His name is Dillon. He's really good-looking in a kind of nothing-but-trouble kind of way."

Her friend was laughing. "When it rains it pours. Seriously? You have two handsome men who are crazy about you?"

She had to laugh. "Crazy might be the perfect word. They met the other day and sparks flew. I still love Chase, but when we broke up he didn't stay and fight for me. He just left. What's to keep him from doing it again?"

"And Dillon?"

"It's too new to say. They both sent me flowers today though."

"That's a good start," Kara said with a laugh.

"Chase sent daisies because he knows I love them."

"And Dillon?"

"A rose to let me know he was thinking about me."

"Mary! Who says you have to choose between them?"

"My father doesn't like me dating either one of them."

"Which makes you want to date them even more, knowing you."

"You *do* know me," she said, and laughed again. "How are you and your adorable husband and the kids?"

"I was going to call you. I'm pregnant again!"

"Congrats," she said, and meant it. Kara was made to be a mother.

"I have morning sickness, and I'm already starting to waddle."

Mary felt a stab of envy and said as much.

"Excuse me? If anyone is envious, it's me of you. You should see me right now. Sweats and a T-shirt with a vomit stain on it—my daughter's not mine."

She laughed. "And I'll bet you look beautiful as always."

A shriek and then loud crying could be heard in the background.

"I'll let you go," Mary said. "Congrats again."

"Same to you."

She sat for a moment, idly finishing her coffee and considering her flowers before going back to work. A while later, she picked up her phone and called Chase. "Thank you for the daisies. They're beautiful. If you have some time, I thought maybe you could stop by if you're free. Like I said, I have your package here at the office. I can tell you how to find the place."

Chase chuckled. "I know how to find you. I'll be right there."

LUCY LOOKED OUT the window of the coffee shop and with a start saw Chase's truck pull up across the street. Her heart squeezed as if crushed in a large fist. Had he seen Mary before this? Had they been meeting at night on the ranch? Jealousy made her stomach roil.

Chase had been hers. At least he had until Mary wrote him that letter. She was why he'd dumped her. To come back here to his precious cowgirl. She wasn't sure at that moment whom she hated more, him or Mary, as she watched him disappear into her office.

"Excuse me?" A woman stepped in front of her, blocking her view. It was all she could do not to reach across the counter and shove her out of the way. She wanted to see what was going on across the street. "I'd like to order."

Fortunately, she got control of herself. She needed this job to get closer to Mary and pull off her plan. If she hoped to pay back Chase, she couldn't lose her cool. She plastered a smile on her face.

"I'm sorry, what can I get you?" She hadn't even realized that her Texas accent had come back until that day when she'd finally met Mary Cardwell Savage. She'd thought she'd put Texas and her childhood behind her. But apparently all of this had brought it back—along with her accent.

As she made the woman a latte, she thought about spitting in her cup, but didn't. Instead, she let herself think about the apartment in Mary's building. Of course she was going to take it. She had already gained the woman's trust. It didn't matter that Chase was over there with Mary. Soon enough she would end their little romance.

She would just have to be careful to avoid Chase. The changes in her appearance were striking, but given what they'd shared, he would know her. He would sense her beneath her disguise. He'd feel the chemistry between them. So she needed to avoid him until she was ready to make her dramatic reveal.

Smiling to herself, she considered all the ways she could make their lives miserable, before she took care of both of them. As she'd told Christy Shores, she was lucky when it came to getting what she wanted. Hadn't she gotten this job and was about to get Christy's apartment, as well?

She wanted Chase and his precious Mary to suffer. She just had to be patient.

CHASE REMOVED HIS Stetson as he stepped into Mary's office. He couldn't help but admire the building and what she'd done with it. Hardwood floors shone beneath a large warm-colored rug. The walls were recycled brick, terra-cotta in color, with paintings and photographs of the area on the walls.

"Your office is beautiful," he said. "This place suits you."

Mary smiled at the compliment, but clearly she hadn't thawed much when it came to him.

"I heard you have a couple of apartments upstairs that you rent and live on the third floor," he said. "Wise investment."

That made her chuckle. "Thank you. I'm glad you approve."

"Mary, can we please stop this?" He took a step toward her, hating this impersonal wall between them. They knew each other. Intimately. They'd once been best friends—let alone lovers.

"Thank you again for the daisies." She picked up a package from her desk and held it out to him, blocking his advance. "This is what was dropped off for you."

He chewed at the side of his cheek, his gaze on her not on the package. "Okay, if this is the way you want it. I'll wait as long as it takes." He could see that she didn't believe that. She'd lost faith in him and he couldn't blame her. For a while, he'd lost faith in himself.

"So you're working for Beth Anne's father at their ranch."

So that was it. "It's temporary. I have a job as a finish carpenter for a company that builds houses like the upscale ones here in Big Sky. It's a good job, but since it doesn't start for a week, I took what I could get in the meantime." He didn't mention that buying a new engine for his pickup had set him back some.

His gaze went to the daisies he'd had sent to her, but quickly shifted to the vase with the rose in it. "Is that from your deputy?"

MARY RAISED HER CHIN. "Don't start, Chase." She was still holding the package out to him.

He took it without even bothering to look at it. He was so close now that she could smell his masculine scent mixed with the outdoors. "I can be patient, Mary," he said, his voice low, seductive. "Remember when we couldn't keep our hands off each other?" He took another step toward her, his voice dropping even more dangerously low. "I remember the taste of you, the feel of you, the way your breath quickens when you're naked in my arms and—"

His words sent an arrow of heat to her center. "Chase—"

He closed the distance, but she didn't step back as if under the cowboy's spell. With his free hand, he ran his fingertips leisurely down her cheek to the hollow of her throat toward the V of her blouse.

She shivered and instinctively she leaned her head back, remembering his lips making that same journey. Her nipples puckered, hard and aching against her bra. "Chase—" This time, she said his name more like a plea for him not to stop.

As he pulled his hand back, he smiled. "You and I will be together again come hell or high water because that's where we belong. Tell me I'm wrong."

When she said nothing, couldn't speak, he nodded, took the package and walked out, leaving her trembling with a need for him that seemed to have grown even more potent.

Chapter Nine

Chase still hadn't paid any attention to the package Mary had given him until he tossed it on the seat of his pickup. The lightweight contents made a soft rustling sound, drawing his attention from thoughts of Mary for a moment.

As he climbed behind the wheel of his pickup, he considered what might be inside. It appeared to be an old shoebox that had been tied up with string. Both the box and the string were discolored, giving the impression of age. Why would someone leave him this? Mary had said the woman claimed to be a friend of his mother's.

His thoughts quickly returned to Mary as he drove back to the Jensen Ranch. He remembered the way she'd trembled under his touch. The chemistry was still there between them, stronger than ever. He'd wanted desperately to take her in his arms, to kiss her, to make love to her. If only she could remember how good they were together.

At the ranch, he took the shoebox inside the bunkhouse, where he was staying, tossing it on his bed. He told himself that he didn't care what was inside. But he couldn't help being curious. He sat down on the edge of the bed and drew the box toward him. It wasn't until then that he saw the faded lettering on the top and recognized his mother's handwriting.

For Chase. Only after I'm gone.

His heart thumped hard against his ribs. This was from his mother?

He dug out his pocketknife from his jeans pocket and with trembling fingers cut the string. He hesitated, bracing himself for what he would find inside, and lifted the lid. A musty scent rose up as the papers inside rustled softly.

Chase wasn't sure what he'd expected. Old photos? Maybe his real birth certificate with his father's name on it? A letter to him telling him the things his mother couldn't or wouldn't while she was alive?

What he saw confused him. It appeared to be pages torn from a notebook. Most were yellowed and curled. His mother's handwriting was overly loopy, youthful. Nothing like her usual very small neat writing that had always been slow with painstaking precision.

He picked up one of the pages and began to read. A curse escaped his lips as he realized what he was reading. These were diary pages. His mother had left him her diary? He'd never known her to keep one.

His gaze shot to the date on the top page. It took him only a moment to do the math. This was written just weeks before he was conceived.

His pulse pounded. Finally he would know the truth about his father.

WHEN HER OFFICE door opened, Mary looked up, startled from her thoughts. Chase had left her shaken. She still wanted him desperately. But she was afraid, as much as she hated to admit it. She'd trusted her heart to Chase once. Did she dare do it again?

That's what she kept thinking even as she tried to get some work done. So when her door had opened, she was startled to realize how much time had gone by.

"Lucy." She'd forgotten all about her saying she might stop by later to discuss the apartment. Mary was glad for the distraction. "Come in."

The young woman took the chair she offered her on the other side of her desk. "Did you mean what you said earlier about renting me the apartment? It's just so convenient being right across the street, but I wanted to make sure you hadn't had second thoughts. After all, we just met."

Mary nodded since she'd *had* second thoughts. But as she looked into the young woman's eager face, she pushed them aside and reached into the drawer for the apartment key. "Why don't I show it to you." She rose from her desk. "We can either go up this way," she said, pointing to the back of her office, "or in from the outside entrance. Let's go this way." They went out of the back of her office to where a hallway wound around to the front stairs.

"The apartment is on the second floor," Mary told her as they climbed. "I live upstairs on the third floor. Some people don't want to live that close to their landlady," she said.

"I think I can handle it," Lucy said with a chuckle.

They stopped at the landing on the second floor, and Mary opened the door to the first apartment. "As you can see, it's pretty basic," she said as she pushed open the door. "Living room, kitchen, bedroom and bath." She watched Lucy take it in.

"It's perfect," the young woman said as she walked over to the window and looked out.

"There's a fire escape in the back, and a small balcony if you want to barbecue and not a bad view of Lone Peak." Mary walked to door and opened it so Lucy could see the view."

"That's perfect." She stepped past Mary out onto the small balcony to lean over the railing, before looking up. "So the fire escape goes on up to your apartment and balcony?"

"It does. I wouldn't use the fire escape except in an emergency so you will have privacy out here on your balcony."

Lucy stepped back in and closed the door. "I didn't even ask what the rent was." Mary told her. "That's really reasonable."

"I like providing housing for those working here in Big Sky. Most of the employees have to commute from the valley because there is so little affordable housing for them." She shrugged. "And it's nice to have someone else in the building at night. This area is isolated since it is mostly businesses that close by nine. The other apartment on this floor is rented to a man who travels a lot so I seldom see him."

Lucy ambled into the bedroom to pull down the Murphy bed. "This is great."

"You can use this room as an office as well as a bedroom. Since it has a closet, I call it a one bedroom."

"And it comes furnished?"

"Yes, but you can add anything you like to make it more yours."

Lucy turned to look at her. "I can really see myself living here. It's perfect. I would love it."

Mary smiled. "Then it's yours. You can move in right away if you want to."

"That's ideal because I've been staying in a motel down in the valley just hoping something opened up before I went broke."

"I'll need first and last month's rent, and a security deposit. Is that going to be a problem?"

Lucy grinned. "Fortunately, I'm not that broke yet, so no problem at all. I promise to be the perfect tenant."

Mary laughed. "I've yet to have one of those."

Back downstairs, Lucy paid in cash. Seeing her surprise, the young woman explained that she'd had the cash ready should she find a place. "They go so fast. I didn't want to miss a good opportunity. I feel as if I've hit the lottery getting first the job and now this apartment."

Mary smiled as she handed over the key. "It's nice to have you here."

"I wouldn't want to be anywhere else."

After Lucy left, Mary went back down to her office and called her mother. "I have a new tenant. It's a bit strange, but she's the barista who took Christy's place."

"That is odd. What do you know about her?"

Mary thought about it for a moment. Nothing really. "She's nice." She told her how Lucy had run across the street to bring her coffee twice when Mary had gotten busy and forgotten.

"She sounds thoughtful."

"I like her so I hope it works out." Most of her tenants had, but there was always that one who caused problems.

"Guess who sent me flowers?" she said, changing the subject and putting her new tenant out of her mind.

LUCY COULDN'T BELIEVE how easy that had been. She smiled to herself as she drove back to her motel to get her things.

Mary would be living right upstairs. It would be like taking candy from a baby. She thought of the fire escape and balconies on the two levels behind the apartment. It would be so easy to climb up to Mary's on the third floor, anytime, day or night. While there was a railing around the stairs—and the balconies—still it could be dangerous, especially if Mary had been drinking.

Her thoughts turned sour though when she recalled the two sets of flowers that had been delivered this morning. Anger set off a blaze in her chest. They had to be from Chase, right? She would have loved to have seen what he'd written on the cards. Now that she would be living in the building, maybe she would get her chance.

She still felt surprised at just how easy it had been. Then again, Mary was just too sweet for words, she thought. Also too trusting. At first, she'd just wanted to meet the woman who'd taken Chase from her. At least that's what she'd told herself. Maybe she'd planned to kill her from the very beginning. Maybe it really had been in the back of her mind from the moment she decided to go to Montana and find her—find Chase.

Her feeling had been that if she couldn't have Chase, then no one else could. She'd had dreams of killing them both. Of killing Mary and making him watch, knowing there was nothing Chase could do to save her.

But in her heart of hearts, when she was being honest with herself, she knew what she wanted was for him to fall in love with her again. Otherwise, she would have no choice. It would be his own fault. He would have to die, but only after he mourned for the loss of his precious Mary. She would kill him only after she shattered his life like he'd done hers.

Living just one floor below the woman would provide the perfect opportunity to get closer to Mary—and Chase—until she was ready to end this.

It would be dangerous. She smiled to herself. There was nothing wrong with a little danger. Eventually she and Chase would cross paths. Lucy smiled in anticipation. She couldn't wait to see the look on his face when he realized she wasn't dead. Far from it. She'd never been more alive.

Chapter Ten

After the first sentence, Chase couldn't believe it. The pages in the shoebox were from a diary. His mother's. His fingers trembled as he picked up another page. All these years he'd wanted answers. Was he finally going to get them?

He thumbed through the random pages, looking for names. There were none. But he did find initials. He scooped up the box and pages and sat down, leaning against the headboard as he read what was written before the initials. "I woke up this morning so excited. Today was going to be wonderful. I was going to see J.M. today. He told me to meet him in our secret spot. Maybe he's changed his mind. I can only hope."

Changed his mind about what?

Chase took out another page, but it was clear from reading it that the page wasn't the next day. He began to sort them by date. Some weren't marked except by the day of the week.

But he found one that began "Christmas Day." Whoever J.M. was, his mother had been in love with the man. And since his birthday was in September—nine months from Christmas...

The entry read: "Christmas Day! I thought I wouldn't

get to see him, but he surprised me with a present—a beautiful heart-shaped locket."

Chase felt his heart clench. His mother had worn such a locket. She never took it off. It was with the few things of hers that he'd kept. But he knew there was nothing but a photo of him in the locket. On the back were the words: *To my love always*.

He picked up the phone.

Mary answered on the second ring. "Chase?"

"I don't mean to bother you. But I had to tell you. It's my mother's diary."

"What's your mother's diary?"

"In the shoebox. It's pages from my mother's diary during the time that she got pregnant with me." Silence. "I really could use your help. I think the answer is somewhere in these pages but they're all mixed up. Some have dates, some don't and—"

"Bring them over. We can go through them in my apartment."

A short time later, Mary let him into the door on the side of the building, the shoebox tucked under his arm as they climbed to the third floor.

"Do you want something to drink?" she asked as he closed the door behind them.

The apartment was done in bright cheery colors that reminded him of Mary. "No, thanks." He felt nervous now that he was here.

She motioned to the dining-room table standing in a shaft of morning sun. Through the window, he could see Lone Peak. "Your apartment is wonderful," he said as he put the shoebox on the table and sat down.

"Thanks." Mary pulled out a chair opposite him. "May I?" she asked, and pulled the box toward her.

He nodded. "I looked at some of it, but truthfully, I didn't want to do this alone."

She took out the diary pages, treating them as if they were made of glass. "There had to be a reason her friend was told to give you this after she was gone." She picked up one page and read aloud, "'Friday, I saw him again at Buck's T-4. He didn't see me but I think he knew I was there. He kept looking around as if looking for me.'"

"She met him here in Big Sky!" Mary exclaimed as she flipped the page over. "'Saturday. I hate that we can't be together. He hates it too so that makes me feel a little better.'"

She looked up at Chase. "They were star-crossed lovers right here in Montana."

"Star-crossed lovers?" He scoffed. "From what I've read, it's clear that he was a married man." He raked a hand through his hair. "What if my father has been here in Big Sky all this time, and I never knew it?"

MARY COULD SEE how hard this was on him, just as she could tell that a part of him wasn't sure he wanted to know the truth. "Are you sure you want to find him?"

Chase had been fifteen when his mother had gotten sick the first time, and he'd come to the area to work on a neighboring ranch. Later, Mary's family had put him to work on their ranch, giving him a place to live while he and Mary finished school.

They'd both believed that he'd been sent to Montana because of one of Hud's law-enforcement connections. Her father had never spelled it out, but she now realized that both of her parents must have known Chase's mother back when she'd lived here. She must have been the one who'd asked them to look out for him.

Mary and Chase had been close from the very start. From as far back as she could remember, he'd been haunted by the fact that he didn't know who his father was. He'd been born in Arizona. He'd just assumed that was where his mother met his father. He hadn't known that there was much more of a Montana connection than either he or Mary had known. Until now.

"Truthfully? I'm not sure of anything." His gaze met hers. "Except how I feel about you."

"Chase—"

He waved a hand through the air. "Sorry. As for my…father… I have to know who he is and why he did what he did."

She nodded. "So we'll find him," she said, and picked up another page of the diary. "There has to be some reason he couldn't marry your mother."

He swore under his breath. "I told you. He was already married. It's the only thing that's ever made sense. It's why my mother refused to tell me who he is."

"Maybe she mentions his name on one of the pages," Mary suggested. "If we put them in order." She went to work, sorting through them, but quickly realized that she never mentioned him by name, only J.M.

She stopped sorting to look at him. "J.M.? He shouldn't be hard to find if he still lives here." She got up and went to a desk, returning with a laptop. "Maybe we should read through them first though. It doesn't look as if she wrote something every day." She counted the diary sheets. "There are forty-two of them with days on both sides, so eight-four days."

"About three months," Chase said. "If we knew when the affair started…" They quickly began going through the pages. "This might help," he said as he held up one of the pages.

Something in his voice caught her attention more than his words. "What is it?"

"Christmas Eve." He read what his mother had written. "'It was so romantic. I never dreamed it could be like this. But he reminded me that I didn't have much to compare it with. He said it would get better. I can't imagine.'"

Chase looked up. "I was born nine months later."

"I'm sorry," she said.

He shrugged as if it didn't matter, but it was clear that it mattered a whole lot. "I have to know who he is."

She heard the fury in his voice as he told her about the heart-shaped necklace that his mother had never taken off. "Maybe he loved her."

He scoffed at that. "If he'd loved her, he wouldn't have abandoned her. She was alone, broke and struggling to raise his child."

"Maybe the answer is in these pages, and we just missed something," Mary said after they finished going through them.

He shook his head and scooped up the diary pages, stuffing them roughly back into the shoebox and slamming down the lid.

Mary wanted to know the whole story. She looked at the box longingly. It was clear that Chase had already made up his mind. Even after reading all the diary entries, she knew it was his mother's view of the relationship, and clearly Muriel's head had been in the stars.

"What are you going to do?" she asked, worried.

"Find him. J.M. The Big Sky area isn't that large." He stepped over to the laptop and called up local phone listings from the browser and started with the *M*s. "We can surmise from what she wrote that he's older, more experienced and married. The necklace he gave her wasn't some cheap dime-store one. He had money, probably owned a business in town."

She hesitated, worried now what he would do once he found the man in question. "I think you should let me go with you once we narrow down the list of men."

He looked at her, hope in his expression. "You would do that?"

"Of course." She picked up the phone to call her mother. Dana had known Chase's mother Muriel. That was clearly why Chase had come to live on the ranch at fifteen. "I need to know how Chase came to live with us."

She listened, and after a moment hung up and said to Chase, "Your mother worked in Meadow Village at the grocery store. She says she didn't know who Muriel was seeing, and I believe her. She would have told us if she'd known. She did say that your mother rented a place on the edge of town. So your mother could have met your father at the grocery store or on her way to work or just about anywhere around here."

Chase shook his head. "His wife probably did the grocery shopping."

"We don't know that he had a wife. We're just assuming…" But Chase wasn't listening. He was going through the phone listings.

GRADY BIRCH HAD been leaving when Hud pulled into the drive in front of the cabin. For just a moment, he thought the man might make a run for it. Grady's expression had been like a deer caught in his headlights.

Hud suspected the man always looked like that when he saw the law—and for good reason.

It amused the marshal that Grady pretended nonchalance, leaning against the doorframe as if he had nothing to hide. As Hud exited his patrol SUV and moved toward the man, Grady's nerves got the better of him. His elbow slid off the doorframe, throwing the man off balance. He stumbled to catch himself, looking even more agitated.

"Marshal," he said, his voice high and strained before he cleared his throat. "What brings you out this way?"

"Why don't we step into your cabin and talk?" Hud suggested.

Grady shot a look behind him through the doorway as if he wasn't sure what evidence might be lying around in there. "I'd just as soon talk out here. Unless you have a warrant. I know my rights."

"Why would I have a warrant, Mr. Birch? I just drove out here to talk to you about Christy Shores."

Grady frowned. That hadn't been what he'd expected. The man's relief showed on his ferret-thin face. Grady's relief that this was about Christy told Hud that this had been a wasted trip. The man hadn't killed the barista. Grady was more worried about being arrested for cattle rustling.

"I just have a couple of quick questions," Hud said, hoping Grady gave him something to go on. "You dated Christy?"

"I wouldn't call it dating exactly."

"You were involved with her."

Grady shook his head. "I wouldn't say that either."

Hud sighed and shifted on his feet. "What would you say?"

"I knew who she was."

"You knew her well enough to get in a fight over her at Charley's the night she was killed."

"Let's say I had a good thing going with her, and Chet tried to horn in."

"What did Christy have to say about all this?"

Grady frowned as if he didn't understand the question. He was leaning against the doorframe again, only this time he looked a lot more comfortable.

Hud rephrased it. "What did she get out of this...relationship with you?"

"Other than the obvious?" Grady asked with a laugh. "It was a place to sleep so she didn't have to go back to her mother's in Bozeman."

"Is that where she was headed that night, to your cabin?"

Grady shook his head. "I told her it wasn't happening. I saw her making eyes at Chet. Let him put her up out at his place. I won't be used by any woman."

Hud had to bite his tongue. The way men like Grady treated women made his teeth ache. "When was the last time you saw her?"

"When Chet told her to scram and she ran into the bathroom crying."

"That was before the two of you got thrown out of the bar?" the marshal asked.

Grady nodded. "So have you found out who ran her down?"

"Not yet."

"Probably some tourist traveling through. I was in Yellowstone once, and there was this woman walking along the edge of the highway and this motor home came along. You know how those big old things have those huge side mirrors? One of them caught her in the back of the head." Grady made a disgusted sound. "Killed her deader than a doornail. Could have taken her head off if the driver had been going faster."

"Christy Shores wasn't killed by a motor home. She was murdered by someone locally."

Grady's eyes widened. "Seriously? You don't think Chet…"

"Chet has an alibi for the time of the murder. Can anyone verify that you came straight here to this cabin and didn't leave again?"

"I was alone, but I can assure you I didn't leave again."

Hud knew the value of an assurance by Grady Birch. "You wouldn't know anyone who might have wanted to harm her, do you?"

He wagged his head, still looking shocked. "Christy was all right, you know. She didn't deserve that." He sounded as if he'd just realized that if he'd brought her back to his cabin that night, she would still be alive.

DILLON WAS HEADED to Grady's when he saw the marshal's SUV coming out of the dirt road into the cabin. He waved and kept going as if headed to Bozeman, his pulse thundering in his ears. What had the marshal been doing out at the cabin? Was he investigating the cattle rustling?

He glanced in his rearview mirror. The marshal hadn't slowed or turned around as if headed back to Big Sky, and as far as Dillon could tell, Grady wasn't handcuffed in the back. He kept going until he couldn't see the patrol SUV in his rearview anymore before he pulled over, did a highway patrol turn and headed back toward the cabin.

His instincts told him not to. The marshal might circle back. Right now, he especially didn't want Hud knowing about his association with Grady Birch. But he had to find out what was going on. If he needed to skip the state, he wanted to at least get a running start.

He drove to the cabin, parking behind it. As he did, he saw Grady peer out the window. Had he thought the marshal had reason to return? The back door flew open. Grady looked pale and shaken. Dillon swore under his breath. It must be bad. But how bad?

"What—" He didn't get to finish his question before Grady began to talk, his words tumbling over each other. He caught enough of it to realize that the marshal's visit had nothing to do with cattle. Relief washed over him.

Pushing past Grady, he went into the cabin, opened the refrigerator and took the last beer. He guzzled it like a man dying of thirst. That had been too close of a call. He'd been so sure that Hud was on to them.

"Did you hear what I said?" Grady demanded. "She was *murdered*. Marshal said so himself."

Dillon couldn't care less about some girl Grady had been hanging with, and said as much.

"You really are a coldhearted bastard," Grady snapped. "And you drank the last beer," he said as he opened the refrigerator. "How about you bring a six-pack or two out for a change? I do all the heavy lifting and you—"

"Put a sock in it or I will." He wasn't in the mood for any whining. "I have my own problems."

"The marshal sniffing around you?"

He finished the beer and tossed the can into the

corner with the others piled there. "It's the marshal's daughter. Things aren't progressing like I planned."

Grady let out a disgusting sound. "I really don't care about your love life. I've never understood why you were messing with her to start with."

"Because she could be valuable, but I don't have to explain myself to you."

His partner in crime bristled. "You know I'm getting damned tired of you talking down to me. Why don't you rustle your own cattle? I'm finished."

"Where do you think you're going?" Dillon asked, noticing a flyer on the table that he hadn't seen before. With a shock, he saw that it advertised a reward from local ranchers for any information about the recent cattle rustling.

"I'm going into Charley's to have a few, maybe pick up some money shooting pool, might even find me a woman."

"You've already jeopardized the entire operation because of the last woman you brought out here."

Grady turned to look back at him. "What are you talking about?"

"Where'd you get that notice about the reward being offered by the ranchers?"

"They're all over town."

"So you just picked up one. Did the marshal see it?"

Grady colored. "No, I wouldn't let him in. I'm not a fool."

But Dillon realized that he *was* a fool, one that he could no longer afford. "I'm just saying that maybe you should lie low."

"I was headed into town when the marshal drove up. He doesn't suspect me of anything, all right? I've got cabin fever. You stay here and see how you like it." He turned to go out the door.

Dillon picked up the hatchet from the kindling pile next to the woodstove. He took two steps and hit Grady with the blunt end. The man went down like a felled pine, his face smashing into the back porch floor. When he didn't move, Dillon set about wiping any surface he had touched on his visits. He'd always been careful, he thought as he wiped the refrigerator door and the hatchet's handle.

His gaze went to the pile of beer cans in the corner and realized that his prints were all over those cans. Finding an old burlap bag, he began to pick up the cans when he saw an old fishing pole next to the door. Smiling, he knew how he could dispose of Grady's body.

Chapter Eleven

Dillon touched Mary's cheek, making her jump. "I didn't mean to startle you. It's just that you seemed a million miles away."

Actually only five miles away, on the ranch where Chase was working.

She couldn't quit thinking about him, which is why she hadn't wanted to go out with Dillon tonight, especially after she'd told him that she needed more time.

"I guess you forgot," he'd said. "The tickets to the concert I bought after the last time we went out? You said you loved that band, and I said I should try to get us some tickets. Well I did. For tonight."

She'd recalled the conversation. It hadn't been definite, but she hadn't been up to arguing about it. Anyway, she knew that if she stayed home, all she'd do was mope around and worry about Chase.

"You've been distracted this whole night."

"Sorry," she said. "But you're right. I have a lot on my mind. Which is why I need to call it a night."

"Anything I can help you with?" he asked.

She shook her head.

"It wouldn't be some blond cowboy named Chase

Steele, would it?" There was an edge to his voice. She wasn't in the mood for his jealousy.

"Chase is a friend of mine."

"Is that all?"

She turned to look at him, not liking his tone. "I can go out with anyone I want to."

"Oh, it's like that, is it?"

She reached for her door handle, but he grabbed her arm before she could get out.

"Slow down," he said. "I was just asking." He quickly let go of her. "Like you said, you can date anyone you please. But then, so can I. What if I decided to ask out that barista friend of yours?"

"Lucy?" She was surprised he even knew about her.

"Yeah, Lucy."

If he was trying to make her jealous, he was failing badly. "Be my guest," she said, and opened her door and climbed out before he could stop her again.

She heard him get out the driver's side and come after her. "Good night Dillon," she said pointedly. But he didn't take the hint.

As she pulled out her keys to open her office door, he grabbed her and shoved her back, caging her against the side of the building.

"I won't put up with you giving me the runaround."

"Let me go," she said from between gritted teeth. Her voice sounded much stronger than she felt at that moment. Her heart was beating as if she'd just run a mile. Dillon was more than wild. She could see that he could be dangerous—more dangerous than she was interested in.

CHANCE HAD BEEN parked down the street, waiting for Mary to return home. He needed to talk to her about earlier. Since getting the box his mother had left for him, he'd been so focused on finding his father that he wanted to apologize. She'd offered to help. He wanted to get it over with as soon as possible since he'd managed to narrow it down to three names.

It wasn't until he saw the pickup stop in front of her building that he realized she had been on a date with that deputy.

He growled under his breath. There was something about that guy that he didn't like. And it wasn't just that he was going out with Mary, he told himself.

Now he mentally kicked himself for sitting down the street watching her place. If she saw him, she'd think he was spying on her. He reached to key the ignition and leave when he saw the passenger door of the deputy's rig open. From where he sat, he couldn't miss the deputy grabbing Mary as she tried to get out. What the hell?

He was already opening his door and heading toward her building when he saw Dillon get out and go after her. He could tell by her body language that she wasn't happy. What had the deputy done to upset her?

Chase saw that Dillon had pinned her against the side of her building. Mary appeared to be trying to get her keys out and go inside.

"Let her go!" he yelled as he advanced on the man.

Both Mary and Dillon turned at the sound of his voice. Both looked surprised, then angry.

"This is none of your business," the two almost said in unison.

"Let go of her," he said again to the deputy.

Mary pushed free of Dillon's arms and, keys palmed, turned to face Chase as he approached. "What are you doing here?"

"I needed to talk to you, but I'm glad I was here to run interference for you. If he's giving you trouble—"

"I can handle this," she said.

Chase could see how upset she was at Dillon and now him. "Date's over. You should go," he said to the deputy.

Dillon started to come at him. Chase was ready, knowing he could take him in a fair fight. He just doubted the man had ever fought fair. Dillon threw the first punch and charged. Chase took only a glancing blow before he slugged the deputy square in the face, driving him back, but only for a moment.

The man charged again, leading with a right and then a quick left that caught Chase on the cheek. He hit Dillon hard in the stomach, doubling him over before shoving him back. The deputy sprawled on the ground, but was scrambling to his feet reaching for something in his boot when Chase heard Mary screaming for them to stop.

"Stop it!" Mary cried. "Both of you need to leave. Now."

Dillon slowly slide the knife back into its scabbard, but not before Chase had seen it. He realized how quickly the fight could have gotten ugly if Mary hadn't stopped it when she did.

The deputy got up from the ground, cussing and spitting out blood. His lip was cut and bleeding. Chase's jaw and cheek were tender. He suspected he'd have a black eye by morning.

The look Dillon gave him made it clear that this wasn't over. The next time they saw each other, if Mary wasn't around, they would settle things. At least now Chase knew what he would be facing. A man who carried a blade in his boot.

"Leave now," Mary repeated.

"We'll finish our discussion some other time," Dillon said to her pointedly, making Chase wish he knew what had been said before Mary had gotten upset and tried to go inside. Now, she said nothing as Dillon started toward his pickup.

"That man is dangerous, Mary. If he—"

She spun on him. "Are you spying on me, Chase?"

"No, I needed to talk to you. I was just waiting..." He knew he sounded lame. It had been weak to wait down the street for her.

She didn't cut him any slack. "I'm sure whatever you need to talk to me about can wait until tomorrow." She turned to open her door.

"I'm sorry," he said behind her, glad he'd been here, even though he'd made her angry. He hated to think what could have happened if he hadn't intervened.

Mary didn't answer as she went inside and closed the door.

As he walked back to his pickup, he knew he had only himself to blame for all of this. He'd made so many mistakes, and he could add tonight's to the list.

Still, he worried. Mary thought she could handle Dillon. But the deputy didn't seem like a man who would take no for an answer.

TORN BETWEEN ANGER and fear, Mary closed and locked the door behind her with trembling fingers. What was wrong with her? Tears burned her eyes. She hadn't wanted to go out with Dillon tonight. So why had she let him persuade her into it?

And Chase. Parked down the street watching her, spying on her? She shook her head. If he thought he could come back after all this time and just walk in and start—

"Is everything okay?" asked a voice behind her, making her jump. "I didn't mean to startle you," Lucy said, coming up beside her in the hallway of her building.

Mary was actually glad to see Lucy. She'd had it with men tonight. She wiped her eyes, angry at herself on so many levels, but especially for shedding more tears over Chase. Her life had felt empty without him, before Dillon, but now she missed that simple world.

Even as she told herself that, she knew she was lying. Chase was back. She loved him. She wanted him. So why did she keep pushing him away?

"What was that about?" Lucy asked, wide-eyed as they both watched the two men leave, Dillon in a hail of gravel as he spun out, and Chase limping a little as he headed for his truck.

"Nothing," she said, and took a deep breath before letting it out. She was glad to have Lucy in the building tonight.

Lucy laughed. "*Nothing?* They were fighting over you. Two men were just fighting over you." She was looking at her with awe.

Mary had to smile. "It had more to do with male ego than me, trust me." She thought about saying something to Lucy about Dillon's warning to Mary that he'd ask her out, but realized it was probably a hollow threat. Anyway, she was betting that Lucy could take care of herself.

LUCY TRIED TO keep the glee out of her voice. She'd witnessed the whole thing. Poor Chase. What struck her as ironic was that she'd had nothing to do with any of it. This was all Mary's own doing.

"Would you like to come up to my apartment for a drink? Sometimes I've found talking also helps." She shrugged.

Mary hesitated only a moment before she gave Lucy an embarrassed smile. "Do you have beer?"

Lucy laughed. "Beer, vodka, ice cream. I'm prepared for every heartbreak."

They climbed the stairs, Lucy opened the door and they entered her apartment. "I haven't done much with the space," Lucy said as she retrieved two beers from the refrigerator and handed one to Mary. "But I'm excited to pick up a few things to make it more mine. It really doesn't need anything. You've done such a good job of appointing it."

"Thank you," Mary said, taking the chair in the living room. "I'm just glad you're enjoying staying here. I'm happy to have you." Mary took a sip of her beer, looking a little uneasy now that she was here.

Lucy curled her legs under her on the couch, getting comfortable, and broke the ice, first talking about decorating and finally getting to the good part. "I had to laugh earlier. I once had two men fight over me. It was in high school at a dance. At the time I'd been mortified with embarrassment." She chuckled. "But my friends all thought it was cool."

"That was high school. It's different at this age," Mary said, and took another drink of her beer.

Lucy cocked her head at her as she licked beer foam from her lips and got up to get them another. "But I'm betting there was one of those men who you wanted to win the fight for you."

Mary looked surprised, then embarrassed.

"I wager it wasn't the deputy."

"You're right," her landlady admitted as she took the second beer. "Chase was my first love since the age of fifteen when he came to Montana to work on the ranch. We became best friends before..." Mary mugged a face. "Before we fell in love."

"So what happened to your happy ending?" Lucy asked as she took her beer back to the couch. She leaned toward Mary expectantly.

"I caught him kissing another woman. He swore the woman kissed him, but I guess I realized then that maybe what my parents had been saying was true. We were too young to be that in love. Only twenty-four. I let Chase go. He left Montana to...find himself," Mary said, and took another sip.

"*Find himself?* I'm guessing you didn't know he was lost."

Mary shook her head with a laugh. "We *were* too young to make any big decisions until we'd lived more. My father said that I had to let Chase sow some wild oats. But I didn't want him to leave."

Lucy groaned. "If he wanted to date other women, you didn't really want him to do it here, did you?"

"I wanted him to tell me that he didn't need to go see what else was out there. That all he wanted was me. But he didn't."

"And now it's too late?"

Mary shook her head. "I still love him."

Lucy traced her fingers around the top of her beer can for a moment. "Why do you think he came back now?"

Mary shook her head. "It's my fault." She sighed.

"Have you ever had a weak moment when you did something stupid?"

She laughed. "Are you kidding? Especially when it comes to men."

"I found his address online since I didn't have his cell phone number or email, and he wasn't anywhere on social media. I wrote him a letter, late at night in a nostalgic mood." Mary shook her head. "Even as I wrote it, I knew I'd never mail it."

This was news. "You didn't mail it?"

"I did put it in an envelope with his address on it. I was staying out at the ranch because my horse was due to have her colt that night. I forgot about the letter— until I realized it was gone. My aunt Stacy saw it and thought I meant to mail it, so she did it for me."

Lucy leaned back, almost too surprised to speak. "So if your aunt hadn't done that…"

Mary nodded. "None of this would have probably happened, although Chase says he was planning to come back anyway. But who knows?"

The woman had no idea, Lucy thought. "So, he's back and he's ready to settle down finally?"

"I guess."

She sipped her beer for a moment. "Is that what you want?"

"Yes, I still love him. But…"

"But there is that adorable deputy," Lucy said with a laugh. "Sounds like a problem we should all have. And it's driving Chase crazy with jealousy."

"You're right about that. He can hardly be civil to Dillon when they cross paths. He says there's something about the guy that he doesn't trust."

"Obviously, he doesn't want you dating the guy."

"I'm not going out with Dillon again, and it has nothing to do with what Chase wants. I didn't date for a long time after Chase left. I was too heartbroken. I finally felt ready to move on, and I wrote that stupid letter." She drained her beer, and Lucy got up to get her another.

"What about you?" Mary asked, seeming more comfortable now that she'd gotten that off her chest and consumed two beers.

"Me?" Lucy curled up on the couch again. "There was someone. I thought we were perfect for each other. But in the end, I was more serious than he was." She shook her head. "You know what I think is wrong with men? They don't know what they want. They want you one day, especially if there is another guy in the picture, but ultimately how can you trust them when the next minute they're waffling again? Aren't you afraid that could happen if Dillon is out of the picture?"

Mary shook her head. "I'd rather find out now than later. Trust. That is what it comes down to. Chase broke my trust when he left, when he didn't answer my letter right away or even bother to call." She seemed to hesitate. "There was this woman he was seeing."

Her ears perked up. "He told you about her?"

"He had to after I told him that she'd called me. Apparently, she'd read my letter to him. She called to tell me to leave him alone because they were engaged."

"Were they?"

"No, he says that she's delusional."

"Wow, it does sound like she was emotionally involved in a big way. He must have cared about her a little for her to react that way."

Mary shrugged. "I know he feels guilty. He certainly didn't want her to die. He admitted that he slept with her one night. But that now just the sound of her name is like fingernails on a blackboard for me. *Fiona*." She dragged out the pronunciation of the name.

Lucy laughed. "*He even told you her name?* Men. Sometimes they aren't very smart. Now you'll always wonder about her and if there is more to the story."

Chapter Twelve

Mary couldn't remember the last time she'd drunk three beers. But as she'd taken the stairs to her third-floor apartment, she'd been smiling. She'd enjoyed the girl-time with Lucy. It made her realize how cut off she'd been from her friends.

A lot of them had moved away after college, and not come back except for a week at Christmas or in the summer. They'd married, had children or careers that they had to get back to. Even though they often promised to stay in touch, they hadn't. Life went on. People changed.

Mary also knew that some of them thought staying in a place where they'd grown up had a stigma attached to it as if, like Chase, they thought the grass was greener away from Big Sky, away from Montana. They went to cities where there were more opportunities. They had wanted more. Just like Chase.

They had wanted something Mary had never yearned for. Everything she needed was right here, she told herself as she drove out to the ranch. She'd wandered past the state line enough during her college days that she knew there was nothing better out there than what she had right here.

So why hadn't she been able to understand Chase's need to leave? Why had she taken it so personally? He'd wanted her to go with him, she reminded herself. But she'd had no need to search for more, not realizing that losing Chase would make her question everything she held dear.

Mary found her mother in the kitchen alone. The moment Dana saw her she said, "What's wrong?"

She and her mother had always been close. While her male siblings had left Montana, she'd been the one to stay. Probably since she'd been the one most like her mother and grandmother.

"Nothing really," she said as she poured herself a cup of coffee and dropped into a chair at the large kitchen table. Sunshine streamed in the open window along with the scent of pine and the river. "Can't I just come by to see my mother?"

Dana cocked an eyebrow at her.

She sighed and said, "It's *everything*. Chase's mother left him this shoebox with diary pages from what appears to be the time she became pregnant with him."

"About his father? That's why you called me and asked me if I knew. Isn't his name in the diary pages?"

She shook her head. "Muriel didn't mention his name, just his initials, J.M. Does that ring any bells?"

"No, I'm sorry. I didn't know Muriel well. I'd see her at the grocery store. She came out to the ranch a couple of times. We went horseback riding. Then I heard that she'd left town. Fifteen years later, she contacted me, thanked me for my kindness back when she lived in Big Sky and asked for our help with Chase."

Mary nodded. "Well, we know why she left. It appears her lover might have been married or otherwise unavailable."

"That would explain a lot," Dana said. "How is Chase taking all of this?"

Mary shook her head. "Not well. He's determined to find him. But with only the man's initials…"

"That's not much help I wouldn't think."

"I'm afraid what he'll do when he finds him," Mary said. "He has such animosity toward him."

"It's understandable. If the man knew Muriel was pregnant and didn't step up, I can see how that has hurt Chase. But is that what happened?"

"That's just it. We don't know. Either she didn't include the diary pages at the end or she never wrote down what happened. The last page we found she was going to meet him at their special place and was very nervous about telling him the news. But that she believed their love could conquer anything."

Dana shook her head. "So Chase is assuming she told him and he turned her away."

Mary nodded. "It's the obvious assumption given that his mother refused to tell him anything about his father."

Dana got up to refill her cup. When she returned to the table, she asked, "How was your date with Dillon last night?"

Mary looked away. "I'm not going out with him again."

"Did something happen?" Dana sounded alarmed, and Mary knew if she didn't downplay it, her mother would tell her father, and who knew what he would do. He already didn't like Dillon.

"It was fine, but that's the problem. He's not Chase."

Her mother was giving her the side-eye, clearly not believing any of it.

She realized that she had to give her more or her mother would worry. "Dillon doesn't like me seeing Chase."

"I see." She probably did. "So that's it?"

She nodded. "Chase isn't wild about me seeing Dillon, but he's smart enough not to try to stop me." Mary tried to laugh it all off as she got up to take her cup to the sink. "Kara says it's a terrible problem to have, two men who both want me."

"Yes," her mother said. "If Dillon gives you a hard time—"

"Do not say a word to Dad about this. You know how he is. I just don't want to go out with Dillon again. That should make Dad happy."

"Only if it is your choice."

"It is. I need to get to work."

Dana got up to hug her daughter before she left. "We just want you to be happy. Right now it doesn't sound like either man is making you so."

"His mother's diary has blindsided Chase, but it would anyone. This whole mystery about who his father is…" She glanced at the clock. "I have to get going. Remember, nothing about this to Dad."

Her mother nodded even though Mary knew there were few secrets between them.

LUCY COULDN'T HAVE been more pleased with the way things had gone last night. Mary had been furious with Chase. The cowboy had done it to himself. *Fiona* hadn't even had a hand in it.

She was still chuckling about it this morning when

the bell over the coffee shop door jangled and she turned to see the deputy come in.

Dillon Ramsey. She immediately picked up a vibe from him that made her feel a kinship. They might have more in common than Mary.

"Good morning," she said, wondering what kind of night he'd had after everything that had happened. How serious was he about Mary? Not that much, she thought as he gave her the eye. He had a cut lip and bruise on his jaw, but he didn't seem any the worse for wear.

"What can I get you?" she asked, and he turned on a grin that told her he'd come in for more than coffee. What was this about?

"I'd take a coffee, your choice, surprise me."

Oh, she could surprise him in ways he never dreamed of. But she'd play along. "You got it," she said, and went to work on his coffee while he ambled over to the window to stare across the street at Mary's building.

She made him something strong enough to take paint off the walls, added a little sweetness and said, "I think I have just what you need this morning."

He chuckled as he turned back to her. "I think you're right about that." He blatantly looked her up and down. "Go out with me."

Okay, she hadn't been expecting that. But all things considered, the idea intrigued her. "I'm sorry, but aren't you dating my landlady?"

"Who says I can't date you too?"

She raised an eyebrow. Clearly, he wanted to use her to make Mary jealous. He could mess up her plans. She couldn't let him do that. Realizing he could be a problem, she recalled that Mary had plans tonight so she wouldn't be around.

"I'll tell you what. I'm working the late shift tonight. I wouldn't be free until midnight." She wrote down the number of her burner phone and handed him the slip of paper. "Why don't you give me a call sometime."

He grinned as he paid for his coffee. "I'll do that."

Lucy grinned back. "I'm looking forward to it," she said, meaning it. Dillon thought he could use her. The thought made her laugh. He seriously had no idea who he was dealing with.

MARY LOOKED UP as Chase came in the front door of her building.

He held up his hands in surrender. "I don't want to keep you from your work, but I thought maybe we could have lunch together if you don't have other plans. I really need to talk to you. Not about us. You asked for space, and I'm giving it to you. But I do need your help."

She glanced at her watch, surprised to see that it was almost noon. Which meant that all the restaurants would be packed. She said as much to him.

He grinned, which was always her undoing with him. "I packed us a picnic lunch. I know you're busy, so I thought we would just go down by the river. I'll have you back within the hour. If it won't work out, no sweat. I'll leave."

She hadn't been on a picnic in years. But more important, Chase wasn't pressuring her. There was a spot on the river on the ranch that used to be one of their favorite places. The memory of the two of them down by the river blew in like a warm summer breeze, a caress filled with an aching need.

"It's a beautiful day out. I thought you could use a little sunshine and fresh air," he said.

She glanced at the work on her desk. "It is tempting." *He* was tempting.

"I didn't just come here about lunch," he said as if confessing. "I've narrowed down the search for my father to three names." That caught her attention. "I was hoping—"

"Just give me a minute to change."

They drove the short distance to the Gallatin River and walked down to a spot with a sandy shore. A breeze whispered in the pines and off the water to keep the summer day cool.

Chase carried a picnic basket that Mary knew he'd gotten from her mother. "Was this my mother's idea?"

He laughed. "I do have a few ideas of my own." His blue gaze locked with hers, sending a delicious shiver through her. She remembered some of his ideas.

She sighed and took a step away from him. Being so close to Chase with him looking at her like that, she couldn't think straight. "It makes me nervous, the two of you with your heads together." When he said nothing, she'd looked over at him.

He grinned. She did love that grin. "Your mom and I have always gotten along great. I like her."

She eyed him for a moment and let it go. Did he think that getting closer to her mother was going to make her trust him again? "How is work going on the Jensen Ranch?"

"I've been helping with fencing so if you're asking about Beth Anne? I haven't even seen her." He shook his head. "Like I told you, it's temporary. I start as finish carpenter with Reclaimed Timber Construction next week. I'll also be moving into my own place in a few days. I was just helping out at the Jensens' ranch. Since

I left, I've saved my money. I'm planning to build my own home here in the canyon." He shrugged and then must have seen her surprised expression. "Mary, I told you, I'm not leaving. I love you. I'm going to fight like hell to get you back. Whatever it takes. Even if I have to run off that deputy of yours."

"Don't talk crazy." She noticed the bruise on his cheek from last night reminding her of their fight.

"Seriously, there is something about him I don't like."

"That was obvious, but I don't want to talk about him. Especially with you."

"Not a problem," he said as he spread out a blanket in the sand and opened the picnic basket "Fresh lemonade. I made it myself."

"With my mother's help," she said as he held up the jug. She could hear the ice cubes rattling.

"I know it's your favorite," he said as he produced a plastic glass and poured her some. As he handed it to her, he smiled. "You look beautiful today, by the way."

She took the glass, her fingers brushing against his. A tingle rushed through her arm to her center in a heartbeat. She took a sip of the lemonade. "It's wonderful. Thank you."

"That's not all." He brought out fried chicken, potato salad and deviled eggs.

"If I eat all this, I won't get any work done this afternoon," she said, laughing.

"Would that be so terrible?"

She smiled at him as she leaned back on the blanket. The tops of the dark pines swayed in the clear blue overhead. The sound of the flowing clear water of the Gallatin River next to them was like a lullaby. It really was an amazing day, and it had been so long since she'd been here with Chase.

"I haven't done this since…"

"I left. I'm sorry."

"Not sorry you left," she said, hating that she'd brought it up.

"Just sorry it wasn't with you."

She nodded and sat up as he handed her a plate. "I guess we'll never agree on that."

"Maybe not. But we agree on most everything else," he said. "We want the same things."

"Do we?" she asked, meeting his gaze. Those old feelings rushed at her, making her melt inside. She loved this cowboy.

"We do. Try the chicken. I fried it myself."

She took a bite and felt her eyes widen. "It's delicious." It wasn't her mother's. "There's a spice on it I'm having trouble placing."

"It's my own recipe."

"It really is good."

"I wish you didn't sound so surprised." But he grinned as he said, "Now the potato salad."

"Equally delicious. So you cook?"

His face broke in a wide smile. "You really underestimate me. Cooking isn't that tough."

They ate to the sound of the river, the occasional birdsong and the chatter of a distant squirrel. It was so enjoyable that she hated to bring up a subject that she knew concerned him. But he'd said he needed to talk to her about the names of men he thought might be his father.

"You said you've narrowed your search to three names?" she asked.

He nodded. "J.M. I've searched phone listings. Since it was someone in the Big Sky area that helps narrow the scope."

Unless the man had just been passing through. Or if he'd left. But she didn't voice her doubts. "What is your plan? Are you going to knock on the door of the men with the initials J.M.?"

He laughed. "You have a better suggestion?"

She studied him. "You're sure you want to do this?"

Chase looked away for a moment. "I wish I could let it go. But I have to know."

"What will you do when you find him?"

He chuckled. "I have no idea."

"I don't believe that."

Chase met her gaze. "This man used my mother and when she got pregnant, he dumped her."

"That isn't what she said in her diary."

"No, she didn't spell it out, if that's what you mean. But I know how it ended. With her being penniless trying to raise me on her own. It's what killed her, working like a dog all those years. I want to look him in the face and— " His voice broke.

She moved to him. As he drew her into his arms, she rested her head against the solid rock wall of his chest. She listened to the steady beat of his heart as tears burned her eyes. She knew how important family was. She'd always known hers. She could feel the hole in his heart, and wanted more than anything to fill it. "Then let's find him."

As they started to pack up the picnic supplies, Chase took her in his arms again. "You know I've never been that good with words."

"Oh, I think you're just fine with words," she said, and laughed.

"I love you," he said simply.

She met his gaze. Those blue eyes said so much that he didn't need words to convince her of that. "I love you."

"That's enough. For now," he said, and released her. The promise in his words sent a shiver of desire racing through her. Her skin tingled from his touch as well as his words. She'd wanted this cowboy more than she wanted her next breath.

Still, she let him finish picking up the picnic supplies. He smiled at her. "Ready?"

Just about, she thought.

LUCY HAD BEEN shocked when Chase had stopped by Mary's and the two had left together. She'd thought Mary was angry with him. Clearly, not enough.

Where had they been? Not far away because he'd brought her back so soon. But something was different. She could sense it, see it in the way they were with each other as he walked her to her door. They seemed closer. She tried to breathe. Her hands ached from being balled up into fists.

Watching from the window of the coffee shop, she saw Mary touch his hand. Chase immediately took hers in his large, sun-browned one. The two looked at each other as if... As if they shared a secret. Surely they weren't lovers again already. Then Chase kissed her.

Lucy brought her fist down on the counter. Cups rattled and Amy, who'd been cashing out for the day, looked over at her. "Sorry. I was trying to kill a pesky fly."

Amy didn't look convinced, but she did go back to

what she was doing, leaving Lucy alone to stare out the window at the couple across the street. Chase had stepped closer. His hands were now on her shoulders. Lucy remembered his scent, his touch. He was hers. Not Mary's.

Chase leaned in and kissed her again before turning back to his pickup. It wasn't a lover's kiss. It was too quick for that. But there was no doubt that Mary was no longer angry with him. Something had changed.

She watched him drive away, telling herself to bide her time. She couldn't go off half-cocked like she had that night at the river. Timing was everything.

A customer came in. She unfisted her hands as she began to make the woman's coffee order and breathe. But she kept seeing the way Chase had kissed his cowgirl and how Mary had responded. It ate at her heart like acid, and she thought she might retch.

But she held it together as the coffee shop filled with a busload of tourists. Soon Mary would come over for her afternoon caffeine fix. Lucy touched the small white package of powder in her apron pocket. She was ready for her.

MARY TRIED TO concentrate on her work. She had to get this report done. But her mind kept going back to Chase and the picnic and the kisses.

She touched the tip of her tongue to her lower lip and couldn't help but smile. Some things didn't change. Being in Chase's arms again, feeling his lips on hers. The short kiss was a prelude to what could come.

"Don't get ahead of yourself," she said out loud. "You're only helping him look for his father." But even as she said it, she knew today they'd crossed one of the barriers she'd erected between them.

She shook her head and went back to work, losing herself in the report until she heard her front door open. Looking up, she saw Lucy holding a cup of coffee from Lone Peak Perk.

"I hope I'm not disturbing you," she said. "When it got late, I realized you might need this." She held out the cup.

"What time is it?"

"Five thirty. I'm sorry. You probably don't want it today." She started to back out.

"No, it's just what I need if I hope to get this finished today," Mary said, rising from her desk. "I lost track of time and I had a big lunch. It's a wonder I haven't already dozed off."

Lucy smiled as she handed her the coffee. "I saw your cowboy come by and pick you up. Fun lunch?"

Mary nodded, grinning in spite of herself. "Very fun." She reached for her purse.

"I put it on your account."

She smiled. "Thank you." She took a sip. "I probably won't be able to sleep tonight from all this sugar and caffeine this late in the day, but at least I should be able to get this report done now. Thank you again. What would I do without you?"

Chapter Thirteen

Mary thought she was going to die. She'd retched until there was nothing more inside her, and yet her stomach continued to roil.

When it had first hit, she'd rushed to the restroom at the back of her office. She'd thought it might have been the potato salad, but Chased had ice packs around everything in the basket.

Still, she couldn't imagine what else it could have been. Flu? It seemed early in the season, but it was possible.

After retching a few times, she thought it had passed. The report was almost finished. She wasn't feeling great. Maybe she should go upstairs to her apartment and lie down for a while.

But it had hit again and again. Now she sat on the cool floor of the office bathroom, wet paper towels held to her forehead, as she waited for another stomach spasm. She couldn't remember ever feeling this sick, and it scared her. She felt so weak that she didn't have the strength to get up off this floor, let alone make it up to her third-floor apartment.

She closed her eyes, debating if she could reach her

desk where she'd left her cell phone. If she could call her mother…

"Mary? Mary, are you here?"

Relieved and afraid Lucy would leave before she could call her, Mary crawled over to the door to the hallway and, reaching up, her arm trembling, opened it. "Lucy." Her throat hurt. When her voice came out, the words were barely audible. "Lucy!" she called again, straining to be heard since she knew she couldn't get to her feet as weak as she was.

For a moment it seemed that Lucy hadn't heard her. Tears burned her eyes, and she had to fight breaking down and sobbing.

"Mary?"

She heard footfalls and a moment later Lucy was standing over her, looking down at her with an expression of shock.

"I'm sick."

"I can see that." Lucy leaned down. "Do you want me to call you an ambulance?"

"No, if you could just help me up to my apartment. I think it must be food poisoning."

"Oh no. What did you have for lunch?" Lucy asked as she reached down to lift her into a standing position. "You're as weak as a kitten."

Mary leaned against the wall for a moment, feeling as if she needed to catch her breath. "Chase made us a picnic lunch. It must have been the chicken or the potato salad."

"That's awful. Here, put your arm around me. Do you think you can walk?"

They went out the back of the office and down the hallway to the stairs.

"Let me know if you need to rest," Lucy said as they started up the steps.

Her stomach empty, the spasms seemed to have stopped—at least for the moment. Having Lucy here made her feel less scared. She was sure that she'd be fine if she could just get to her apartment and lie down.

"I'm all right." But she was sweating profusely by the time they'd reached her door.

"I didn't think to ask," Lucy said. "Are your keys downstairs?"

Mary let out a groan of frustration. "On my desk."

"If you think you can stand while I run back down—"

"No, there's a spare key under the carpet on the last stair at the top," she said. "I sometimes forget when I just run up from the office for lunch."

"Smart."

She watched Lucy retrieve the key. "I can't tell you how glad I was to see you."

"I saw that your lights were still on in your office, but there was no sign of you. I thought I'd better check to make sure everything was all right. When I found your office door open and you weren't there…" She opened the door and helped her inside.

"I think I want to go straight to my bedroom. I need to lie down."

"Let me help you." Lucy got her to the bed. "Can you undress on your own?"

"If you would just help me with my boots, I think I can manage everything else."

Lucy knelt down and pulled off her Western boots. "Here, unbutton your jeans and let me pull them off. You'll be more comfortable without them."

Mary fumbled with the buttons, realizing the woman

was right. She felt so helpless, and was grateful when Lucy pulled off her jeans and helped tuck her into bed. "Thank you so much."

"I'm just glad I could help. Would you like some ginger ale? My mother always gave me that when I had a stomachache."

Mary shook her head. "I think I just need to rest."

"Okay, I'll leave you to it. I don't see your phone."

"It's downstairs on my desk too."

"I'll get it so you can call if you need anything, and I mean anything, you call me, all right? I'll be just downstairs."

Mary nodded. Suddenly she felt exhausted and just wanted to close her eyes.

"Don't worry. I'll lock your apartment door, put the key back, lock up downstairs—after I get your phone. You just rest. You look like something the cat dragged in."

Even as sick as she was, Mary had to smile because she figured that was exactly what she looked like given the way she felt.

Lucy started to step away from the bed, when Mary grabbed her hand. "Thank you again. You're a lifesaver."

"Yep, that's me."

Unable to fight it any longer, Mary closed her eyes, dropping into oblivion.

Lucy HAD TAKEN her time earlier when she'd finished work. She'd casually crossed the street, whistling a tune to herself. There'd been no reason to hurry. She'd known exactly what she was going to find when she got to Mary's office.

Now as Mary closed her eyes, she stood over the woman, simply looking down into her angelic face. She didn't have to wonder what Chase saw in Mary. She was everything Lucy was not.

That was enough to make her want to take one of the pillows, force it down on Mary's face and hold it there until the life ebbed out of her.

She listened to Mary's soft breaths thinking how Mary had it all. A business, a building in a town where she was liked and respected, not to mention rentals and Chase. Lucy reminded herself that she used to have a great profession, where she was respected, where she had friends. What was missing was a man in her life. Then along came Chase.

With a curse, she shook her head and looked around the room as she fought back tears. The bedroom was done in pastel colors and small floral prints, so like Mary. She wondered what Chase thought of this room— or if he'd seen it yet. Not very manly. Nor was it her style, she thought as she left, closing the bedroom door softly behind her, and checked out the rest of the place.

She'd been sincere about Mary's decorating abilities. The woman had talent when it came to design and colors. It made her jealous as she took in the living room with its overstuffed furniture in bright cheery colors. Like the bedroom, there was a soft comfort about the room that made her want to curl up in the chair by the window and put her feet up.

But with a silent curse, she realized that what she really wanted was to be Mary Savage for a little while. To try out her life. To have it all, including Chase.

Shaking herself out of such ridiculous thinking, she left the apartment, leaving the door unlocked. As she put the spare key back, she told herself that it would come in handy in the future.

Smiling at the thought, she headed downstairs to Mary's office. It looked like any other office except for the large oak desk. The brick walls had been exposed to give the place a rustic look. The floor was bamboo, a rich color that went perfectly with the brick and the simple but obviously expensive furnishings.

She would have liked an office like this, she thought as she found Mary's cell phone on her desk and quickly pocketed it before picking up the woman's purse. It felt heavy. She heard the jingle of keys inside. Slipping the strap over her shoulder, she went to the front door and locked it.

Across the street she saw that the coffee shop was still busy and the other baristas were clearly slammed with orders. She wondered if anyone had seen her and quickly left by the back way again, turning out the lights behind her after locking the door. That's when she realized that she couldn't kill Mary here. She would be the first suspect.

Once on the stairs, out of view of anyone outside or across the street, she sat down on a step and went through Mary's purse. She found a wallet with photos of people she assumed must be relatives. Brothers and sisters? Cousins? Her parents?

Friends? She realized how little she knew about the woman.

There was eighty-two dollars in cash in the wallet, a few credit cards, some coupons… Seriously? The woman clipped coupons? Other than mints, a small hairbrush, a paperback and miscellaneous cosmetics there was nothing of interest.

She turned to Mary's cell phone.

Password protected. Swearing softly, she tried various combinations of words, letters, numbers. Nothing worked.

A thought struck her like a brick. She tried Chase. When that didn't work, she tried Chase Steele. Nope.

She had another thought, and taking the keys to the office, she went back inside. Turning on a small lamp on the desk, she quickly began a search. She found the list of passwords on a pull-out tray over the right-hand top drawer. The passwords were on an index card and taped down. Some had been scratched out and replaced.

Lucy ran her finger down until she found the word cell. Next to it was written Homeranch#1. She tried the password and the phone unlocked.

Quickly she scanned through contacts, emails and finally messages. She found a cell phone number for Chase and on impulse tried it, just needing to hear his voice.

It was no longer in service.

Surely he had a cell phone, not that she'd ever had his number. Wouldn't he have given it to Mary though?

She went through recent phone calls, and there it was. She touched the screen as she memorized the number. It began to ring. She held her breath. He would think it was Mary calling. He would call back.

Lucy quickly hit the hang-up button but not quick enough. "Hello, Mary, I was just thinking of you." She disconnected, wishing she hadn't done that. He'd sounded so happy that Mary was calling him that she felt sick to her stomach.

Just as she'd feared, he called right back. She blocked his call. He tried again. What if he decided to come check on Mary? This was the kind of mistake she couldn't make.

She answered the phone, swallowed and did her best imitation of Mary's voice, going with tired and busy. "Working. Didn't mean to call."

"Well, I'm glad you did. Don't work too late."

"Right. Talk tomorrow." She disconnected, pretty sure she'd pulled it off. He wouldn't question the difference in their voices since he'd called Mary's phone. At least she hoped she'd sounded enough like the woman. Sweet, quiet, tired, busy. When the phone didn't ring again, she told herself that she'd done it.

Hurrying back upstairs, she picked up Mary's purse from where she'd left it on the step on her way. Outside the third-floor apartment, she stopped to catch her breath. Putting Mary's cell on mute, she carefully opened the door, even though she didn't think Mary would be mobile for hours.

An eerie quiet hung in the air. She stepped in and headed for the bedroom. The door was still closed. She eased it open. The room had darkened to a shadowy black with the drapes closed. Mary lay exactly where she'd left her, breathing rhythmically.

Taking the cell phone, she stepped in just far enough to place the now turned off phone next to her bed. Then she left, easing the bedroom door closed behind her. The apartment was deathly quiet and growing darker. It no longer felt cozy and she no longer wanted to stay. Leaving Mary's purse on the table by the door, she left, locking it behind her.

It had been an emotional day, Lucy thought. She took the stairs down to her apartment, unlocked her door and, turning on a light, stepped in. The apartment was in stark contrast to Mary's. While everything was nice, it was stark. Cold.

"That's because you're cold," she whispered as she locked the door behind her. "Anyway, it's temporary." But even as she said it, she was thinking that she should at least buy a plant.

The apartment had come furnished right down to two sets of sheets and two throw pillows that matched the couch. Suddenly Lucy hated the pillows. She tossed them into the near empty closet and closed the door. Tomorrow was her day off. After she checked on Mary, she'd go into Bozeman and do some shopping.

She needed this apartment to feel a whole lot less like Mary Savage. Now that she had Chase's cell number, it was time for her to make him pay.

Chapter Fourteen

Lucy tapped lightly at Mary's door the next morning. Given how sick the woman had been the evening before, she thought she still might be in bed.

So she was a little surprised when Mary answered the door looking as if she'd already showered and dressed for the day.

"Oh good, you look like you're feeling better," she said.

"Much. Thank you again for yesterday."

"Just glad I could help." She started to turn away.

"Do you ride horses?" Mary asked.

Lucy stopped, taken aback by the question. She'd hoped to get close to Mary, befriend her, gain her trust and then finish this. She'd thought it would take more time. "I used to ride when I was younger."

"Would you like to come out to the ranch sometime, maybe on your day off, and go for ride?"

"I would love to." The moment she said it, she knew how dangerous it could be. Chase might show up. She'd managed not to come face-to-face with him. Even with the changes in her appearance, he could recognize her. They'd been lovers. Soul mates. He would sense who she was the moment they were in the same room.

"Good," Mary was saying. "Let's plan on it. Just let me know what day you're free. And thank you again for yesterday. I don't know what I would have done without you."

Lucy nodded, still taken aback. "I'm glad I was here." She took a step toward the door, feeling strangely uncomfortable. "Off to work," she said as she walked backward for a few steps, smiling like a fool.

Could this really be going as well as she thought it was? She couldn't believe how far she'd come from that night in Arizona when she'd gone into the river. She had Mary Savage, the woman who'd stolen Chase from her, right where she'd wanted her. So why wasn't she more euphoric about it? Her plan was working. There was no reason to be feeling the way she was, which was almost…guilty.

The thought made her laugh as she crossed the street. Guilt wasn't something she normally felt. She was enjoying herself. Maybe too much. She'd thought it would take longer, and she'd been okay with that.

As she settled into work, she realized that she would have to move up her revenge schedule. She was starting to like Mary and that was dangerous. No way could she go on a horseback ride with her, and not just because she might run into Chase. She couldn't let herself start liking Mary. If she weakened… She told herself that wouldn't happen.

But realizing this was almost over, she felt a start. She hadn't given any thought as to what she would do after she was finished here. Where would she go? What would she do? She'd been so focused on destroying Chase and his cowgirl that she hadn't thought about what to do when it was over.

That thought was nagging at her when she looked up to find Chase standing in front of her counter. Panic made her limbs go weak. He wasn't looking at her, but at the board with the day's specials hanging over her head. Could she duck in the back before he saw her? Let the other barista wait on him?

But Amy was busy with another customer. Lucy knew she couldn't hide out in the back until Chase left. All her fears rushed through her, making her skin itch. She'd come so far. She was so close to finishing this. What would she do when he recognized her?

He'd know what she was up to. He'd tell Mary. All of this would have been for nothing. Mary's father was the marshal. It wouldn't take long before he'd know about what had happened in Texas, about the suspicions that had followed her from town to town and finally to Big Sky, Montana. Once he saw through her disguise, and he would. Just like that and it would be all over. She wanted to scream.

"Good morning," he said, and finally looked at her.

"Morning." She held her breath as she met his blue eyes and gave him an embarrassed gap-toothed smile.

He smiled back, his gaze intent on her, but she realized with a start that she saw no recognition in his face. *It's me*, she wanted to say. *The love of your life. Don't tell me you don't see me, don't sense me, don't feel me standing right here in front of you.*

"I hope you can help me. I want to buy my girlfriend the kind of coffee she loves, but I forgot what it's called. She lives right across the street. I thought you might know what she orders. It's for Mary Savage."

Girlfriend? "Sorry, I'm new."

"That's all right. It was a shot in the dark anyway.

Then I guess I'll take one caramel latte and a plain black coffee please."

She stared at him for a moment in disbelief. She'd been so sure he would know her—instinctively—even the way she looked now. But there was no recognition. *None.*

Fury shook her to her core. They'd made *love*. They had a connection. *How could he not know her?*

"You do have plain black coffee, don't you?" he asked when she didn't speak, didn't move.

She let out a sound that was supposed to be a chuckle and turned her back on him. Her insides trembled, a volcano of emotions bubbling up, ready to blow. She fisted her hands, wanting to launch herself across the counter and rip out his throat.

Instead, she thought of Mary and something much better. Ripping out Mary's heart, the heart he was so desperately trying to win back.

She made the latte and poured him a cup of plain black coffee. He handed her a ten and told her to keep the change.

Thanking him, she smiled at the thought of him standing over Mary Savage's grave. "You have a nice day now."

"You too," he said as he left.

She watched him go, still shocked and furious that the fool hadn't known her. She promised herself that his nice days were about to end, and very soon.

IT WASN'T UNTIL he was headed across the street to Mary's office that Chase looked back at the woman working in the Lone Peak Perk. What was it about her…? He frowned until it hit him. Her voice. Even with the slight lisp and Southern drawl, the cadence of her voice was enough like Fiona's to give him the creeps.

He shuddered, wondering if he would ever be able to put the Fiona nightmare behind him. Yesterday he'd called Rick, and Patty had answered.

"I'm so sorry about what happened with you and Fiona," she'd said. "I just feel so sorry for her. I know it's no excuse, but she had a really rough childhood. Her mother remarried a man who sexually abused her. When she told her mother, the woman didn't believe her. That had to break her heart."

"Did she have anyone else?"

"No siblings or relatives she could turn to. On top of that, her stepfather had three sons."

He had sworn under his breath "So they could have been abusing her too."

"Or Fiona could have lied about all of it. When her mother, stepfather and the three sons died in a fire, I had to wonder. Fiona could have been behind it. I wouldn't put anything past her, would you?"

"Or she could have lied about the sexual abuse and then been racked with guilt when they all died."

Patty had laughed. "You really do try to see the best in people, and even after the number she pulled on you. You're a good guy, Chase. You take care of yourself."

He didn't feel like a good guy. He'd made so many mistakes. Fiona for one. Mary for another. He couldn't do much about Fiona, but he still had a chance to right things with Mary.

Patty had put Rick on the phone. The news was the same. Fiona's body still hadn't turned up.

"Some fisherman will find her downstream. It will be gruesome. A body that's been in the water that long…"

Chase hadn't wanted to think about it.

Like now, he tried to put it behind him as he neared Mary's office door. He wanted to surprise her with coffee. He just wished the barista had known the kind of coffee she drank. Mary was helping him today with his search for a man with the initials J.M. She understood his need to find his father even though there were days when he didn't. Why couldn't he just let it go? His mother apparently had forgiven the man if not forgotten him.

For all he knew, the man could have moved away by now. Or his mother hadn't used his real initials. Or... He shook off the negative thoughts. He would be spending the day with the woman he loved. Did it really matter if they found his father today?

As Chase came in the front door of her office, Mary saw him look back toward the coffee shop and frown. "Is something wrong?" she asked.

He started as if his thoughts had been miles away. "There's a woman working over there. Lucy?"

"I know her." She took the coffee he handed her. Not her usual, but definitely something she liked.

"She just reminded me of someone I used to know— and not in a good way," he said.

"She just started working at Lone Peak Perk only a week or two ago. Why?"

He shook his head. "Just a feeling I got." He seemed to hesitate. "That dangerous woman, Fiona, who I told you about from Arizona. Lucy doesn't look anything like her, but she reminds me of her for some reason."

Mary shook her head. She really did not want to hear anything more about Fiona. "You do realize how crazy that sounds. I know Lucy. She's really sweet. I like her. I rented one of my apartments to her. I'm sure she's nothing like *your...* Fiona."

"She wasn't *my* Fiona. Look, you've never asked, but I didn't date for a long time after I left. I wasn't interested in anyone else. That wasn't why I left and you know it. If I hadn't been drinking, if I hadn't just picked up my mother's ashes the day of the barbecue at my boss's house..."

Mary stood up. "I don't need to hear this."

"Maybe you do," he said, and raked a hand through his hair as he met her gaze. "It was one drunken night. I regretted it right away. She became...obsessed, manufacturing a relationship that didn't exist. She must have stolen my extra house key and copied it. I came home several times to find her in my apartment. She knew I was in love with someone else. But that seemed to make her even more determined to change my mind." He shook his head. "She wouldn't stop. She tried to move some of her stuff into my apartment. Needless to say it got ugly. The last time I saw her..." He hesitated as if he'd never wanted to tell her the details about Fiona and she didn't want to hear them now.

But before she could stop him, he said, "She tried to kill me."

Mary gasped. "You can't be serious."

"She knew I was leaving. She said she wanted to give me a hug goodbye, but when she started to put her arms around me, I saw the knife she'd pulled from her pocket. I would have gotten to Montana weeks sooner, but she sabotaged my pickup. I had to have a new engine put in it." He shook his head. "What I'm saying is that I wouldn't put anything past her. She supposedly drowned in the Colorado River after driving her car into it. But her body was never found."

Mary couldn't believe what she was hearing.

"Lucy doesn't look anything like her except..." He glanced up at her and must have seen the shock and disbelief in her eyes. Couldn't he tell that she didn't want to know anything more about Fiona?

She shook her head, wished this wasn't making her so upset. He'd said Fiona was obsessed with him? It sounded like he was just as obsessed. "This woman really did a number on you, didn't she?"

He held up both hands in surrender. "Sorry. I thought you should know."

About a woman he'd made love to who was now dead? But certainly not forgotten. Even Lucy reminded him of her even though, as he said, she looked nothing like Fiona? Her heart pounded hard in her chest. She pushed her coffee away, feeling nauseous. "We should get going. I need to come back and work."

He nodded. She could tell that he regretted bringing up the subject. So why had he? She never wanted to hear the name Fiona again. Ever.

"I'm sorry. You're right. Forget I mentioned it. I promise not to say another word about her."

But she saw him steal a look toward the coffee shop as they were leaving. He might not mention Fiona's name again, but he was definitely still thinking about her.

Chapter Fifteen

With Mary's mother's help, Chase had narrowed down their search to three local men—Jack Martin, Jason Morrison and Jonathan Mason. Dana had helped him weed out the ones that she knew were too young, too old or hadn't been around at the time.

His mother had been eighteen when she'd given birth to him. If her lover had been older, say twenty-five or thirty as Chase suspected, then his father would now be in his fifties.

Jack Martin owned a variety of businesses in Big Sky, including the art shop where his wife sold her pottery. A bell tinkled over the door as Mary and Chase entered. A woman passed them holding a large box as if what was inside was breakable. Chase held the door for her, before he and Mary moved deeper in the shop.

The place smelled of mulberry candles, a sickeningly sweet fragrance that Mary had never liked. She tried not to breathe too deeply as they moved past displays of pottery toward the back counter.

Jack had begun helping out at the shop during the busiest time, summer, Mary knew. She spotted his gray head coming out of the back with a large pottery bowl, which he set on an open space on a display table. There was a young woman showing several ladies a set of pottery dishes in an adjoining room, and several visitors were looking at pottery lamps at the front of the shop.

As Mary approached, Jack turned and smiled broadly. "Afternoon, is there something I can help you with?"

Mary knew Jack from chamber of commerce meetings, but it took him a second before he said, "Mary Savage. I'm sorry, I didn't recognize you right away."

"This is my friend Chase Steele." She watched for a reaction. For all they knew, Chase's father could have kept track of his son all these years. But she saw no reaction. "Is there a private area where we could speak with you for a moment?"

Jack frowned, but nodded. "We could step into the back." He glanced around to see if there were customers who needed to be waited on. There didn't appear to be for the moment.

"We won't take much of your time," she promised.

Chase tensed next to her as if to say, if Jack Martin was his father, he'd damned sure take as much of his time as he wanted.

Mary was glad that she'd come along. She knew how important this was, and could feel how nervous Chase had become the moment they stepped into the shop.

In the back it was cool and smelled less like the burning candles. "Did you know a woman named Muriel Steele?" Chase asked the moment they reached a back storage and work area.

Jack blinked in surprised. "Who?"

"Muriel Steele," Mary said with less accusation. "It would have been close to thirty years ago."

Jack looked taken aback. "You expect me to remember that long ago? Who was this woman?"

"One you had an affair with," Chase said, making her cringe. She'd hoped he would let her handle this since he was too emotionally involved.

"That I would remember," the man snapped. "I was married to Clara thirty years ago. We just celebrated our fortieth anniversary." Jack was shaking his head. "I'm not sure what this is about or what this Muriel woman told you, but I have never cheated on my wife."

Mary believed him. She looked to Chase, whom she could tell wasn't quite as convinced.

"Would you be willing to take a DNA test to prove it?" Chase demanded.

"A DNA test? How would that prove..." Realization crossed his face. "I see." His gaze softened. "I'm sorry young man, but I'm not related to you."

"But you'd take the test," Chase pressed.

Jack grew quiet for a moment, his expression sad. "If it would help you, yes, I would."

Mary saw all the tension leave Chase's body. He looked as if the strain had left him exhausted.

"Thank you," Mary said as she heard more customers coming into the shop. "We won't keep you any longer."

"It's not him," Chase said as he climbed behind the wheel and started the pickup's engine. A floodgate of emotions warred inside him. He wasn't sure what he'd hoped for. That he could find his father that quickly and it would be over? He'd wanted to hate the man. Worse, he'd wanted to punch him. But when realization had struck Jack Martin, Chase had seen the pity in the man's eyes.

"No, it wasn't Jack," she said. "Are you up to visiting the rest of them?"

He pulled off his Stetson and raked a hand through his hair. "I'm not sure I can do this. I thought I could but…" He glanced over at her.

"It's all right."

He shook his head. For a moment, they merely sat there, each lost in their own thoughts. Then Chase smiled over at her. "Could we drive up to Mountain Village and have an early lunch and forget all this for a while? Then I promise to take you back to work. I shouldn't have dragged you into this."

She reached over and placed a hand on his arm. He felt the heat of her fingers through his Western shirt. They warmed him straight to his heart and lower. What he wanted was this woman in his arms, in his bed, in his life. He felt as if he had made so many mistakes and was still making them.

"My stomach is still a little upset. I was really sick last night." He looked at her with concern. "I'm sure it was just some twenty-four-hour flu," she said quickly.

"I hope that's all it was," he said. "I was really careful with our picnic lunch."

"And you didn't get sick, so like I said, probably just a flu bug." He must not have looked convinced. "I was just going to eat some yogurt for lunch. Maybe some other time?"

He studied her for a moment, so filled with love for this woman. "You're the best friend I've ever had."

She laughed at that, and took her hand from his arm.

"Is it any wonder that I haven't been able to stop loving you?" he asked.

Their gazes met across the narrow space between

them. He could feel the heat, the chemistry. He reached over and cupped the back of her neck, pulling her into the kiss. He heard her breath catch. His pulse quickened. A shaft of desire cut through him, molten hot.

Mary leaned into him and the kiss. It felt like coming home. Chase had always been a great kisser.

As he drew back, he looked into her eyes as if the kiss had also transported him back to when they were lovers.

"You're just full of surprises today, aren't you," she said, smiling at him as she tried to catch her breath. She loved seeing Chase like this, relaxed, content, happy, a man who knew who he was and what he wanted.

The cowboy who'd left her and Montana had been antsy, filled with a need she couldn't understand. Just like he'd been only minutes ago when they'd gone looking for his father.

He needed to find him. She would help him. And then what?

"You have work to do, and I'm keeping you from it," he said. "We can have lunch another day when you feel better and aren't as busy. I've already taken up too much of your morning."

She shook her head as she met his gaze. "If I didn't have this report due—"

"You don't have to explain. You took off this morning to help me. I appreciate that." His smile filled her with joy as much as his words. "We have a lot of lunches in our future. I hope you know how serious I am about us, about our future. I'll do whatever it takes because I know you, Mary Savage. I know your heart."

She felt her eyes burn with tears at the truth in his

words. "Tomorrow. Let's go talk to the other two men tomorrow morning."

"Are you sure?" Chase asked. "I don't like keeping you from your work."

She managed to nod. "I'm sure." Swallowing the lump in her throat, she reached to open her door. If she stayed out here with him a minute longer, she feared what she might say. Worse, what she might do. It would have been too easy to fall into his arms and take up where they'd left off and forget all about the report that was due.

But she climbed out of the pickup, knowing it was too soon. She had to know for sure that Chase wouldn't hurt her again. Her heart couldn't take being broken by him again.

As Chase was leaving, he glanced toward the coffee shop. Was Lucy working? He swung his pickup around and parked in front of Lone Peak Perk. Getting out, he told himself to play it cool. He had to see her again. He had to know. But just the thought that he might be right...

As he walked in, Lucy looked up. Surprise registered in those dark eyes. Nothing like Fiona's big blue ones. Still, he walked to the counter. She looked nervous. "Is it possible to get a cup of coffee in a real cup?" he asked. "Just black."

She looked less nervous, but that too could have been his imagination. He wondered what he'd been thinking. The woman looked nothing like Fiona and yet... She was much skinnier, the gapped two front teeth, the short dark hair, the brown eyes. What was it about her that reminded him of Fiona? Mary was right. He was obsessed with the disturbed, irrational woman.

Lucy picked up a white porcelain coffee cup and took her time filling it with black coffee. "Can I get you anything else?" she said with that slight lisp, slight Southern accent. Nothing like Fiona. She flashed him a smile, clearly flirting.

He grinned. "Maybe later." He took the coffee cup by the handle over to an empty spot near the door. Sitting with his back to her, he took a sip. Coffee was the last thing he wanted right now. But he drank it as quickly as the hot beverage allowed.

Taking advantage of a rush of people coming in for their afternoon caffeine fix, he carefully slipped the now empty cup under his jacket and walked out. He'd expected to be stopped, but neither Lucy or the other barista noticed. When he reached his pickup, he carefully set the cup on the center console and headed to the marshal's office.

He would get Hud to run the prints because he had to know what it was about the woman that turned his stomach, and left him feeling like something evil had come to Big Sky.

LUCY COULDN'T BELIEVE that Chase had come back into the coffee shop. She smiled to herself as she whipped up one of the shop's special coffees for a good-tipping patron. As she finished the drink, she turned expecting to see Chase's strong back at the corner table. To her surprise, he'd left during the rush. He'd certainly finished his coffee quickly enough. She frowned as concern slithered slowly through her.

It took her a moment to realize why the hair was now

standing up on the back of her neck. The table where
Chase had been sitting. His empty porcelain cup wasn't
where he should have left it.

She hurriedly glanced around, thinking he must have
brought it back to the counter. Otherwise…

Her heart kicked up to double time. Otherwise… He
wouldn't have tossed the cup in the trash and she could
see from here that he hadn't put it in the tray with the
few other dishes by the door.

Which left only one conclusion.

He'd taken the cup.

Why would he—

The reason struck her hard and fast. *He had recognized her.* Warring emotions washed over her. Of course
he'd sensed her behind the disguise. She hadn't been
wrong about that. It was that unique chemistry that they
shared. But at the same time, fear numbed her, left her
dumbstruck. She could hear the patron asking her a
question, but nothing was registering.

Chase would go to the marshal, Mary's father, have
him run the prints. Once that happened… She told herself that there was time. And, there was Deputy Dillon Ramsey.

"Miss! I need a receipt, please."

Lucy shook her head and smiled. "Sorry," she said
to the woman, printed out the receipt and handed it to
her. "You have a nice day now."

AFTER HIS INITIAL surprise at seeing the cowboy, Hud
waved Chase into a chair across from his desk. As the
young man came in, he carefully set a white porcelain coffee cup on the edge of the desk. Hud eyed it, then Chase.

"I need you to run the fingerprints on this cup."

The marshal lifted a brow. "For any particular reason?"

"I really don't want to get into it. I'm hoping I'm wrong."

Hud leaned back in his chair. "That's not enough reason to waste the county's time running fingerprints."

"If I'm right, this person could be a danger to Mary. Isn't that enough?"

Rubbing his jaw, he studied the cowboy. "You do understand that unless this person has fingerprints on file—"

"They'll be on file if I'm right."

Intrigued, Hud sighed and said, "Okay. I'll let you know, but it might take a few days."

A deputy was walking past. Hud called to him as he bagged the cup Chase had brought in. "Dillon, run the fingerprints on this cup when you have a minute. Report back to me."

"WE'RE STILL ON for tonight, right?" Lucy asked when Dillon called. The last thing she wanted him to do was cancel.

"You know it."

"Then I have a small favor," she said. "It's one that only you can grant." She could almost hear the man's chest puff out. "And I'll make it worth your while."

"Really?" He sounded intrigued. She reminded herself that he was only doing this to get back at Mary. The thought did nothing for her disposition, but she kept the contempt out of her voice. She needed his help.

"Really. But then maybe you don't have access to what I need down there at the marshal's office."

"Name it. I have the run of the place."

"I believe Chase Steele might have brought in a cup and asked that fingerprints be run on it?"

Dillon chuckled. "The marshal asked me to do it when I had time and report back to him."

"Have you had time?" she asked, her heart in her throat.

"I like to do whatever the marshal asks right away."

She closed her eyes and tried to breathe. Her prints were on file. Chase must have suspected as much.

"I haven't seen him though to give him the report."

Lucy took a breath and let it out slowly. "Is there any way that the report could get lost?"

He snickered. "Now you've got me curious. Why would you care about prints run on a Fiona Barkley?"

So her prints had come back that quickly? "If that report gets lost, I'd be happy to tell you when I see you. Like I said, I'll make it worth your while."

"Are we talking money?" he asked quietly. "Or something else?"

"Or both," she said, her heart pounding. "I can be quite...creative."

He laughed. "What time shall I pick you up?"

"I have a better idea. Why don't I meet you later tonight after I get off my shift? I know just the spot." She told him how to get to the secluded area up in the mountains. She'd spent her free time checking out places for when it came time to end this little charade.

Dillon thought he was going to get lucky—and use her to bring Mary into line. She'd known men like him. He would blackmail her into the next century if she let him.

"I have to work late. Is midnight too late for you?" she asked sweetly.

"Midnight is perfect. I can't wait."

"Me either." The deputy had no idea that he'd walked right into her plot, and now he had a leading role.

Chapter Sixteen

Later that night, as Lucy prepared for her date with Dillon, she couldn't help being excited. She'd spent too much time waiting around, not rushing her plan, being patient and pretending to be someone she wasn't.

Tonight she could let Fiona out. The thought made her laugh. Wait until Dillon met her.

She had to work only until ten, but she needed time to prepare. She knew all about forensics. While she had little faith in the local law being able to solve its way out of a paper bag, she wasn't taking any chances. Amy, who worked at the coffee shop, had seen her talking to Dillon when he'd asked her out, but as far as the other barista knew, he was just another customer visiting after buying a coffee.

If Amy had heard anything, she would have thought he had been asking her for directions. There was no law in him flirting with her, Lucy thought with a grin. That exchange would be the only connection she had to Dillon Ramsey.

At least as far as anyone knew.

She didn't drive to the meeting spot. Instead, she came in the back way. It hadn't rained in weeks, but a thunderstorm was predicted for the next morning. Any tire or foot tracks she left would be altered if not destroyed. She had worn an old pair of shoes that would be going into the river tonight. Tucked under her arm was a blanket she'd pulled out of a commercial waste bin earlier today.

The hike itself wasn't long as the crow flew, but the route wound through trees and rocks. The waning moon and all the stars in the heavens did little to light her way. She'd never known such a blackness as there was under the dense pines. That's why she was almost on top of Dillon's pickup before she knew it.

As she approached the driver's-side door, she could hear tinny sounding country music coming from his pickup's stereo. He was drumming on his steering wheel and glancing at his watch. From his expression, she could tell that he was beginning to wonder if he'd been stood up.

When she tapped on his driver's-side window, he jumped. His expression changed from surprise to relief. He motioned for her to go around to the passenger side.

She shook her head and motioned for him to get out of the truck.

He put his window down partway, letting out a nose-wrinkling gust of cheap aftershave and male sweat. "It's warmer in here."

"I'm not going to let you get cold."

Dillon gave that a moment's thought before he whirred up the window, killed the engine and music, and climbed out.

Lucy had considered the best way to do this. He had his motivation for asking her out. She had hers for being here. Everyone knew about Dillon and Chase's fight. The two couldn't stand each other. So whom would the marshal's first suspect be if anything happened to Dillon?

She tossed down the blanket she'd brought onto the bed of dried pine needles. Dillon reached for her. He would be a poor lover, one who rushed. "Not yet, baby," she said, holding him at arm's length. "Why don't you strip down, have a seat and let me get ready for you. Turn your back. I want this to be a surprise."

It was like leading a bull to the slaughterhouse.

"Well hurry, because it's cold out tonight," he said as he began to undress. She'd brought her own knife, but when she'd seen his sticking out of his boot, she'd changed her plans.

The moment he sat down, his back to her, she came up behind him, grabbed a handful of his hair and his knife, and slit his throat from ear to ear. It happened so fast that he didn't put up a fight. He gurgled, his hand going to his throat before falling to one side.

She stared down at him, hoping he'd done what he promised and lost the report on her fingerprints. Her only regret was that she hadn't gotten to see the surprise and realization on his smug face. He'd gotten what was coming to him, but she doubted he would have seen it that way.

As she wiped her prints from the knife and stepped away, she kicked pine needles onto her tracks until she was in the woods and headed for the small creek she'd had to cross to get there. She washed her hands, rinsing away his blood. She'd worn a short-sleeved shirt, and with his back to her, she hadn't gotten any of his blood on anything but her hands and wrists.

She scrubbed though, up to her elbows, the ice-cold water making her hands ache. She let them air-dry as she walked the rest of the way back to her vehicle. Once she got rid of the shoes she had on, no one would be able to put her at the murder scene.

THE MOMENT MARY saw her father's face, she knew something horrible had happened. Was it her mother? One of her brothers or someone else in the family? Chase? She rose behind her desk as her father came into her office, his Stetson in hand, his marshal face on.

"Tell me," she said on a ragged breath, her chest aching with dread. She'd seen this look before. She knew when her father had bad news to impart.

"It's Dillon Ramsey."

She frowned, thinking she'd heard him wrong. "Dillon?"

"You weren't with him last night, were you?"

"No, why?"

"He was found dead this morning."

Her first thought was a car accident. The Gallatin Canyon two-lane highway was one of the most danger ous highways in the state with all its traffic and curves through the canyon along the river.

"He was found murdered next to his truck up by Goose Creek."

She stared at him, trying to make sense of this. "How?"

He hesitated but only a moment, as if he knew the details would get out soon enough and he wanted to be the one to tell her. "He was naked, lying on a blanket as if he'd been with someone before that. His throat had been cut."

Her stomach roiled. "Why would someone want to kill him?"

"That's what I'm trying to find out. I'm looking for a friend of his, Grady Birch. Do you know him?"

Mary shook her head. "I never met any of his friends."

Her father scratched the back of his neck for a moment. "I understand that Dillon and Chase got into a confrontation that turned physical."

"Chase? You can't think that Chase… You're wrong. Chase didn't trust him, but then neither did you."

"With good reason as it turns out. I believe that Dillon was involved in the cattle rustling along with his friend Grady Birch."

Mary had to sit back down. All of this was making her sick to her stomach. "I'd broken up with him. I had no plans to see him again. He'd threatened to ask out one of my tenants." She shook her head. "But Chase had nothing to do with this."

The marshal started for the door. "I just wanted you to hear about it from me rather than the Canyon grapevine."

She nodded and watched him leave. Dillon was dead. Murdered. She shuddered.

GRADY BIRCH'S BODY washed up on the rocks near Beckman's Flat later that morning. It was found by a fisherman. The body had been in the water for at least a few days. Even though the Gallatin River never got what anyone would call warm, it had been warm enough to do damage over that length of time.

Hud rubbed the back of his neck as he watched the coroner put the second body that day into a body bag. Dillon was dead; Grady had been dead even longer. What was going on?

He would have sworn that it was just the two of them in on the cattle rustling. But maybe there was someone else who didn't want to share the haul. He'd send a tech crew out to the cabin to see what prints they came up with. But something felt all wrong about this. Killers, he'd found, tended to stay with the same method and not improvise. A drowning was much different from cutting a person's throat. The drowning had been made to look like an accident. But Grady's body had been held down with rocks.

"I'll stop by later," he told the coroner as he walked to his patrol SUV. There was someone he needed to talk to.

Hud found Chase fixing fences on the Sherman Jensen ranch. He could understand why Sherman needed the help and why Chase had agreed to working for board. He was a good worker and Sherman's son was not.

Chase looked up as Hud drove in. He put down the tool he'd been using to stretch the barbed wire and took off his gloves as he walked over to the patrol SUV.

"Did you get the prints off the cup back?" Chase asked.

Hud shook his head. He'd been a little busy, but he'd check on them the first chance he got. He studied the man his daughter had been in love with as far back as he could remember. Out here in his element, Chase looked strong and capable. Hud had thought of him as a boy for so long. At twenty-four, he'd still been green behind the years. He could see something he hadn't noticed when he saw him at the marshal's office. Chase had grown into a man.

Still he found himself taking the man's measure.

"Marshal," Chase said. "If you've come out here to ask me what my intentions are toward your daughter…" He grinned.

"As a matter of fact, I would like to know, even though that's not why I'm here."

Chase pushed back his Stetson. "I'm going to marry her. With your permission, of course."

Hud chuckled. "Of course. Well, that's good to hear, as far as intentions go, but I'm here on another matter. When was the last time you saw Dillon Ramsey?"

Chase grimaced. "Did he think that's why I was in your office the other day?" He shook his head. "That I'd come there to report our fight? So he decided to tell you his side of it?"

"Actually no. But I heard about it. Heard that if Mary hadn't broken it up, it could have gotten lethal."

"Only because Dillon was going for a knife he had in his boot," Chase said.

Hud nodded. Chase had known about the man's knife. The knife Dillon had been killed with. "So the trouble between you was left unfinished." Chase didn't deny it. "That's the last time you saw him?"

Chase nodded and frowned. "Why? What did he say? I saw the way he was trying to intimidate Mary."

"Not much. Someone cut his throat last night." He saw the cowboy's shocked expression.

"What the hell?"

"Exactly. Where were you last night?"

"Here on the ranch."

"Can anyone verify that you were here the whole time?"

"You can't really believe that I—"

"Can anyone verify where you were?" Hud asked again.

Chase shook his head. "Can't you track my cell phone or something? Better yet, you know me. If I saw Dillon again, I might get in the first punch because I knew he'd fight dirty. But use a knife?" He shook his head. "Not me. That would be Dillon."

Hud tended to believe him. But he also knew about the knife Dillon kept in his boot, and he hadn't seen Chase in years. People change. "You aren't planning to leave town, are you?"

Chase groaned. "I have a carpenter job in Paradise Valley. I was leaving tomorrow to go to work. But I can give you the name of my employer. I really don't want to pass up this job."

Hud studied him for a moment. "Call me with your employer's name. I don't have to warn you not to take off, right?"

Chase smiled. "I'm not going anywhere. Like I told you, I'm marrying your daughter and staying right here."

Hud couldn't help but smile. "Does Mary know that?"

The cowboy laughed. "She knows. That doesn't mean she's said yes yet."

"Are you all right? I just heard the news about the deputy," Chase asked when he called Mary after her father left. "I'm so sorry."

"Dillon and I had broken up, but I still can't believe it. Who would want to kill him?"

"Your father thought I might," he said. "I just had a visit from him."

"What? You can't be serious."

"He'd heard about the fight Dillon and I had in front of your building," Chase said. "I thought maybe you'd mentioned it to him."

"I didn't tell him, but he can't believe that you'd kill anyone."

Chase said nothing for a moment. "The word around town according to Beth Anne is that Dillon had been with someone in the woods. A woman. You have any idea who?"

She thought of Lucy, but quickly pushed the idea away. Dillon had said he was going to ask her out, but she doubted he'd even had time to do that—if he'd been serious. Clearly, he'd been seeing someone else while he was seeing her.

"I'll understand if you don't want to go with me late to see the next man on my list," Chase said.

"No, I'm going. I'm having trouble getting any work done. I'm still in shock. I know how much finding your father means to you. Pick me up?"

"You know it. I'm going to get cleaned up. Give me thirty minutes."

"YOU QUESTIONED CHASE about Dillon's murder?" Mary cried when he father answered the phone.

He made an impatient sound. "I'm the marshal, and I'm investigating everyone with a grudge against Dillon Ramsey."

"Chase doesn't hold grudges," she said indignantly, making Hud laugh.

"He's a man, and the woman he's in love with was seeing another man who is now dead. Also, he was in an altercation with the dead man less that forty-eight hours ago."

"How did you know about the fi—"

"I got an anonymous call."

"I didn't think anyone but me…" She thought of Lucy. No, Lucy wouldn't do that. Someone else in the area that night must have witnessed it.

"You can't possibly think that Chase would…" She shook her head adamantly. "It wasn't Chase."

"Actually, I think you're right," her father said. "I just got the coroner's report. The killer was right-handed. I noticed Chase is left-handed."

Mary felt herself relax. Not that she'd ever let herself think Chase was capable of murder, but she'd been scared that he would be a suspect because of their altercation.

As she looked up, she saw Lucy on her way to work. The woman turned as if sensing she was being watched, and waved before coming back to the front door of the office to stick her head in.

"Mary, are you all right? I just heard the news on the radio about that deputy you were seeing, the one your cowboy got into a fight with the other night."

"I know, it's terrible, isn't it?"

"You don't think Chase—"

"No." She shook her head. "My dad already talked to him. It wasn't him."

Lucy lifted a brow. "Chase sure was angry the other night."

"Yes, but the forensics proved that Chase couldn't have done it." Mary waved a hand through the air as if she couldn't talk about it, which she couldn't. "Not that I ever thought Chase could kill someone."

Lucy still didn't look convinced. "I think everyone is capable. It just has to be the right circumstances."

"You mean the wrong ones," Mary said, the conversation making her uncomfortable. She no longer wanted to think about how Dillon had died or who might have killed him.

"Yes," Lucy said, and laughed.

"Did you ever go out with Dillon?" Mary asked, and wished she hadn't at Lucy's expression.

"Seriously?" The woman laughed. "Definitely not my type. Why would you ask me that?"

"He mentioned that he might ask you out. I thought maybe—"

Lucy sighed. "Clearly, he was just trying to make you jealous. I think he came into the coffee shop once that I can remember. You really thought I was the woman who had sex with him in the woods?"

"We don't know that's what happened."

"It's what everyone in town is saying. They all think that the killer followed the deputy out to the spot where he was meeting some woman. That's why I asked about Chase. If your cowboy thought it was you on that blanket with him…"

"That's ridiculous. Anyway, it wasn't me."

"But maybe in the dark, Chase didn't know that."

"Seriously, Lucy, you don't know him. I do. Chase wouldn't hurt anyone."

"Sorry. Not something you want to dwell on at this time of the morning. I can't believe you thought I could be the woman with him."

And yet Lucy seemed determine to believe that Chase had been the killer.

"Coming over for your coffee?" Lucy asked. "I can have it ready for you as soon as I get in."

"No, actually. I have an errand to run this morning."

Lucy frowned but then brightened. "Well, have a nice day. Maybe I'll see you later."

From the window, Mary saw her hesitate as if she wanted to talk longer before she closed the door and started across the street. She seemed to quicken her pace as Chase drove up.

Mary hurried out, locking her office door behind her before climbing into his pickup. He smiled over at her. "You okay? I saw Lucy talking to you as I drove up."

"Nothing important."

"Then let's get it over with. I never realized how… draining this could be," Chase said.

"Who's next?"

"Jason Morrison."

Morrison was a local attorney. His office was only a few doors down from Mary's. They'd called to make an appointment and were shown in a little before time.

Jason was tall and slim with an athletic build. He spent a lot of time on the slopes or mountain biking, and had stayed in good shape at fifty-five. He was a nice looking man with salt and pepper dark hair and blue eyes. When his secretary called back to say that his eleven o'clock was waiting, he said to send them on back.

Jason stood as they entered and came around his desk to shake Mary's hand and then Chase's.

Mary watched as he shook Chase's hand a little too long, his gaze locked on the younger man's.

Was it Chase's blue eyes, or did Jason see something in him he recognized?

"Please, have a seat," the attorney said, going behind his desk and sitting down. "What can I do for the two of you?"

"We're inquiring about a woman named Muriel Steele," Mary said. "We thought you might have known her twenty-seven years ago."

Jason leaned back in his chair and looked from Mary to Chase and back. "Muriel. Has it been that long ago?" He shook his head. "Yes, I knew her." He frowned. "Why are you asking?"

"I'm her son," Chase said.

Jason's gaze swung back to him. "I thought there was something about you that was familiar when we shook hands. Maybe it's the eyes. Your mother had the most lovely blue eyes."

As Chase started to rise, Mary put a hand on his thigh to keep him in his chair. "Chase is looking for his father."

"His father?" He glanced at Mary and back to Chase.

"When my mother left Big Sky, she was pregnant with me, but I suspect you already know that," Chase said through clenched teeth.

The attorney looked alarmed. "I had no idea. Wait a minute. You think I was the one who…" He held up his hands. "I knew your mother, but I was already married by then. Linda was pregnant with our daughter Becky." He was shaking his head.

"My mother left a diary," Chase said.

Jason went still. "If she said it was me…" He shook his head. "I'm sorry, but I'm not your father."

"She didn't name her married lover," Chase said. "Just his initials. J.M. Quite a coincidence you knew her and you have the exact initials."

A strange look crossed the man's face. "I'm sorry. Like I said, you have the wrong man."

"Then you wouldn't mind submitting to a DNA test," Mary said.

"I'm a lawyer. No good can come of submitting to a DNA test, not with the legal system like it is. No offense to your father the marshal, ma'am," he added quickly.

"So you're saying no?" Chase asked as he got to his feet.

Jason sighed. "I want to help you, all right? If it comes to that, I'd get a DNA test. I assume there are others you're talking to?"

"Actually, a friend of yours," Mary said. "Jonathan Mason."

Jason groaned. He looked as if he wanted to say more, but changed his mind. "My heart goes out to you. But maybe there was a reason your mother never told you who your father was."

"Other than she wanted to protect him?" Chase demanded.

Jason sighed again. "I wish I could help you. I really do. But after all this time…"

"You think I should let it go?" Chase leaned toward the man threateningly.

Jason held up his hands. "I can see your frustration."

"It's not frustration. It's anger. The man knocked up my mother, broke her heart and her spirit, and let her raise me alone. She was only seventeen when she became pregnant, had no education and no way to support herself but menial jobs. So, I'm furious with this man who fathered me."

"Then why find him? What good will it do?" the lawyer asked.

Chase leaned back some. "Because I want to look him in the eye and tell him what I think of him."

Mary rose and so did the attorney. "We'll probably be back about that DNA test," she said.

Jason nodded, but he didn't look happy about it. His gaze went to Chase and softened. "I cared about your mother, but I wasn't her lover."

"I guess we'll see," Chase said as they left.

"IT'S HIM," CHASE SAID as they left the attorney's office. His heart was pounding. He thought about what the man had said. "It's him, I'm telling you."

"I don't know."

"He admitted knowing her. You saw the way he looked at me. He knew the moment he shook my hand. He practically admitted it."

"But he didn't admit it," Mary pointed out.

"He's a lawyer. He's too smart to admit anything."

"He admitted that he knew her, that he cared about her. Chase, I think he's telling the truth."

He stopped walking to sigh deeply. Taking off his Stetson, he raked a hand through his hair and tried to calm down. "I don't know why I'm putting myself through this. I'm twenty-eight years old. He's right. What do I hope to get out of this?"

"A father."

He let out a bark of a laugh. "That ship has sailed. I don't need a father."

"We all need family."

He shook his head. "When I find him, I want to tell him off—not bond with him. Hell, I want to punch him in his face."

At a sound behind them, they turned to see Jason hurrying toward his car.

"I think we should follow him," Mary said as they watched him speed away.

Chase nodded, his gaze and attention on the attorney. "I think you're right. He certainly took off fast enough right after we talked to him. Let's go."

They climbed into his pickup, turned around in the middle of the street and followed at a distance. "Where do you think he's going?"

"Good question. Maybe home to talk to his wife."

Mary shook her head. "He doesn't live in this direction."

"What if he is going to warn Jonathan Mason?"

"Maybe. But only if Jonathan is up at the mountain resort." Chase drove up the road toward Lone Peak.

"Maybe he's going to lunch," he suggested.

"Maybe." After a few miles, the lawyer turned into the Alpine Bar parking lot.

Jason parked, leaped out and went inside.

"He could have called someone to meet him," Chase said.

She nodded. "Let's give him a minute and go inside."

Chase pulled into the lot next to the attorney's car. It was early so there were only three cars out front. During ski season, the place would have been packed. "Recognize any of the rigs?"

She shook her head.

"Have I thanked you for doing this for me? I really do appreciate it."

She smiled over at him. "You have thanked me. I'm glad to help, you know that. But Chase—"

"I know. Try not to lose my temper."

"I don't want to have to bail you out of jail," she said, still smiling.

"But you would, wouldn't you?" He reached out and stroked her cheek, his gaze locking with hers. "I've never loved you more than I do right now, Mary Cardwell Savage." He drew back his hand. "Marry me when this is all over."

She laughed and shook her head.

"I'm serious. What is it going to take to make you realize that you're crazy about me? I want to make you Mrs. Chase Steele. We can have the big wedding I know your mother wants. But I was thinking—"

"You're stalling. Come on, let's go in," she said, and they climbed out. He caught up with her and, taking her arm, pulled her around to face him.

"For the record? I was serious about asking you to marry me. Soon." As he pushed open the door, country music from the jukebox spilled out. Chase heard a familiar song, and wished he and Mary were there to dance—not track down his no-count biological father.

He spotted Jason at the bar talking to the bartender, a gray-haired man with wire-rimmed glasses. As the door closed behind them, a man came through the back door. He caught a glimpse of a residence through the doorway and a ramp before the door closed.

The man motioned to Jason to join him at one of the tables in the back.

"Do you recognize him?" he asked Mary.

"It's Jim Harris," Mary said, and grabbed Chase's arm to stop him. "What if the initials J.M. were short for Jim? Jim Harris owns this bar. He and his wife live in a house behind it."

Chase stared at the man the attorney had joined.

Blond, blue-eyed, midfifties. The scary part was that as he watched the man, he saw himself in Jim Harris's expression, in the line of his nose, the way he stroked his jaw as he listened.

Chase didn't know that he'd stopped in the middle of the room and was still staring until the man looked up. Their gazes met across the expanse of the bar.

Jim Harris froze.

Chapter Seventeen

Chase felt as if he'd been punched in the stomach. He couldn't breathe, had no idea how he'd gotten out of the bar. He found himself standing outside, bent over, gasping for breath, Mary at his side.

The bar door opened behind him. Sucking in as much air as he could, he straightened and turned. He was a good two inches taller than his father, but the similarities were all too apparent. He stared at the man who was staring just as intensely back at him.

"I didn't know," Jim said, his voice breaking. "I had no idea."

"You didn't know my mother was pregnant? Or you didn't know you had a son?" Chase demanded, surprised he could speak.

"Neither." The man suddenly dropped to the front steps of the bar and put his head in his hands. "When Jason told me…" He lifted his head. "I didn't believe him until I saw you."

"How was it you didn't know?" Mary asked. For a moment, Chase had forgotten she was there.

"She never told me…" Jim moaned.

"You weren't at all curious why she left?" Chase said,

his voice breaking. His strength was coming back. So was his anger.

"I knew why Muriel left," the man said, meeting his gaze. "I separated from my wife when I met your mother. We fell in love. I was in the process of filing for divorce to marry Muriel when…" His voice broke and he looked away. "My wife was in a car accident. She almost died."

"And you decided not to leave her," Chase said, nodding as if he could feel his mother's pain. She'd been young and foolish, fallen for a man who was taken only to realize all his promises had come to nothing—and she was pregnant with his child. So she hadn't told him. What would have been the point since by then she knew he was staying with his wife?

The door behind Jim opened. Chase heard a creak and looked up to see a woman in a wheelchair framed in the doorway. The woman had graying hair that hung limp around her face. She stared at him for a long moment before she wheeled back and let the door close behind her. He looked at his father, who was looking at him.

"She's been in a wheelchair since the accident," Jim said quietly as he got to his feet. "I blamed myself since she had her accident after an argument we had over the bar. The bar," he said with disgust. "We both wanted the divorce. That wasn't the problem. It was the bar. I wanted to keep it. She wanted it sold, and half the money. If only I'd let her have it…" His voice dropped off. "I wanted to be with your mother. Muriel was the love of my life. If I'd known she was pregnant…"

"But she didn't tell you after she heard about your wife's accident," Chase said more to himself than his father.

Jim nodded. "If I'd known where your mother had

gone…" He didn't finish because it was clear he didn't know what he would have done.

Chase thought of how close his father had been in the years from fifteen on that he'd lived and worked on the Cardwell Ranch. All that time, his father had been not that far away. But there was no reason for their paths to cross. His father's bar was up on the mountain at the resort and Chase had lived down in the canyon.

He looked at his father and could see that the man had paid the price for all these years, just as his mother had. Jim Harris stood for a moment, his hands hanging at his sides, a broken man. "I'm sorry you didn't find a better father than me." With that he turned and went back inside.

Chase felt Mary touch his arm. "I can drive," she said, and took his pickup keys from his hand.

HOURS LATER, SHE and Chase lay curled up in her apartment bed, his strong arms around her. They'd stayed up and talked until nearly daylight, and finally exhausted had climbed into her bed.

Chase had found his father. Not the man he'd thought he was going to find. Not a man he'd wanted to punch. A man who looked like him. A man who'd made mistakes, especially when it came to love.

Mary had told him what she knew about Jim and his wife, Cheryl. They'd gotten married young when Cheryl had been pregnant, but she'd lost the baby and couldn't have another. It had been a rocky marriage.

"Jim said they were separated when he met your mother, but they must have kept it quiet. She wandered down in Meadow Village and he lived up on the mountain behind the bar." She'd called her mother to ask her what she knew and Jim and Cheryl.

Dana had said she remembered that Cheryl had been staying with a sister down in Gateway near Bozeman when she'd had her accident.

"So no one knew about my mother and Jim," Chase had said.

"Apparently not. I guess they hadn't wanted it to be an issue in the divorce, especially since the bar was already one."

When it got late and they'd talked the subject nearly to death, she'd suggested they go to bed.

"Mary, I—"

"Not to make love. Sleep. I don't want you leaving after what you've been through. Also, it won't be long before morning. We both need sleep and you have to leave for you carpentry job tomorrow."

Now as they lay in bed, Chase said, "I don't want to be like him, a coward, a man who never followed his heart."

"You're not like him."

He made a groaning sound. "I have been. Out of fear. I should have stayed in Montana and fought for you. Instead, I left. I was miserable the whole time. I missed you and Montana so much. I didn't think I was good enough for you. I'm still not sure I am."

She touched her finger to his lips. "That's ridiculous and all behind us."

"Is it? Because I still feel like you don't trust me," Chase whispered in the dark room as he pulled her closer. "What is it going to take to make you trust me again?"

Lucy lay in bed listening to the noises coming from upstairs. She hadn't been able to sleep since she'd heard Mary come in with Chase. They'd gone right upstairs.

She had heard them moving around and the low murmur of voices, but she hadn't been able to tell what was going on until minutes ago when they'd gone into the bedroom. It was right over her own.

Not that she could hear what they were doing. The building was solid enough that she'd had to strain to hear anything at all. But she'd heard enough to know that they were still in the bedroom. Both of them. She knew exactly what they were doing, and it was driving her mad.

Getting up, she went into the living room, got herself a stiff drink and sprawled on the couch. She had hoped that Mary wouldn't fall for him again. What was wrong with the woman? How could she trust a man like that? Lucy fumed and consumed another couple of shots until she'd fallen asleep on the couch only to be awakened by movement upstairs later in the morning.

She sat up and listened. Chase's boots on the stairs. Mary's steps right behind him. Lucy listened to them descend the stairs as she fought the urge to charge out into the hall and attack them both with her bare hands. Mary was a fool.

She cracked her door open to listen and heard them talking about Chase leaving the area for a carpenter job he was taking. Leaving? She tiptoed to the top of the stairs, keeping to the shadows. They had stopped on the main floor landing.

"I don't like leaving you," he said. "But I'll be back every weekend. This job will only last about six weeks, and then my boss said we have work around Big Sky so I'll see you every night. That's if you want to see me."

Lucy couldn't hear what Mary said, but she could

hear the rustle of clothing. Had Mary stepped into his arms? Were they kissing? She felt her blood boil.

"You'll be careful?" Chase said.

"Please, don't start that again."

Lucy heard the tension in her voice and moved down a few steps so she could hear better.

"I'm sorry, but there is still something about Lucy that bothers me," Chase said. "Doesn't it seem strange that three people have died since she came to town?"

"You can't believe that she had anything to do with that."

"Lucy just walks into the job at the coffee shop after the last new hire gets run down on the road? Then she moves into the same apartment Christy Shores was going to rent before she was murdered? A coincidence?"

"Big Sky is a small place, so not that much of a co-incidence since I live across the street from the coffee shop and had an apartment for rent."

"And didn't you tell me that Dillon was going to ask Lucy out?"

She rolled her eyes. "And that was reason enough to kill him? She said he hadn't and she wouldn't have gone out with him if he had."

Chase shrugged. "It's…creepy."

"What's creepy is that she reminds you of an old girlfriend."

"Fiona wasn't my girlfriend. But Lucy definitely reminds me of her. Fiona went after what she wanted at all costs and the consequences be damned."

"I really don't want to talk about this."

"I just want you to be careful, that's all. Don't put so much trust in her. Promise?"

"I promise. I don't want to argue with you right before you leave me."

Lucy could hear the two of them smooching again.

"I'll be back Friday night. I'd love to take you to dinner."

"I'd love that."

Lucy pressed herself against the wall as the door opened and light raced up the stairs toward her. She stayed where she was and tried to catch her breath. Chase suspected she was Fiona. So far he hadn't convinced Mary. Nor had the marshal gotten her prints off the cup and found out she was Fiona Barkley. The deputy had done his job. She almost felt bad about killing him.

But it was only a matter of time before Mary started getting suspicious.

After hearing her go into her office, Lucy inched her way back to her apartment. She wanted to scream, to destroy the apartment, anything to rid herself of the fury boiling up inside her. She'd tried to be patient, but the more she was around Mary, the more she hated seeing her with Chase.

She clenched her fists. Mary had said she wasn't sure about the two of them. Liar. But Lucy knew Chase was to blame. He'd somehow tricked his way into Mary's bed. Chase was the one chasing the cowgirl.

She'd come here planning to kill them both. It wasn't Mary's fault that Chase went around breaking women's hearts. But even as she thought it, she knew that Mary had disappointed her by falling for Chase all over again.

Not that it mattered, she thought as she calmly walked into the kitchen, opened the top drawer and took out the knife she'd planned to use on the deputy.

She stared at it, telling herself it was time to end this and move on. And there was only one way to finish it.

"IT'S MY DAY OFF," Lucy announced as she came out of her apartment as Mary was headed downstairs a few days later.

Mary couldn't help but look confused as she took in Lucy's Western attire and tried to make sense of the words. She knew that she'd been avoiding her tenant since their conversation about Dillon and Chase and felt guilty for it.

"Oh no, I'm sorry," Lucy said quickly. "You forgot. That's all right." She started to turn back toward her apartment.

"Horseback riding." Mary racked her brain, trying to remember if they'd made a definite date to go.

"You said on my day off. I thought I'd mentioned that I would be off today. Don't worry about it. I'm sure we can go some other time."

"No," Mary said quickly. "I did forget, but it will only take me a moment to change." She was thinking about what work she'd promised to do today, but she could get it done this afternoon or even work late if she had to. She didn't want to disappoint Lucy. The woman had looked so excited when she'd first mentioned it.

The more Chase had said Lucy reminded him of the woman he'd known in Arizona, the more Mary had defended her. If she never heard the name Fiona again, she'd be ecstatic.

And yet she found herself pulling away from Lucy, questioning the small things, like how close they'd become so quickly. Also she'd always tried to keep tenants as just that and not friends. More than anything, it was Chase's concern that had her trying to put distance between her and Lucy. Mary didn't want the woman always reminding him of Fiona.

So the last thing she wanted to do today was go horseback riding with the woman. But it had been her idea, and she had invited her. If anything, she prided herself on keeping her word. After this though, she would put more distance between them.

"I'll run across the street and get us some coffee," Lucy said, all smiles. "I'm so excited. It's been so long since I've been on a horse."

Mary hurried back upstairs to change. She missed Chase. He called every night and they talked for hours. He never mentioned his father, and she didn't bring it up. But she'd felt a change in him since discovering that Jim Harris was his biological father. He seemed stronger, more confident, more sure of what he wanted. He said he didn't want to be like the man. She wasn't sure exactly what he'd meant. Jim Harris was an unhappy man who'd made bad decisions before finding himself between a rock and hard place. She wondered if Chase could ever forgive him. Or if he already had.

When she came back downstairs, dressed for horseback riding, she found Lucy sitting at her desk. Two coffees sat on the edge away from the paperwork. Mary stopped in the doorway and watched for a moment as Lucy glanced through the papers on her desk before taking the card with the daisies that Chase had sent her, reading it and putting it back. As she did, she caught one of the daisies in her fingers.

Mary watched her crush it in her hand before dropping it into the trash can. She felt a fissure of irritation that the woman had been so nosy as to read the card let alone destroy one of the daisies. It was clear that Lucy resented Chase. Was she jealous? Did she not want Mary to have any other relationships in her life?

She cleared her voice, and Lucy got up from her desk quickly.

"Sorry, I was just resting for a moment." Lucy flashed her a gap-toothed smile. "I'm on my feet all day. It will be nice to sit on the back of a horse for a while."

HUD HAD THREE unsolved murders within weeks of each other and no clues. He got up to get himself some coffee when he remembered the cup Chase had brought in to be fingerprinted.

With a curse, he recalled that he'd given the cup to Dillon. Back in his office, he called down to the lab. "Last week a cup was brought down to be fingerprinted. I haven't seen the results yet."

The lab tech asked him to hold for a moment. "I have the order right here. I did the test myself, but I don't see my report on file. You didn't get a copy?"

"No, who did you give it to?"

"Dillon Ramsey, the deputy who brought it down. He asked that I give it to him personally. I did."

Hud swore. "You don't happen to remember—"

"The prints *were* on file," the tech said. Just as Chase had thought they would be. "Give me a minute. It was an unusual name. Fiona. Fiona Barkley."

Hud wrote it down and quickly went online. Fiona Barkley had been fingerprinted several times when questioned by police, starting with a house fire when she was eleven. Her entire family died in the fire.

The marshal shook his head as he saw that she'd been

questioned and fingerprinted in a half dozen other incidents involving males that she'd dated.

Where had Chase gotten this cup? He put in a call to the cowboy's number. It went straight to voice mail. He didn't leave a message. Mary had said that Chase would be home Friday night. Hud would ask him then.

As CHASE TOOK a break, he noticed that Rick had left several messages for him to call. Tired from a long day, he almost didn't call him back. He wasn't sure he could stay awake long enough to talk to both Mary and Rick, and he much preferred to talk to Mary before he fell asleep. But the last message Rick had left said it was important.

Chase figured that Fiona's body had been found, and Rick wanted him to know. So why hadn't he just left that message? The phone rang three times before Rick answered. Chase could hear a party going on in the background and almost hung up.

"Chase, I'm so glad you called back. Hold on." He waited and a few moments later, Rick came back on, the background noise much lower. "Hey, I hate to call you with bad news."

"They found her body?"

"Ah, no. Just the opposite. Some dentist down on the border recognized Fiona's photograph from a story in the newspaper about her disappearance. He contacted authorities. Chase, it looks like Fiona is alive. Not just that. She had the dentist change her appearance. Apparently, the Mexican dentist thought it was strange since she'd obviously been in some kind of accident. But he gave her a gap between her two front teeth."

Chase felt his heart stop dead. Lucy. The woman

living on the floor below Mary. Lucy. The barista who Mary had befriended. He tried to take a breathe, his mind racing. Hadn't he known? He'd sensed it gut deep, as if the woman radiated evil. Why hadn't he listened to his intuition?

"I have to go." He disconnected and quickly dialed Mary's cell phone number. It went straight to voice mail. "When you get this, call me at once. It's urgent. Don't go near Lucy. I'll explain when I see you. I'm on my way to Big Sky now." He hung up and called the ranch. Mary's mother answered.

"Dana, it's Chase. Have you seen Mary?"

"No. Chase, what's wrong?"

"I'm on my way there. If you see or hear from Mary, keep her there. Don't let her near Lucy, the barista at Lone Peak Perk, okay? Tell Hud. She's not who she is pretending to be. She's come to Montana to hurt me. I'm terrified that she will hurt Mary." He hung up and ran out to his pickup. He could be home within the hour. But would that be soon enough?

Or was it already too late?

Chapter Eighteen

"You haven't touched your coffee," Lucy said, glancing over at her as Mary drove her pickup to the ranch. Lucy had wanted to see the place and asked if they could take the back roads—unless Mary was in a hurry.

She'd taken a sip of the coffee. It had tasted bitter. Or maybe the bitter taste in her mouth had nothing to do with the coffee and more to do with what she'd seen earlier in her office—Lucy going through her things.

Now she took another sip. It wasn't just bitter. It had a distinct chalky taste—one that she remembered only too well. Even as she thought it, though, she was arguing that she was only imagining it. Otherwise, it would mean that there'd been something in the coffee that Lucy had brought her that day that had made her deathly ill—and again today.

"My stomach is a little upset," she said, putting the coffee cup back into the pickup's beverage holder.

Lucy looked away, her feelings obviously hurt. "Maybe we should do this some other day. I feel like you're not really into it."

"No, I asked you and this is the first day you've had off," Mary said, hating that she'd apparently forgotten. Worse, hating that she'd let Chase's suspicions about

Lucy get to her. Not that the woman hadn't raised more suspicions by her actions earlier.

Lucy turned away as if watching the scenery out the window. Mary pretended to take a sip of her coffee, telling herself that after today, she would distance herself from the woman and the coffee shop—at least for a while. It wasn't good to get too involved with a tenant, maybe especially this one.

Even the little bit of the coffee on the tip of her tongue had that chalky taste and made her want to gag. She looked over at Lucy as she settled her cup back into the pickup's beverage holder. She'd taken the long way to the ranch for Lucy but now she regretted it, just wanting to get this trip over with.

As she slowed for a gate blocking the road, she asked, "Lucy, would you mind getting the gate?"

Without a word, the woman climbed out as soon as Mary stopped the vehicle. Easing open her door, Mary poured half of the coffee onto the ground and quietly closed her door again. Lucy pushed the gate back and stepped aside as Mary drove through and then waited for her to close it.

Would she notice the spot on the ground where the coffee had been dumped? She hoped not. She also hoped that she was wrong about the chalky taste and what might have caused it. She didn't want to be wrong about Lucy, she thought as she watched the young woman close the gate and climb back in the truck.

Mary saw her glance at the half-empty coffee cup. Did she believe that Mary had drunk it?

Looking away again, Lucy asked, "How much farther to where you keep the horses?"

"Just over the next hill." Mary had called ahead and

asked one of the wranglers to saddle up her horse and a gentle one for Lucy. As they topped the hill, she could see two horses waiting for them tied up next to the barn. She tried to breathe a sigh of relief. Maybe Lucy had gotten up on the wrong side of the bed this morning. Or maybe she had drugged Mary's coffee and was angry that she hadn't drunk it.

"Is everything all right?" Lucy asked. "You seem upset with me."

Mary shot her a look. "I'm sorry. I just feel bad that I forgot about our horseback ride today. That's all."

"Not just your upset stomach?" the woman asked pointedly.

"That too, but I'm feeling better. There is no place I like better than the back of a horse."

Lucy said no more as Mary parked behind the bar and they got out. She helped the woman into the saddle. After she swung up onto her mount, they headed off on a trail that would take them to the top of the mountain. Mary was already planning on cutting the horseback ride short as she led the way up the trail.

"I'm out of sorts this morning too," Lucy said behind her. "I haven't slept well worrying about you."

Mary turned in her saddle to look back at her. "Worrying about *me*?"

"I probably shouldn't say anything, but there is something about Chase that bothers me."

She wanted to laugh out loud. Or at least say, *There's something about you that bothers him.* Instead, she said, "There is nothing to worry about."

"You just seem to be falling back into his arms so quickly. I heard him up in your apartment. He didn't leave until the next morning."

Mary felt a sliver of anger ripple through her. Chase was right about one thing. Lucy had become too involved in her life. "Lucy, that is none of your business."

"I'm sorry, I thought we were friends. You told me that night in my apartment all about him and the deputy."

"Yes." That, she saw now had been a mistake. "Then you know I never stopped loving him."

"But he stopped loving you."

She brought her horse up short as the trail widened, and Lucy rode up beside her. "Lucy—"

"You're the one who told me about this Fiona woman he had the affair with," she said, cutting Mary off.

"It was *one* night."

Lucy shrugged. "Or so he says. You said this woman called you. Said they were engaged. Why would she do that if they'd only had one date?"

Had Mary told her about that? She couldn't remember.

Lucy must have seen the steam coming out of her ears. "Don't get angry. I'm only saying this because you need someone who doesn't have a dog in the fight to tell you the truth."

She had to bite her tongue not to say that they didn't have that kind of friendship. "I appreciate your concern. But I know what I'm doing."

"It's just that he hurt you. I don't want to see him do it again."

"We probably shouldn't talk about this," Mary said, and spurred her horse forward. The sooner they got to the top of the mountain and finished this ride, the better. Chase was right. Somehow Lucy had wormed her way deep into Mary's life. Too deep for the short time they had known each other.

Lucy was jealous of her being with Chase, she realized. Had he sensed that? Is that why he didn't like Lucy? Why she reminded him of Fiona?

They rode in silence as the trail narrowed again, and Lucy was forced to fall in behind her. When they finally reached the top of the mountain, Mary felt as if she could breathe again. She blamed herself. Lucy had been kind to her. Lucy had managed to somehow always be there when needed. Mary had let her get too close, and now it was going to be awkward having her for a tenant directly below her apartment.

She just had to make it clear that her love life was none of Lucy's business. When they rode back to town, she'd talk to her.

HUD LISTENED TO his wife's frantic call. He thought of the cup that Chase had brought him wanting the fingerprints checked. "Lucy? You're sure that's what he said?" "She's a barista at a coffee shop across the street from Mary's building and one of her tenants." He thought of the plain white cup.

"Chase sounded terrified. He's on his way here. I tried to call Mary before I called you. Her phone went straight to voice mail. I'm scared."

"Okay, don't worry," Hud said. "I'll find this Lucy woman and see what's going on. If you see Mary, call me. Keep her there until I get to the bottom of this."

He disconnected, fear making his heart pound, and headed for his patrol SUV. The town of Big Sky had spread out some since the early days when few would have called it a real town. Still, it didn't take him but a few minutes to get to the coffee shop. As he walked in, he looked about for a barista with the name tag Lucy. There was an Amy and a Faith, but no Lucy.

"Excuse me," he said to the one called Amy. "Is Lucy working today?"

"Day off," she called over her shoulder as she continued to make a coffee that required a lot of noise.

"Do you know where she might have gone?" A headshake. He looked to the other barista. Faith shook her head as well and shrugged.

Dana had said that Lucy rented an apartment across the street. He headed over to Mary's building. With his master key, he opened the door and started up the stairs. An eerie quiet settled over him as he reached the second floor. He knocked at the first door. No answer. He tried the other one. No answer.

He was thinking about busting down the doors when the second one opened. A young man peered out. "I was looking for Lucy," he said.

"Lucy? The woman who is renting the apartment next door? I haven't met her but I overheard her and Mary talking about going horseback riding."

"Do you know where?"

"On Mary's family ranch, I would assume."

Lucy had gone horseback riding with Mary? He quickly called the ranch as he took the stairs three at a time down to his patrol SUV. "Dana," he said when she answered, "a tenant in the building said that Lucy and Mary went horseback riding. You're sure they aren't there?"

"I don't see her rig parked by the barn unless..." He could hear Dana leaving the house and running toward the barn. "She parked in back. They must have come in the back way," she said, out of breath. "Oh, Hud, they're up in the mountains somewhere alone." He heard the sound of a vehicle come roaring up.

"Who is that?" he demanded.

"Chase."

The marshal swore. "Tell him to wait until I get there. Don't let him go off half-cocked." But even as he said the words, he knew nothing was going to stop Chase. "I'm on my way." The moment he disconnected, he raced toward his patrol SUV.

Hud swore as he climbed behind the wheel, started the engine and headed for the ranch. It didn't take much to put the coffee cup and the barista named Lucy together with an apparently disturbed woman named Fiona Barkley who had a lot of priors in her past. His dead deputy had seen the report and kept the results to himself. He had the tie-in with Dillon and the barista, he thought his stomach roiling. His daughter was on a horseback ride with a killer.

LUCY GRITTED HER teeth as she watched Mary ride to the edge of the mountain and dismount. As she stared at her back, there was nothing more Lucy could say. She could tell that Mary was angry with her. Angry at a friend who was just trying to help her. Mary thought she knew Chase better than her.

Lucy wanted to laugh at that. She knew the cowboy better than Mary assumed. Maybe it was time to enlighten her. Look how easily Chase had cast her aside. How he'd gotten that irritated look whenever he saw her after that first night. He'd wanted her to go away. He'd gotten what he wanted from her and no longer needed her.

Instead, he thought he needed Mary. Sweet, precious Mary. She glared at the woman's back as she rode toward her, reined in and dismounted. She told herself that she'd tried to save Mary. It was Mary's own fault if she wouldn't listen. Now the cowgirl would need to die. It would have to look like an accident. Earlier, she'd thought about pulling the pocketknife she'd brought and jamming it into the side of her horse.

But she'd realized that Mary had been raised on horses. She probably wouldn't get bucked off when the horse reared or even when it galloped down the narrow trail in pain.

No, it had been a chance she couldn't take. But one way or another Mary wasn't getting off this mountain alive, she thought as she stepped over to stand beside her.

The view was just as Mary had said it was. They stood on a precipice overlooking a dozen mountains that stretched far into the horizon.

Below them was the canyon with its green-tone river snaking through the pines and canyon walls. It would have been so easy to push Mary off and watch her tumble down the mountain. But there was always the chance that the fall wouldn't kill her.

Lucy reached into her pocket and fingered the gun as she said, "I slept with Chase in Arizona."

Chapter Nineteen

Chase roared up in his pickup and leaped out as Dana ran toward him.

"The wrangler had horses saddled for them. He said they headed up the road into the mountains," she told him as he rushed toward her. He could see that she'd been saddling horses. "Hud wants you to wait for him. If this woman is as dangerous as you say she is—"

"I'm the one she wants. Not Mary. If I wait, it might be too late." He swung up into the horse she'd finished saddling and spurred it forward. Dana grabbed the reins to stop him.

"I know I can't talk you out of going. Here, take this." She handed him the pistol he knew she kept in the barn. "It's loaded and ready to fire. Be careful." Her voice broke. "Help Mary."

He rode off up the road headed for the mountaintop. He knew where Mary would take Lucy. It was her favorite spot—and the most dangerous.

As he rode at a full-out gallop, he thought of his misgivings about Lucy. Fiona must have loved the fact that she'd fooled him. That she'd fooled them all, especially trusting Mary. The woman had known exactly how to worm her way into Mary's life, how to get her claws into her and make her believe that she was her friend.

What Fiona didn't know how to do was let go.

He took the trail, riding fast and hard, staying low in the saddle to avoid the pine tree limbs. His heart was in his throat, his fear for Mary a thunderous beat in his chest and his abhorrence for Fiona a bitter taste in his mouth. He prayed as he rode that he would reach them in time. That the woman Fiona had become would spare Mary who'd done nothing to her.

But he had little hope. He knew Fiona. She had come all the way to Montana to extract her vengeance. She'd become another person, Lucy, taking her time, playing Mary. Did she know that they were on to her? That's what frightened him the most. If she thought that Mary was turning against her or that the authorities knew

MARY TURNED TO the woman in surprise, telling herself she must have heard wrong. "What did you just say?"

"I slept with Chase before you sent the letter."

She stared at the woman even as her heart began to pound. "What are you talking about?"

"I'm Fiona."

Mary took a step back as the woman she'd known as Lucy pulled a gun and pointed it at her heart.

Lucy laughed. "Surprise! I read your pathetic letter, and I hated you for taking him from me. You're the reason Chase broke up with me. Instead, the accident helped me become Lucy. You liked Lucy, didn't you? We could have been such good friends. But then Chase showed up—just as I knew he would."

Mary's mind was reeling. This was Lucy. And yet as she stared at her, she knew this was the woman who

Chase said had tried to kill him before he left Arizona. The woman he'd said was delusional.

"You think you know him so well." Lucy shook her head. "I was in love with him. He and I were so good together. You don't want to believe that, do you? Well, it's true. There was something between us, something real and amazing, but then you wrote that letter." Lucy's face twisted in disgust. "You ruined my life. You ruined Chase's."

Mary was shaking her head, still having trouble believing this was happening. Chase had tried to warn her, but she'd thought she knew Lucy. She'd really thought she was a friend.

Until she'd taken a sip of the coffee this morning and tasted that horribly familiar chalky taste. "You drugged me."

Lucy shrugged. "You shouldn't have poured out your coffee this morning. That was really rude. I was nice enough to get it for you."

"You wanted to make me sick again?"

"I was being kind," Lucy said, looking confused. "This would have been so much easier if you'd been sick. Now, it's going to get messy." She jabbed the gun at her. "If you had just stayed mad at Chase, this wouldn't be happening either."

Mary didn't know what to say or do. She'd never dealt with someone this unbalanced. "You want to make him suffer. Is that what this is about?"

Lucy smiled her gap-toothed smile. "For starters."

"You want him to fall in love with you again." She saw at once that was exactly what Lucy wanted. "But if you hurt me, that won't happen."

"It won't happen anyway and we both know it. Because of you." The woman sounded close to tears. "I could have made him happy. Before the letter came from you, he needed me. I could tell. He would have fallen in love with me."

Mary doubted that, but she kept the thought to herself. "If you hurt me, you will lose any chance you have for happiness."

Lucy laughed, sounding more like the woman she'd thought she knew. "Women like me don't find happiness. That's what my mother used to say. But then she let my stepfather and brothers physically and sexually abuse me."

Mary felt her heart go out to the woman despite the situation. "I'm so sorry. That's horrible. You deserved so much better."

Lucy laughed. "I took care of all of them, sending them to hell on earth, and for a while, I was happy, now that I think about it."

"Lucy—"

"Call me Fiona. I know how much you hate hearing that name. Fiona. Fiona. Fiona." She let out a high-pitched laugh that drowned out birdsong but not the thunder of hooves as a horse and rider came barreling across the mountaintop.

CHASE REINED IN his horse as all his fears were realized. The women had been standing at the edge of the mountaintop, Fiona holding a gun pointed at Mary's heart. But when they'd heard him coming, Fiona had grabbed Mary and pressed the muzzle of the weapon to her rival's throat.

"Nice you could join us," Fiona said as he slowly dismounted. "I wondered how long it would take before you realized who I was."

"I sensed it the first time I saw you," he said as he walked toward the pair, his gaze on Fiona and the gun. He couldn't bear to look into Mary's eyes. Fear and disgust. This was all his fault. He'd brought Fiona into their lives. Whatever happened, it was on him.

"I knew it was you," he said, and she smiled.

"It's the chemistry between us. When you pretended not to know me, well, that hurt, Chase. After everything we meant to each other…"

"Exactly," he said. "That's why you need to let Mary go. This is between you and me, Fiona."

Her face clouded. "Please, you think I don't know that you came riding up like that to save her?"

"Maybe I came to save you."

Fiona laughed, a harsh bitter sound. "Save me from what?"

"Yourself. Have any of the men you've known tried to save you, Fiona?" The question seemed to catch her off guard. "Did any of them care what happened to you?"

She met his gaze. "Don't pretend you care."

"I'm not pretending. I never wanted to hurt you. When I heard they found your car in the river, I was devastated. I didn't want things to end that way for you." He saw her weaken a little and took a step toward her and Mary.

"But you don't love me."

That was true and he knew better than to lie. "No. I'd already given away my heart when I met you. It wasn't fair, but it's the truth."

"But you picked me up at that party and brought me back to your place."

He shook his head as he took another step closer. "Rick asked you to drive me home because I'd had too much to drink."

She stared at him as if she'd told herself the story so many times, she didn't remember the truth. "But we made love."

"Did we? I remember you pulling off my boots and jeans right before I passed out."

Fiona let out a nervous laugh. "We woke up in the same bed."

"We did," he agreed as he stepped even closer. "But I suspect that's all that happened that night."

She swallowed and shook her head, tears welling in her eyes. "I liked you. I thought you and I—"

"But you knew better once I told you that I was in love with someone else."

"Still, if you had given us a chance." Fiona made a pleading sound.

"Let Mary go. She had nothing to do with what happened between us."

Fiona seemed to realize how close he was to the two of them. She started to take a step back, dragging Mary along with her. The earth crumbled under her feet and she began to fall.

Chase could see that she planned to take Mary with her. He dived for the gun, for Mary, praying Fiona didn't pull the trigger as she fell. He caught Mary with one hand and reached for the gun barrel with the other. The report of the handgun filled the air as he yanked Mary forward, breaking Fiona's hold on her. But Mary still teetered on the sheer edge of the cliff as he felt a searing pain in his shoulder. His momentum had carried him forward. He shoved Mary toward the safety of the mountain top as was propelled over the edge of the drop-off.

He felt a hand grab his sleeve. He looked up to see Mary, clinging to him, determined not to let him fall.

Below him, he saw Fiona tumbling down the mountainside over boulders. Her body crashed into a tree trunk, but kept falling until it finally landed in a pile of huge rocks at the bottom.

As Mary helped pull him back up to safety, he saw that Fiona wasn't moving, her body a rag doll finally at rest. Behind them he heard horses. Pulling Mary to him, he buried his face in her neck, ignoring the pain in his shoulder as he breathed in the scent of her.

"He's shot," Chase heard Dana cry before everything went black.

Chapter Twenty

Chase opened his eyes to see Mary sitting next to his hospital bed as the horror of what had happened came racing back. "Are you—"

"I'm fine," she said quickly, and rose to reach for his hand. "How are you?"

He glanced down at the bandage on his shoulder. "Apparently, I'm going to live. How long have I been out?"

"Not long. You were rushed into surgery to remove the bullet. Fortunately, it didn't hit anything vital."

He stared into her beautiful blue eyes. "I was so worried about you. I'm so sorry."

She shook her head. "I should have listened to you."

Chase laughed. "I wouldn't make a habit of that."

"I'm serious. You tried to warn me."

He sobered. "This is all my fault."

"You didn't make her do the things she did." Her voice broke. Tears filled her eyes. "I thought we were both going to die. You saved my life."

"You saved mine," he said, and squeezed her hand. "Once I'm out of this bed—"

"Slow down, cowboy," the doctor said as he came into the room. "It will be a while before you get out of that bed."

"I need to get well soon, Doc. I'm going to marry this woman."

Mary laughed. "I think he's delirious," she joked, her cheeks flushed.

"I've never been more serious," he called after her as the doctor shooed her from the room. "I love that woman. I've always loved Mary Cardwell Savage," he called before the door closed. He was smiling as he lay back, even though the effort of sitting up had left him in pain. "I need to get well, Doc. I have to buy a ring."

HUD LEANED BACK in his office chair and read the note Fiona-Lucy had left in her apartment. That the woman had lived just a floor below his daughter still made his heart race with terror.

By the time, you find this, I will probably be dead. Or with luck, long gone. Probably dead because I'm tired of living this life. Anyway, I have nowhere to go. I came here to make Chase Steele pay for breaking my heart. Sometimes I can see that it wasn't him that made me do the things I've done. That it started long before him. It's the story of my life. It's the people who have hurt me. It's the desperation I feel to be like other people, happy, content, loved.

But there is an anger in me that takes over the rest of the time. I want to hurt people the way I've been hurt and much worse. I killed my mother, stepfather and stepbrothers in a fire. Since then, I've hurt other people who hurt me—and some who didn't. Some, like Deputy Dillon Ramsey, deserved to die. Christy Shores, not so much.

Today, I will kill a woman who doesn't deserve it in order to hurt a man who I could have loved if only he had loved me. He will die too. If not today, then soon. And then... I have no idea. I just know that I'm tired. I can't keep doing this.

Then again, I might feel differently tomorrow.

Hud carefully put the letter back into the evidence bag and sealed it. Fiona was gone. She'd died of her injuries after falling off the mountain. Because she had no family, her body would be cremated. Chase had suggested that her ashes be sent back to Arizona to her friend, Patty, the one person who'd stuck by her.

Two of his murders had been solved by the letter. The third, Grady Birch, was also about to be put to rest. A witness with a cabin not far from where Grady's body was found had come forward. He'd seen a man dragging what he now suspected was a body down to the river. That man had been Deputy Dillon Ramsey, who the witness identified after Dillon's photo had run in the newspaper following his murder.

According to the law, everything would soon be neatly tied up, Hud thought as he put away the evidence bag. But crimes left scars. He could only hope that his daughter would be able to overcome hers. He had a feeling that Chase would be able to help her move on. He wouldn't mind a wedding out at the ranch. It had been a while, and he was thinking how much his wife loved weddings—and family—when his phone rang. It was Dana.

"I just got the oddest call from our son Hank," his wife said without preamble. "He says he's coming home for a visit and that he's bringing someone with him. A woman."

Hud could hear the joy in Dana's voice. "I told you that it would just take time, didn't I? This is great news."

"I never thought he'd get over Naomi," she said, but quickly brightened again. "I can't wait to meet this woman and see our son. It's been too long."

He couldn't have agreed more. "How's Mary?"

"She's picking up Chase at the hospital. Given the big smile on her face when she left the ranch, I'd say she's going to be just fine. How do you feel about a wedding or two in our future?"

He chuckled. "You just read my mind, but don't go counting your chickens before they hatch. Let's take it one at a time." But he found himself smiling as he hung up. Hank was coming home. He'd missed his son more than he could even tell Dana. He just hoped Hank really was moving on.

CHASE COULDN'T WAIT to see Mary. He was champing at the bit to get out of the hospital. He'd called a local jewelry store and had someone bring up a tray of engagement rings for him to choose one. He refused to put it off until he was released. The velvet box was in his pocket. Now he was only waiting for the nurse to wheel him down to the first floor—and Mary—since it was hospital policy, he'd been told.

Earlier, his father had stopped by. Chase had been glad to see him. Like his father, he'd made mistakes. They were both human. He'd been angry with a man who hadn't even known he existed. But he could understand why his mother had kept the truth from not only him, but also Jim Harris.

He didn't know what kind of relationship they could have, but he no longer felt as if there was a hole in his heart where a father should have been. Everyone said Jim was a good man who'd had some bad luck in his life. Chase couldn't hold that against him.

When his hospital room door opened, he heard the creak of the wheelchair and practically leaped off the bed in his excitement. He and Mary had been apart for far too long. He didn't want to spend another minute away from her. What they had was too special to let it go. He would never take their love for each for granted again.

To his surprise, it wasn't the nurse who brought in the wheelchair. "Mary?"

She looked different today. He was trying to put his finger on what it was when she grinned and shoved the wheelchair to one side as she approached.

MARY COULDN'T EXPLAIN the way she felt. But she was emboldened by everything that had happened. When Chase had first come back, she'd told herself that she couldn't trust him after he'd left Montana. But in her heart, she'd known better. Still, she'd pushed him away, letting her pride keep her from the man she loved.

Instead, she'd trusted Lucy. The red flags had been there, but she'd ignored them because she'd wanted to like her. She'd missed her friends who had moved away. She'd been vulnerable, and she'd let a psychopath into her life.

But now she was tired of being a victim, of not going after what she wanted. What she wanted was Chase.

She stepped to him, grabbed the collar of his Western shirt and pulled him into a searing kiss. She heard his intake of breath. The kiss had taken him by surprise. But also his shoulder was still healing.

"Oh, I'm so sorry," she said, drawing back, her face heating with embarrassment.

"I'm not," he said as he pulled her to him with his good arm and kissed her. When she drew back he started to say something, but she hushed him with a finger across his lips. "I have to know, Chase Steele. Are you going to be mine or not?"

He let out a bark of a laugh. "I've always been yours, Mary Savage."

She sighed and said, "Right answer."

His grin went straight to her heart. He pulled her close again and this time his kiss was fireworks. She melted into his arms. "Welcome home, Chase."

* * * * *

The Cardwell Ranch: Montana Legacy series by New York Times *bestselling author B.J. Daniels continues with Hank's Story. Read on for a sneak peek.*

Hank Savage squinted into the sun glaring off the dirty windshield of his pickup as Cardwell Ranch came into view. He slowed the truck to a stop, resting one sun-browned arm over the top of the steering wheel as he took it all in.

The ranch, with its log and stone structures, didn't appear to have changed in the least. Nor had the two-story house where he'd grown up. Memories flooded him of hours spent on the back of a horse, of building forts in the woods around the creek, of the family sitting around the large table in the kitchen in the mornings, the sun pouring in, the sound of laughter. He saw and felt everything he'd given up, everything he'd run from, everything he'd lost.

"Been a while?" asked the sultry dark-haired woman in the passenger seat.

He nodded around the lump in his throat, shoved back his Stetson and wondered what the hell he was doing back here. This was a bad idea, probably his worst ever.

"Having second thoughts?" He'd warned Frankie

about his big family, but she'd said she could handle it. He wasn't all that sure *he* could handle this. He prided himself on being fearless about most things. Give him a bull that hadn't been ridden, and he wouldn't hesitate to climb right on. Same with his job as a lineman. He'd faced gale winds hanging from a pole to get the power back on, braved getting fried more times than he liked to remember.

But coming back here, facing the past? He'd never been more afraid. He knew it was just a matter of time before he saw Naomi—just as he had in his dreams, in his nightmares. She was here, right where he'd left her, waiting for him as she had been for eight long years. Waiting for him to come back and make things right.

He looked over at Frankie. "You sure about this?"

She sat up straighter to take in the ranch and him, took a breath and let it out. "I am if you are. After all, this was your idea."

Like she had to remind him. "Then I suggest you slide over here." He patted the seat between them and she moved over, cuddling against him as he put his free arm around her. She felt small and fragile, certainly not strong enough for what was to come. For a moment, he almost changed his mind. It wasn't too late. He didn't have the right to involve her in his past.

"It's going to be okay," she said, and nuzzled his neck where his dark hair curled at his collar. "Trust me."

He pulled her closer and let his foot up off the brake. The pickup began to roll toward the ranch. It wasn't that he didn't trust Frankie. He just knew that it was only a matter of time before Naomi came to him, pleading with him to do what he should have done eight years ago. He felt a shiver even though the summer day was unseasonably warm.

I'm here.

Available August 2019 wherever
Harlequin books are sold.

CRIME SCENE
AT CARDWELL RANCH

When I think of the Gallatin Canyon,
I remember rubber gun fights at our cabin,
hikes to Lava Lake and stopping by
Bessie and Russell Rehm's place near the current
Big Sky. Russell is gone now, but I will always
remember Bessie's cooking—and the treat
she used to make me at her ranch in Texas:
a mixture of peanut butter and molasses.
I still make it and I always think of Bessie.

This book is for you, Bessie.
Thanks for all the memories!

Prologue

Seventeen years earlier

The fall knocked the air out of her. She'd landed badly, one leg bent under her. On the way down, she'd hit her head and the skin on her arms and legs was scraped raw.

Stunned, she tried to get to her feet in the darkness of the tight, confined space. She'd lost both shoes, her body ached and her left hand was in terrible pain, her fingers definitely broken.

She managed to get herself upright in the pitch-blackness of the hole. Bracing herself on the cold earth around her, she looked up, still dazed.

Above her, she could see a pale circle of starlit sky. She started to open her mouth to call out when she heard him stagger to the edge of the old dry well and fall to his knees. His shadow silhouetted over part of the opening.

She stared up at him in confusion. He hadn't meant to push her. He'd just been angry with her. He wouldn't hurt her. Not on purpose.

The beam of a flashlight suddenly blinded her. "Help me."

He made a sound, an eerie, low-keening wail like a wounded animal. "You're alive?"

His words pierced her heart like a cold blade. He'd thought the fall would kill her? *Hoped* it would?

The flashlight went out. She heard him stumble to his feet and knew he was standing looking down at her. She could see his shadow etched against the night sky. She felt dizzy and sick, still too stunned by what had happened.

His shadow disappeared. She could see the circle of dim light above her again. She listened, knowing he hadn't left. He wouldn't leave her. He was just upset, afraid she would tell.

If she pleaded with him the way she had the other times, he would forgive her. He'd tried to break it off before, but he'd always come back to her. He loved her.

She stared up until, with relief, she saw again his dark shape against the starlit sky. He'd gone to get a rope or something to get her out. "I'm sorry. Please, just help me. I won't cause you any more trouble."

"No, you won't." His voice sounded so strange, so foreign. Not the voice of the man she'd fallen so desperately in love with.

She watched him raise his arm. In the glint of starlight she saw it wasn't a rope in his hand.

Her heart caught in her throat. "No!" The gunshot boomed, a deafening roar in the cramped space.

She must have blacked out. When she woke, she was curled in an awkward position in the bottom of the dry well. Over the blinding pain in her head, she could hear the sound of the pickup's engine. He was driving away!

"No!" she cried as she dragged herself up onto her feet again. "Don't leave me here!" As she looked up to the opening high above her, she felt something wet and sticky run down into her eye. Blood.

He'd shot her. The pain in her skull was excruciating. She dropped to her knees on the cold, hard earth. He'd said he loved her. He'd promised to take care of her. Tonight, she'd even worn the red dress he loved.

"Don't leave! Please!" But she knew he couldn't hear her. As she listened, the sound of the engine grew fainter and fainter, then nothing.

She shivered in the damp, cold blackness, her right hand going to her stomach.

He'd come back.

He couldn't just leave her here to die. How could he live with himself if he did?

He'd come back.

Chapter One

As the pickup bounced along the muddy track to the old homestead, Dana Cardwell stared out at the wind-scoured Montana landscape, haunted by the premonition she'd had the night before.

She had awakened in the darkness to the howl of the unusually warm wind against her bedroom window and the steady drip of melting snow from the eaves. A chinook had blown in.

When she'd looked out, she'd seen the bare old aspens vibrating in the wind, limbs etched black against the clear night sky. It felt as if something had awakened her to warn her.

The feeling had been so strong that she'd had trouble getting back to sleep only to wake this morning to Warren Fitzpatrick banging on the door downstairs.

"There's something you'd better see," the elderly ranch manager had said.

And now, as Warren drove them up the bumpy road from the ranch house to the old homestead, she felt a chill at the thought of what waited for her at the top of the hill. Was this what she'd been warned about?

Warren pulled up next to the crumbling foundation and cut the engine. The wind howled across the open hillside, making the tall yellowed grass keel over and gently rocking the pickup.

It was called the January Thaw. Without the blanket of white snow, the land looked wrung out, all color washed from the hills until everything was a dull brown-gray. The only green was a few lone pines swaying against the wind-rinsed sky.

Little remained of the homestead house. Just part of the rock foundation and the fireplace, the chimney as stark as the pines against the horizon.

Past it, in the soft, wet earth, Dana saw Warren's tracks where he had walked to the old well earlier this morning. All that marked the well was a circle of rock and a few weathered boards that covered part of the opening.

Warren cocked his head as if he already heard the marshal's SUV coming up the ranch road. Dana strained her ears but heard nothing over the pounding of her heart.

She was glad Warren had always been a man of few words. She was already on edge without having to talk about what he'd found.

The ranch manager was as dried out as a stick of jerky and just as tough, but he knew more about cattle than any man Dana had ever known. And he was as loyal as an old dog. Until recently, he and Dana had run the ranch together. She knew Warren wouldn't have gotten her up here unless it was serious.

As Dana caught the whine of the approaching vehicle over the wind, the sound growing louder, her dread grew with it.

Warren had told her last night that he'd noticed the

boards were off the old dry well again. "I think I'll just fill it in. Safer that way. Give me something to do."

Like a lot of Montana homesteads, the well was just a hole in the ground, unmarked except for maybe a few old boards thrown over it, and because of that, dangerous to anyone who didn't know it was there.

"Whatever you think," she'd told him the night before. She'd been distracted and really hadn't cared.

But she cared now. She just hoped Warren was wrong about what he'd seen in the bottom of the well.

They'd know soon enough, she thought as she turned to watch the Gallatin Canyon marshal's black SUV come roaring up the road from the river.

"Scrappy's driving faster than usual," she said, frowning. "You must have lit a fire under him when you called him this morning."

"Scrappy Morgan isn't marshal anymore," Warren said.

"What?" She glanced over at him. He had a strange look on his weathered face.

"Scrappy just up and quit. They had to hire a temporary marshal to fill in for a while."

"How come I never hear about these things?" But she knew the answer to that. She'd always been too busy on the ranch to keep up with canyon gossip. Even now that she worked down in Big Sky, her ties were still more with the ranching community—what little of it was left in the Gallatin Canyon since the town of Big Sky had sprung up at the base of Lone Mountain. A lot of the ranchers had sold out or subdivided to take advantage of having a ski and summer resort so close by.

"So who's the interim marshal?" she asked as the Sheriff's Department SUV bounded up the road, the morning sun glinting off the windshield. She groaned.

"Not Scrappy's nephew Franklin? Tell me it's anyone but him."

Warren didn't answer as the new marshal brought the black SUV with the Montana State marshal logo on the side to a stop right next to her side of the pickup.

All the breath rushed from her as she looked over and saw the man behind the wheel.

"Maybe I should have warned you," Warren said, sounding sheepish.

"That would've been nice," she muttered between gritted teeth as she met Hudson Savage's clear blue gaze. His look gave nothing away. The two of them might have been strangers—instead of former lovers—for all the expression that showed in his handsome face.

Her emotions boiled up like one of the Yellowstone geysers just down the road. First shock and right on its heels came fury. When Hud had left town five years ago, she'd convinced herself she'd never have to lay eyes on that sorry son of a bitch again. And here he was. Damn, just when she thought things couldn't get any worse.

OVER THE YEARS as a policeman in L.A., Hudson "Hud" Savage had stared down men who were bigger and stronger. Some had guns, some knives and baseball bats.

But none unnerved him like the look in Dana Cardwell's whiskey-brown glare.

He dragged his gaze away, turning to pick up the heavy-duty flashlight from the seat next to him. *Coward*. If just seeing her had this effect on him, he hated to think what talking would do.

Her reaction to him was pretty much what he'd expected. He'd known she would be far from happy to see him. But he had hoped she wouldn't be as furious as she'd been when he'd left town. But given the look in her eyes, he'd say that was one wasted hope.

And damn if it was no less painful than it had been five years ago seeing her anger, her hurt.

Not that he blamed her. He hadn't just left town, he'd flat-out run, tail tucked between his legs.

But he was back now.

He picked up the flashlight and, bracing himself against the wind and Dana Cardwell, he opened his door and stepped out.

The sun glinted off the truck's windshield so he couldn't see her face as he walked to the front of the SUV. But he could feel her gaze boring into him like a bullet as he snugged his Stetson down to keep it from sailing off in the wind.

When Warren had called the office this morning, Hud had instructed him not to go near the well again. The ranch foreman's original tracks to and from the well were the only ones in the soft dirt. It surprised Hud, though, that Dana hadn't gotten out to take a look before he arrived. She obviously hadn't known the order was from him or she would have defied it sure as the devil.

As he looked out across the ranch, memories of the two of them seemed to blow through on the breeze. He could see them galloping on horseback across that far field of wild grasses, her long, dark hair blowing back, face lit by sunlight, eyes bright, grinning at him as they raced back to the barn.

They'd been so young, so in love. He felt that old ache, desire now coupled with heartbreak and regret.

Behind him, he heard first one pickup door open, then the other. The first one closed with a click, the second slammed hard. He didn't have to guess whose door that had been.

Out of the corner of his eye, he saw Warren hang back, waiting by the side of his pickup, out of the way— and out of earshot as well as the line of fire. Warren was no fool.

"Are we goin' to stand here all day admiring the scenery or are we goin' to take a look in the damned well?" Dana asked as she joined Hud.

He let out a bark of nervous laughter and looked over at her, surprised how little she'd changed and glad of it. She was small, five-four compared to his six-six. She couldn't weigh a hundred and ten pounds soaking wet, but what there was of her was a combination of soft curves and hard-edged stubborn determination. To say he'd never known anyone like her was putting it mildly.

He wanted to tell her why he'd come back, but the glint in her eye warned him she was no more ready to hear it than she'd been when he'd left.

"Best take a look in that well then," he said.

"Good idea." She stood back as he trailed Warren's tracks to the hole in the ground.

A half-dozen boards had once covered the well. Now only a couple remained on the single row of rocks rimming the edge. The other boards appeared to have been knocked off by the wind or fallen into the well.

He flipped on the flashlight and shone the beam down into the hole. The well wasn't deep, about fifteen feet, like looking off the roof of a two-story house. Had it been deeper, Warren would never have seen what lay in the bottom.

Hud leaned over the opening, the wind whistling in

his ears, the flashlight beam a pale gold as it skimmed the dirt bottom—and the bones.

Hunting with his father as a boy, Hud had seen his share of remains over the years. The sun-bleached skeletons of deer, elk, moose, cattle and coyotes were strewn all over rural Montana.

But just as Warren had feared, the bones lying at the bottom of the Cardwell Ranch dry well weren't from any wild animal.

DANA STOOD BACK, her hands in the pockets of her coat, as she stared at Hud's broad back.

She wished she didn't know him so well. The moment he'd turned on the flashlight and looked down, she'd read the answer in his shoulders. Her already upset stomach did a slow roll and she thought for a moment she might be sick.

Dear God, what was in the well? *Who* was in the well?

Hud glanced back at her, his blue eyes drilling her to the spot where she stood, all the past burning there like a hot blue flame.

But instead of heat, she shivered as if a cold wind blew up from the bottom of the well. A cold that could chill in ways they hadn't yet imagined as Hud straightened and walked back to her.

"Looks like remains of something, all right," Hud said, giving her that same noncommittal look he had when he'd driven up.

The wind whipped her long dark hair around her face. She took a painful breath and let it go, fighting the wind, fighting a weakness in herself that made her angry and scared. "They're human bones, aren't they?"

Hud dragged his hat off and raked a hand through his hair, making her fingers tingle remembering the feel of that thick sun-streaked mop of his. "Won't be certain until we get the bones to the lab."

She looked away, angry at him on so many levels that it made it hard to be civil. "I *know* there are human remains down there. Warren said he saw a human skull. So stop lying to me."

Hud's eyes locked with hers and she saw anger spark in all that blue. He didn't like being called a liar. But then, she could call him much worse if she got started.

"From what I can see, the skull appears to be human. Satisfied?" he said.

She turned away from the only man who had ever satisfied her. She tried not to panic. If having Hud back—let alone the interim marshal—wasn't bad enough, there was a body in the well on her family ranch. She tried to assure herself that the bones could have been in the well for years. The well had been dug more than a hundred years ago. Who knew how long the bones had been there?

But the big question, the same one she knew Hud had to be asking, was *why* the bones were there.

"I'm going to need to cordon this area off," he said. "I would imagine with it being calving season, you have some cattle moving through here?"

"No cattle in here to worry about," Warren said.

Hud frowned and glanced out across the ranch. "I didn't notice any cattle on the way in, either."

Dana felt his gaze shift to her. She pulled a hand from her pocket to brush a strand of her hair from her face before looking at him. The words stuck in her throat and she was grateful to Warren when he said,

"The cattle were all auctioned this fall to get the ranch ready to sell."

Hud looked stunned, his gaze never leaving hers. "You wouldn't sell the ranch."

She turned her face away from him. He was the one person who knew just what this ranch meant to her and yet she didn't want him to see that selling it was breaking her heart just as he had. She could feel his gaze on her as if waiting for her to explain.

When she didn't, he said, "I have to warn you, Dana, this investigation might hold up a sale."

She hadn't thought of that. She hadn't thought of anything but the bones—and her added bad luck in finding out that Hud was acting marshal.

"Word is going to get out, if it hasn't already," he continued. "Once we get the bones up, we'll know more, but this investigation could take some time."

"You do whatever you have to do, Hud." She hadn't said his name out loud in years. It sounded odd and felt even stranger on her tongue. Amazing that such a small word could hurt so much.

She turned and walked back to Warren's pickup, surprised her legs held her up. Her mind was reeling. There was a body in a well on her ranch? And Hud Savage was back after all this time of believing him long gone? She wasn't sure which shocked or terrified her more.

She didn't hear him behind her until he spoke.

"I was sorry to hear about your mother," he said so close she felt his warm breath on her neck and caught a whiff of his aftershave. The same kind he'd used when he was hers.

Without turning, she gave a nod of her head, the wind burning her eyes, and jerked open the pickup door, sending a glance to Warren across the hood that she was more than ready to leave.

As she climbed into the truck and started to pull the door shut behind her, Hud dropped one large palm over the top of the door to keep it from closing. "Dana…"

She shot him a look she thought he might still remember, the same one a rattler gives right before it strikes.

"I just wanted to say…happy birthday."

She tried not to show her surprise—or her pleasure—that he'd remembered. That he had, though, made it all the worse. She swallowed and looked up at him, knifed with that old familiar pain, the kind that just never went away no matter how hard you fought it.

"Dana, listen—"

"I'm engaged." The lie was out before she could call it back.

Hud's eyebrows rose. "To anyone I know?"

She took guilty pleasure from the pain she heard in his voice, saw in his face. "Lanny Rankin."

"Lanny? The *lawyer?*" Hud didn't sound surprised, just contemptuous. He must have heard that she'd been dating Lanny. "He still saving up for the ring?"

"What?"

"An engagement ring. You're not wearing one." He motioned to her ring finger.

Silently she swore at her own stupidity. She'd wanted to hurt him and at the same time keep him at a safe distance. Unfortunately she hadn't given a thought to the consequences.

"I just forgot to put it on this morning," she said.

"Oh, you take it off at night?"

Another mistake. When Hud had put the engagement

ring on her finger so many years ago now, she'd sworn she'd never take it off.

"If you must know," she said, "the diamond got caught in my glove, so I took it off to free it and must have laid it down."

His brows went up again.

Why didn't she just shut up? "I was in a hurry this morning. Not that it's any of your business."

"You're right," he agreed. "Must be a big diamond to get stuck in a glove." Not like the small chip he'd been able to afford for her, his tone said.

"Look, as far as I'm concerned, you and I have nothing to say to each other."

"Sorry, didn't mean to pry into your personal life." A muscle bunched in his jaw and he took on that all-business marshal look again. "I'd appreciate it if you and Warren wouldn't mention what you found in the well to anyone. I know it's going to get out, but I'd like to try to keep a lid on it as long as we can."

He had to be joking. The marshal's office dispatcher was the worst gossip in the canyon.

"Anything else?" she asked pointedly as his hand remained on the door.

His gaze softened again and she felt her heart do that pitter-patter thing it hadn't done since Hud.

"It's good seeing you again, Dana," he said.

"I wish I could say the same, Hud."

His lips turned up in a rueful smile as she jerked hard on the door, forcing him to relinquish his hold. If only she could free herself as easily.

The pickup door slammed hard. Warren got in and started the engine without a word. She knew he'd heard her lie about being engaged, but Warren was too smart to call her on it.

As sun streamed into the cab, Warren swung the pickup around. Dana rolled down her window, flushed with a heat that had nothing to do with the warmth of the sun or the January Thaw. She could see the ranch house down the hillside. Feel the rattle of the tires over the rough road, hear the wind in the pines.

She promised herself she wouldn't do it even as she reached out, her fingers trembling, and adjusted the side mirror to look back.

Hud was still standing where she'd left him, looking after them.

Happy birthday.

Chapter Two

Well, that had gone better than he'd expected, Hud thought with his usual self-deprecating sarcasm.

She was *engaged* to Lanny Rankin?

What did you expect? It's been years. I'm surprised she isn't married by now. But Lanny Rankin?

He watched the pickup disappear over the hill, listening until the sound of the engine died away and all he could hear was the wind again.

Yeah, why *isn't* she married?

Lanny Rankin had gone after Dana before Hud had even driven out past the city limit sign. He'd had five years. So why weren't the two of them married?

He felt a glimmer of hope.

Was it possible Dana was dragging her feet because she was still in love with him—not Lanny Rankin?

And why wasn't she wearing her ring? Maybe she didn't even have one. Maybe she wasn't engaged—at least not officially.

Maybe you're clutching at straws.

Maybe, but his instincts told him that if she was going to marry Lanny, she would have by now.

A half mile down the hillside, he could see Warren's pickup stop in a cloud of dust. Hud watched Dana get out. She was still beautiful. Still prickly as a porcupine. Still strong and determined. Still wishing him dead.

He couldn't blame her for that, though.

He had a terrible thought. What if she married Lanny now just out of spite?

And what was this about selling the ranch? The old Dana Cardwell he knew would never put the ranch up for sale. Was she thinking about leaving after it sold? Worse, after she married Lanny?

She disappeared into the ranch house. This place was her heart. She'd always said she would die here and be buried up on the hill with the rest of her mother's family, the Justices.

He'd loved that about her, her pride in her family's past, her determination to give that lifestyle to her children—to *their* children.

Hud felt that gut-deep ache of regret. God, how he hated what he'd done to her. What he'd done to himself. It didn't help that he'd spent the past five years trying to make sense of it.

Water under the bridge, his old man would have said. But then his old man didn't have a conscience. Made life easier that way, Hud thought, cursing at even the thought of Brick Savage. He thought of all the wasted years he'd spent trying to please his father—and the equally wasted years he'd spent hating him.

Hud turned, disgusted with himself, and tried to lose himself in the one thing that gave him any peace, his work.

He put in a call to Coroner Rupert Milligan. While he waited for Rupert, he shot both digital photographs and video of the site, trying not to speculate on the bones in the well or how they had gotten there.

Rupert drove up not thirty minutes later. He was dressed in a suit and tie, which in Montana meant either a funeral or a wedding. "Toastmasters, if you have to know," he said as he walked past Hud to the well, grabbing the flashlight from Hud's hand on his way.

Rupert Milligan was older than God and more powerful in this county. Tall, white-haired, with a head like a buffalo, he had a gruff voice and little patience for stupidity. He'd retired as a country doctor but still worked as coroner. He'd gotten hooked on murder mysteries—and forensics. Rupert loved nothing better than a good case and while Hud was still hoping the bones weren't human, he knew that Rupert was pitching for the other team.

Rupert shone the flashlight down into the well, leaning one way then the other. He froze, holding the flashlight still as he leaned down even farther. Hud figured he'd seen the skull partially exposed at one edge of the well.

"You got yourself a human body down there, but then I reckon you already knew that," he said, sounding too cheerful as he straightened.

Hud nodded.

"Let's get it out of there." Rupert had already started toward his rig.

Hud would have offered to go down in Rupert's place but he knew the elderly coroner wouldn't have stood for it. All he needed Hud for was to document it if the case ever went to trial—and help winch him and the bones out of the well.

He followed Rupert over to his pickup where the coroner had taken off his suit jacket and was pulling on a pair of overalls.

"Wanna put some money on what we got down there?" Rupert asked with a grin. Among his other eclectic traits, Rupert was a gambler. To his credit, he seldom lost.

"Those bones could have been down there for fifty years or more," Hud said, knowing that if that was the case, there was a really good chance they would never know the identity of the person or how he'd ended up down there.

Rupert shook his head as he walked around to the back of the truck and dropped the tailgate. "Those aren't fifty-year-old bones down there. Not even close."

The coroner had come prepared. There was a pulley system in the back and a large plastic box with a body bag, latex gloves, a variety of different size containers, a video camera and a small shovel.

He handed Hud the pulley then stuffed the needed items into a backpack, which he slung over his shoulder before slipping a headlamp over his white hair and snapping it on.

"True, it's dry down there, probably been covered most of the time since the bones haven't been bleached by the sun," Rupert said as he walked back to the well and Hud followed. "Sides of the well are too steep for most carnivores. Insects would have been working on the bones, though. Maggots." He took another look into the well. "Spot me five years and I'll bet you fifty bucks that those bones have been down there two decades or less," he said with his usual confidence, a confidence based on years of experience.

Twenty years ago Hud would have been thirteen. Rupert would have been maybe forty-five. With a jolt Hud realized that Rupert wasn't that much older than his father. It felt odd to think of Brick Savage as old. In Hud's mind's eye he saw his father at his prime, a large, broad-shouldered man who could have been an actor. Or even a model. He was that good-looking.

"I got a hundred that says whoever's down there didn't fall down there by accident," Rupert said.

"Good thing I'm not a betting man," Hud said, distracted. His mind on the fact that twenty years ago, his father was marshal.

"TELL ME YOU DIDN'T," Dana said as she walked into Needles and Pins and heard giggling in the back beyond the racks of fabric.

Her best friend and partner in the small sewing shop gave her a grin and a hug. "It's your birthday, kiddo," Hilde whispered. "Gotta celebrate."

"Birthdays after thirty should not be celebrated," Dana whispered back.

"Are you kidding? And miss seeing what thirty-one candles on a cake looks like?"

"You didn't."

Hilde had her arm and was tugging her toward the back. "Smile. I promise this won't kill you, though you do look like you think it will." She slowed. "You're shaking. Seriously, are you all right?"

As much as she hated it, Dana was still a wreck after seeing Hud again. She'd hoped to get to work at the shop and forget about everything that had happened this morning, including not only what might be in the old well—but also who. The last thing she wanted was to even be reminded of her birthday. It only reminded her that Hud had remembered.

"Hud's back," she said, the words coming out in a rush.

Hilde stopped dead so that Dana almost collided with her.

Her best friend's surprise made her feel better. Dana had been worried all morning that everyone had known about Hud's return—and just hadn't told her to protect her. She hated being protected. Especially from news like that. If she'd known he was back, she could have prepared herself for seeing him— Even as she thought it, she knew nothing could have prepared her for that initial shock of seeing Hud after five long years.

"Hud's back in the canyon?" Hilde whispered, sounding shocked. The Gallatin Canyon, a fifty-mile strip of winding highway and blue-ribbon river, had been mostly ranches, the cattle and dude kind, a few summer cabins and homes—that is until Big Sky resort and the small town that followed at the foot of Lone Mountain. But the "canyon" was still its own little community.

"Hud's the new temporary marshal," Dana whispered, her throat suddenly dry.

"Hello?" came the familiar voice of Margo from the back of the store. "We've got candles burning up in here."

"Hud? Back here? Oh, man, what a birthday present," Hilde said, giving her another hug. "I'm so sorry, sweetie. I can imagine what seeing him again did to you."

"I still want to kill him," Dana whispered.

"Not on your birthday." Hilde frowned. "Does Lanny know yet?" she whispered.

"Lanny? Lanny and I are just friends."

"Does Lanny know that?" her friend asked, giving her a sympathetic smile.

"He knows." Dana sighed, remembering the night

Lanny had asked her to marry him and she'd had to turn him down. Things hadn't been the same between them since. "I did something really stupid. I told Hud I was engaged to Lanny."

"You didn't."

Dana nodded miserably. "I don't know what I was thinking."

Margo called from the back room. "Major wax guttering back here."

"Let's get this over with," Dana said, and she and Hilde stepped into the back of the shop where a dozen of Dana's friends and store patrons had gathered around a cake that looked like it was on fire.

"Quick! Make a wish!" her friend Margo cried.

Dana closed her eyes for an instant, made a wish, then braving the heat of thirty-one candles flickering on a sheet cake, blew as hard as she could, snuffing out every last one of them to the second chorus of "Happy Birthday."

"Tell me you didn't wish Hud dead," Hilde whispered next to her as the smoke started to dissipate.

"And have my wish not come true? No way."

HUD WATCHED RUPERT, the glow of the coroner's headlamp flickering eerily on the dark dirt walls as he descended into the well. Hud tried not to think about remains down there or the fact that Brick might have investigated the disappearance. Might even have known the victim. Just as Hud and Rupert might have.

Rupert stopped the pulley just feet above the bones to video the scene on the bottom of the well. The light flickered and Hud looked away as he tried to corral his thoughts. Sure as hell this investigation would force him to deal with his father. The thought turned his stomach. The last time he'd seen his father, more than five years ago now, they'd almost ended up in a brawl, burning every bridge between them—both content with the understanding that the next time Hud saw his father it would be to make sure Brick was buried.

When Hud had decided to come back, he'd thought at least he wouldn't have to see his father. Word was that Brick had moved to a place up on Hebgen Lake near West Yellowstone—a good fifty miles away.

The wind seemed cooler now and in the distance Hud could see dark clouds rolling up over the mountains. He turned his face up to the pale sun knowing it wouldn't be long before it was snowing again. After all, this was January in Montana.

The rope on the pulley groaned and he looked down again into the well as Rupert settled gently on the bottom, the headlamp now focused on the human remains.

Because of the steep sides of the well, the body was contained, none of the bones had been scattered by critters or carried off. The coroner had pulled on a pair of the latex gloves. He opened the body bag and began to carefully fill it with the bones.

"Good thing you didn't bet with me," Rupert said. "I'd say the bones have been here closer to fifteen years." He held up a pelvic bone in his gloved hands. "A woman. White. Late twenties, early thirties."

In the light from the headlamp, Hud watched Rupert pick up the skull and turn it slowly in his hands.

"Well, how about that," he heard Rupert say, then glance up at him. "You got a murder on your hands, son," the coroner said solemnly. He held up the skull, his headlamp shining through a small round hole in it.

"The bullet entered this side, passed through the brain and lodged in the mastoid bone behind the left ear," Rupert said, still turning the skull in his hands. "The bullet lead is flattened and deformed from impact but there will be enough lands and grooves to match the weapon. Looks like a .38."

"If we could find the weapon after all this time," Hud said. He let out an oath under his breath. Murder. And the body found on the Cardwell Ranch.

"Get one of those containers out of my rig so I can bag the skull separately," Rupert said, his voice echoing up.

Hud ran back to Rupert's truck and returned to lower the container down to him. A few minutes later Rupert sent the filled container up and Hud found himself looking at the dead woman's skull. A patch of hair clung to the top. The hair, although covered with dirt, was still reddish in color. He stared at the hair, at the shape of the skull, and tried to picture the face.

"You think she was young, huh?" he called down.

In the well, Rupert stopped to inspect one of the bones in the light from his headlamp. "Based on growth lines, I'd say twenty-eight to thirty-five years of age." He put down one bone to pick up what appeared to be a leg bone. "Hmm, that's interesting. The bony prominences show muscle development, indicating she spent a lot of time on her feet. Probably made her living as a hairdresser, grocery clerk, nurse, waitress, something like that." He put the bone into the body bag and picked up another shorter one. "Same bony prominences on the arms as if she often carried something heavy. My money's on waitress or nurse."

Few coroners would go out on a limb with such conjecture. Most left this part up to the forensics team at the state crime lab. But then, Rupert Milligan wasn't like most coroners. Add to that the fact that he was seldom wrong.

"What about height and weight?" Hud asked, feeling a chill even in the sun. His father had always liked waitresses. Hell, his father chased skirts no matter who wore them.

Rupert seemed to study the dirt where the bones had been. "I'd say she was between five-four and five-seven. A hundred and twenty to a hundred and forty pounds."

That covered a lot of women, Hud thought as he carried the container with the skull in it over to Rupert's pickup and placed it carefully on the front seat. All the teeth were still intact. With luck, they'd be able to identify her from dental records if she'd been local.

He tried to remember if he'd heard his father talking about a missing person's case about fifteen years ago. Rodrick "Brick" Savage loved to brag about his cases especially the ones he solved.

But then this one wouldn't have been one he'd solved. And fifteen years ago, Hud had been eighteen and away at college. He wondered if Dana had mentioned a missing woman in one of her letters to him. She'd written him every week, but the letters were more about what was happening on the ranch, I-miss-you letters, love letters.

Leaving the skull at the pickup, he went back to watch Rupert dig through the dirt on the well floor. The coroner slowed as he hit something, then stooped and shook dirt from what he'd found.

Hud felt his chest heave as Rupert held up a bright red high-heeled shoe.

AFTER THE BIRTHDAY party and in between customers, Dana defied Hud's orders and told Hilde about what Warren had found in the old dry well by the original homestead's foundation.

Dana was sure the news was all over the canyon by now. But still she'd waited, not wanting to say anything to anyone but Hilde, her best friend.

"He really thinks the bones are human?" Hilde asked with a shiver. "Who could it be?"

Dana shook her head. "Probably some ancestor of mine."

Hilde looked skeptical. "You think the bones have been down there that long?" She hugged herself as if she could feel the cold coming up from the well just as Dana had earlier.

"It's horrible to think that someone might have fallen in and been unable to get out, died down there," Dana said.

Hilde nodded. "It's just odd that you found them now." Her eyes lit. "You think the investigation will hold up the sale of the ranch?"

"Maybe, but ultimately the ranch will be sold, trust me," Dana said, and changed the subject. "Thank you for the birthday party. I love the purse you made me."

"You're welcome. I'm sorry you've had such a lousy day. Why don't you go on home? I can handle things here. It's your birthday."

Dana groaned. "I hate to imagine what other horrible things could happen before this day is over."

"Always the optimist, aren't you."

Dana smiled in spite of herself. "I think I will go home." She looked outside. Clouds scudded across the pale sky, taking the earlier warmth with them. The sign over the door pendulumed in the wind and she could almost feel the cold trying to get in.

Across the way from the shop, the top of the mountain had disappeared, shrouded in white clouds. The first snowflakes, blown by the wind, swept across the window. Apparently the weatherman had been right when he'd called for snow before midnight.

Dana would be lucky to get home before the roads iced over.

FROM DOWN IN THE WELL, Rupert signaled for Hud to pull up the body bag. It was heavy, but mostly from the layer of dirt retrieved from the bottom of the well. The dirt would be sifted for evidence later at the state crime lab.

He put down the body bag, noting that the weather had turned. Snowflakes danced around him, pelting him on gusts of wind and momentarily blinding him. He barely felt the cold as he squatted near the edge of the well, pulling up the hood on his marshal's jacket as he watched Rupert finish.

The red high-heeled shoe had triggered something. Not a real memory since he couldn't recall when, where or if he'd even actually seen a woman in a red dress and bright red high-heeled shoes. It could have been a photograph. Even a television show or a movie.

But for just an instant he'd had a flash of a woman in a bright red dress and shoes. She was spinning around in a circle, laughing, her long red hair whirling around her head, her face hidden from view.

That split-second image had left him shaken. Had he known this woman?

The canyon was like a small town except for a few

months when the out-of-staters spent time in their vacation homes or condos to take advantage of the skiing or the mild summer weather.

But if the woman had been one of those, Hud knew he'd have heard about her disappearance. More than likely she was someone who'd worked at the resort or one of the local businesses. She might not have even been missed as seasonal workers were pretty transient.

"I'm going to need another container from the truck," Rupert called up.

The wind had a bite to it now. Snowflakes swirled around him as Hud lowered the container down and watched the coroner place what appeared to be a dirt-caked piece of once-red fabric inside. Just as in his memory, the woman had worn a red dress. Rupert continued to sift through the dirt, stooped over in the small area, intent on his work.

Hud pulled his coat around him. The mountains across the canyon were no longer visible through the falling snow. And to think he'd actually missed winters while working for the police department in Los Angeles.

From down in the well, Rupert let out a curse, calling Hud's attention back to the dark hole in the ground.

"What is it?" Hud called down.

Rupert had the video camera out and seemed to be trying to steady his hands as he photographed the well wall.

"You aren't going to believe this." The older man's voice sounded strained as if he'd just found something that had shaken him—a man who'd bragged that he'd seen the worst of everything. "She was still alive."

"What?" Hud asked, his blood running cold.

"Neither the gunshot wound nor being thrown down the well killed her right away," Rupert said. "There are deep gouges in the earth where she tried to climb out."

Chapter Three

Long after Rupert came up out of the well, neither he nor Hud said anything. Snow whirled on the wind, the bank of clouds dropping over them, the sun only a memory.

Hud sat behind the wheel of the SUV, motor running, heater cranked up, drinking coffee from the thermos Rupert had brought. Next to him, Rupert turned the SUV's heater vent so it blew into his face.

The older man looked pale, his eyes hollow. Hud imagined that, like him, Rupert had been picturing what it must have been like being left in the bottom of that well to die a slow death.

The yellow crime scene tape Hud had strung up now bowed in the wind and snow. The hillside was a blur of white, the snow falling diagonally.

"I suppose the murder weapon could still be up here," Hud said to Rupert, more to break the silence than anything else. Even with the wind and the motor and heater going, the day felt too quiet, the hillside too desolate. Anything was better than thinking about the woman in the well—even remembering Dana's reaction to seeing him again.

"Doubt you'll ever find that gun," Rupert said without looking at him. The old coroner had been unusually quiet since coming up out of the well.

Hud had called the sheriff's department in Bozeman and asked for help searching the area. It was procedure, but Hud agreed with Rupert. He doubted the weapon would ever turn up.

Except they had to search for it. Unfortunately this was Montana. A lot of men drove trucks with at least one firearm hanging on the back window gun rack and another in the glove box or under the seat.

"So did he shoot her before or after she went into the well?" Hud asked.

"After, based on the angle the bullet entered her skull." Rupert took a sip of his coffee.

"He must have thought he killed her."

Rupert said nothing as he stared in the direction of the well.

"Had to have known about the well," Hud said. Which meant he had knowledge of the Cardwell Ranch. Hud groaned to himself as he saw where he was headed with this. The old homestead was a good mile off Highway 191 that ran through the Gallatin Canyon. The killer could have accessed the old homestead by two ways. One was the Cardwells' private bridge, which would mean driving right by the ranch house.

Or…he could have taken the Piney Creek Bridge, following a twisted route of old logging roads. The same way he and Dana used when he was late getting her home.

Either way, the killer had to be local to know about the well, let alone the back way. Unless, of course, the killer was a member of the Cardwell family and had just driven in past the ranch house bold as brass.

Why bring the woman here, though? Why the Cardwell Ranch well?

"You know what bothers me?" Hud said, taking a sip of his coffee. "The red high heel. Just one in the well. What happened to the other one? And what was she doing up here dressed like that?" He couldn't shake that flash of memory of a woman in a red dress any more than he could nail down its source.

He felt his stomach tighten when Rupert didn't jump in. It wasn't like Rupert. Did his silence have something to do with realizing the woman in the well hadn't been dead and tried to save herself? Or was it possible Rupert suspected who she was and for some reason was keeping it to himself?

"The heels, the dress, it's almost like she was on a date," Hud said. "Or out for a special occasion."

Rupert glanced over at him. "You might make as good a marshal as your father some day." High praise to Rupert's way of thinking, so Hud tried hard not to take offense.

"Odd place to bring your date, though," Hud commented. But then maybe not. The spot was isolated. Not like a trailhead where anyone could come along. No one would be on this section of the ranch at night and you could see the ranch house and part of the road up the hillside. You would know if anyone was headed in your direction in plenty of time to get away.

And yet it wasn't close enough that anyone could hear a woman's cries for help.

"Still, someone had to have reported her missing," Hud persisted. "A roommate. A boss. A friend. A husband."

Rupert finished his coffee and started to screw the cup back on the thermos. "Want any more?"

Hud shook his head. "You worked with my father for a lot of years."

Rupert looked over at him, eyes narrowing. "Brick Savage was the best damned marshal I've ever known." He said it as if he knew only too well that there were others who would have argued that, Hud among them, and Rupert wasn't going to have it.

Brick Savage was a lot of things. A colorful marshal, loved and respected by supporters, feared and detested by his adversaries. Hud knew him as a stubborn, rigid father who he'd feared as a boy and despised as a man. Hud hated to think of the years he'd tried to prove himself to his father—only to fail.

He could feel Rupert's gaze on him, daring him to say anything against Brick. "If you're right about how long she's been down there…"

Rupert made a rude sound under his breath, making it clear he was right.

"…then Brick would have been marshal and you would have been assistant coroner."

"Your point?" Rupert asked.

Hud eyed him, wondering why Rupert was getting his back up. Because Hud had brought up Brick? "I just thought you might remember a missing person's case during that time."

"You'd have to ask your father. Since no body was found, I might not even have heard about it." Rupert zipped up his coroner jacket he'd pulled from behind the seat of his truck. "I need to get to the crime lab."

Hud handed Rupert the coffee cup he'd lent him. "Just seems odd, doesn't it? Someone had to have missed her. You would think the whole area would have been talking about it."

The coroner smiled ruefully. "Some women come and go more often than a Greyhound bus."

Hud remembered hearing that Rupert's first wife had run off on numerous occasions before she'd finally cleared out with a long-haul truck driver.

"You think this woman was like that?" Hud asked, his suspicion growing that Rupert knew more than he was saying.

"If she was, then your suspect list could be as long as your arm." Rupert opened his door.

"You almost sound as if you have an idea who she was," Hud said over the wind.

Rupert climbed out of the truck. "I'll call you when I know something definite."

Hud watched the older man move through the falling snow and wondered why Rupert, who was ready to bet on the bones earlier, seemed to be backpedaling now. It wasn't like the old coroner. Unless Rupert suspected who the bones belonged to—and it hit a little too close to home.

THE PHONE WAS ringing as Dana walked through the ranch house door. She dropped the stack of mail she'd picked up at the large metal box down by the highway and rushed to answer the phone, not bothering to check caller ID, something she regretted the moment she heard her older brother's voice.

"Dana, what the hell's going on?" Jordan demanded without even a hello let alone a "happy birthday." Clearly he had been calling for some time, not thinking to try her at her new job.

"Where are you?"

"Where do you think I am?" he shot back. "In case

you forgot, I live in New York. What the hell is going on out there?"

She slumped into a chair, weak with relief. For a moment she'd thought he was in Montana, that he'd somehow heard about the bones in the well and had caught a flight out. The last thing she needed today was her brother Jordan to deal with in the flesh. Unfortunately it seemed she would have to deal with him on the phone, though.

Her relief was quickly replaced by irritation with him. "I'm fine, Jordan. Thanks for asking, considering it's my birthday and it's been a rough day." She'd seen the sheriff's department cars go up the road toward the old homestead, making her even more aware of what was happening not a mile from the ranch house.

Jordan let out a weary sigh. "Dana, if this is about the ranch—"

"Jordan, let's not. Not today. Is there a reason you called?"

"Hell yes! I want to know why the marshal thinks there's a body in a well on our ranch."

Our ranch? She gritted her teeth. Jordan had hated everything about the ranch and ranching, distancing himself as far as he could from both.

How had he heard about the bones already? She sighed, thinking of Franklin Morgan's sister, Shirley, who worked as dispatcher. Shirley had dated Jordan in high school and still drooled over him whenever Jordan returned to the canyon. Well, at least Dana didn't have to wonder anymore how long it would take for the word to get out.

She didn't dare tell him that it had been Warren who'd found the bones. Jordan would never understand why Warren hadn't just filled in the well and kept his mouth shut. "I found some bones in the old dry well at the homestead."

"So?"

"I called the marshal's office to report them."

"For God's sake, why?"

"Because it's both legally and morally the thing to do." She really wasn't in the mood for Jordan today.

"This is going to hold up the sale of the ranch."

"Jordan, some poor soul is in the bottom of our well. Whoever it is deserves to be buried properly."

"It's probably just animal bones. I'm flying out there to see what the hell is really going on."

"No!" The word was out before she could call it back. Telling Jordan no was like waving a red blanket in front of a rodeo bull.

"You're up to something. This is just another ploy on your part."

She closed her eyes and groaned inwardly. "I just think it would be better if you didn't come out. I can handle this. You'll only make matters worse."

"I have another call coming in. I'll call you back." He hung up.

Dana gritted her teeth as she put down the phone and picked up her mail and began sorting through it. All she needed was Jordan coming out here now. She thought about leaving so she didn't have to talk to him when he called back.

Or she could just not answer the phone. But she knew that wouldn't accomplish anything other than making him more angry. And Jordan wasn't someone you wanted to deal with when he was angry.

She opened a letter from Kitty Randolph asking

her to help chair another fundraiser. Kitty and Dana's mother had been friends and since Mary's death, Kitty had seemed to think that Dana would take her mother's place. Dana put the letter aside. She knew she would probably call Kitty in a day or so and agree to do it. She always did.

She picked up the rest of the mail and froze at the sight of the pale yellow envelope. No return address, but she knew who it was from the moment she saw the handwriting.

Throw it away. Don't even open it.

The last thing she needed was to get something from her sister, Stacy, today.

The envelope was card-shaped. Probably just a birthday card. But considering that she and Stacy hadn't spoken to each other in five years...

She started to toss the envelope in the trash but stopped. Why would her sister decide to contact her now? Certainly not because it was her birthday. No, Stacy was trying to butter her up. Kind of like good cop, bad cop with Jordan opting of course for the bad cop role. Her other brother Clay was more of the duck-for-cover type when there was conflict in the family.

Dana couldn't help herself. She ripped open the envelope, not surprised to find she'd been right. A birthday card.

On the front was a garden full of flowers and the words, *For My Sister.* Dana opened the card.

"Wishing you happiness on your birthday and always."

"Right. Your big concern has always been my happiness," Dana muttered.

The card was signed, Stacy. Then in small print under it were the words, *I am so sorry.*

Dana balled up the card and hurled it across the room, remembering a time when she'd idolized her older sister. Stacy was everything Dana had once wanted to be. Beautiful, popular, the perfect older sister to emulate. She'd envied the way Stacy made everything look easy. On the other hand, Dana had been a tomboy, scuffed knees, unruly hair and not a clue when it came to boys.

What Dana hadn't realized once she grew up was how much Stacy had envied *her.* Or what lengths she would go to to hurt her.

The phone rang. She let it ring twice more before she forced herself to pick up the receiver, not bothering to check caller ID for the second time. "Yes?"

"Dana?"

"Lanny. I thought it…was someone else," she said lamely.

"Is everything all right?" he asked.

She could picture him sitting in his office in his three-piece, pin-striped suit, leaning back in his leather chair, with that slight frown he got when he was in lawyer mode.

"Fine. Just…busy." She rolled her eyes at how stupid she sounded. But she could feel what wasn't being said between them like a speech barrier. Lanny had to have heard that Hud was back in town. Wasn't that why he'd called?

"Well, then I won't keep you. I just wanted to make sure we were still on for tonight," he said.

"Of course." She'd completely forgotten about their date. The last thing she wanted to do was to go out tonight. But she'd made this birthday dinner date weeks ago.

"Great, then I'll see you at eight." He seemed to hesitate, as if waiting for her to say something, then hung up.

Why hadn't she told him the truth? That she was exhausted, that there was a dead body in her well, that she just wanted to stay home and lick her wounds? Lanny would have understood.

But she knew why she hadn't. Because Lanny would think her canceling their date had something to do with Hud.

ONCE THE TEAM of deputies on loan from the sheriff's department in Bozeman arrived and began searching the old homestead, Hud drove back to his office at Big Sky.

Big Sky didn't really resemble a town. Condos had sprung up after construction on the famous resort began on the West Fork of the Gallatin River in the early 1970s. A few businesses had followed, along with other resort amenities such as a golf course in the lower meadow and ski area on the spectacular Lone Mountain peak.

The marshal's office was in the lower meadow in a nondescript small wooden building, manned with a marshal, two deputies and a dispatcher. After hours, all calls were routed to the sheriff's office in Bozeman.

Hud had inherited two green deputies and a dispatcher who was the cousin of the former sheriff and the worst gossip in the state. Not much to work with, especially now that he had a murder on his hands.

He parked in the back and entered the rear door, so lost in thought that he didn't hear them at first. He stopped just inside the door at the sound of his name being brandished about.

"Well, you know darned well that he had some kind of pull to get this job, even temporarily." Hud recognized Franklin Morgan's voice. Franklin was the nephew of former marshal Scott "Scrappy" Morgan. Franklin was a sheriff's deputy in Bozeman, some forty miles away.

Hud had been warned that Franklin wasn't happy about not getting the interim marshal job after his uncle left and that there might be some hard feelings. Hud smiled at that understatement as he heard Franklin continue.

"At first I thought he must have bought the job, but hell, the Savages haven't ever had any money." This from Shirley Morgan, the dispatcher, and Franklin's sister. Nepotism was alive and well in the canyon.

"Didn't his mother's family have money?" Franklin asked.

"Well, if they did, they didn't leave it to their daughter after she married Brick Savage," Shirley said. "But then, can you blame them?"

"Hud seems like he knows what he's doing," countered Deputy Norm Turner. Norm was a tall, skinny, shy kid with little to no experience at life or law enforcement from what Hud could tell.

"Maybe Brick pulled some strings to get Hud the job," Franklin said.

Hud scoffed. Brick wouldn't pull on the end of a rope if his son was hanging off it from a cliff on the other end.

"Not a chance," Shirley said with a scornful laugh. "It was that damned Dana Cardwell."

Hud felt a jolt. Dana?

"Everyone in the canyon does what she wants just

like they did when her mother was alive. Hell, those Cardwell women have been running things in this canyon for years. Them and Kitty Randolph. You can bet Dana Cardwell got him the job."

Hud couldn't help but smile just thinking how Dana would love to hear that she was responsible for getting him back to town.

Franklin took a drink of his coffee and happened to look up and see Hud standing just inside the doorway. The deputy's eyes went wide, coffee spewing from his mouth. Hud could see the wheels turning. Franklin was wondering how long Hud had been there and just what he'd overheard.

Norm swung around and about choked on the doughnut he'd just shoved into his mouth.

Shirley, who'd been caught before, didn't even bother to look innocent. She just scooted her chair through the open doorway to the room that housed the switchboard, closing the door behind her.

Hud watched with no small amount of amusement as the two deputies tried to regain their composure. "Any word from the crime lab?" Hud asked as he proceeded to his office.

Both men answered at the same time.

"Haven't heard a word."

"Nothing from our end." Franklin tossed his foam coffee cup in the trash as if he suddenly remembered something urgent he needed to do. He hightailed it out of the office.

Deputy Turner didn't have that luxury. "Marshal, about what was being said…"

Hud could have bailed him out, could have pretended he hadn't heard a word, but he didn't. He'd been young once himself. He liked to think he'd learned from his mistakes, but coming back here might prove him wrong.

"It's just that I—I…wanted to say…" The young deputy looked as if he might break down.

"Deputy Turner, don't you think I know that everyone in the canyon is wondering how I got this job, even temporarily, after what happened five years ago? I'm as surprised as anyone that I'm the marshal for the time being. All I can do is prove that I deserve it. How about you?"

"Yes, sir, that's exactly how I feel," he said, his face turning scarlet.

"That's what I thought," Hud said, and continued on to his office.

He was anxious to go through the missing person's file from around fifteen years back. But he quickly saw that all but the past ten years of files had been moved to the Bozeman office.

"We don't have any records back that far," the clerk told him when he called. "We had a fire. All the records were destroyed."

Twelve years ago. He'd completely forgotten about the fire. He hung up. All he could hope was that Rupert was wrong. That the woman hadn't been in the well more than twelve years. Otherwise… He swore.

Otherwise, he would be forced to talk to the former marshal. After all this time, the last thing Hud wanted was to see his father.

"I'M TAKING THE FIRST flight out," Jordan said without preamble when he called Dana back. "I'll let you know what time I arrive so you can pick me up at the airport."

Dana bit down on her tongue, determined not to let

him get to her. He seemed to just assume she wouldn't have anything else to do but pick him up at Gallatin Field, a good fifty miles away. "Jordan, you must have forgotten. I have a job."

"You're half owner of a...fabric shop. Don't tell me you can't get away."

She wasn't going to chauffeur him around the whole time he was here, or worse, let him commandeer her vehicle. She took a breath. She would have loved to have lost her temper and told him just what she thought of him. He was in no position to be asking anything of her.

She let out the breath. "You'll have to rent a car, Jordan. I'll be working." A thought struck her like the back of a hand. "Where will you be staying in case I need to reach you?" Not with her. Please not with her at the ranch.

She heard the knife edge in his voice. "Don't worry, I'm not going to stay at that old run-down ranch house with you."

She almost slumped with relief. She'd suspected for some time that he was in financial trouble. Ever since two years ago when he'd married Jill, an out-of-work model, Jordan had seemed desperate for money.

"I assume Jill is coming with you?" Dana said, assuming just the opposite.

"Jill can't make it this time."

"Oh?" Dana bit her tongue again, just not quick enough. Jill had set foot in Montana only once and found it too backwoodsy.

"You have something to say, Dana? We all know what an authority you are on romantic relationships."

The jab felt all the more painful given that Hud was back in town. "At least I had the sense not to marry him." Instantly she wished she could snatch back the words. "Jordan, I don't want to fight with you." It was true. She hated how quickly this had escalated into something ugly. "Let's not do this."

"No, Dana, you brought it up," Jordan said. "If you have something to say, let's hear it."

"Jordan, you know this isn't what Mom wanted, us fighting like this."

He let out a cruel laugh. "You think I care what she wanted? The only thing she ever loved was that damned ranch. And just like her, you chose it over a man."

"Mom didn't choose the ranch over Dad," Dana said. "She tried to make their marriage work. It was Dad who—"

"Don't be naive, Dana. She drove him away. The same way you did Hud."

She wasn't going to discuss this with him. Especially today. Especially with Hud back. "I have to go, Jordan."

He didn't seem to hear her. "At least I have someone to warm my bed at night. Can your precious ranch do that?"

"Enjoy it while it lasts," Dana snapped. "Jill will be long gone once you don't have anything else you can pillage to appease her."

She knew at once that she'd gone too far. Jordan had never liked to hear the truth.

Dana smacked herself on the forehead, wishing she could take back the angry words. He'd always known how to push her buttons. Isn't that what siblings were especially adept at because they knew each other's weaknesses so well?

"Jordan, I'm sorry," she said, meaning it.

"I'll have Dad pick me up. But, dear sister, I will deal

with you when I see you. And at least buy a damned answering machine." He ended the call abruptly.

She felt dirty, as if she'd been wrestling in the mud, as she hung up. She hadn't wanted the conversation to end like that. It would only make matters worse once he hit town.

She told herself that with luck maybe she wouldn't have to see him. She wouldn't have to see any of her siblings. The only one she'd been even a little close to was Clay, the youngest, but she wasn't even talking to *him* lately.

And she didn't want an answering machine. Anyone who needed to reach her, would. Eventually. She could just imagine the kind of messages Jordan would leave her.

She shuddered at the thought. As bad as she felt about the argument and her angry words, she was relieved. At least Jordan wasn't staying at the ranch, she thought with a rueful smile as she went into the kitchen and poured herself a glass of wine.

As she did, she heard the sound of a vehicle coming up the road to the house and groaned. Now what?

Glancing out the window she saw the marshal's black SUV barreling toward her.

This day just kept getting better.

Chapter Four

Across the river and a half mile back up a wide valley, the Cardwell ranch house sat against a backdrop of granite cliffs and towering dark pines. The house was a big, two-story rambling affair with a wide front porch and a new brick-red metal roof.

Behind it stood a huge weathered barn and some outbuildings and corrals. The dark shapes loomed out of the falling snow and darkness as Hud swung the SUV into the ranch yard.

He shut off the engine. Out of habit, he looked up at Dana's bedroom window. There was nothing but darkness behind the glass but in his mind he could see her waving to him as she'd done so many times years before.

As he got out of the patrol car, ducking deep into his coat against the falling snow, he ran to the porch, half expecting Dana's mother, Mary Justice Cardwell, to answer the door. Mary had been a ranch woman through and through. No one had ever understood why she'd married Angus Cardwell. He'd been too handsome and charming for his own good, with little ambition and even less regard for ranch work. But he'd also been heir to the C-Bar Ranch adjacent to the Justice Ranch.

When the two had married, so had the ranches. The combined spread became the Cardwell Ranch.

No one had been surprised when the two divorced. Or when Angus gave up the ranch to Mary.

People were just surprised that the two stayed together long enough to have four children.

And Angus and Mary had certainly produced beautiful children.

Jordan, the oldest, was almost too good-looking and had definitely taken after his father. Clay was the youngest, a slim, quiet young man who worked in local theater groups.

Then there was Stacy, two years older than Dana, cheerleader cute. Stacy had cashed in on her looks her whole life, trading up in three marriages so far. He didn't like to think about Stacy.

There was no comparison between the two sisters. While Dana also had the Justice-Cardwell good looks, she had something more going for her. She'd been the good student, the hard worker, the one who wanted to carry on the family tradition at the ranch, while the others had cut and run the first chance they got.

Dana, like her mother, loved everything about ranching. It and breathing were one and the same to her. That's why he couldn't understand why Dana would be selling the place. It scared him.

He couldn't stand the thought that he'd come back too late. Or worse that he'd been carrying a torch for a woman who no longer existed.

As he started to knock, he heard a dog growl and looked over to see a gray-muzzled, white-and-liver springer spaniel.

"Joe?" He couldn't believe his eyes. He knelt as the

dog lumbered over to him, tail wagging with recognition. "Joe, hey, old boy. I didn't think you'd still be around." He petted the dog, happy to see a friendly face from the past.

"Was there something you wanted?"

He hadn't heard the front door open. Dana stood leaning against the frame, a glass of wine in her hand and a look that said she was in no mood for whatever he was selling.

He wished like hell that he wasn't going to add to her troubles. "Evening," he said, tipping his hat as he gave Joe a pat and straightened. "Mind if I come in for a few minutes? I need to talk to you."

"If this has something to do with you and me…"

"No." He gave her a rueful smile. There was no "you and me"—not anymore. Not ever again from the look in her brown eyes. "It's about what we found in the well."

All the starch seemed to go out of her. She stepped back, motioning him in.

He took off his hat and stepped in to slip off his boots and his jacket before following her through the very Western living area with its stone and wood to the bright, big airy kitchen. Joe followed at his heels.

"Have a seat."

Hud pulled out a chair at the large worn oak table, put his Stetson on an adjacent chair and sat.

Dana frowned as Joe curled up at his feet. "Traitor," she mouthed at the dog.

Hud looked around, memories of all the times he'd sat in this kitchen threatening to drown him. Mary Justice Cardwell at the stove making dinner, Dana helping, all of them chatting about the goings-on at the ranch, a new foal, a broken-down tractor, cows to be moved.

He could almost smell the roast and homemade rolls baking and hear Dana's laughter, see the secret, knowing looks she'd sent him, feel the warmth of being a part of this family.

And Dana would have made her mother's double chocolate brownies for dessert—especially for him.

Dana set a bottle of wine and a glass in front of him, putting it down a little too hard and snapping him back to the present. "Unless you think we're both going to need something stronger?" she asked.

"Wine will do." He poured himself some and topped off her glass as she took a chair across from him. She curled her bare feet under her but not before he noticed that her toenails were painted coral. She wore jeans and an autumn gold sweater that hugged her curves and lit her eyes.

He lifted his glass, but words failed him as he looked at her. The faint scent of her wafted over to him as she took a drink of her wine. She'd always smelled of summer to him, an indefinable scent that filled his heart like helium.

Feeling awkward, he took another drink, his throat tight. He'd known being in this house again would bring it all back. It did. But just being here alone with Dana, not being able to touch her or to say all the things he wanted to say to her, was killing him. She didn't want to hear his excuses. Hell, clearly she'd hoped to never lay eyes on him again.

But a part of him, he knew, was still hoping she'd been the one who'd sent him the anonymous note that had brought him back.

"So what did you find in the well?" she asked as if she wanted this over with as quickly as possible. She took another sip of wine, watching him over the rim of her glass, her eyes growing dark with a rage born of pain that he recognized only too well.

Dana hadn't sent the note. He'd only been fooling himself. She still believed he'd betrayed her.

"The bones are human but you already knew that," he said, finding his voice.

She nodded, waiting.

"We won't know for certain until Rupert calls from the crime lab, but his opinion is that the body belonged to a Caucasian woman between the ages of twenty-eight and thirty-five and that she's been down there about fifteen years." He met her gaze and saw the shock register.

"Only fifteen years?"

Hud nodded. It seemed that, like him, she'd hoped the bones were very old and had no recent connection to their lives.

Dana let out a breath. "How did she get there?"

"She was murdered. Rupert thinks she was thrown down the well and then shot."

Dana sat up, her feet dropping to the floor with a slap. "No." She set the wineglass down on the table, the wine almost spilling.

Without thinking, Hud reached over to steady the glass, steady her. His fingers brushed hers. She jerked her hand back as if he'd sliced her fingers with a knife.

He pulled back his hand and picked up his wineglass, wishing now that he'd asked for something stronger.

Dana was sitting back in the chair, her arms crossed, feet on the floor. She looked shaken. He wondered how much of it was from what he'd told her about the bones in the well and how much from his touch. Did she ever wonder what their lives might have been like if she hadn't broken off the engagement? They would be husband and wife now. Something he always thought about. It never failed to bring a wave of regret with it.

He didn't tell Dana that the woman had still been alive, maybe even calling to her attacker for help as he left her down there.

"I'm going to have to question your family and anyone else who had access to the property or who might have known about the dry well," he said.

She didn't seem to hear him. Her gaze went to the large window. Outside, the snow fell in huge feathery flakes, obscuring the mountains. "What was she shot with?"

He hesitated, then said, "Rupert thinks it was a .38." He waited a beat before he added, "Does your father still have that .38 of his?"

She seemed startled by the question, her gaze flying back to him. "I have no idea. Why—" Her look turned to stone. "You can't really believe—"

"Do you have any guns in the house?" he asked in his official tone.

Her eyes narrowed in reaction. "Just the double-barreled shotgun by the door. But you're welcome to search the house if you don't believe me."

He remembered the shotgun. Mary Justice Cardwell had kept it by the door, loaded with buckshot, to chase away bears from her chicken coop.

"You have any idea who this woman in the well might have been?" he asked.

"Fifteen years ago I was sixteen." She met his gaze. Something hot flashed there as if she, too, remembered her sixteenth birthday and their first kiss.

"You recall a woman going missing about that time?" he asked, his voice sounding strange to his ears.

She shook her head, her gaze never leaving his face. "Won't there be a missing person's report?"

"The law and justice center fire in Bozeman destroyed all the records twelve years ago," he said.

"So we might never know who she was?" Dana asked.

"Maybe not. But if she was local, someone might remember her." He pulled his notebook and pen from his pocket. "I'm going to need Jordan's phone number so I can contact him."

"He's flying in tomorrow. He'll probably stay with Angus, but I'm sure he'll be contacting you."

He thought it strange she referred to her father as Angus. He wondered what had been going on in the years he'd been gone.

"You know where to find them," she continued. "Angus on the nearest bar stool. Clay at his studio in the old Emerson in Bozeman. And Stacy—" Her voice broke. "Well, she's where you left her."

Hud surprised himself by taking the jab without flinching.

"I was really sorry to hear about your mom's accident." He'd heard that Mary had been bucked off a horse and suffered severe brain damage. She'd lived for a short while, but never regained consciousness.

Dana locked eyes with him. "She always liked you." She said it as if it was the one mistake her mother ever made.

"Is that why you're selling the ranch?"

She got up from the table. "Is there anything else?"

He could see that he shouldn't have mentioned the

sale. Not only was it none of his business, but he also got the feeling today really wasn't the day to ask.

He finished his wine and pushed himself up from the chair. Picking up his Stetson, he settled it on his head. "I see you forgot your ring again."

DANA CURSED HERSELF for ever lying about the engagement let alone the ring. "The stone was loose," she said, compounding the lies. She'd spent thirty-one years telling the truth and Hud came back to town and she became an instant liar.

"You're not engaged to Lanny Rankin," he said softly. "Are you?"

She lifted her chin ready to defend her lie to the death. "Not that it's any of your business—"

"Why did you lie to me, Dana?"

Something in his tone stopped her cold. Obviously he thought she'd done it to make him jealous because she still cared. This was turning out to be the worst day of her life.

"I didn't want you thinking there was any chance for you and me."

He smiled. "Oh, your attitude toward me made that pretty clear. You didn't have to come up with a fiancé." His eyes suddenly narrowed. "Why *hasn't* the guy asked you to marry him? Something wrong with him?"

"No," she snapped. "My relationship with Lanny is none of your business." She could see the wheels turning in his stubborn head. He thought more than ever that she was still carrying a torch for him.

"You're the most annoying man I've ever known," she said as she headed for the door to show him out.

His soft chuckle chased after her, piercing her heart

with memory. So many memories of the two of them together.

"At least I still have that distinction," he said as she snatched open the front door and he stepped through it.

Joe, she noticed, had followed them and now stood by her feet. The old dog might be deaf and barely getting around anymore, but he was no fool. When push came to shove, he knew where his loyalties lay.

Hud turned in the doorway to look at her, all humor gone from his expression. "At some point, I'll need to talk to you about this investigation. I can come here or you can come down to the Big Sky office—"

"The office would be fine," she said. "Just let me know when."

"Dana, I really am sorry about—" he waved a hand "—everything."

Her smile felt as sharp as a blade. "Good night, Hud." She closed the door in his face but not before she heard him say, "Good night, Dana," the way he used to say it after they'd kissed.

She leaned against the door, her knees as weak as water. Damn it, she wasn't going to cry. She'd shed too many tears for Hud Savage. He wasn't getting even one more out of her.

But she felt hot tears course down her cheeks. She wiped at the sudden wetness, biting her lip to keep from breaking down and bawling. What a lousy day this had been. This birthday was destined to go down as the worst.

Joe let out a bark, his old eyes on her, tail wagging.

"I'm not mad at you," she said, and squatted to wrap her arms around him. "I know you always liked Hud. Didn't we all?"

Dana had never been one to wallow in self-pity. At least not for long. She'd gone on with her life after Hud left. His coming back now wasn't going to send her into another tailspin.

She rose and walked to the kitchen window, drawn to it by what she now knew had been in the old well all these years. The horror of it sent a shudder through her. Was it possible she had known the woman? Or worse, she thought, with a jolt, that Angus had? Hud had reminded her that her father had owned a .38.

With a groan, she recalled the time her father had let her and Hud shoot tin cans off the ranch fence with the gun.

Through the falling snow, she looked toward the hillside and hugged herself against the chill of her thoughts before glancing at the kitchen clock.

There was time if she hurried. She'd heard that her dad and uncle were playing with their band at the Corral Bar tonight. If she left now she might be able to talk to both of them and still get back in time for her date with Lanny.

She was anxious to talk to her father—before he and her uncle had time to come up with a convincing story. The thought surprised her. Why had she just assumed he had something to hide? Because, she thought with a rueful grin, he was her father and she knew him.

By now the canyon grapevine would be humming with the news about the body in the well. After all, Jordan had heard all the way back in New York City.

She'd just have to weather the blizzard—the storm outside as well as the arrival of her brother tomorrow from New York.

She groaned at the thought as she took her coat from

a hook by the door. It was a good ten miles down the road to the bar and the roads would be slick, the visibility poor. But she knew she wouldn't be able to get any sleep until she talked to her father.

She just hoped it was early enough for him to be halfway sober, but she wasn't counting on it.

As HUD DROVE away from the ranch, he kept saying the words over and over in her head.

She isn't engaged. She isn't engaged.

He smiled to himself. Admittedly, it was a small victory. But he'd been right. She wasn't engaged to Lanny.

Maybe even after all this time, he knew Dana better than she'd thought.

As snow continued to fall, he drove across the narrow bridge that spanned the Gallatin River and turned onto Highway 191 headed south down the Gallatin Canyon, feeling better than he had in years.

The "canyon," as it was known, ran from the mouth just south of Gallatin Gateway almost to West Yellowstone, ninety miles of winding road that trailed the river in a deep cut through the steep mountains on each side.

It had changed a lot since Hud was a boy. Luxury houses had sprouted up all around the resort. Fortunately some of the original cabins still remained and the majority of the canyon was national forest so it would always remain undeveloped.

The drive along the river had always been breathtaking, a winding strip of highway that followed the river up over the Continental Divide and down the other side to West Yellowstone.

Hud had rented a cabin a few miles up the canyon from Big Sky. But as he started up the highway, his headlights doing little to cut through the thick falling snow, his radio squawked.

He pulled over into one of the wide spots along the river. "Savage here."

The dispatcher in Bozeman, an elderly woman named Lorraine, announced she was patching through a call.

"Marshal Savage?" asked a voice he didn't recognize. "This is Dr. Gerald Cross with the crime lab in Missoula."

"Yes." Hud wondered why it wasn't Rupert calling.

"I have information on the evidence you sent us that I thought you'd want to hear about right away." There was the fluttering sound of papers, then the doctor's voice again. "We got lucky. Normally something like this takes weeks if not months, but your coroner was so insistent that we run the tests ASAP... The bullet lodged in the skull of the victim matches a bullet used in a shooting in your area."

Hud blinked in confusion. "What shooting?"

Another shuffle of papers. "A Judge Raymond Randolph. He was murdered in his home. An apparent robbery?"

Hud felt the air rush from his lungs. Judge Randolph. And the night Hud had been trying to forget for the past five years.

He cleared his throat. "You're saying the same gun that killed the Jane Doe from the well was used in the Randolph case?"

"The striations match. No doubt about it. Same gun used for both murders," the doctor said.

"The Randolph case was only five years ago. Hasn't

this body been down in the well longer than that? The coroner estimated about fifteen years."

"Our preliminary findings support that time period," Dr. Cross said.

Hud tried to take it in: two murders, years apart, but the same gun was used for both?

"We found further evidence in the dirt that was recovered around the body," the doctor was saying. "An emerald ring. The good news is that it was custom-made by a jeweler in your area. Should be easy to track."

Hud felt hopeful. "Can you fax me the information on the ring along with digital photos?"

"I'll have that done right away," the doctor said. "Also, three fingers on her left hand were broken, the ring finger in two places. Broken in the fall, I would assume, unless she tried to fight off her assailant.

"But what also might be helpful in identifying the woman is the prior break in the Jane Doe's radius, right wrist," the doctor continued. "It appears it was broken and healed shortly before her death. The break had been set, indicating she sought medical attention. She would have been wearing a cast in the weeks prior to her death."

A woman with a broken wrist in a cast.

"I've sent the information to both the dentists and doctors in your area," Dr. Cross said. "All her teeth were intact and she'd had dental work done on several molars not long before her death, as well. You got lucky on this one."

Lucky? Hud didn't feel lucky. Again he wondered why Rupert hadn't made the call. "Is Dr. Milligan still there? I wanted to ask him something."

"Sorry, but Rupert left some time ago. He said he had an appointment."

Hud thanked him and hung up the radio, wondering what was going on with Rupert. Why hadn't he been the one to call? It wasn't like him. Especially since he'd been right about everything. He would have called if for nothing else than to say, "Good thing you didn't bet me."

Because, Hud thought, Rupert wanted to get the information to someone else first? For instance, his friend the former marshal, Brick Savage?

Hud stared out at the falling snow. The night was bright, the scene past the windshield a tableau of varying shades of white and gray. Next to him the Gallatin River ran under a thick layer of ice. He couldn't remember ever feeling this cold.

He reached over and kicked up the heat, letting the vent blow into his face.

The same gun used to murder the woman in a red dress was used during what had appeared to be a robbery of Judge Randolph's residence. The judge had been shot and killed—the two incidents years apart.

Hud rubbed his hand over his face. No, he didn't feel lucky in the least. Judge Randolph had been one of Brick Savage's most outspoken opponents. Hud had never known what had spurred the judge's hatred of Marshal Brick Savage. The two had butted heads on more than one occasion, but then his father butted heads with a lot of people, Hud thought.

The difference was the judge had been in a position to make his threats come true. There had been talk that Judge Randolph was determined to see Marshal Brick Savage fired.

If the judge hadn't met such an untimely demise, who knows what would have happened, Hud thought as he pulled back onto the highway, the snow falling now in a dizzying white blur.

He hadn't been looking forward to going back to the cabin he'd rented near Big Sky. The cabin was small with just the bare essentials—exactly what he'd thought he wanted.

Except tonight he had too much on his mind to go back there yet. He turned around and headed for Bozeman. He wouldn't be able to sleep until he looked at the case file on Judge Raymond Randolph's robbery-murder.

He thought again about the anonymous note he'd received. Someone had wanted him back here. Someone with an agenda of their own?

As he drove down the canyon, the snow falling in a blinding wall of white, he feared he was being manipulated—just as he'd been five years ago.

Chapter Five

Dana brushed snow from her coat as she pushed open the door to the Corral Bar. The scent of beer and smoke hit her as she stepped in, pulled off her hat and, shaking the snow from it, looked around the bar for her father.

It was early. The place was relatively empty, only a few locals at the bar and a half-dozen others in booths eating the burgers the Corral was famous for.

A Country-Western song played on the jukebox, competing with the hum of conversation. The bartender was busy talking with a couple at her end of the bar.

Dana spotted her father and uncle at the far end on adjacent stools. They each had two beers in front of them and hadn't seemed to notice her come in. That was because they had their heads together in deep conversation.

As she approached, she saw her father look up and catch her reflection in the mirror. He sat up straighter, pulling back but mouthing something to Harlan as if warning him of her approach. Uncle Harlan turned on his stool to flash her a smile, both men appearing nervous. Clearly she had interrupted something.

"Dana," Harlan said, sounding surprised. "Haven't seen you for a while." Like his brother, he was a big man with a head of dark hair peppered with gray.

"Uncle Harlan." She patted his arm as she passed, her gaze on her father.

While Angus Cardwell resembled his brother, he'd definitely gotten the looks in the family. He'd been a devastatingly handsome young man and Dana could see why her mother had fallen for him.

Angus was still handsome and would have been quite the catch in the canyon if it wasn't for his love of alcohol. Thanks to the healthy settlement he'd received from Dana's mother in the divorce, he didn't have to work.

"How's my baby girl?" Angus asked, and leaned over to kiss her cheek. She smelled the familiar scent of beer on his breath. "Happy birthday."

Dana had always been his baby girl and still was—even at thirty-one. "Fine. Thank you.

"Is there someplace we could talk for a minute?" she asked. Angus shot a look at Harlan.

"We could probably step into the back room," her father said. "I'm sure Bob wouldn't mind." Bob owned the place and since Angus was likely the most regular of the regulars who frequented the bar, Bob probably wouldn't mind.

"Guess I'll tag along," Uncle Harlan said, already sliding off his stool.

The back room was part office, part spare room. It had a small desk and an office chair along with a threadbare overstuffed chair and a sofa that looked like it might pull out into a bed. The room smelled of stale cigarette smoke and beer.

"So what's up?" Angus asked. Both he and Harlan had brought along their beers.

She studied them for a moment, then said, "I'm sure

you've heard about what happened at the ranch today." She could see by their expressions that they had.

"Hell of a thing," Angus said.

Harlan nodded in agreement and tipped his beer bottle to his lips.

"Any idea how the bones got into our well?" she asked, wondering how much they'd heard on the canyon grapevine.

"Us?" Harlan said, looking puzzled. "Why would we know anything about her?"

Her. So they'd heard it was a woman. She couldn't believe how quickly word spread.

She hadn't meant to sound so accusing. "I just thought you might have some idea since you were both on the ranch during that time." Her parents were still together then, kind of, and her uncle had been working on the ranch and living in one of the spare bedrooms.

A look passed between them.

"What?" she asked.

"We were just talking about this," her father said.

"And?" she prodded.

"And nothing," Angus said.

"Anyone could have come onto the ranch and done it," Harlan said. "Could have driven right by the house or come in the back on one of the old loggin' roads. Could have been anyone." He looked embarrassed, as if he'd spoken out of turn. Or maybe said too much. He took a drink of his beer.

"So you two have it all figured out," she said, studying them. "That mean you've figured out who she was? Seems she went into the well about fifteen years ago."

"Fifteen years?" Clearly, Angus was surprised by that.

"Bunch of cowhands on the ranch back then," Harlan

said. "Anyone could have known about the well. There's old wells and mine shafts all over Montana. Usually an old foundation nearby. Not that hard to find if you're looking for one."

Dana thought about the homestead chimney still standing and part of the foundation visible from the ranch house. Stood to reason, she supposed, there would be an old well nearby.

"All this seasonal help around here, the woman didn't have to be a local," Harlan said. "She could have been working in the canyon for the summer or even at the ski hill for the winter."

"Wouldn't someone have missed her, though?" Dana said, noticing her father was nursing his beer and saying little.

Harlan shrugged. "If she had family. If her family knew where she'd gone to in the first place. You know how these kids are who show up for the seasonal employment. Most move on within a few weeks. Could have been a runaway even. Wasn't there some bones found in the canyon a few years ago and they never did find out who that guy was?"

She nodded. The other remains that had been found were male and no identification had ever been made. Was the same thing going to happen with the woman's bones from the well?

She started to ask her father about his .38, but changed her mind. "You all right?" she asked her father.

Angus smiled and tossed his now empty beer bottle into the trash. "Fine, baby girl. I just hate to see you upset over this. How about I buy you a drink to celebrate your birthday and we talk about something else?" he asked as he opened the door to the bar. The blare of the jukebox swept in along with a blue haze of smoke and the smell of burgers and beer.

Dana met his gaze. His eyes were shiny with alcohol and something else. Whatever he was hiding, he was keeping it to himself whether she liked it or not.

"Maybe some other time," she said. "I have a date tonight."

"I heard Hud was back," he said, and grinned at her.

"I'm not with Hud, Dad." How many times did she have to tell him that she was never getting back together with Hud? "Lanny's taking me out to dinner for my birthday."

"Oh," Angus said. He'd never been fond of Lanny Rankin and she'd never understood why. All her father had ever said was, "I just don't think he's the right man for you."

AT THE LAW AND JUSTICE CENTER, Hud sat with the file on the Judge Raymond Randolph killing, still haunted by that night. Most of the night was nothing but a black hole in his memory. He couldn't account for too many hours and had spent years trying to remember what he'd done that night.

He shook his head. It was one of the questions he was bound and determined to get answered now that he was back in Montana.

How strange that his first case as acting Gallatin Canyon marshal was tied to that night. Coincidence? He had to wonder.

He opened the file. Since he'd left town right after the judge's death, he knew little about the case.

The first thing that hit him was the sight of his father's notes neatly printed on sheets of eight-and-a-half-by-eleven, lined white paper. Brick Savage had never learned to type.

Hud felt a chill at just the sight of his father's neat printing, the writing short and to the point.

The judge had been at his annual Toastmasters dinner; his wife, Katherine "Kitty" Randolph, was away visiting her sister in Butte. The judge had returned home early, reason unknown, and was believed to have interrupted an alleged robbery in progress. He was shot twice, point-blank in the heart with a .38-caliber pistol.

A neighbor heard the shots and called the sheriff's department. A young new deputy by the name of Hudson Savage was on duty that night. But when he couldn't be reached, Marshal Brick Savage took the call.

Hud felt his hands begin to shake. He'd known he was going to have to face that night again when he'd come back, but seeing it in black-and-white rattled him more than he wanted to admit.

Brick reported that as he neared the Randolph house, he spotted two suspects fleeing the residence. He gave chase. The high-speed chase ended near what was known as the 35-mile-an-hour curve, one of the worst sections in the winding canyon road because it ended in a bridge and another curve in the opposite direction.

The suspect driving the car lost control after which the car rolled several times before coming to a stop upside down in the middle of the Gallatin River.

Both the driver and the passenger were killed.

Marshal Brick Savage called for an ambulance, wrecker and the coroner before returning to the Randolph house where he discovered signs of a break-in and the judge lying dead in the foyer.

According to Brick's account, evidence was later found in the suspects' car that connected the two to the robbery-murder. The suspects were Ty and Mason Kirk, two local brothers who had been in trouble pretty much all of their lives.

The case seemed cut-and-dried. Except now the murder weapon appeared to have been used in the murder of a woman in a well a good decade before.

Tired and discouraged, he photocopied the file and drove back up the canyon. Still, he couldn't face the small cabin he'd rented. Not yet.

He drove to his office in the deepening snow. His headlights shone on the evergreens along each side of the road, their branches bent under the weight of the snowfall. A white silence had filled the night. The streets were so quiet, he felt as if there wasn't another soul within miles as he neared his office.

Had he made a terrible mistake coming back here, taking the job as marshal even temporarily? It had been instantaneous. When he'd gotten the offer, he'd said yes without a moment's hesitation, thinking it was fate. After the note he'd received, he was coming back anyway. But to have a job. Not just a job, but the job he'd always said he wanted....

He pulled up to the office, turned off the engine and lights, and sat for a moment in the snowy darkness, trying to put his finger on what was bothering him.

Something about the Judge Raymond Randolph murder case. Something was wrong. He could feel it deep in his bones, like a sliver buried under the skin.

As he picked up the copied file from the seat next to him, he had that same sick feeling he'd had when he'd looked down into the dry well and seen human bones.

IT WASN'T UNTIL Dana returned home from the bar that she noticed the tracks on the porch. She stopped and turned to look back out through the falling snow.

Someone had been here. The tire tracks had filled with snow and were barely visible. That's why she hadn't noticed them on her way in. Plus she'd had other things on her mind.

But now, standing on the porch, she saw the boot tracks where someone had come to the door. She checked her watch. Too early for it to have been Lanny.

Her breath caught in her throat as she realized the tracks went right into the house. She'd never locked the front door in her life. Just as she hadn't tonight. This was rural Montana. No one locked their doors.

Carefully she touched the knob. It was cold even through her gloves. The door swung open.

The living room looked just as she'd left it. Except for a few puddles of melted snow where someone had gone inside. Her heart rate tripled as she trailed the wet footprints across the floor to the kitchen.

That's when she saw it. A small wrapped package on the kitchen table.

A birthday present. Her relief was quickly replaced by anger. She had a pretty good idea who'd left it. Hud. He'd returned and, knowing the door would be unlocked, had come in and left it.

Damn him. Why did he have to come back? Tears burned her eyes. She wouldn't cry. She…would…not…cry.

Her heart was still pounding too hard, the tears too close after the day she'd had. She turned on the lights, shrugged out of her coat to hang it on the hook by the door and wiped angrily at her eyes. *Damn you, Hud.*

She had to get ready for her date. Stumbling up the

stairs, she went to the bathroom, stripped down and stepped into the shower. She turned her face up to the water for a moment. The memory of the Hud she'd loved filled her with a pain that almost doubled her over. A sob broke loose, opening the dam. Leaning against the shower stall she couldn't hold back the pain any longer. It came in a flood. She was helpless to stop it.

After a while she got control again, finished showering and got out. She'd have to take care of the package on the kitchen table. She quickly dressed. Her eyes were red from crying, her face flushed. She dug in the drawer looking for makeup she seldom if ever wore, but it did little to hide her swollen eyes.

The doorbell rang. Lanny was early. She'd hoped to get back downstairs and throw away Hud's birthday present before Lanny arrived.

She ran downstairs without glancing toward the kitchen and Hud's present, unhooking her coat from the hook as she opened the door and flipped on the porch light.

Lanny looked up from where he stood about to ring the doorbell again. He was tall and slim with sandy-colored hair and thick-lashed brown eyes. Any woman with good eyesight would agree he was handsome. Even Dana.

But she'd never felt that thumpity-thump in her pulse when she saw him. She didn't go weak in the knees when they kissed, hardly thought about him when they were apart.

She enjoyed his company when they were together, which over the past five years hadn't been very often. Her fault. She'd put Lanny off for a long time after Hud left because she hadn't been ready to date. And then she'd been busy much of the time.

She'd thought that in time she would feel about him the way he felt about her. She'd wished she could feel more for him, especially after he'd confessed that he'd had a crush on her since first grade.

"So it's true," he said, now looking into her face.

She knew her eyes were still red, her face puffy from crying and she'd done enough lying for one day. "It's been a rough birthday."

"It's all over town," Lanny said. "According to the rumor mill, you and I've been upgraded."

She groaned. Hud must have asked someone about the engagement. That's all it would take to get the rumor going. "Sorry. I got a little carried away."

He nodded ruefully. "Then it's not true?"

She shook her head and saw the hurt in his expression. For the first time she had to admit to herself that no matter how long she dated Lanny, she was never going to fall in love with him. She'd only been kidding herself. And giving Lanny false hope. She couldn't keep doing that.

"I figured I'd probably have heard if it was true," he said. "But you never know."

Yeah, she did know. "I'm sorry," she said again, unable to think of anything else to say. She hated to break it off tonight. He would think she was going back to Hud and that's the last rumor she wanted circulating. But she had to get it over with. She didn't think it would come as too big of a surprise to Lanny.

"You still want to go out tonight?" he asked, as if he sensed what was coming.

"Nothing's changed," she said too quickly.

"Yeah, that's kind of the problem, huh?" He glanced into the house.

She didn't want to have this discussion here, on her doorstep, and she didn't want to invite him inside. She didn't want him to see the present Hud had left her. It would only hurt him worse and that was something she didn't want to do.

"Ready?" she asked.

Lanny hesitated for only a moment, then walked her through the falling snow to his large SUV.

She chattered on about the weather, then the sewing shop and Hilde, finally running out of safe conversation as he pulled into the restaurant.

Once inside, Dana found herself watching the door. She couldn't help it. Now that she knew Hud was back in the canyon, she expected to run into him at every turn, which kept him on her mind. Damn him.

"Hud's working late tonight," Lanny said.

She jerked her head around. "I wasn't—" The beginning of a lie died on her lips. "I just hate running into him," she said sheepishly.

Lanny nodded, his smile indulgent. "After all this time, it must be a shock, him coming back." He wiped a line of sweat off his water glass, not looking at her. "He say what brought him back?"

"No." That was one of the things that bothered her. Why after so long?

"He must think he has a chance with you." He met her gaze.

"Well, he doesn't." She picked up her menu, the words swimming in front of her. "What did Sally say was the special tonight?"

Lanny reached over and pulled down the menu so

he could see her face. "I need you to be honest with me," he said, his voice low even though because of the weather there were only a couple of people in the restaurant and they weren't close by.

She nodded, her throat a desert.

"Dana, I thought you'd gotten over Hud. I thought after he hurt you the way he did, you'd never want to see him again. Am I wrong about that or—" He looked past her, his expression telling her before she turned that Hud had come into the restaurant.

Her heart took off at a gallop at just the sight of him. She looked to see if he was alone, afraid he wouldn't be. He was. He stepped up to the counter and started to sit down, instantly changing his mind when he saw her and Lanny.

"You need a table, Hud?" Sally asked him from behind the counter.

"Nah, just wanted to get a burger," he said, turning his back to Dana and Lanny. "Working late tonight."

Dana recalled now that Lanny had said Hud was working tonight. How had he known that?

"Working, huh," Sally said, glancing toward Dana's table. "You want fries with that?" She chuckled. "Daddy always said if I didn't pay more attention in school I'd be saying that. He was right."

"No fries. Just the burger." He sat at the counter, his shoulders hunched, head down. Dana felt her traitorous heart weaken at the sight. She'd thought she wanted to hurt him, hurt him badly, the way he'd hurt her. Seeing her on a date with Lanny was killing him. She should have taken pleasure in that.

Sally must have seen his discomfort. "You know I can have that sent over to you since you have work to do."

"I'd appreciate that," he said, getting up quickly, his relief so apparent it made Dana hurt. He laid some money on the counter and, without looking in her direction, pulled his coat collar up around his neck as he stepped out into the snowstorm.

A gust of winter washed through the restaurant and he was gone. Just like that. Just like five years ago. Dana felt that same emptiness, that same terrible loss.

"We don't have to do this," Lanny said as she turned back to the table and him.

Her heart ached and her eyes burned. "I'm sorry."

"Please, stop apologizing," Lanny snapped, then softened his expression. "You and I have spent too long apologizing for how we feel."

"Can we just have dinner as friends?" she asked.

His smile never reached his eyes. "Sure. Friends. Why not? Two friends having dinner." The words hit her like thrown stones. Anger burned in his gaze as he picked up his menu.

"Lanny—"

"It's your birthday, Dana. Let's not say anything to spoil it."

She almost laughed. Her birthday had been spoiled from the moment she'd opened her eyes this morning.

They ordered, then sat in silence until Sally arrived with their salads.

Dana felt terrible on so many levels. She just wanted to get through this dinner. She asked him about his work and got him talking a little.

But by the time they left, they'd exhausted all topics of conversation. Lanny said nothing on the drive back to the ranch. He didn't offer to walk her to her door.

"Goodbye, Dana," he said, and waited for her to get

out of the car. He met her gaze for an instant in the yard light and she saw rage burning in his eyes.

There was nothing she could say. She opened her door. "Thank you for dinner."

He nodded without looking at her and she got out, hurrying through the falling snow to the porch before she turned to watch him drive away.

It wasn't until she entered the house that she remembered the present on her kitchen table.

The box, the size of a thick paperback book, was wrapped in red foil. There was a red bow on top with a tag that read Happy Birthday!

She knew exactly what was inside—which gave her every reason not to touch it. But still she picked up the box, disappointed in herself.

She felt the weight of the chocolates inside, felt the weight of their lost love. She'd tried to get over Hud. Tried so hard. Why did he have to come back and remind her of everything—including how much she had loved him?

Still loved him.

All the old feelings rained down on her like a summer downpour, drowning her in regret.

Damn Hud.

She set the box down, heard the chocolates rattle inside. Not just any chocolate. Only the richest, most wonderful, hard-to-find chocolates in the world. These chocolates were dark and creamy and melted the instant they touched your tongue. These chocolates made you close your eyes and moan and were right up there with sex. Well, not sex with Hud. Nothing could beat that.

Making love with Hud was a whole other experience—and she hated him even more now for reminding her of it.

Knowing her weakness, Hud had found these amazing chocolates and had given them to her on her twenty-fifth birthday—the night he'd asked her to marry him.

She glared down at the box and, like niggling at a sore tooth with her tongue, she reminded herself of how Hud had betrayed her five years ago. That did the trick.

Grabbing up the box of chocolates, she stormed over to the trash. The container was empty except for the balled up card from her sister that she'd retrieved from the floor and thrown away. She dropped the box of chocolates into the clean, white plastic trash bag, struck by how appropriate it was that the card from Stacy and the chocolates from Hud ended up together in the trash.

The chocolates rattled again when they hit the bottom of the bag and for just a moment she was tempted. What would it hurt to eat one? Or even two? Hud would never have to know.

No, that's exactly what he was counting on. That she wouldn't be able to resist the chocolates—just as there was a time when she couldn't resist him.

Angrily she slammed the cupboard door. He'd broken her heart in the worst possible way and if he thought he could worm his way back in, he was sadly mistaken.

She stormed over to the phone and called his office. "Hello?"

"It didn't work," she said, her voice cracking. Tears burned her eyes. She made a swipe at them.

"Dana?"

"Your…present… The one you left me after sneaking into my house like a thief. It didn't work. I threw the chocolates away."

"Dana." His voice sounded strange. "I didn't give you a present."

Her breath caught. Suddenly the kitchen went as cold as if she'd left the front door wide-open. "Then who…?"

"Dana, you haven't eaten any of them, have you?"

"No." Who had left them if not Hud? She walked back over to the sink and was about to open the cabinet door to retrieve the box, when her eye was caught by something out the window.

Through the snow she saw a light flickering up on the hillside near the old homestead. Near the well.

She stepped over and shut off the kitchen light, plunging the kitchen into darkness. Back at the window she saw the light again. There was someone up there with a flashlight.

"Dana? Did you hear what I said? Don't eat any of the chocolates."

"Do you still have men up on the mountain at the well?" she asked.

"No, why?"

"There's someone up there with a flashlight."

She heard the rattle of keys on Hud's end of the line. "Stay where you are. I'll be right there."

Chapter Six

Dana hung up the phone and sneaked into the living room to turn out that light, as well. She stood for a moment in total darkness, waiting for her eyes to adjust.

Through the front window, the sky outside was light with falling snow. She listened for any sound and heard nothing but the tick of the mantel clock over the fireplace. After locking the front door, she crept back into the kitchen to the window again.

No light. Had she only imagined it? And now Hud was on his way over—

There it was. A faint golden flicker through the falling snow. The light disappeared again and she realized that the person must have stepped behind the old chimney.

She stared, waiting for the light to reappear and feeling foolish even with her pulse still hammering in her ears. If she hadn't been on the phone with Hud when she'd seen the light, she wouldn't have called for help.

She'd had trespassers on the ranch before. Usually they just moved along with a warning. A few needed to see the shotgun she kept by the door.

Obviously this was just some morbid person who'd heard about the body in the well and had sneaked in the back way to the ranch hoping to find…what? A souvenir?

She really wished she hadn't told Hud about the light. She could handle this herself. The light appeared again. The person moved back and forth, flashing the light around. Didn't the fool realize he could be seen from the house?

A thought struck her. What if it was a member of her family? She could just imagine her father or uncle up there looking around. Hud wasn't one to shoot first and ask questions later, but if he startled whoever was up there— Even if he didn't kill them, he'd at least think them guilty of something.

Or…what if it was the killer returning to the scene of the crime? What if he was looking for evidence he believed the marshal hadn't found?

The thought sent a chill running up her spine. She stepped away from the window and moved carefully to the front door again in the darkness. The roads were icy; she didn't know how long it would take Hud to get here.

She found the shotgun by the door, then moved to the locked cabinet, found the hidden key and opened the drawer to take out four shells. Cracking the double-barreled shotgun open, she slipped two shells in and snapped it closed again, clicking on the safety. Pocketing the other two shells, she returned to the kitchen.

No light again. She waited, thinking whoever it was had gone behind the chimney again. Or left. Or…

Her heart began to pound. Had he seen the lights go out in the ranch house and realized he'd been spotted? He could be headed for the house right now.

She'd never been afraid on the ranch. But then, she

hadn't known there was a murdered woman's remains in the well.

The shotgun felt heavy in her hands as she started to move toward the back door, realizing too late that she'd failed to lock it. She heard the creak of a footfall on the back porch steps. Another creak. The knob on the back door started to turn.

She raised the shotgun.

"Dana?"

The shotgun sagged in her arms as the back door opened and she saw Hud's familiar outline in the doorway.

He froze at the sight of the shotgun.

"I didn't hear you drive up," she whispered, even though there wasn't any need to.

"I walked the last way so your visitor wouldn't hear my vehicle coming and run. When I didn't see any lights on, I circled the house and found the back door unlocked..." His voice broke as he stepped to her and she saw how afraid he'd been for her.

He took the shotgun from her and set it aside before cupping her shoulders in his large palms. She could feel his heat even through the thick gloves he wore and smell his scent mixed with the cold night air. It felt so natural, she almost stepped into his arms.

Instead he dropped his hands, leaving her aching for the feel of him against her, yearning for his warmth, his strength, even for the few seconds she would have allowed herself to enjoy it before she pushed him away.

She stepped past him to the window and stared up the hillside. There was only falling snow and darkness now. "I don't see the light now."

"I want you to stay here," Hud said. "Lock the door behind me."

"You aren't going up there alone?"

He smiled at her. "Does that mean you're not wishing me dead anymore?"

She flushed, realizing she *had* wished that. And fairly recently, too. But she hadn't meant it and now she was afraid that foolish wish might come true if he went up that hillside alone. "I'm serious. I don't want you going up there. I have a bad feeling about this."

He touched her cheek. Just a brush of his gloved fingertips across her skin. "I'll be all right. Is that thing loaded?" he asked, tilting his head toward the shotgun where he'd left it.

"It would be pretty useless if it weren't."

He grinned. "Good. Try not to shoot me when I come back." And with that, he was gone.

HUD MOVED STEALTHILY through the snowy night, keeping to the shadows of the house, then the barn and outbuildings as he made his way toward the pines along the mountainside.

Earlier, he'd caught glimpses of the light flickering through the falling snow as he'd run up the road toward the ranch house, his heart in his throat.

Now, the falling snow illuminated the night with an eerie cold glow. No light showed by the well, but he didn't think whoever it was had left. He hadn't heard a vehicle. More to the point, he didn't think whoever it was had finished what he'd come here to do.

His breath puffed out in a cloud around his face as he half ran through the fallen snow in the darkness of the pines.

He stopped at the edge of the trees in view of the old homestead. Snow fell silently around him in the freezing night air. He watched the play of shadows over the new snow. A quiet settled into his bones as he stilled his breathing to listen.

From this position, the dark shape of the chimney blocked his view of the well. He could see no light. No movement through the blur of snow.

The night felt colder up here, the sky darker. No breeze stirred the flakes as they tumbled down. He moved as soundlessly as possible, edging his way toward the dark chimney.

He hadn't gone far when he saw the impression of tracks in the new snow. He stopped, surprised to find that the footprints had formed a path back and forth along the edge of the old homestead's foundation as if the person had paced here. Making sure Dana saw the light and went to investigate? he thought with a start.

Again Hud listened and heard nothing but the occasional semi on the highway as it sped by into the night. The snow was falling harder, visibility only a few feet in front of him now.

If any place could be haunted, this would be the place, he thought. A gust of sudden wind whirled the snow around him and he felt a chill as if the woman from the well reached out to him, demanding justice.

He pulled his weapon and made his way toward the chimney, staying in the shadow it cast.

That's when he saw it. Something lying in the snow. A rope. As he moved closer, he saw that it was tied to the base of the old chimney and ran across the snow in the direction of the well.

Hud stared into the falling snow, but he couldn't see

the top of the well at this distance. He took the flashlight from his coat pocket but didn't turn it on yet. Holding his gun in one hand and the flashlight in the other, he moved soundlessly along the length of rope toward the well opening.

DANA COULDN'T STAND STILL. She'd lost sight of Hud as well as the old homestead chimney as the storm worsened. Nor had she seen the light again.

She couldn't stand it any longer. She couldn't wait here for Hud.

She knew he'd be furious with her and had even tried to talk herself out of going up there as she pulled on her boots, hat, coat and gloves.

But ever since last night, she hadn't been able to shake the feeling that something horrible was going to happen. This morning when she'd found out about the bones in the well and that Hud was back in town, she'd thought that was the something horrible the premonition had tried to warn her about.

But as she picked up the shotgun and stepped out the back door into the darkness and snow, she was still plagued with the feeling that the worst was yet to come. And then there was her stupid birthday wish!

She took the road, feeling fairly safe that she couldn't be seen since she couldn't see her hand in front of her face through the snowfall. Sometimes she would catch a glimpse of the mountainside as a gust of wind whirled the snow away. But they were fleeting sightings and she was still too far away to be seen, so she kept moving.

The air was cold. It burned her throat, the snow getting in her eyes. She stared upward, straining to see the chimney, reminded of ranchers' stories about stringing clotheslines from the house to the barn so they didn't get lost in a blizzard.

She'd always prided herself on her sense of direction but she didn't chance it tonight. She could feel the rut of the road on the edge of her boot as she walked, the shotgun heavy in her hands, but at the same time reassuring.

As she neared the homestead, the wind swirled the snow around her and for an instant she saw the chimney dark against the white background. It quickly disappeared but not before she'd seen a figure crouched at the edge of the old homestead foundation.

HUD FOLLOWED THE ROPE to the well, stopping just short of the edge to listen. He edged closer to the hole. The rope dropped over the side into blackness. Still hearing nothing, he pointed the flashlight down into the well, snapped on the light and jerked back, startled.

He wasn't sure what he'd expected to see dangling from the rope. Possibly a person climbing down. Or trying to climb out.

He holstered his weapon, then kneeling, he shone the flashlight to get a better look. It was a doll, the rope looped like a noose around its neck.

What the hell?

He picked up the rope and pulled it until the doll was within a few feet of the top. Its face caught in the beam of his flashlight and he let out a gasp, all his breath rushing from him.

The doll had Dana's face.

He lost his grasp on the rope. The doll dropped back into the well. As he reached for the rope to stop its fall, he sensed rather than heard someone behind him.

Half turning, he caught movement as a large dark figure, the face in shadow, lunged at him, swinging one of the boards from the well.

A shotgun discharged close by as he tried to pull his weapon but wasn't quick enough. The board slammed into his shoulder, pitching him forward toward the gaping hole in the earth.

Hud dropped the flashlight and grabbed for the rope with both hands, hoping to break his fall if not stop it.

His gloved hands wrapped around the rope, but the weight of his falling body propelled him over the side and partway down into the cold darkness of the well. He banged against the well wall with his left shoulder and felt pain shoot up his arm. But he'd managed to catch himself.

He dangled from the rope, the doll hanging below him. He was breathing hard, his mind racing. Where the hell had the shotgun blast come from? He had a bad feeling he knew.

Bracing his feet against the wall, he managed to pull the gun from his holster, telling himself it couldn't have been Dana. He'd told her to stay in the ranch house.

He looked up, pointing the gun toward the well opening. He could wait for his attacker or climb out. Snowflakes spiraled down from a sky that seemed to shimmer above him iridescent white. He squinted, listening.

Another shotgun blast, this one closer.

Hud climbed as best he could without relinquishing his weapon. Only seconds had passed since the attack. But now time seemed to stand still.

Then in the distance he heard the growl of an engine

turning over and, a moment later, another shadow fell over the top of the well above him.

He looked up through the falling snow and saw the most beautiful woman in the world lay down her shotgun and reach for him.

DANA'S HEART WAS in her throat as she looked down into the well and saw Hud hanging there.

He was alive, not broken at the bottom, but partway down a rope. That's all that registered at first. Then she saw him wince as he tried to use his left arm to holster his gun and pull himself up.

"You're hurt," she said, as if the pain were her own. "Here, let me help you."

She managed to get him up to the edge and drag him out into the snow. They lay sprawled for a few moments, both breathing hard from the exertion.

"Thanks," Hud said, turning his head to look over at her.

She nodded, more shaken now than she'd been when she'd looked over the edge of the well and had seen him hanging down there. Aftershock, she supposed. The time when you think about what could have happened. Realized how close it had been. She breathed in the night air as the sound of a vehicle engine died off until there was nothing but the sound of their labored breaths.

They were alone. Entirely alone, as if the rest of the world didn't exist.

Hud sat up and looked at her. He was favoring his left arm and she saw now that his jacket was ripped and dark with blood.

"Your arm… It's bleeding!"

He shook his head. "I'm fine. What about you?"

"Fine." She pushed herself up, her arms trembling with the effort.

His gaze met hers and he shook his head. Couldn't fool him.

She started to get to her feet, but he caught her sleeve, pulling her back to the ground beside him.

"Dana."

Her face crumpled as he encircled her with his good arm and pulled her tightly against him. His hug was fierce.

She buried her face into his chest, the snow falling around them.

When she pulled back, the kiss was as natural as sunrise. Soft, salty, sweet and tentative. And for a moment nothing mattered. Not the past, the pain, the betrayal. In that moment, she only recalled the love.

The snow stopped. Just like that. And the moment passed.

Dana pulled back, drowning in all the reasons she shouldn't love this man—wouldn't love this man. Not again.

Hud saw the change in her eyes. A quick cooling, as if her gaze had filmed over with ice. Just as her heart had five years ago.

She pulled away to pick up the shotgun from where she'd dropped it earlier. He watched her rise, keeping her back to him.

He got to his feet, searching the snow for his flashlight. His left arm ached from where he'd smacked it against one of the rocks embedded in the side of the well and split it open. The pain was nothing compared to what he'd seen in Dana's eyes.

Maybe he couldn't make up for what he'd done to her five years ago, but he sure as hell would find whoever had put the doll down the well. Whoever had tried to kill him tonight.

He heard a sound from Dana, part cry, part gasp, and realized that she'd found his flashlight and was now shining it down into the well.

Stepping to her side, he took the light from her, seeing the shock on her face as well as the recognition. "It's your doll?"

She nodded. "My father gave it to me for my sixth birthday. He thought it looked like me. How…" She met his gaze. "It was on a shelf in my old playroom along with the rest of the toys Mom saved for her—" Dana's voice broke "—grandchildren."

Mary Cardwell hadn't lived long enough to see any grandchildren be born. He could see what a huge hole losing her mother had left in Dana. Desperately he wanted to take her in his arms again. The need to protect her was so strong he felt sick with it.

He wanted to believe the doll had been put in the well as just a cruel prank meant to frighten her, but he feared it had been a trap. If Dana had come up here alone to investigate after seeing the light on the hillside, she would have been the one knocked into the well and there wouldn't have been anyone here with a shotgun to scare the would-be killer away. The thought was like a knife to his heart but as he stepped past her, pulled the doll the rest of the way up and removed the noose from its neck, he told himself that Dana needed a marshal now more than she needed a former lover.

"When was the last time you saw the doll?" he asked. The doll's hair was flattened with snow. Careful not to disturb any fingerprints that might be on it, he brushed the snow away, shocked again how much the face resembled Dana's.

"I don't know. The toys have been on the shelves in the playroom for so long I hardly notice. I don't go into that room much." Another catch in her voice. The playroom would only remind her of her mother, he thought. "I'd forgotten about the doll."

Well, someone else hadn't.

She shivered as if she'd had the same thought.

"Let's get back to the house and out of this weather," he said.

The sky over their heads was a deep, cold midnight-blue as they walked back toward the ranch house. A few stars glittered like ice crystals as a sliver of moon peeked out from behind a cloud.

He made her wait on the porch, leaving her still armed with the reloaded shotgun while he searched the house. There was no sign that anyone had been there—not to drop off a box of chocolates or to steal a doll from a shelf in her old playroom.

"All clear," he said, opening the front door.

She stepped in, breaking down the shotgun and removing the shells. He watched her put the shotgun by the door, pocket the shells and turn toward him again. "Let me see your arm," she ordered.

He started to protest, but she was already helping him off with his jacket. His uniform shirt was also torn and bloodied, though the cut in his upper arm didn't look deep from what he could see.

"Come in here," she said, and he followed her to the kitchen where she motioned to a chair.

He sat, watching her as she brought out a first aid kit.

He rolled his shirtsleeve up as she sat next to him, all her attention on the three-inch gash in his arm.

"You shouldn't have come up there, but I appreciate what you did," he said, his voice hoarse with emotion. "You quite possibly saved my life tonight."

"You should get stitches," she said as if she hadn't heard him. "Otherwise it will leave a scar."

"It won't be my first," he said.

She mugged a disapproving face and said, "This is going to sting." Her fingers gripped his upper arm.

He winced, the disinfectant burning into the cut.

"I warned you," she said, glancing up into his face. "Sure you don't want a ride to the emergency room?"

"Positive. A few butterfly bandages and I'll be as good as new."

She looked doubtful but went to work. He'd seen her doctor horses and cows before. He doubted doctoring him was any different for her. Except she liked the horses and cows better.

He couldn't help but think about the kiss. Man, how he had missed her.

"There, that should at least keep it from getting infected," she said, slamming the lid on her first aid kit and rising from the chair.

He touched her wrist and she met his gaze again. "Thanks."

She nodded and went to put the kit away.

He rose from the chair. "Mind if I take a look where that doll was kept?"

"I don't see how—" She stopped, then shrugged as if she didn't have the energy to argue.

He reminded himself that it was her birthday for a few more hours. What a lousy birthday.

He followed her up the stairs to what had once been her playroom. Mary had left it just as it had been when the kids were little.

The room was large with a table at its center surrounded by small chairs. There were books everywhere in the room and several huge toy boxes. The Cardwell kids had been blessed. One wall was filled with shelves and toys. There was a small tea set, stuffed animals, dolls and large trucks.

In the center, high on the wall, was a gaping hole where something had been removed. "That's where she has always been," Dana said, hugging herself as she stared at the empty spot on the shelf as if the realization that someone had to have come into the house and taken the doll had finally hit home.

"Who knew about the doll?" he asked.

She shook her head. "Only everyone who knew me. Angus probably showed it off at the bar for days before my sixth birthday. You know how he is."

Hud nodded. Anyone in the canyon could have known about the doll. "But how many people knew where you kept it?"

"Anyone who ever visited when we were kids knew about the playroom," she said.

"Or anyone in the family," he said, not liking what he was thinking.

"No one in my family would do this." Her face fell the instant the denial was out. It was a blood instinct to take up for your brothers and sister. But clearly, Dana wasn't entirely convinced her siblings were innocent of this.

She reached out for the doll he hadn't even realized he'd carried up the stairs.

He held it back. "Sorry, it's evidence. But I'll make sure you get it back. I want to take the chocolates you received, too."

She nodded, then turned and headed for the playroom doorway, moving like a sleepwalker. The day had obviously taken its toll on her. He looked around the room, then down at the doll in his gloved hand, thinking about Dana's siblings before following her to the kitchen.

She opened the cabinet doors under the sink and pulled out the trash can. Their gazes met. She'd thrown the candy away believing it had come from him. He never thought he'd be thankful for that.

"Mind if I take the plastic bag and all?" he asked.

"Be my guest."

"I could use another bag for the doll."

She got him one. He lowered the doll inside and tightened the drawstring, then pulled the other trash bag with the present in it from the container.

"I'll have the gift box dusted for prints and the candy tested," he said.

Her eyes widened. "You think the chocolates might have been…poisoned?"

He shrugged, the gesture hurting his arm.

The phone rang. She picked it up. He watched her face pale, her gaze darting to him, eyes suddenly huge.

He reached for the phone and she let him take it. But when he put the receiver to his ear, he heard only the dial tone. "Who was it?"

She shook her head. "Just a voice. A hoarse whisper. I didn't recognize it." She grabbed the back of the chair, her knuckles white.

"What did the caller say to you?" he asked, his stomach a hard knot.

"'It should have been you in the bottom of that well.'"

Hud checked caller ID and jotted down the number. He hit star 69. The phone rang and rang and finally was answered.

"Yeah?" said a young male voice.

"What number have I reached?" Hud asked.

What sounded like a kid read the number on the phone back to him. Hud could hear traffic on the street and what sounded like skateboarders nearby. A pay phone near the covered skate park in Bozeman?

"Did you see someone just make a call from that phone?" he asked the boy.

"Nope. No one was around when I heard it ringing. Gotta go." He hung up.

"I'm not leaving you alone in this house tonight," Hud said to Dana as he replaced the receiver. "Either you're coming with me or I'm staying here. What's it going to be?"

Chapter Seven

"You look like you've seen better days," Hilde said the next morning when Dana walked into the shop. "I heard you were at the Corral. So you decided to celebrate your birthday, after all."

"Who told you I was at the Corral?" Dana hadn't meant her tone to sound so accusing.

Hilde lifted a brow. "Lanny. I ran into him this morning at the convenience store." She tilted her head toward the two coffee cups on the counter. "I brought you a latte. I thought you might need it."

How had Lanny known that she was at the Corral last night? she wondered as she placed her purse behind the counter. "Thanks for the coffee. I really could use it."

Hilde handed her one of the lattes. She held it in both hands, trying to soak up some of the heat. Lanny had also known that Hud was working late. With a shiver, she realized he'd been checking up on her. And Hud.

"Are you all right?" Hilde asked, looking concerned.

Dana shook her head. "I went by the Corral last night to talk to Dad, then Lanny took me to dinner for my birthday."

"Oh, you didn't mention you were going out with Lanny."

"I'd forgotten we had a date."

Hilde gave her a look she recognized only too well.

"It was our *last* date. I'd hoped we could be friends...."

"I hate to say this, but it's just as well," Hilde said.

Dana couldn't believe her ears.

Hilde raised her hands in surrender. "Hey, you were never going to fall in love with Lanny and we both know it."

Dana started to protest, but saved her breath. It was true.

"Maybe Hud coming back was a good thing."

Dana eyed her friend. "I beg your pardon?"

"I mean it. You need to resolve your issues with him."

"Resolve my issues? He slept with my sister when we were engaged!"

"Maybe."

"Maybe? There is no maybe about it. I caught them in bed together."

"Going at it?"

"No." Dana stepped back as if afraid she would ring her friend's neck.

"That's my point. You caught him in her bed, but you don't know what happened. If anything. Stacy has always been jealous of you. I wouldn't put anything past her."

"And what ready excuse do you have for Hud?" She held up her hands. "No, that's right, he was drunk and didn't know what he was doing."

"I know it sounds clichéd—"

"It sounds like what it is, a lie. Even if Stacy threw herself at him. Even if he was falling-down drunk—"

"Which would mean nothing happened."

Dana shook her head. "Hud wouldn't have left town the way he did if he'd been innocent."

"Did you ever give him a chance to explain?" Hilde asked.

"There was nothing that needed explaining. End of story." She turned and walked to the back of the store, surprised how close she was to tears. Again.

A few moments later she heard Hilde come up behind her. "Sorry."

Dana shook her head. "It's just seeing him again. It brings it all back."

"I know. I just hate to see you like this."

Dana turned, biting her lip and nodding as tears spilled out.

Hilde pulled her into a hug. "Maybe you're right. Maybe you should just kill the bastard. Maybe that's the only way you'll ever be free of him."

Hilde was joking but Dana knew that even in death she would still be haunted by Hud Savage. And after last night, she knew she didn't want him dead. Far from it.

She dried her tears and said, "Hud spent the night at my place last night."

Her friend's eyebrows shot up. "No way."

"He slept on the couch." She practically groaned at the memory of Hud's bare chest when she'd gone downstairs earlier. The quilt she'd given him down around his waist. His bare skin tanned from living in southern California. Muscled from working out.

"Dana, what's going on?"

She shook off the image and took a sip of the latte. It was wonderful. Just like her friend. "It's a long story." She filled Hilde in on what had happened last night. "That's why I look like I didn't get any sleep. I didn't."

She shook her head. "Hilde, I can't understand why anyone would do those things."

"This voice on the phone, was it a man or a woman?"

"I don't know. It was obviously disguised." She shivered and took another drink of the coffee. It warmed her from her throat to her toes and she began to relax a little. In the daylight, she wasn't quite so scared. "You know what bothers me the most is that whoever put that doll in the well had to have taken it from the house. Just like whoever left the chocolates."

"Everyone knows you never lock your doors," Hilde said.

"I do now. I just can't understand why I'm being threatened. It has to have something to do with the woman whose remains were found in the well."

There was a soft knock on the door and both women turned to see their first customer—Kitty Randolph—looking at her watch.

"She's early but we're going to have to let her in, huh," Hilde said with a laugh. "You sure you're up to this today?"

"I would go crazy if I stayed home, believe me," Dana said as she started toward the door to unlock it and put up the open sign. "Good morning, Mrs. Randolph."

"Dana," the older woman said, then added, "Hilde," by way of greeting. Kitty Randolph was a petite gray-haired woman with a round cheery face and bright blue eyes.

"I was going to get back to you about the fundraiser," Dana said, instantly feeling guilty for not doing so.

Kitty patted her hand with a cool wrinkled one of her own. "Now, dear, don't you worry about that. I know something dreadful happened out at the ranch. You must tell me all about it while you match this color thread." She pulled the leg of a pair of blue slacks from a bag hooked on her arm. "I need to raise the hem. I hate it, but I'm shrinking and getting shorter every day." She chuckled. "Now what's this about a body being in the well?" she asked conspiratorially as she took Dana's arm and steered her toward the thread rack.

Dana picked up several spools of thread and held them to the pants in Kitty Randolph's bag.

She gave the elderly woman a short version of the discovery in the well.

"Any idea who she was?" Kitty asked.

Dana shook her head. "We might never know."

Kitty purchased her thread and left, promising to bring some of her wonderful chocolate chip cookies the next time she stopped by.

ARMED WITH PHOTOGRAPHS and information about the emerald ring found in the well, Hud drove to Bozeman first thing.

The jewelry store was one of those small, exclusive shops on Main Street. Hud tapped at the door just over the closed sign and a fit-looking, gray-haired man unlocked the door.

"Marshal Savage," the jeweler said, extending his hand. "You made good time."

Hud handed him the photographs and information taken from the ring.

"Oh, yes," Brad Andrews said as he examined the photos. "I remember this ring very well. A one-carat emerald set in a pear-shape with two half-carat diamonds on each side. A beautiful ring. Something you would notice a woman wearing." He looked up, still nodding.

"You can tell me who purchased the ring?" Hud asked.

"Of course. I remember this ring well. It was a twenty-fifth anniversary present. Judge Randolph purchased it for his wife, Kitty."

As KITTY RANDOLPH LEFT Needles and Pins, several other ladies from the canyon entered the shop, also using the excuse of needing fabric or patterns or thread when they were really just interested in the latest goings-on at the Cardwell Ranch.

Dana could see how her day was going to go, but better here than being at the ranch. Especially alone.

At least that's what she thought until the bell over the door at Needles and Pins jangled and the last person she wanted to see came through the door.

Dana looked up from the fabric she was pricing and swore under her breath. Hilde had gone to the post office to mail a special fabric order so Dana was alone with no place to run as her sister, Stacy, stepped into the shop.

Stacy glanced around, looking almost afraid as she moved slowly to the counter and Dana.

Dana waited, wondering what her sister was doing here. Stacy didn't sew and, as far as Dana knew, had never been in the store before.

Stacy was two years her senior, with the same dark hair, the same dark eyes, and that was where the similarities ended. Stacy was willowy-thin, a true beauty and all girl. She'd never been a tomboy like Dana, just the opposite. Stacy had hated growing up on the ranch, wanting even from a very young age to live on a street in town that had sidewalks. "I never want to smell cow manure again," she'd said when she'd left home at eighteen. "And I will *never* marry a cowboy."

Dana always thought Stacy should have been more specific about the type of man she would marry. She'd married at nineteen, divorced at twenty-two, married again at twenty-four, divorced at twenty-nine, married again at thirty-two and divorced. None of them were cowboys.

"Hi, Dana," Stacy said quietly.

"Is there something I can help you with?" Dana asked in her store-owner tone.

Stacy flushed. "I...no...that is I don't want to buy anything." She clutched her purse, her fingers working the expensive leather. "I just wanted to talk to you."

Dana hadn't seen Stacy since their mother's funeral and they hadn't spoken then. Nor did she want to speak to her now. "I don't think we have anything to talk about."

"Jordan asked me to stop by," Stacy said, looking very uncomfortable.

Jordan. Perfect. "He didn't have the guts to do it himself?"

Stacy sighed. *"Dana."*

"What is it Jordan couldn't ask me?" She hated to think what it would be since her brother hadn't seemed to have any trouble making demands of her yesterday on the phone.

"He would like us all to get together and talk at the ranch this evening," Stacy said.

"About what?" As if she didn't know, but she wanted to hear Stacy say it. So far Jordan had been the one who'd spoken for both Clay and Stacy. Not that Dana doubted the three were in agreement. Especially when it came to money.

But Stacy ignored the question. "We're all going to be there at seven, even Clay," Stacy continued as if she'd memorized her spiel and just had to get the words out.

That was so like Jordan to not ask if it was convenient for Dana. She wanted to tell her sister that she was busy and that Jordan would have to have his family meeting somewhere else—and without her.

Stacy looked down at her purse. Her fingers were still working the leather nervously. As she slowly lifted her gaze, she said, "I was hoping you and I could talk sometime. I know now isn't good." Her eyes filled with tears and for a moment Dana thought her sister might cry.

The tears would have been wasted on Dana. "Now definitely isn't good." She'd gotten by for five years without talking to Stacy. Recently, she'd added her brothers to that list. Most of the time, she felt she could go the rest of her life without even seeing or hearing from them.

Stacy seemed to be searching her face. Of course, her sister would have heard Hud was back in town. For all Dana knew, Hud might even have tried to see Stacy. The thought curdled her stomach. She felt her skin heat.

"Mother came by to see me before she died," Stacy said abruptly.

It was the last thing Dana expected her sister to say. A lump instantly formed in her throat. "I don't want to hear this." But she didn't move.

"I promised her I would try to make things right between us," Stacy said, her voice breaking.

"And how would you do that?"

The bell over the door of the shop jangled. Kitty Randolph again. "This blue still isn't quite right," the older woman said, eyeing Stacy then Dana, her nose for news practically twitching.

"Let me see what else we have," Dana said, coming out from behind the counter.

"I hope I didn't interrupt anything," Mrs. Randolph said, stealing a look at Stacy who was still standing at the counter.

"No, Mrs. Randolph, your timing was perfect," Dana said, turning her back on her sister as she went to the thread display and began to look through the blues. She'd already picked the perfect shade for the slacks, but pretended to look again.

She suspected that Kitty had seen Stacy come into the shop and was only using the thread color as an excuse to see what was going on.

"How about this one, Mrs. Randolph?" Dana asked, holding up the thread the woman had already purchased.

"That looks more like it. But, please, call me Kitty. You remind me so much of your mother, dear."

Dana caught a glimpse of Stacy. Her face seemed even paler than before. She stumbled to the door and practically ran to her car. Unfortunately, Mrs. Randolph witnessed Stacy's hasty exit.

"Is your sister all right? She seems upset," Kitty said.

"Who wouldn't be upset after a body's been found in the family well," Dana said.

"Yes, who isn't upset about that," Kitty Randolph said, watching Stacy drive away.

Dana sighed, feeling guilty and then angry with her-

336 Crime Scene at Cardwell Ranch

self for only upsetting her sister worse. But damn it, she had every reason to hate her sister.

She could practically hear her mother's voice filled with disapproval. "Families stick together. It isn't always easy. Everyone makes mistakes. Dana, you have to find forgiveness in your heart. If not for them, for yourself."

Well, Mom, now all three of them have banned together against me. So much for family.

And there was no getting out of the family meeting— or probably having to listen to her sister say she was sorry again. She just hoped Stacy didn't think that saying she was sorry over and over was going to fix things between them. Not even when hell froze over.

Sorry, Mom.

WHEN HUD RETURNED to his office, he had a message to call Coroner Rupert Milligan.

"Got an ID on your woman from the well," Rupert said, then cleared his throat. "It's Ginger Adams."

Hud had to sit down. He moved the files stacked on his chair and dropped into it.

"The doctor and dental records the crime lab sent down came back with a match on both dental and emergency room records," Rupert said.

Good God. Ginger Adams. In a flash, Hud saw her. A pretty redhead with a stunning body and the morals of an alley cat.

Hud closed his eyes as he kneaded his forehead. "You're sure it's Ginger?"

"It's a ringer," Rupert said, not sounding any happier about it than Hud. "I told you your suspect list could be as long as your arm, didn't I?"

"You were right about her being a waitress, too," Hud noted. Was that why Rupert had been acting strangely after coming out of the well yesterday? Because he'd suspected it was Ginger?

Ginger had waited tables at the Roadside Café, the place where locals hung out every morning, gossiping over coffee. Both of his deputies had been there just this morning. It was an old hangout for sheriff's department deputies, the local coroner—and the marshal.

Hud swore softly under his breath. "I thought she left town with some guy."

"Guess that's what we were supposed to think," Rupert said. "I gotta go. Calving season."

"I didn't realize you were still running cattle on your place."

"Helping a friend."

Hud had that feeling again that Rupert knew more about this case than he was saying. "Thanks for letting me know."

"Good luck with your investigation."

"Yeah." Hud didn't mention that he'd found the owner of the ring. He was still trying to figure out how it ended up in the same well as Ginger Adams— years later.

Holy hell. The woman had been rumored to have broken up more marriages in the canyon than Hud could shake a stick at. But there was at least one marriage that had definitely bit the dust because of Ginger—the marriage of Mary and Angus Cardwell.

Damn. As he hung up, he wondered how Dana was going to take the news. He started to dial her number. But he realized he couldn't tell her this over the phone.

Everyone knew the Cardwell marriage had been on

the rocks, but Ginger, it seemed, had been the last straw. And now her body had turned up on the ranch. Add to that, someone was targeting Dana.

He picked up his hat, grabbing his new marshal jacket on the way out the door. His left arm still ached, the skin around the cut bruised, but Dana had done a good job of patching him up.

It was only a few blocks to Needles and Pins. He knew he had more than one reason for wanting to tell Dana the news in person. He wanted to see how she was doing. She'd left the ranch house so quickly this morning he hadn't even had a chance to talk to her.

Clearly she'd been avoiding him. Last night after he'd announced he wasn't leaving her alone, she'd started to argue, but then got him some bedding from the closet and pointed at the couch.

She'd gone to bed and he hadn't seen her again until this morning—and only for the length of time it had taken her to grab her coat and leave.

He was her least favorite person in the world, true enough. Except maybe for whoever had put that doll in the well—and called and threatened her afterward.

But he also wanted to see her reaction to the news that the body had been Ginger's. He was the marshal and he needed to find Ginger's killer as fast as possible so he could put a stop to whoever was threatening Dana. He couldn't help but believe the two incidents were connected somehow.

As he started to cross the street to Needles and Pins, Lanny Rankin stepped into his path.

Hud hadn't seen Lanny since he'd returned, but he'd

known eventually he'd run into him. The canyon wasn't wide or long enough for their paths not to cross.

"Lanny," he said, seeing the set of the man's broad shoulders, the fire in his eyes. There'd been bad blood between the two of them as far back as Hud could remember. Lanny seemed to have a chip on his shoulder and it didn't help when Hud had started dating Dana.

Hud had known that Lanny would move in on Dana as soon as he was out of the picture. He'd seen the way Lanny had looked at Dana back in high school. In fact, Hud had wondered over the past five years if Lanny hadn't just been waiting for Hud to screw up so he would have his chance with Dana.

"Stay away from Dana," Lanny said. "I don't want her hurt again."

"Lanny, I don't want to get into this with you but my relationship with Dana is none of your business."

"Like hell," Lanny said, advancing on him. "I know you're the marshal now and you think you can hide behind that badge…"

"Go ahead. Take your best shot," Hud said, removing the marshal star from his coat and pocketing it.

Lanny's eyes narrowed as if he thought it was a trick. "You think you can get her back after everything you did to her?" He took a wide roundhouse swing.

The punch caught Hud on the left side of his jaw, a staggering blow that about took his feet out from under him.

He rubbed his jaw, nodding at Lanny who was breathing hard. "That's the end of it, Lanny." He reached into his pocket, took out the silver star and reattached it to his coat. "Dana's a grown woman with a mind of her own. She'll do whatever it is she wants to do no matter what either of us has to say about it."

Lanny rubbed his bruised knuckles.

Hud waited. He wanted this over with right here, right now.

"What the hell are you doing back here anyway?" Lanny asked, cradling his hand, which looked broken the way it was swelling up. "I would have thought you wouldn't have the nerve to show your face around here after what you did to her."

Hud ignored him. "Might want to have Doc Grady take a look at that hand, Lanny," he said, gingerly touching his jaw. Fortunately it wasn't broken but it hurt like hell. Lanny packed quite a wallop for a lawyer.

"She wasn't worth it," Lanny snarled, evening his gaze at him.

Hud knew Lanny was talking about Stacy now. And he couldn't have agreed more.

"She used you. She wanted a divorce in the worst way, but Emery didn't want to lose her. The old fool loved her for some crazy reason. But then she found a way to force his hand. After what happened between the two of you while he was out of town, he couldn't wait to get rid of her. Better than being the laughing-stock of the canyon."

This was news to Hud. For years he'd tried to remember that night. He'd been told he got stinking drunk. He remembered wanting to. But after that, there was nothing in his memory banks until he woke up the next morning—in Dana's sister's bed.

After getting the anonymous note, Hud had come back to Montana convinced Stacy had somehow manipulated the incident just to get back at Dana. It was no secret that Stacy was jealous of her younger sister. He'd just never considered there might be more to it.

The thought gave him hope that he really had been set up. Maybe nothing had happened that night, just as he'd always wanted to believe. More to the point, maybe there was a way to prove it.

"You played right into Stacy's hands," Lanny said.

Hud nodded, saying nothing because he had no defense.

Lanny seemed to consider hitting him again, but must have changed his mind. "You hurt Dana again and that badge isn't going to stop me." With that, he turned and stormed off.

Hud watched Lanny go, hoping this really would be the end of it. But he couldn't get what Lanny had said about Stacy out of his head.

He needed to know what had happened that night. Nothing could have gotten him into Stacy's bed. At least nothing he remembered.

With a curse, he turned and saw Dana standing in the doorway of the sewing shop. From the expression on her face, she'd not only witnessed the ugly display between him and Lanny, she'd overheard it, as well.

DANA QUICKLY TURNED and went back inside the shop, not wanting Hud to see her shock.

It was bad enough that everyone in the canyon knew about Hud and Stacy, but to hear Lanny talking about it... And could it be true that Stacy had done it—not to spite her—but to force Emery to give her a divorce?

She had to remind herself that whatever her sister's reasoning, Hud had gone along with it. So why was it getting harder and harder to call on that old anger?

She heard Hud come into the shop and tried to quit shaking. She was the one who should have left here and never come back, she thought. Instead it had been Hud who'd taken off, a sure sign of his guilt, everyone had said. While she'd stayed and faced all the wagging tongues.

"Dana?"

She turned to Hud, just as she'd faced the gossip that had swept through the canyon like wildfire.

"I'm sorry you heard that," he said.

"I'm sure you are. You'd much rather pretend it never happened."

"As far as I'm concerned, it didn't," he said.

"Let me guess," she said with a humorless laugh. "Your story is you don't remember anything."

"No, I don't."

All the anger of his betrayal burned fire-hot as if she'd just found out about it. "I really don't want to talk about this."

"We're going to have to at some point," he said.

She gave him a look that she hoped seared his skin. "I don't think so."

He shifted on his feet, then held up his hands in surrender. "That isn't why I came by." He glanced around the shop as if trying to lasso his emotions. In an instant, his expression had transformed. He was the marshal again. And she was... She saw something in his gaze. Something that warned her.

"We got an ID on the remains found in the well," he said. "Is there someplace we could sit down?"

She gripped the edge of the counter. If he thought she needed to sit, the news must be bad. But what could be worse than having a murdered woman's body found on your property?

Meeting Hud's gaze, she knew the answer at once— *having the marshal suspect that someone in your family killed her.*

Chapter Eight

Hud had expected more resistance but Dana led him to the back of the shop where there was a small kitchen with a table and chairs. The room smelled of chocolate.

"Hilde made some brownies," she said, then seemed to remember brownies were his favorite and something *she* used to make for him using a special recipe of her mother's.

"I'll pass on the brownies, but take some coffee," he said, spotting the coffeemaker and the full pot.

She poured them both some, her fingers trembling as she put down the mugs, and took a chair across from him. He watched her cup her mug in both hands, huddling over it as if it were a fire.

"So who is she?" Dana asked.

"Ginger Adams."

Dana paled as the name registered. She took a sip of the coffee, her hands shaking. "Ginger," she said on a breath, and closed her eyes.

He got up to get some sugar and cream for his coffee. He'd never really liked coffee. How could something that smelled so good taste so awful?

He took his time adding the cream and sugar before taking a sip. Her eyes were open again and she was watching him intently, almost as if she was trying to read his mind. If she could have, she'd know that all he could think about was how she used to feel in his arms.

"Have you talked to my father?" she asked.

"Not yet."

Her spine seemed to take on a core of steel. "It was over between them almost before it began. Ginger wasn't the reason my mother divorced Angus."

He said nothing, but wondered if she was defending her father. Or her mother. He'd known Mary Justice Cardwell. He couldn't imagine her killing anyone. But he knew everyone had the capability if pushed far enough.

And Mary was a crack shot. He doubted she would have only wounded Ginger Adams.

"I know it sounds like I'm defending him, but Ginger dumped him months before she supposedly left town with some other woman's husband," Dana said.

"Ginger dumped *him*?"

Dana seemed to realize her mistake. She'd just given her father a motive for murder. No man liked being dumped. Especially if he felt the woman had cost him his marriage. And then there was her father's old .38.

"Did Angus tell you Ginger was involved with a married man?" he asked.

She shrugged. "I can't remember where I heard that."

He studied her. Was there a grain of truth to Ginger being involved with another woman's husband? Maybe, given Ginger's propensity for married men. But he got the feeling Dana might be covering for someone.

"Any idea who the man was?" Hud asked.

Dana shook her head and looked down into her coffee mug. Whatever she was hiding would come out. Sooner or later, he thought.

In the meantime, he needed to talk to Kitty Randolph about her emerald ring.

"I NEED TO RUN an errand," Dana said the moment Hilde returned. "Can you watch the shop?"

"Are you all right? I saw Hud leaving as I was pulling in," her friend said.

"The woman in the well was Ginger Adams. That's what he came by to tell me."

Hilde frowned. "Ginger Adams? Not the Ginger who your dad…"

"Exactly," Dana said, pulling on her coat. "I'll be back."

Her father had a small place along the river on the way to Bozeman.

Dana took the narrow dirt road back into his cabin. His truck was parked out back. She pulled up next to it and got out. A squirrel chirped at her from a nearby towering evergreen; the air smelled of river and pine.

When she got no answer to her knock, she tried the door. Of course it opened. No one locked their doors around here. She stepped inside, struck by a wash of cool air, and saw that the door leading to the river was open. He must have gone fishing.

She walked out onto the deck, looked down the river and didn't see him. Turning, she spotted her father's gun cabinet and moved to it.

There were numerous rifles, several shotguns and a half-dozen different boxes of cartridges and shells. No .38 pistol, though.

"What are you looking for?"

Dana jumped at the sound of her father's voice behind her. She turned, surprised by his tone. "You startled me." She saw his expression just before it changed. Fear?

"You need to borrow a gun?" he asked, stepping past her to close the gun cabinet.

"I was looking for your .38."

He stared at her as if she'd spoken in a foreign language.

"The one you always kept locked in the cabinet."

He glanced at the gun cabinet. "I see you found the key."

"You've hidden it in the same place since I was nine." She waited. He seemed to be stalling. "The .38?"

"Why do you want the .38?"

"Are you going to tell me where it is or not?" she said, fear making a hard knot in her stomach.

"I don't know where it is. Wasn't it in the cabinet?"

Her father had never been a good liar. "Dad, are you telling me you don't have it?" She could well imagine what Hud was going to think about that.

"Why do you care? It wasn't like it was worth anything."

She shook her head. "Do I have to remind you that Ginger Adams was killed with a .38 and her remains were found on our property?"

All the color drained from his face in an instant. "Ginger?" He fumbled behind him, feeling for a chair and finding one, dropped into it. "Ginger?"

His shock was real. Also his surprise. He hadn't known it was Ginger in the well. "They're sure it's Ginger?" he asked, looking up at her.

She nodded. Had her father really cared about the

woman? "Dad, you know Hud will want to see a .38 owned by someone with a connection to Ginger."

"Well, I don't know where it is. I guess I lost it."

"That's it?" Dana said, aghast, thinking what Hud would think.

Angus frowned and shrugged, but this time she saw something in his expression that made her wonder again what he was hiding from her. Was he protecting someone?

When she didn't say anything, he said, "I don't know what you want from me."

Her heart caught in her throat. She wanted him to tell her he was sorry for what he'd done. Splitting up their family. What she didn't want was for him to have killed Ginger Adams. Or be covering for someone else.

"I know that you and Jordan were both interested in Ginger," Dana said, the words coming hard.

His head jerked up in shock. "You knew?"

She'd found out quite by accident when she'd seen Jordan kissing a woman in the alley behind the building that would one day be Needles and Pins. Who could have missed Ginger Adams in that outfit she was wearing? The dress and shoes were bright red—just like her hair.

"It isn't what you think," her father said defensively. "I was never..." He waved a hand through the air. "You know. I can't speak for Jordan."

Like father like son. She shook her head in disgust as she sat in a chair next to him.

"Ginger was a nice young woman."

"You were *married*," she pointed out. "And Jordan was just a kid."

"Your mother and I were separated. I only lived at

the ranch so you kids wouldn't know. Jordan was eighteen. I wouldn't say he was a kid."

"And you were forty."

He must have heard the accusation in her tone.

"And you're wondering what she could have seen in a forty-year-old man?" He laughed. "Sometimes you are too naive, sweetheart." He patted her head as he'd done when she was a child. "Dana," he said patiently, his eyes taking on a faraway look. "We can't change the past even if we'd like to." He got up from his chair, glancing at his watch. "I'm going to have a beer. I'm sure you won't join me but can I get you a cola?"

She stared at his back as he headed into the kitchen and after a moment she followed him. Sometimes he amazed her. Talk about naive.

"I don't think the past is going to stay buried, Dad, now that Ginger has turned up murdered and at the family ranch well. You and Jordan *are* suspects."

He glanced around the fridge door at her, a beer can in one hand, a cola in the other. He raised the cola can. She shook her head.

"If I were you I'd come up with a better story than you lost the .38," she continued, angry at him for thinking this would just pass. But that had been his attitude for as long as she'd known him. Just ignore the problem and it will fix itself—one way or another. That was her father.

Only this time, the problem wasn't going to go away, she feared. "Hud knows you had the gun. You used to let the two of us shoot it, remember?"

Her father nodded as he popped the top on his beer and took a drink. "Ahh-hh," he said, then smiled. "Of course I remember. I remember everything about those days, baby girl. Truthfully, honey? I don't know what happened to the gun. Or how long it's been gone. One day it just wasn't in the cabinet."

She was thankful that Hud didn't know about Ginger and Jordan. She'd never told Hud about the kiss in the alley she'd witnessed. And she doubted Jordan would be forthcoming about it.

She watched her father take a long drink and lick the foam from his lips. His gaze settled on her and a strange look came into his eyes. It was gentle and sad and almost regretful. "Sometimes you look so much like your mother."

HUD CALLED THE judge's number, a little surprised to learn that Kitty Randolph still lived in the same house she had shared with her husband. The same house where he'd been murdered five years before.

The maid answered. Mrs. Randolph had gone out to run a few errands and wasn't expected back until after lunch.

Lunch. Hud felt his stomach growl as he hung up. He hadn't eaten all day, but he knew a good place to get a blue plate special—and information at the same time.

Leroy Perkins had been a cook at the Roadside Café back when Ginger had been a waitress there. Now he owned the place, but hung out there most days keeping an eye on his investment.

Leroy was tall and thin and as stooped as a dogwood twig. His hair, what was left of it, was gray and buzz-cut short. He was drinking coffee at the end stool and apparently visiting with whoever stopped by and was willing to talk to him.

Hud slid onto the stool next to him.

"Get you a menu?" a young, blonde, ponytailed waitress asked him. She looked all of eighteen.

"I'll take the lunch special and a cola, thanks," Hud said.

She was back in a jiffy with a cola and a glass of ice along with the pot of coffee. She refilled Leroy's cup then went back into the kitchen to flirt with the young cook.

Leroy was shaking his head as he watched the cook. "Hard to find anyone who knows anything about the grill. There's a knack to cooking on a grill."

Hud was sure there was. "Leroy, I was wondering if you remember a waitress who used to work here back about twenty years ago."

"Twenty years? You must be kidding. I can barely remember what I had for breakfast."

"Her name was Ginger Adams."

Leroy let out a laugh. "Ginger? Well, hell yes. That cute little redhead? Who could forget *her*?" He frowned. "Why would you be asking about her? It's been...how many years? It was the year we got the new grill. Hell, that was seventeen years ago, the last time I saw her."

There was no avoiding it. Everyone in the canyon knew about the bones. Once he started asking about Ginger, any fool would put two and two together. "It was her bones that were found in the Cardwell Ranch well."

"No kiddin'." Leroy seemed genuinely surprised.

"You ever date her?" Hud asked.

The old cook let out a cackle. "She wasn't interested in some cook. Not that girl. She was looking for a husband—and one who could take care of her."

"Someone with money."

"Money. Position. Power. And it didn't matter how old he was, either," Leroy said grudgingly.

"Like Angus Cardwell."

Leroy nodded. "He was old enough to be her daddy, too. Guess she thought the Cardwell Ranch was his. Dropped him like a hot potato once she found out Mary Cardwell wasn't going to let loose of that land, though."

"Know who she dated after Angus?" Hud asked.

Leroy chuckled and took a sip of his coffee before he said, "Sure do. Went after the eldest son."

Hud couldn't hide his surprise. "Jordan?"

"Oh, yeah," Leroy said.

He wondered why he'd never heard about this. "You're sure? You said you could barely remember what you had for breakfast this morning...."

"I was here the night Jordan came by and the two had quite the row," Leroy said. "They didn't see me. I was just getting ready to bust the two of them up when he shoved her and she fell and broke her arm."

Hud felt a start. The broken wrist bone. "Jordan broke her arm?" he asked in surprise. "How, in this canyon, did something like that happen and not be public knowledge within hours?"

Leroy flushed. "Well, that could be because she was ready to file an assault charge against Jordan—until he promised to pay for all her expenses, including medical costs and lost wages."

"He paid you off, too," Hud guessed.

Leroy shrugged. "Cooking is the most underpaid profession there is."

So that's how Leroy started his nest egg to buy the café. "So what were Jordan and Ginger arguing about?"

"Seems he thought they had something going on,"

Leroy said. "She, however, had moved on to higher ground, so to speak."

The waitress returned and slid a huge plate covered with thick-sliced roast beef and a pile of real mashed potatoes covered with brown gravy and a side of green beans and a roll.

"So they didn't patch things up?" Hud asked in between bites.

Leroy laughed again. "Not a chance. Jordan tried to make it up to her, but she wasn't having any of it. Nope, Jordan was history after that."

"And this higher ground you spoke of?" Hud asked.

Leroy wrinkled his brow. "I just knew Ginger. She'd found herself someone else, probably someone with more potential than Jordan. Ginger didn't go five minutes without a man."

"But you don't know who he was?"

Leroy shook his head. "She took off time from the café while her arm healed. Didn't see much of her and then…she was just gone. I assumed she'd taken off with the guy. Her roommate said she packed up what she wanted of her things, even gave away her car, and left."

"Her roommate?"

"A bunch of girls bunked in one of those cheap cabins near the café but you know how it is, some last a day on the job, some a week. Very few last a summer. I barely remember the one roommate that Ginger used to hang with. A kind of plain girl, not a bad waitress, though."

"This friend never heard from her again?" Hud asked as he ate. The food was excellent.

Leroy shrugged. "None of us did, but we didn't think

anything of it. Girls like Ginger come and go. The only thing they leave behind is broken hearts."

"Ginger have any family?" Hud asked.

"Doubt it or wouldn't someone have come looking for her? I got the feeling she might not have left home under the most congenial circumstances."

Hud had the same feeling. "Try to remember something more about this girl who befriended Ginger."

"She didn't work at the café long." He slapped his forehead. "I can almost think of her name. It was something odd."

"If you remember it, call me," Hud said, throwing down enough money to cover his meal and cola. "I wish you wouldn't mention this to anyone."

Leroy shook his head, but Hud could tell that the moment he left, Leroy would be spreading the word.

"Wait a minute," Leroy said. "There might be someone you could ask about Ginger." He seemed to hesitate. "Ginger used to flirt with him all the time when he came in." The cook's eyes narrowed. "You're probably not going to want to hear this…"

Hud let out a snort. "Let me guess. Marshal Brick Savage."

"Yeah, how'd you know?" Leroy asked, sounding surprised.

Hud smiled. "Because I know my father." He had another flash of memory of a woman in red. Only this time, he heard her laughter dying off down the street.

As Hud climbed into his patrol SUV, he turned south onto the highway and headed toward West Yellowstone and the lake house his father had bought on Hebgen Lake.

He couldn't put off talking to his father any longer.

Chapter Nine

"I wondered when I'd be seeing you," Brick Savage said when he answered the door. The former marshal shoved the door open wider and without another word, turned and walked back into the house.

Hud stepped in, closed the door, then followed his father to the back part of the house to the kitchen and small dining nook in front of a bank of windows.

He studied his father under the unkind glare of the fluorescent lights, surprised how much the elder Savage had aged. Hud remembered him as being much more imposing. Brick seemed shrunken, half the man he'd once been. Age hadn't been kind to him.

Brick opened the refrigerator door and took out two root beers. Hud watched him take down two tall glasses and fill each with ice cubes.

"You still drink root beer," Brick said. Not really a question. Root beer was about the only thing Hud had in common with his father, he thought as he took the filled glass.

"Sit down," Brick said.

Hud pulled up one of the chairs at the table, his gaze going to the window. Beyond it was a huge, flat, white expanse that Hud knew was the frozen snow-covered surface of Hebgen Lake. Not far to the southeast was Yellowstone Park.

He wondered why Brick had moved up here. For the solitude? For the fishing? Or had his father just wanted out of the canyon for some reason? Bad memories maybe.

"So what can I do for you?" Brick asked and took a long swig of his root beer.

Hud doubted his father was so out of touch that he hadn't heard about the woman's body that was found in the Cardwell Ranch well. In fact, Hud suspected the coroner had filled him in on every facet of the case.

"I'm investigating the murder of Ginger Adams," Hud said, watching his father's expression.

Nothing. Brick seemed to be waiting for more.

"Ginger Adams, a pretty redheaded waitress who worked at the Roadside Café seventeen years ago?" Hud said.

"What does that have to do with me?" Brick asked, sounding baffled.

"You knew her."

Brick shrugged. "I'm sorry, but I don't remember her. I don't remember most of them."

Hud cursed under his breath. "Well, I remember. I keep seeing Ginger in a slinky red dress and red high heels. And for some reason, I keep seeing you with her."

"Could have been me," he admitted congenially. "That was how many years ago?"

"Seventeen according to Leroy at the café."

Brick nodded. "The year your mother died. Oh, yeah, it could have been me." Brick looked down at his half-empty glass of root beer.

Hud rubbed a hand over his face, feeling the old anger toward his father. "You broke her heart, you know."

"I broke your mother's heart long before she got sick," his father said. "I was your mother's number one disappointment." He looked up at Hud. "Isn't that what she always told you?"

"She loved you."

Brick laughed. "Maybe. At one time. You won't believe this, but your mother was the only woman I ever loved."

"You had an odd way of showing it."

"You disappoint a woman enough times and you quit trying not to. But you didn't drive all this way to talk about this, did you?"

Hud cleared his throat. There was no point getting into the past. He couldn't change it. He couldn't change his father and his mother was dead. He dropped the case file on the table between them. "I need to ask you some questions about Judge Raymond Randolph's killing."

Something showed in Brick's face. "Is there something new in that case?"

Hud thought he heard a slight waver in his father's voice, but then he might have imagined it.

"If you read my report, you know as much as I do about the case," Brick said, glancing down at the file but not reaching for it.

"I've read the file," Hud said.

"Then you know what happened that night," Brick said. "I took the call from a neighbor who heard gunshots at the judge's house. I tried to reach you and couldn't, so I went instead."

Hud knew Brick would remind him of that.

"According to your report, you saw the Kirk brothers coming out of the judge's house and gave chase."

His father eyed him, no doubt bristling at the use of his exact words. "That's exactly what happened."

"The vehicle, an older model car, was being driven by one of the Kirk brothers, Ty. Mason was with him in the passenger seat."

"That's right," Brick said. "I chased them down the canyon almost to Gallatin Gateway."

"Almost. According to your report, Ty lost control of the car at the 35-mile-an-hour curve just before the bridge. Both men were killed. Later you reported that several items from the judge's house were found in the car. The conclusion was that the judge had come home early, caught the Kirk brothers in the act of burglarizing the house and was fatally injured when one of the brothers panicked and shot him with a .38-caliber pistol. The judge's wife, Kitty, was out of town. The boys ran, you chased them, they both died in the car wreck."

"You have a problem with my report?"

Hud rubbed his bruised jaw, never taking his eyes off his father. "It's just a little too cut-and-dried, because now, something stolen from the judge's house that night has turned up in the Cardwell Ranch well—along with the remains of Ginger Adams."

The older man's shock was real. Rupert couldn't have told him about the owner of the ring because the coroner hadn't known.

"If Ginger was killed the night she allegedly left town seventeen years ago and the robbery was only five years ago, then how did Kitty Randolph's ring end up in the well?"

Brick shook his head. "I'm supposed to know?"

"You know what bothers me about this case?" Hud said. "Nowhere in the original report does it say that there was any item found on the brothers that connected them to the robbery and murder of the judge."

"Doesn't it say that a pair of gold cuff links and a pocket watch were found in the glove box of the car?" Brick said.

Hud nodded. "That information was added later." Both items were small and could easily have been put in the car—after the accident. "You know what else is missing? The .38. What happened to the gun? And where did they get a gun that had been used in a murder years before—back when both brothers were barely out of diapers?"

"They could have found the gun. Then after using it, threw it in the river during the chase," Brick said with a shrug.

"Maybe..." Hud agreed "...but I'm sure you had deputies looking for the gun, right?" His father nodded, a muscle bunching in his jaw. "Never found, right?" Again his father nodded. "Leaves a lot of questions since both Kirk boys are dead and the gun is missing."

"Life is like that sometimes," Brick said. "You don't always find the answers."

"Weren't drugs found in their car after the accident?"

His father nodded slowly and picked up his glass to take a drink.

"If the Kirks had gotten caught with drugs again wouldn't they both have been sent to Deer Lodge? It would have been the third offense for both of them. They would have been looking at some hard time."

"Rather a moot point since they were both killed," Brick said.

"My point exactly. Isn't it possible that the drugs were the reason they ran that night and not that they'd just burglarized Judge Randolph's house and murdered him?"

Brick put down his glass a little too hard. "Son, what exactly are you accusing me of?"

What was he accusing his father of? "I'm not sure justice was done that night."

"Justice?" His father let out a laugh. "For years I chased down the bad guys and did my best to get them taken off the street. The Kirk brothers are just one example. Those boys should have been locked up. Instead, because of overcrowding in corrections, they got probation for the first offense and saw very little jail time for the second. The law put them back on the street and they ended up killing Judge Randolph. I saw them come running out of his house, no matter what you believe."

"You sure you didn't see a chance to get Ty and Mason Kirk off the streets for good?"

Brick shook his head sadly. "You're wrong, but let me ask you this. This murder you got on your hands, what if you find out who killed her but you can't prove it? You think you'll be able to pass that killer on the street every day knowing he did it and him thinking he got away with it?"

"We aren't talking about the Kirk brothers now, are we."

Brick took a drink of his root beer. "Just hypothetical, son."

"Right before he was killed five years ago, Judge Randolph was threatening to have you fired from your job," Hud said. "He seemed to think you'd been playing fast and loose with your position of power."

"Five years ago, I was getting ready to retire, you know that. What would I care if the judge got me fired?"

"If you'd gotten fired, you would have lost your pension," Hud said.

Brick laughed. "And you think I'd kill someone for that measly amount of money?" He shook his head still smiling as if he thought this was a joke.

"Maybe the judge had something on you that would have sent you to jail."

He laughed again. "Hell, you would have gotten the marshal job if I had gone to jail."

Hud knew now that he'd only taken the deputy job to show his father. Brick had been dead set against it and done everything he could to keep Hud out of the department. But his father was right about one thing, Hud would have been up for marshal in the canyon.

"Tell me something," Hud said. "Why were you so dead set against me being a deputy?"

"I knew what kind of life it was. I didn't want that for you. Maybe I especially didn't want it for Dana. I know how much your mama hated me being in law enforcement. Isn't it possible that I was trying to protect you?"

It was Hud's turn to laugh. "I think you were protecting yourself. You knew I'd be watching you like a hawk. I think you were worried I'd find out what the judge had on you."

"I hate to burst your bubble, but the judge had nothing on me. In fact, he was about to be removed from the bench," Brick said. "He had Alzheimer's. He was losing his mind. His allegations against me were just part of his irrational behavior."

Hud stared at his father. Could that possibly be true? Brick picked up their empty glasses and took them to the sink. "I'll admit I've made my share of mistakes," he said, his back to Hud. "I thought you only took the deputy job to prove something to me. I didn't want you following in my footsteps for the wrong reasons."

Hud *had* taken the job for all the wrong reasons. But law enforcement must have been in his blood. It had turned out to be the right career for him.

His father turned to look back at him. "Did you know your mother wanted me to go into business with her father? She married beneath her. We both knew it. Everyone told her she could do better than me. She just wouldn't listen. She thought I'd change my mind once you were born." He turned back to the sink.

Hud stared at his father's back, thinking about the things his mother used to say about Brick. She'd been angry at her husband as far back as Hud could remember. Now he wondered if a lot of that anger and resentment hadn't stemmed from Brick not going to work for her father. Had she been embarrassed being married to a small-town marshal?

Brick shut off the water and dried his hands. "I know you think I killed your mother, not cancer. Maybe I did. Maybe her disappointment in me caused the cancer." He stood against the sink, looking small and insubstantial. "I was sorry to hear about you and Dana. I always thought you made a nice couple."

Hud picked up the Judge Randolph case file from the kitchen table. He'd thought coming up here to see his father would be an end to all his questions. Now he had even more questions. "I'm going to solve these murders."

"I don't doubt you will," Brick said. "You were always a damned good deputy. I thought after what happened five years ago, you'd be soured on the profession. You know I had to suspend you the night the judge was killed just like I would have had to any deputy who blew his shift. I couldn't protect you because you were my son."

He studied his father. "It must have been a shock to you then to hear that I'm the temporary marshal until they can advertise the job."

Brick smiled but said nothing.

Hud started toward the door, stopped and turned. "You didn't seem surprised."

"About what?"

"About the ring that was found in the well with Ginger's remains." He studied his father. "Because you already knew, didn't you?"

"Good luck with your investigation, son."

DANA RETURNED TO the shop to find it packed with customers. She met Hilde's eye as she came in the door and saw her friend wink mischievously. They hadn't even had this much business during the rush before Christmas—and January was when most businesses felt a slump.

But here it was January and the shop was full of women. It didn't take a genius to figure out what was up.

Hilde cut fabric while Dana rang up purchases and answered questions relating to the bones found in the ranch well and a rumor that was circulating that the bones belonged to Ginger Adams.

Dana fudged a little. "Ginger Adams? *Really?*"

The afternoon whizzed by. Dana tried not to watch the door, afraid Hud would pay her another visit. But by closing, he hadn't shown and she breathed a sigh of relief when Hilde offered to take the deposit to the bank and let Dana finish closing up.

"Can you believe this?" Hilde said, hefting the deposit bag. She grimaced. "Sorry. I do feel bad making money at your expense. And Ginger's."

"S'all right," Dana said, laughing. "It's a windfall for the store. At least something good is coming out of it."

Hilde left and Dana straightened the counter before going to lock up. As she put the closed sign up on the front door, she was surprised how dark it was outside. It got dark early this time of year. Plus it had snowed off and on most of the day, the clouds low, the day gloomy. There was no traffic on the street and only a few lights glowed at some of the businesses still open this time of the afternoon.

As she looked out, a movement caught her eye. She stared across the street into the shadowy darkness at the edge of the building. Had she only imagined it or was someone standing there looking in her direction?

She stepped to the side to make sure the light in the back wasn't silhouetting her and waited, unable to shake the feeling that someone had been watching her as intently as she had been staring across the street at them.

Lanny? He'd spied on her last night and on Hud, as well. But surely he wasn't still doing it.

Or Hud? That would be just like him to keep an eye on her.

Another thought struck her. Could it be the person who had left the chocolates for her? The same person who'd taken her doll and put it in the well last night? She shivered, remembering the voice on the phone. Just a prank call, she kept telling herself.

A sick, morbid cruel prank. Was it possible that's all

the chocolates and the doll in the well were meant to be? The prankster had just been having fun at Dana's expense but then she'd had to go and call the marshal and things got out of hand?

That's what she wanted to believe as she stepped to the window again and looked out. Nothing moved. The lights of a car came down the winding street, blinding her for a moment as it swept past.

In that instant as the car passed, the headlights illuminated the building across the street.

No one was there.

She'd been so sure she'd seen a person watching her.

On impulse, she reopened the front door and ran across the street without her coat, leaving the shop door wide-open.

It would only take a second to find out if she was losing her mind or not.

THE MOMENT HUD HIT the highway, he called Judge Raymond Randolph's widow to see if Kitty had returned home. It would have been better to stop by and see her, but she lived at the other end of the canyon. He'd spent longer at his father's than he'd meant to. Now he was running late. He wouldn't be able to drive down to see her and still get back to Needles and Pins before Dana left for the night, and he was worried about Dana.

But he needed to know if anything his father had told him was the truth.

"Hello?" Kitty's voice was small but strong.

"Mrs. Randolph?" He remembered Katherine "Kitty" Randolph as being tiny and gray with smooth pink skin and twinkling blue eyes. She baked the best chocolate chip cookies and always brought them to the church bake sales.

"Yes?"

"My name is Hudson Savage. You probably don't remember me."

"Hud," she said, her tone more cheerful. "Of course I remember you. You and your mother used to sit near me in church. Your mother baked the most wonderful pies. I think her apple pie was my favorite. I couldn't help myself. I always purchased a slice at every sale. For a good cause, I'd tell myself." She let out a soft chuckle, then seemed to sober. "I remember your mother fondly. You must miss her terribly."

He'd forgotten about his mother's pies. Her crust would melt in your mouth. Pies were her one pride.

He cleared his throat. "Yes. I hate to bother you this evening but I'm the new interim marshal in Gallatin Canyon and I'm involved in an investigation." He hesitated, unsure how to proceed.

"That woman's bones that were found in the well on the Cardwell Ranch," Kitty Randolph said. "Yes, I heard about it. How horrible. But I don't see what I—"

"The woman is believed to have been killed with the same gun that killed your husband."

Kitty let out a small gasp and Hud wished he'd been more tactful. He should have done this in person. He should have waited. But since he hadn't, he dove right in.

"I need some information about the last few months the judge was alive." He took a breath. "Did he have Alzheimer's and was he about to be asked to step down from the bench?"

Silence, then a shaky croak. "Yes, I'm afraid so."

Hud let out a breath. "I'm sorry. That must have been very difficult for you. I understand his behavior was sometimes irrational."

"Yes," she repeated. "This is about your father, isn't it?"

Behind the twinkling blue eyes, Kitty had always shown a sharp intelligence.

"Yes. Mrs. Randolph, do you know what the judge had against my father?"

"No, I never understood his animosity toward Marshal Savage," she said, sounding sad. "But the judge was a hard man. Much like your father. And who knows how much of it was just my husband's illness."

"Were there any papers missing after the judge's death?" Hud asked.

"You mean, some evidence my husband might have had on your father?"

That was exactly what he meant.

"No. I doubt any existed." She sounded tired suddenly.

"I know it's late. I just have one more question. In the burglary report, you didn't mention a ring."

"No," she said, sounding tentative.

"Well, Mrs. Randolph, an emerald ring was found." Another gasp. "You found my ring?"

"Yes, I'm afraid it's being held as evidence."

"I don't understand."

He cleared his throat again. "The ring was found in the well with the remains of Ginger Adams."

Another gasp, this one more audible than the first. For a moment he thought she might have dropped the phone. Or even fainted. "Mrs. Randolph?"

"I had to sit down," she said. "I don't understand. How is that possible?"

"I was hoping you might have some idea," Hud said.

"This is very upsetting."

"I'm sorry to have to give you the news on the telephone," he said as he drove. "Do you have any idea how long the ring has been missing?"

"No, I didn't look for it for months after the judge's death and when I did, I realized it was missing. I thought about calling the marshal and letting him know, but your father had retired by then and I just assumed it had been lost when those young men wrecked their vehicle in the river. I never thought I'd see it again." She sounded like she might be crying. "The judge had it made for me in honor of our twenty-fifth wedding anniversary."

"I understand it's an expensive piece of jewelry," Hud said.

"The only piece of real jewelry the judge ever bought me. When we married, he couldn't afford a diamond." Her voice broke.

Hud frowned. "Wouldn't you have kept a piece of expensive jewelry like that in a safe or a safe-deposit box at the bank?"

Ahead he could see the lights of Big Sky. The Kirk brothers hadn't found the safe. Nor would they have known how to open it if they had.

"I thought it was in the safe," Kitty said. "Obviously, I had taken it out to wear it and forgot to put it back. The judge probably saw it and put it in the jewelry box with his cuff links and his father's old pocket watch."

But it didn't explain how the ring ended up in the

well. "I'll see what I can do about getting the ring returned to you as soon as possible," Hud told her.

"Thank you. I can't tell you what your call has meant to me. Good night, Hud."

He disconnected as he turned off and drove up to Big Sky's lower meadow. As he started to turn down the street to Needles and Pins, a car whipped out of the marshal's office parking lot, tossing up gravel.

The driver spotted him and threw on his brakes. The vehicle's door flew open and Jordan Cardwell jumped out.

"I want to talk to you, Savage," he said, storming over to the SUV.

"How about that," Hud said. "I want to talk to you, too, Jordan. Now just isn't a great time."

"Too bad," Jordan said. "I want to know what the hell is going on out at the ranch."

DANA STOPPED AT the edge of the building across the street from the fabric shop, waiting for her eyes to adjust to the darkness. The air was cold, the shadows dark and deep along the side of the building.

She saw that the sidewalk across the front had been shoveled but there was new snow along the side of the closed office building. She stepped into the dark shadows, almost convinced she'd only imagined a figure standing here. What fool would stand in all that snow just to—

She saw the fresh tracks. Her heart lodged in her throat. The snow was tramped where someone had stood. Waiting. She glanced behind her and saw that from this spot, the person had a clear view of the shop.

Behind the spot where the snow was trampled was a

set of tracks that came up the narrow passage alongside the building. Another set returned to the alley.

For one wild moment she thought about following them. She even placed her boot into one track. The shoe size was larger than her own, but the edges caved in after each step the person had taken so it was impossible to gauge a true size of the print.

She shivered as she looked toward the dark alley, seeing nothing but the tracks. Only a fool would follow them. Whoever had been standing here watching the shop only minutes ago might not be gone, she told herself. He'd seen her look out the window. Maybe that's what he'd been waiting for. For her to see him. And follow him?

But why? It made no sense. It was as if someone was just trying to scare her. Unless the chocolates were filled with poison. And she was the one who was supposed to have been knocked down into the well last night.

Just like Ginger Adams had been?

Just like her caller had said.

She hugged herself against the bone-deep cold of her thoughts as she turned and ran back across the street. Halfway across she noticed the shop door. She'd left it wide-open, but now it was closed. The wind must have blown it shut.

But as she opened it and stepped tentatively inside, she tried to remember feeling even the slightest breeze while she was across the street—and couldn't.

As she stood in the darkened shop, she realized someone could have slipped in while she was gone. It had been stupid to run out like that and leave the door wide-open. Worse, she realized, she hadn't locked the back door of the shop because she was planning to go out that way.

She held her breath, listening for a sound. The shop was deathly quiet. The small light still burned in the back room, casting a swath of pale gold over the pine floor.

Her teeth began to chatter. Glancing out into the street, she saw only darkness. Again she looked toward the back of the shop where she'd left her purse, her cell phone, her car keys.

There's no one in here. No one hiding behind the rows of fabric.

Even if the person who'd been across the street *had* been watching her, what were the chances he had circled around and come into the shop when she wasn't watching and was now waiting for her?

She started to take a step toward the back of the shop.

Silent and huge, a shadow loomed up from the darkness and came out of the stacks of fabric. A large silhouette against the light in the back.

She screamed as he reached for her. She shot an elbow out, stumbling backward into one of the fabric rows.

"Dana. It's me."

But it was too late. She'd already driven her elbow into his ribs and sent a kick to his more private parts. Fortunately for Hud, the kick missed its mark.

She heard him let out a curse followed by her name again. "It's me. Hud."

As if she hadn't already recognized his voice.

A flashlight beam illuminated a spot on the floor at their feet.

"What are you doing?" she demanded. "You scared the life out of me."

He rubbed his thigh where her boot had made contact and eyed her suspiciously.

"What are you doing here anyway?" she asked.

"I came in through the back. The door was unlocked. When I saw the front door standing open, I was afraid something had happened to you." He turned on the light and she saw how worried he looked.

She swallowed back a retort. "That wasn't you watching from across the street then?"

"There was someone watching you from across the street?" He was already headed for the door.

"Whoever it was is gone," she called after him.

"Stay in the shop. Lock the doors," he called over his shoulder without looking back as he crossed the street.

Hurriedly, she locked the back door, then the front, and from the window watched the flicker of his flashlight beam moving across the snow.

She saw him stop at the spot she'd discovered between the buildings, no doubt following the footprints she'd seen in the snow.

She waited, hating that Hud had acted so quickly on something that was probably innocent. Maybe it had been someone waiting for a friend who didn't show. Maybe the whole thing had nothing to do with her. Hud taking it seriously only made her more anxious.

Was she really in danger?

What scared her was that he seemed to think so.

He came back across the street and she unlocked the door to let him in. He closed the door behind him, locking it.

"Nothing, right?" she asked hopefully.

"I don't want you going back to the ranch by yourself."

She'd let him stay last night because she'd been as scared for him as for herself. But she hadn't been able to sleep knowing he was downstairs, so close.

She shook her head. "I won't be driven out of my home."

"Then I'm staying with you."

"No. That is, I won't be alone tonight. We're having a family meeting. I'll get Clay or Jordan to stay with me. I'll be fine. Anyway, no one has any reason to harm me," she said, trying to convince herself as well as him. "I didn't put Ginger Adams in that well."

"But someone in your family might have. And quite frankly, having one of the suspects staying in the house with you might not be the best plan." His gaze softened. "Dana, why didn't you tell me that Jordan is forcing you to sell the ranch?"

Dana stared at Hud. "Jordan told you that?"

"In so many words, yes. Is there really a will?"

"I don't know." She sighed. His gaze filled with such tenderness it was like a physical pain for her. "I thought so at first. Mom told me she wrote up a draft and signed and dated it. Unfortunately, I can't find it and since she never got a copy to her lawyer before her death... Jordan is convinced I made up the whole story about Mother's new will."

"So, the ranch goes to all her heirs," Hud said, sympathy in his voice.

"Yes, and they have decided they want the money, which means I have no choice but to sell," Dana said. "I'm fighting to hang on to the house and a little land. That is what has been holding things up."

"Dana, I am so sorry."

She turned away. "Please, I hate talking about this." She remembered something he'd said and frowned as she turned to face him again. "You don't really think someone in my family had anything to do with Ginger's death, do you?"

He had on his cop face again, giving nothing away. "Anyone who had contact with Ginger or access to the ranch is a suspect."

She let out a surprised breath. "So I'm a suspect, too."

He sighed. "Dana, I've been thinking about what happened at the ranch last night. Is there anyone who might want to hurt you?"

She laughed. "What were we just talking about? I'm holding up the sale of the ranch and my three siblings are all chomping at the bit to get their hands on the money from the property."

"You seriously believe one of them would try to hurt you?" he asked.

"You know them." Her gaze locked with his. "There is little they wouldn't do to hurt me. Have done to hurt me."

"I have to ask you this," he said. "Last night, did you see the person who attacked me?"

"Why are you asking me this now?"

"I need to know if the reason you fired that shotgun in the air last night was to help someone in your family get away."

She stared at him, anger rising in her. "How can you ask me that?"

"Dana—" He reached for her, but she stepped back.

"You broke my heart." The words were out, surprising her as much as they did him. They had nothing to do with what he'd accused her of. They were also words she never thought she would admit to him of all people.

"I'll never forgive myself for letting it happen."

"Good." She started to step past him, but he grabbed her wrist.

"I made the worst mistake of my life that night," he said quickly.

Wouldn't Stacy love to hear that?

"You were everything to me."

"Apparently not," she snapped, trying to pull free. But his grip was firm, his fingers warm and strong.

"I truly don't remember that night," he said, his voice low and filled with emotion. "The last thing I remember is having a drink at the bar—"

"I told you I don't want to talk about this," she said.

"You have never let me tell you what happened. At least what I remember."

"Finding you in my sister's bed was sufficient enough."

"Dana, I've thought about this for five years, thought of little else. One drink and then nothing. I remember *nothing*."

"Well, that's your story, isn't it? That lets you off the hook."

"Damn it, why do you think I came back? Because of you and to prove that nothing happened that night."

"I thought you don't remember."

"I don't. I couldn't be sure before but I got a note from someone in the canyon that said I was set up that night."

"Who?"

"It was anonymous, but, Dana, I believe I *was* set up. Otherwise, why can't I remember that night? What I've never been able to understand is why? All I knew for sure is that your sister had to be in on it. But after what Lanny said earlier... Your sister couldn't have acted alone. Someone helped her."

Dana didn't move. Didn't breathe. All she could do was stare at him, remembering what she'd overheard Lanny tell him. That Stacy had used Hud to force Emery into giving her a divorce. Emery had been thirty years Stacy's senior, an older man with money. That was until he hooked up with Stacy. Stacy got her divorce five years ago—and took half of Emery's assets and his home.

What if Stacy had done it not to hurt Dana but for her own selfish reasons?

"Dana, if I was as drunk as everyone at the bar said I was, then believe me, I didn't sleep with your sister," Hud said. "I swear to you. I had one drink at the bar, then the rest of the night is a total blank. What does that sound like to you?"

That he'd been drugged.

"How was it that you showed up at Stacy's house so early the next morning?" he asked.

She swallowed, remembering the strange phone call, the strange voice. *Do you know where your fiancé is? I do. In your sister's bed.* She'd just thought it was some canyon busybody and told Hud about the call.

"I figured it had to be something like that. Which only makes me more convinced Stacy was behind it—and she wasn't working alone. My guess is that Stacy got some man to help her. I don't know why or how they did it, but I'm going to find out." He let go of her wrist, the look in his eyes a painful reminder of the love they'd once shared. "I've never wanted anyone but you. And I'm going to prove it to you."

She stood just looking at him, afraid of what she might say at that moment. Even more afraid of what she might do. They were so close that she could smell the faint hint of his aftershave and the raw maleness of him. She wanted desperately to believe him.

Her gaze went to his lips. The memory of his mouth on hers was like a stabbing pain. All she wanted was for him to take her in his arms, to kiss her again, to make her forget everything that had happened.

He reached for her, his large palm cupping her cheek, as he pulled her to him. She felt her body start to lean toward him like metal to magnet and the next thing she knew their lips brushed then locked.

She clutched the front of his jacket, balling up the fabric in her fists as his arms came around her. His tongue touched hers and desire shot through her. She moaned as he deepened the kiss, so lost in his mouth that she didn't even hear the first ring.

His cell phone rang again, shattering the silence, shattering the moment. She pulled back. He looked at her as if the last thing he wanted to be at that moment was marshal. The phone rang again. Slowly, he withdrew his arms and checked caller ID.

"I have to take this," he said, sounding as disappointed as she felt.

She stepped away from him, taking a deep breath and letting it out slowly. What had she done? She shook her head at how easily she had weakened. What was wrong with her? How could she forget the pain Hud had caused her?

Did she really believe he'd been set up? That nothing had happened that night except someone trying to drive them apart?

"Sheriff's department business. Sorry," he said behind her.

She touched her tongue to her upper lip, then turned to face him and nodded. "I need to get home, too. Wouldn't want to miss the family meeting Jordan's scheduled at the ranch tonight."

Hud swore. "Be careful. I'll call you later. I don't want you staying at the ranch house, especially with Jordan there. He told me just a while ago that he doesn't remember Ginger Adams nor did he have any contact with her." Hud seemed to hesitate. "I have a witness who saw him fighting with her. It was clear they'd had some type of intimate relationship before that and that Ginger was trying to end it. Jordan broke her wrist. This was soon before her death."

Dana couldn't hide her shock.

"It was apparently an accident. Jordan shoved her, she fell and broke her wrist. The thing is, he lied about his relationship with her and my witness says he paid her to keep quiet about the incident." Hud cursed under his breath as he must have seen something in her expression. "You knew about Ginger and Jordan?"

"Dad told me, but years ago I'd seen Ginger and Jordan in the alley kissing."

Hud swore. "I know Jordan is your brother and even with you being on the outs with him right now, you'd still take up for him when push comes to shove. But, Dana, I'm afraid of what Jordan might be capable of when he doesn't get his way. Right now from what I can gather, what he wants more than anything is the Cardwell Ranch. And you're the only thing standing between him and the money from the sale. Watch your back."

Chapter Ten

Dana had stopped off to see Hilde on the way home, putting off the family meeting as long as possible—and trying to keep her mind off Hud and the kiss and everything he'd told her, as well as the person she'd spotted across the street watching the shop. Watching her.

"Someone is trying to scare me," she told Hilde. "Or worse." She filled her in.

"I'm with Hud. You shouldn't be alone out there. Maybe especially with your family. Come stay with me."

"Thanks, but Hud is coming out later," Dana said. "I really think it's just one of my siblings trying to get me out of the house so they can do a thorough search for Mom's new will."

"Didn't you say you looked for it and couldn't find it?"

Dana nodded. "They would be wasting their time and I could tell them that, but they wouldn't believe me."

"You're sure one of them hasn't already found it?"

"I hope not, because then it is long gone," Dana said. "But then how do I explain these threats?"

"That is too creepy about the doll in the well last night. It sounds like something Jordan would do."

She shook her head. "He wasn't in town." She thought about the doll her father had given her. Why that doll? "I just have a feeling that the person at the well wanted me to see the light and come up and investigate. And I would have, if I hadn't been on the phone with Hud."

"Did he find out who left you the chocolates?"

Dana shook her head. "He's having them checked to see if they might have been poisoned."

Hilde shivered. "Dana, someone came into your house to take that doll and leave the chocolates. That person had to know the house. Not just the house. He knows *you*."

"That's why it's probably one of my siblings." She pulled on her coat. "I kissed Hud."

Hilde's eyebrow shot up. "And?"

"And it was…" She groaned. "Wonderful. Oh, Hilde, I want to believe him. He thinks he was set up five years ago. That someone other than just Stacy wanted to see us broken up and that nothing happened."

"Didn't I tell you that was a possibility?"

Dana nodded.

"You're the only woman he's ever loved," Hilde said. "You know that. Why can't you forgive him?"

"Could you if you caught him in your sister's bed?"

Hilde looked uncertain. "It would be hard. But imagine how he must be feeling? If he really believes nothing happened. Have you ever asked Stacy about it?" Hilde asked.

Dana shook her head. "What was there to ask? You should have seen the expression on her face that morning when I caught them. I can't bear to be in the same room with her, let alone talk to her. And anyway, what was there to ask? 'How was my fiancé?'"

"Given everything that's been going on, maybe this family meeting isn't such a bad idea," Hilde said. "If it was me, I'd corner that sister of yours and demand some answers."

On the way to the ranch, Dana thought about what Hilde had said. How many people knew about the chocolates that Hud had always bought for her birthday? Her family, not that any of them seemed to pay much attention or care. All three of her siblings knew about the doll upstairs and that the ranch house was never locked. But so did a lot of other people.

Stacy, Clay and Jordan seemed the most likely suspects. She couldn't imagine any of them hanging out in a blizzard with a flashlight just to scare her away from the house, though.

But if this wasn't about her siblings trying to speed up the sale of the ranch, then what?

Ginger Adams's murder?

Jordan had always had a terrible temper when he didn't get his way, just as Hud had said.

On top of that, Jordan had lied about his relationship with Ginger Adams—and apparently been so angry when she'd dumped him that he'd knocked her down and broken her wrist. And all this right before she'd ended up in the well.

With a shudder, Dana realized that Jordan also had access to their father's .38. And now the gun was missing.

But that didn't explain the incident last night at the well. Unless Jordan hadn't been in New York when he'd called her yesterday.

As she turned into the ranch house yard, she saw a car parked out front with a rental sticker in the back window. Jordan. Apparently he'd arrived early. She could see lights on in the house and a shadow moving around on the second floor—in what had been their mother's bedroom.

HUD FOUND DEPUTY LIZA TURNER waiting for him in his office. "What was so important that you had to see me right away?" he demanded and instantly regretted it. "Sorry."

"Oh, I caught you in the middle of something," she said, stepping tentatively to him to wipe a smudge of lipstick from the corner of his mouth with her thumb. She grinned and he knew he looked sheepish. "But I thought you'd want to see this right away," Liza said, unfazed.

He noticed that her eyes shone with excitement. Then he looked at what she held up. A .38 pistol in a plastic evidence bag. "Where—"

"I was going through the list of names you had me put together, checking to see if I recognized any names on the list of people who owned registered .38 firearms, when Angus Cardwell drove up." She grinned. "I thought it wouldn't hurt to ask him if he had a .38. He told me he did, but he'd lost it. I asked if he'd mind if I took a look in his truck." Her grin broadened. "Don't worry, I got him to sign a release. And lo and behold, the .38 was right under the seat behind some old rags."

"Nice work, Deputy."

"Tomorrow's my day off," she said quickly. "I was wondering if you'd like me to take the gun up to the crime lab."

"You'd drive all the way to Missoula on your day

off?" he asked, amused. She reminded him of the way he'd been when he'd first started working for the sheriff's department.

"Truthfully? I can't stand the suspense," she said. "You should have seen Angus's face when I pulled out the gun— Don't worry, I was careful not to get any of my prints on it. He looked like he might faint. No kidding. He grabbed the side of his pickup. You would have sworn he'd just seen a ghost."

"It might take a while before the lab can run a ballistics test on the pistol," Hud said distractedly, thinking of Angus's reaction.

"I can be pretty persuasive when I need to," Liza said with a grin. "It's about the only advantage of being a woman deputy."

He smiled. Liza was cute, with dark hair, green eyes and freckles. "Call me as soon as you get the results."

"I left the list on your desk," she said as she locked the .38 in the evidence room. "I'll pick it up first thing in the morning."

"One more thing," he said, thinking about what she'd said about being persuasive. "Think you could get the fingerprints of our main suspects before you go off duty?"

She grinned. "Just give me a list."

He jotted down the names: Jordan Cardwell, Clay Cardwell, Angus Cardwell, Stacy Cardwell, Harlan Cardwell. He left off Dana's name. He could get those himself.

She took the list, read down it, then looked at him. "Just about all of the Cardwells, huh?"

He nodded, wishing now that he'd put Dana's name on it.

Liza started for the door. "Oh, I almost forgot. I

found a card in that plastic garbage bag with the box of chocolates when I sent it and the doll to the lab for you this morning. I left the card on your desk. And I just took a phone message for you from the airlines regarding the passenger you'd inquired about." Hud could see curiosity burning in her gaze. "Also on your desk."

"Thanks." Hud stepped into his office and picked up the note Liza had left. His heart began to race.

Jordan Cardwell flew in yesterday—not today. He had taken a morning flight. When Dana said he'd called her to let her know he was flying out—he was probably already in the canyon. Maybe even on the ranch.

He picked up the other item Liza had left him. A wadded-up birthday card. He stared at the front. This had been in Dana's wastebasket? He opened the card and saw Stacy's name. His heart stopped dead in his chest.

He recognized this handwriting. Hurriedly, he pulled out the anonymous note he'd received in California. The handwriting matched.

It had been Stacy who'd gotten him back here?

JORDAN MUST HAVE heard Dana's pickup approaching because as she parked, the lights upstairs went off. A moment later she saw her brother rush past one of the living room windows.

When she entered the house, he was sitting in one of the overstuffed chairs, one shiny new cowboy boot resting on his opposite leg, a drink in his hand.

"Finally," he said. "I thought you got off at six?"

"Not that it's any of your business, but I had a stop to make. Anyway, Stacy told me the family meeting was at seven," she said, taking off her coat. "Aren't you a little early?"

"I wanted us to visit before the others got here."

She turned to look at him. He was trying to give her the impression he'd been sitting there waiting patiently for her—not upstairs snooping around. Her brother really was a liar. She'd always known that Jordan was a lot of things, but she was starting to worry that he could be a lot more than just a liar. He could be a murderer.

"Visit?" she said, unable to keep the sarcasm out of her voice. "Let me guess what you want to visit about."

"Isn't it possible I might just want to see you before the others arrive?" he demanded. Another lie.

"No. Not unless you want to tell me the truth about what you were doing up in Mother's old room."

He made an ugly face in answer to being found out.

"Or I can tell you," she said against the advice of the little voice in her head warning her to be careful. "You were looking for Mom's will. The one you said didn't exist. In fact, you accused me of making up the story to hold up the sale of the ranch."

"I still believe that."

She felt her anger rise. "If I didn't know better I'd swear you staged that scene last night at the well."

Jordan stared at her. "What are you talking about?"

"Last night," Dana said, biting off each word. "Someone tried to trick me into coming up to the well. To kill me. Or just get me away from the house so you could search for the will. Hud was almost killed."

"I have no idea what you're talking about," Jordan snapped. "Remember? I didn't even fly in until today."

"How do I know you aren't lying again."

Jordan downed the rest of his drink and slammed the

glass down on the end table as he launched himself to his feet. "I'm sick of this." He stormed across the room until he stood towering over her. "The ranch is going on the market," he snapped, grabbing both of her shoulders in his hands. "You are going to quit using every legal maneuver possible to hold up the sale."

She tried to pull free, his fingers biting into her flesh.

He gave her a shake. "There is no will. Or if there is, you can't produce it." His words were like the hiss of a snake, his face within inches of hers. "You have no choice, Dana, so stop fighting me or you'll be sorry you were ever born, you stubborn damned—"

The sound of the front door opening killed the rest of his words. He let go of Dana at once and stepped back as Stacy asked, "What's going on?"

"Nothing," Jordan said sullenly. "We were just waiting for you and Clay. Where the hell is Clay, anyway? And what is that?"

Dana never thought she'd be relieved to see her sister. She was also surprised by Stacy's attitude. Her sister never stood up to Jordan but clearly she was angry with him now. Because of what she'd just witnessed?

Her hands trembling, Dana reached for the container in Stacy's hand and instantly regretted taking it.

Through the clear plastic lid she could see the crudely printed words: *Happy Birthday, Dana!* on what was obviously a homemade cake. Stacy had baked?

Dana didn't want to feel touched by the gesture, but she did as she heard the sound of another car coming in from the highway. She realized she and Jordan would have heard Stacy arrive if they hadn't been hollering at each other. Her shoulders still hurt from where he'd grabbed her.

"That must be Clay now," Stacy said, still glaring at Jordan.

He shoved past Stacy and out the front door.

Stacy shrugged out of her coat as she looked around the living room as if she hadn't seen it in a very long time. She hadn't and Dana wondered if her sister might be starting to have doubts about selling the place.

"I wish you hadn't done this," Dana said to her sister, holding up the cake.

"It was nothing," Stacy said, dropping her head.

Dana studied her for a moment wondering if the cake wasn't just a ploy to get back into her good graces so Dana would quit fighting the sale of the ranch. Now that Dana thought about it, she wouldn't have been surprised if the cake was Jordan's idea.

Jordan came back in the house, stomping his feet loudly, Clay at his heels.

"Hi, sis," Clay said quietly. He looked as if he might hug her, but changed his mind. He didn't seem to know what to do with his big hands. They fluttered in the air for a moment before he stuffed them into the pockets of his pants. "Happy birthday."

Had he been in on this? He sounded as if he'd only remembered her birthday when he'd seen the cake in her hands, though.

"Hello, Clay." Clay was what was called lanky. He was tall and thin, his bones seeming too large for his body. His hair was shorter than Dana had ever seen it, a buzz cut, and he wore chinos and a T-shirt. He wasn't so much handsome as he was beautiful.

She saw Jordan give him a disgusted look. He'd always thought Clay weak.

Stacy had taken down plates from their mother's

good china. Dana watched her stop for a moment as if admiring the pattern. Or maybe she was just speculating on how much the china might be worth on the market.

Their mother should have been here, Dana thought as she watched everyone take a seat around the large table. Jordan pulled out a chair and sat at the spot their mother used to sit. Obviously he now considered himself the head of the family.

Clay sat where he always had, near the other end of the table. Stacy put plates and forks on the table, then took the cake Dana realized she was still holding.

As Dana slumped into her chair, Stacy carefully cut the cake. Dana noticed that her sister's hands were trembling. She served everyone a piece, then started to ask, "Should we sing—"

"No," Dana interrupted. "The cake is more than enough."

Stacy looked disheartened but sat and picked up her fork. "I hope it tastes all right. I don't do much baking."

Jordan snorted at the understatement.

Dana studied her older brother as she took a bite of the cake. What would Jordan have done if Stacy hadn't arrived when she had?

"It's good," Dana said, touched by her sister's kind gesture even though she didn't want to be.

Jordan downed his and shoved his plate and fork aside. "Could we please get this settled now?"

Stacy looked angrily at their brother. "You are such a jerk," she snapped, and got up to take everyone's dishes to the sink.

"Leave the dishes. I'll do them," Dana said, getting up from the table. The kitchen felt too small for this discussion, the smell of chocolate cake too strong. "Let's go in the living room."

They all filed into the adjacent room. Clay sat in the corner, Stacy teetered on the edge of the fireplace hearth, Jordan went straight to the bar and poured himself a drink.

"Dana, you're killing us," Jordan said after gulping down half a glass of her bourbon. "All these attorney fees to fight you. You know we're going to win eventually. So why put us through this?"

Dana looked around the room at each of her siblings. "I can't believe any of you are related to me or Mother. If she knew what you were doing—"

"Don't bring her into this," Jordan snapped. "If she wanted you alone to have the ranch then she should have made the proper arrangements."

"She tried to and you know it," Dana said, fighting not to lose her temper. "I know Mother talked to each of you before she drafted her new will and explained how you would be paid over the long term."

"Produce the document," Jordan demanded.

"You know I can't."

He made an angry swipe through the air. "Then stop fighting us. You can't win and you know it. Dragging your feet has only made things worse. Now we have a dead body on the ranch."

"The body's been there for seventeen years," Dana said. "It would have turned up sooner or later."

"Not if Warren had filled in the well like he was supposed to," Jordan snapped.

Dana narrowed her gaze at him. "You told him to fill in the well?"

Jordan glared at her. "I told him to get the ranch

ready to sell. Filling in the well was his idea. How did I know he was going to find human bones in it?"

How indeed?

"We just need to stop fighting among ourselves," Clay said from the corner.

Jordan rolled his eyes. "No, what we need is to get this ranch on the market and hope to hell this investigation is over as quickly as possible. In the meantime, Dana, you could stop being so antagonistic toward the marshal."

Dana felt all the air rush from her lungs as if he'd hit her. "You aren't seriously suggesting that I—"

"Your attitude is making us all look guilty," Jordan said.

"And you think if I'm nice to Hud, it will make you look any less guilty?" she snapped.

"Please, can't we all just quit arguing?" Stacy said, sounding close to tears.

"After the ranch sells, I'm leaving," Clay said out of the blue, making everyone turn to look at him. He seemed embarrassed by the attention. "I have a chance to buy a small theater in Los Angeles."

"You'd leave Montana?" Dana asked, and realized she didn't know her younger brother at all.

Clay gave her a lopsided smile. "You're the one who loves Montana, Dana. I would have left years ago if I could have. And now, with everyone in town talking about our family as if we're murderers... Did you know that a deputy made me stop on the way here to have my fingerprints taken?"

"Stop whining, Clay, I got a call from the deputy, too," Jordan said, and looked at Stacy. She nodded that she had, too.

"What do you expect?" Dana said, tired of her siblings acting so put-upon. "A woman's body was found in our well. We all knew her. She broke up Mom and Dad's marriage. And, Jordan—"

"Maybe Mom killed her and threw her down the well," Jordan interrupted.

The room went deathly quiet.

"Don't give me that look, Dana," he said. "You know Mom was capable of about anything she set her mind to."

"I've heard enough of this," Dana said, and headed for the kitchen.

"Well, that's a surprise," Jordan said to her retreating back. "We knew we couldn't count on you to be reasonable."

Seething with anger, she turned to face him. "I have another month here before the court rules on whether the ranch has to be sold to humor the three of you and I'm taking it. If you don't like it, too bad. I'm fighting to save the ranch my mother loved. All the three of you want is money—any way you can get it. Even by destroying something that has been in our family for generations."

Jordan started to argue but she cut him off. "And as for the murder investigation, you're all on your own. Frankly, I think you're all capable of murder."

Clay and Stacy both denied that they had anything to hide. Jordan just glared at her and said, "You're making a very big mistake, Dana. I hope you don't live to regret it."

She turned and stalked off into the kitchen. Going to the sink, she grabbed the cool porcelain edge and gripped it, Jordan's threat ringing in her ears.

HUD GOT THE call from the crime lab just as he was starting to leave his office.

"We've found some latent prints on both the box of chocolates and the doll," Dr. Cross said. "I decided to do the tests myself since it tied in with your ongoing case. Interesting case."

"Did you come up with a match?" Hud asked.

"No prints on file that matched any of the prints on the doll or the package. We found multiple prints on the doll, all different. As for the gift, only one set."

Hud felt his heart rate quicken. "My deputy is bringing you up some fingerprints to compare those to. What about the chocolates themselves?"

"No prints on them. Also no sign of a drug or poison. As far as I can tell, they were nothing but chocolate."

Relieved, Hud sighed. "Thanks for doing this so quickly." He hung up. There was one set of prints he hadn't asked Liza to get for him. Lanny Rankin's.

Hud planned to get those himself tonight.

He picked up the phone and started calling the local bars on a hunch. The bartender at the second one Hud called said that Lanny was there.

"Try to keep him there. I'm buying," Hud said. "I'll be right down."

DANA WASN'T SURPRISED to hear tentative footfalls behind her and smell her sister's expensive perfume. Standing at the sink with her back to her sister, she closed her eyes, waiting for the next onslaught. Obviously, Jordan and Clay had sent Stacy in to convince her to change her mind.

"Dana," her sister said quietly. "I have to tell you something."

Dana kept her back turned to her sister. She'd planned on asking her sister point-blank what had happened that night five years ago with Hud. But quite frankly, she just wasn't up to the answer tonight.

"You can't just keep ignoring me. I'm your sister."

"Don't remind me," Dana said, finally giving up and turning to look at her.

Tears welled in Stacy's eyes, but she bit her lip to stem them, no doubt realizing that tears would only anger Dana more. Likewise another apology.

"I have to tell you the truth," Stacy said.

"Don't," Dana said. "I told you, I don't want to hear anything you have to say. I know they sent you in here to try to get me to change my mind."

"I didn't come in here to talk about the ranch," she said, and sounded surprised that Dana would think that. "I need to tell you about Hud."

Dana felt her face flush. "I'd rather talk about selling the ranch." She started to step past Stacy, but her sister touched her arm and whispered, "I lied."

Dana froze, her gaze leaping to Stacy's face.

Her sister nodded slowly, the tears in her eyes spilling over. "I didn't sleep with him," she whispered, and looked behind her as if afraid their brothers might be listening.

"What is this? Some ploy to get me to sell the ranch?" Dana couldn't believe how low her sister would stoop.

"This doesn't have anything to do with the ranch." Stacy shook her head, tears now spilling down her cheeks. "I have to tell you the truth, no matter what happens to me. I didn't want to do it."

Dana felt her pulse jump. "What are you talking

about?" she asked, remembering what Hud had said about Stacy not acting alone that night.

Stacy gripped her arm. "I didn't have a choice."

"You always have a choice," Dana said, keeping her voice down. "What happened that night?"

Stacy looked scared as she let go of Dana and glanced over her shoulder again.

"Don't move," Dana ordered, and walked to the doorway to the living room. "Leave," she said to Jordan and Clay. Clay got up at once but Jordan didn't move.

"We're not finished here," Jordan said angrily. "And I'm not leaving until this is settled. One way or the other."

"Stacy and I need to talk," Dana said, letting him believe she had to iron things out with her sister before she would give in on selling the ranch.

Clay was already heading for the door as Jordan reluctantly rose. Clay opened the front door then stopped. Dana saw why. Their father's pickup had just pulled into the yard.

"I'll be outside talking to Dad," Jordan said, and practically shoved Clay out the door.

What was their father doing here? Dana wondered as she hurried back to the kitchen. No doubt her siblings had commandeered his help to convince her to sell the ranch. Bastards.

Stacy had sat at the table, her head in her hands. Dana closed the kitchen door as she heard her brothers and their father talking out on the porch. It almost sounded as if Jordan and Angus were arguing.

What was that about? She'd find out soon enough, she feared. But right now she wanted some answers out of her sister.

Stacy looked up when Dana closed the kitchen door. "I'm so sorry."

"Don't start that again. Just tell me." Dana didn't sit. She stood, her arms folded across her chest to keep her hands from shaking, to keep from strangling Stacy. "Tell me *everything* and whatever you do, don't lie to me."

Stacy started to cry. "I'm telling you I didn't sleep with Hud, isn't that enough?"

"No. I need to know how he got there. Did he pick you up at the bar? Or did you pick him up?"

Stacy was crying harder. "I picked him up."

"How?" Hud swore he'd had only one drink. But she recalled hearing from people at the bar that night that he'd been falling-down drunk when he'd left with Stacy.

"I drugged him."

Dana stared at her sister in disbelief. "You drugged him!"

"I had to do it!" she cried. "Then before the drug could completely knock him out, I got him outside and into my car."

Dana could hear raised voices now coming from the living room. The three had brought their argument in out of the cold. But the fact barely registered. Stacy had admitted that she'd drugged Hud and taken him out to her car.

"I was to take him to my place," Stacy said, the words tumbling out with the tears. "I thought that was all I had to do. I didn't want to do it. I swear. But if I didn't…" She began to sob. Angus and Jordan were yelling at each other in the living room, the words incomprehensible.

"What did you do?" Dana demanded, moving to stand over her.

"I didn't know part of the plan was to make it look like we'd slept together until when you got there the next morning," Stacy cried. "I didn't want to hurt you."

Dana remembered the look of shock on Hud's and Stacy's faces when they'd seen her that morning. She'd thought it was from being caught. But now she recalled it was bewilderment, as well.

"Why tell me now?" Dana demanded. "Why not tell me five years ago before you ruined everything?"

"I couldn't. I was scared. I'm still scared, but I can't live like this anymore." Stacy looked up, her gaze meeting her sister's. The fear was as real as the anguish, Dana thought. "I've hated myself for what I did. No matter what happens to me now, I had to tell you. I couldn't live with what I did."

"What do you mean, no matter what happens to you now?"

Stacy shook her head. "I used to be afraid of going to jail, but even that is better than the hell I've been in these past years. I'm not strong like you. I couldn't stand up to them."

Them? "Jail?" Dana repeated. For just an instant she flashed again on the memory of Stacy's face that morning five years ago. Stacy had looked scared. Or was it trapped? "Are you telling me someone was threatening jail if you didn't go along with setting Hud up?"

The kitchen door banged open and Clay appeared, panicked and breathless. "It's Dad. I think he's having a heart attack!"

Chapter Eleven

Lanny Rankin was anything but happy to see Hud take the stool next to him at the bar.

The lawyer had two drinks in front of him and was clearly on his way to getting drunk.

"What do you want?" Lanny slurred.

"Just thought I'd have a drink." Hud signaled the bartender who brought him a draft beer from the tap. He took a drink and watched Lanny pick up his glass and down half of what appeared to be a vodka tonic.

"Bring Lanny another drink," Hud told the bartender.

Lanny shoved his glass away and picked up the second drink and downed it, as well, before stumbling to his feet. "Save your money, Marshal. I'm not drinking with you."

"I hope you're not driving," Hud said.

Lanny narrowed his gaze. "You'd love to arrest me, wouldn't you? She tell you about us? Is that what you're doing here? Tell you we're engaged? Well, it's all a lie. All a lie." His face turned mean. "She's all yours. But then again, she always has been, hasn't she?"

He turned and stumbled out the back door.

Hud quickly pulled an evidence bag from his jacket pocket and slipped both of the glasses with Lanny's prints on them inside. He paid his bill and went outside to make sure Lanny wasn't driving anywhere.

Lanny was walking down the street toward his condo.

Hud watched him for a moment, then headed for his office. If he hurried, he could get both glasses ready for Liza to take to the crime lab in the morning.

He wondered if Liza had any trouble getting the Cardwell clan's fingerprints.

Just the thought of the family meeting going on at the ranch made him uneasy. Maybe he would swing by there later.

Back at his office, Hud got the drink glasses with Lanny's prints ready and locked the box in the evidence room with the .38 Liza had taken from Angus's pickup.

As he started to leave, he remembered the list of registered owners of .38 pistols in the county Liza had left on his desk. The list was long. He thumbed through it, his mind more on the family meeting going on at the Cardwell Ranch than the blur of names.

This list had probably been a waste of time. There was a very good chance that Liza had already found the murder weapon and it was now locked in the evidence room. By tomorrow, Hud worried that he would be arresting Angus Cardwell. He didn't even want to think what that would do to Dana.

He folded the list and stuck it in his pocket. As he started to leave, planning to go out and check on Dana, no matter how angry it made her, he heard the call come in on the scanner. An ambulance was needed at the Cardwell Ranch.

"How's Dad?" Dana asked when she found Jordan and Clay in the waiting room at Bozeman Deaconess Hospital. She hadn't been able to get any information at the desk on her way in and the roads down the canyon had been icy, traffic slow.

Clay shrugged, looking miserable and nervous in a corner chair.

"The doctor's in with him," Jordan said, pacing the small room, clearly agitated.

"Where's Stacy?" she asked. Earlier Dana had glanced through the open living room doorway and seen her father on the floor, Jordan leaning over him. She'd let out a cry and run into the living room. Behind her she'd heard Clay on the phone calling for an ambulance on the kitchen phone.

It wasn't until later, after the ambulance had rushed Angus to the hospital and Dana began looking for her keys to follow in her pickup, that she'd realized Stacy was gone.

"When did Stacy leave?" Dana asked, glancing around.

Both brothers shrugged. "After I called 911 I turned around and I noticed your back door was open, and when I went out to follow the ambulance, I saw that her car was already gone."

"Stacy just left?" Dana asked in disbelief. Why would her sister do that without a word? Especially with their father in the next room on the floor unconscious?

Stacy's words echoed in Dana's ears. "No matter what happens to me now." Was it possible her sister was in danger because she'd told Dana the truth?

Dana couldn't worry about that now. "What were you and Dad fighting about?" she asked Jordan.

"This is not my fault," Jordan snapped.

"I'll get us some coffee," Clay said, and practically bolted from the room.

Jordan and Angus couldn't have been arguing about the sale of the ranch. Her father had said he wasn't going to take sides, but he did add that he felt the ranch was too much for Dana to handle on her own.

"Sell it, baby girl," he'd said to Dana. "It's an albatross around your neck. Your mother would understand."

"That's how you felt about the ranch, Dad, not me," she'd told him.

But he'd only shook his head and said, "Sell it. Some day you'll be glad you did. And it will keep peace in the family." He'd always been big on keeping peace in the family. Except when it came to his wandering ways.

"I heard the two of you yelling at each other in the other room," Dana said. "What was going on?"

Jordan stopped pacing to look at her. "The stupid fool thinks I killed Ginger."

Ginger Adams, the woman whose wrist he'd broken in an argument. The woman who'd ended up in the Cardwell Ranch well. The floor under her seemed to give way. "Why would Dad think that?"

"Who the hell knows? He's always been a crazy old fool."

Dana bristled. "Dad is a lot of things. Crazy isn't one of them."

Jordan's look was lethal. "Don't play games with me. Dad told me you knew about me and Ginger. What's crazy is that he thinks I took his gun."

She stared at him. "The missing .38?"

"Turns out it wasn't missing," Jordan said. "It was under the seat of his pickup and now the cops have it. He thinks I took the gun and then when Ginger's body was found, I put it under the pickup seat to frame him for her murder."

Dana felt her heart drop to her feet. Hadn't Hud told her that the gun was used in both Ginger's murder and Judge Randolph's? What motive could Jordan have to kill the judge, though? "Jordan, you didn't—"

Jordan let out a curse. "You think I'm a murderer, too?" His angry gaze bore into her. "Not only a murderer, but I framed my own father, as well?" He let out a scornful laugh and shook his head at her. "I guess I didn't realize how little you and Dad thought of me until now." He turned and stormed out of the waiting room, almost colliding with Clay who was carrying a cardboard tray with three cups of coffee on it.

What bothered Dana was the guilty look in Jordan's eyes before he left.

"Thanks," she said as she took one of the foam cups of hot coffee Clay offered her and stepped out in the hallway, fighting the terrible fear that had settled in the pit of her stomach.

At the sound of footfalls, she turned to see her father's doctor coming toward her. She froze. All she could think about was the day of her mother's accident and the doctor coming down the hall to give her the news. She couldn't lose another parent.

Hud spotted Dana the moment he walked into the Bozeman hospital emergency room waiting area. Relief washed through him, making his legs feel boneless. She was all right.

She was talking to the doctor and he could see the concern in her face. He waited, studying her body language, fear closing his throat.

Her shoulders seemed to slump, and he saw her hand go to her mouth then brush at her tears. She was smiling and nodding, and Hud knew that whatever had happened, there had been good news.

She saw him then. He tried not to read anything into her expression. For a moment there she'd actually looked glad to see him.

She said something to the doctor and walked toward him. He caught his breath. Sometimes he forgot how beautiful she was. Her eyes were bright, cheeks flushed from crying, her face glowing with the good news the doctor had given her.

"Dana?" he said as she closed the distance. "What's happened?"

"Dad. He had a heart attack." Her voice broke. "But the doctor says he's stable now." She looked up at him, tears in her eyes. "I have to talk to you."

"Okay." He couldn't help but sound tentative. She hadn't wanted to lay eyes on him—let alone talk to him. "Did you want to talk at the office or—"

She glanced around, making him wonder where her brothers were. And Stacy. "Could we go back to your place?"

His place? "Sure." Whatever she wanted to talk to him about was serious. "You want to follow me?"

She shook her head. "I need to stop by Stacy's. You go on. I'll meet you there."

Whatever that was about he didn't want to know. But at the same time, he didn't like the idea of her going alone.

"I could go with you," he said.

She shook her head again. "I'll meet you at the cabin you're renting." She knew where he lived?

"I'll see you soon," he said.

She nodded distractedly. "Soon."

As he got into his patrol car, he tried not to even guess what this was about. But he had a bad feeling it could have something to do with her father's gun now locked in his evidence cabinet at the office.

The night was clear, stars bright dots in the crystalline cold blue of the sky overhead. Snow covered everything. It sat in puffy white clumps in the branches of the trees and gleamed in the starlight like zillions of diamonds on the open field across the road.

The drive home was interminable. He kept looking in his rearview mirror, hoping to see the headlights of Dana's pickup. She'd said she needed to make a stop by Stacy's. He wished he'd asked how long she might be.

He parked in front of the cabin, the night darker than the inside of a gunny sack. In the cabin, he straightened up, built a fire and put on some coffee.

A wind had come up. It whirled the light fresh snow in a blizzard of white outside the window. He should have insisted she ride with him as upset as she was. But he'd had no desire to go to Stacy's, and Dana hadn't wanted him along.

The sky over the tops of the pines darkened as another storm moved in. He'd forgotten how dark it could be in the dead of winter.

He watched the road—what little of it he could see through the swirling snow. Surprisingly he really had missed winters while in Los Angeles. Missed the seasons that were so dramatic in Montana. Especially winter. Two feet of snow could fall overnight. It wasn't unusual to wake up to the silence and the cold and know that something had changed during the night.

Dana should be here by now. He began to worry, thinking about what he'd heard in her voice. She'd been upset about her father. But that hadn't been all of it. Something had happened. Something she needed to talk to him about. But first she had to see Stacy.

Hud was to the point where he was ready to go looking for her when he spotted headlights through the drifting snow.

She pulled in beside his patrol car and got out, seeming to hesitate. She was wearing a red fleece jacket, her dark hair tucked up under a navy stocking cap. A few strands whipped around her face as she stared at the cabin.

He opened the front door and stood looking at her. A small drift had formed just outside the door and now ran across the porch. The steps down had disappeared, the snow smooth and deep.

He met her gaze through dancing snowflakes, then reached for the shovel. But before he could clean off the steps, she was coming up them, all hesitation gone.

To his utter shock, she rushed to him. He took her in his arms, now truly afraid.

"I'm sorry." Her words were barely audible over the howl of the wind across the roof. "I'm so sorry."

He held her, his heart in his throat. He hugged her to him, breathing in the smell of her. God, how he'd missed that scent. But what could she possibly be sorry about?

Holding her felt so good, he hated it when she stepped from his arms and went inside the cabin. He followed, closing the door to the wind and snow.

She had walked to the fireplace. When she turned, he saw the tears. Dana crying. He could count on one hand the times he'd seen that. His fear escalated.

"Whatever it is, I'll help you," he said, wanting to hold her again but afraid to step toward her.

She let out a laugh at his words and shook her head. Her face was flushed, her eyes bright. "I haven't killed anyone. Although it did cross my mind." She sobered, her gaze locked on his. "I talked to my sister."

His heart dislodged from his throat and dropped to his stomach.

She jerked her cap from her head, shaking off the snow as her hair fell around her shoulders. "She told me everything."

He didn't move—didn't breathe. He'd told himself that he'd come back here to learn everything that had happened that night but now he wasn't so sure he wanted to know.

"You were right. She lied. She was sent to the bar to drug you, get you out of there before the drug completely knocked you out and take you to her place. It was just as you suspected—" her voice broke, eyes shimmering with tears "—nothing happened. You *were* set up." A tear trailed down her cheek. "*We* were set up."

It took him a moment. So it had been just as he'd believed in his heart. No matter how drunk he might have been, he wouldn't have bedded Dana's sister or any other woman for that matter. He'd known it. And yet he'd feared that for that night, he'd lost his mind and his way.

"I'm so sorry I didn't believe you. That I didn't even give you a chance to explain."

He found himself shaking with relief and anger as he stepped to Dana and pulled her into his arms again. "I couldn't have explained it. That's why I left. I thought it would be easier on you if you never had to see me again."

"But you came back."

"Thanks to your sister."

Dana raised her head to look into his face. "Stacy sent you the note?"

He nodded. "I found the birthday card she mailed you, the one you'd thrown away. It was under the box of chocolates. I recognized the handwriting."

"So she was responsible for you coming back." She leaned into him again.

He rested his chin on the top of her head. Her hair felt like silk. Her body softened against his. He could feel his heart pounding. Nothing had happened that night. He closed his eyes and pulled Dana even closer, wishing he could turn back the clock. These wasted years apart felt like a chasm between them.

"I SHOULD HAVE trusted you." Dana hadn't believed that he'd been set up, that nothing had happened. She hadn't loved him enough. If she'd trusted him, if she'd even let him tell her his side of the story...

"Hey, there were times I didn't believe in my innocence myself," he said, holding her at arm's length to look into her face. "I thought maybe I'd lost my mind. Or worse, that I was about to become my father."

The blaze in the fireplace popped and cracked, the flames throwing shadows on the walls. She could hear the wind howling outside. Snow hit the windows, sticking, then melting down. Inside, the fire burned. Outside, the storm raged, the snow piling deeper and deeper.

She looked up into Hud's eyes and saw nothing but

love. All her anger at herself and her sister melted like the snow at the windows.

She covered one of his hands with her own, turning the palm up to kiss the warm center. She heard him let out a breath. Their eyes locked, the heat of his look warming her to her core.

"Oh, Hud," she breathed. She heard his breath catch, saw the spark of desire catch fire in his eyes. "I've never stopped wanting you."

He groaned and took her with a kiss, his mouth capturing hers as he tugged her even closer to him. She could feel the pounding of his heart, felt her body melt into his.

"I didn't want to live without you," he said as he pulled back. "The only way I was able to get through the past five years was to believe that you still loved me."

She touched his cheek, then cupped his face in her hands and kissed him, teasing the tip of his tongue with her own.

He moaned against her lips, then swept her up into his arms, carrying her to the rug in front of the fire.

She pulled him down to her. His kiss was gentle and slow, as if they had all night to make love. They did.

"You are so beautiful," he whispered, his hand trailing down the length of her neck. He leaned in to kiss her, his hand cupping her breast, and she groaned with the exquisite pleasure of his touch.

The fire warmed her skin as he slowly unbuttoned her blouse and pressed his lips to the hard nipple of one breast, then the other. She arched against him, her fingers working at the buttons of his shirt.

Their clothes began to pile up in the corner as the fire popped and crackled, the heat shimmering over their naked bodies, damp with perspiration and wet warm kisses.

Their lovemaking was all heat and fire, a frenzied rush of passion that left them both breathless.

Hud held her, smoothing her hair under his hand, his eyes locked with hers as their bodies cooled.

Dana looked into his eyes, still stunned by the powerful chemistry that arced between them. Nothing had killed it. Not the pain, not the years.

She curled into his strong arms and slept. On this night, no wind woke her with a premonition. She had no warning what the day would bring. If only for one night, she felt safe. She felt loved.

Chapter Twelve

Dana drove to Bozeman to the hospital before daylight the next morning. Her father was still in stable condition, sedated and sleeping. She peeked in on him and then drove back to Big Sky and the shop.

She spent the quiet early morning before the shop opened unloading the latest shipment of fabric and pricing it. Unfortunately the task wasn't difficult enough that it kept her from thinking about last night with Hud.

She wasn't surprised when she heard a knock at the back door and saw him.

"Good morning," he said, but his look said there was nothing good about it.

"Good morning." She couldn't believe how glad she was to see him. She'd never stopped being in love with him and even when she hadn't known the truth, he'd been much harder to hate in the flesh than he'd been in her memory.

He pulled off his hat to rake his fingers through his thick sandy-blond hair. It was a nervous habit. She felt a jolt, wondering what he had to be nervous about.

"You left before I woke up this morning," he said.

She nodded sheepishly. "I needed to think about some things and go see my father."

"Think about some things?"

She sighed, picking up a bolt of fabric and carrying it over to its spot on the wall. "About last night."

"You're afraid I'm going to hurt you again?" he asked behind her.

She turned and looked up into his wonderful face. "Do you blame me? You left me for five years."

"But if you believe that Stacy was finally telling the truth—"

"I do, but..."

"You still can't forget," he said softly.

She reached up to cup his rough jaw. He hadn't taken the time to shave. Instead he'd rushed right over here. "Last night made me feel all those old wonderful feelings again that we shared."

"You know I came back here because of you. Because I still love you. I'm sorry I didn't come back sooner. I should never have left."

"You thought you'd lost everything, your career—"

"Losing you is what devastated my life, Dana. It took a while to get my head on straight."

She nodded. "I just need to take it slow." She dropped her hand and turned her back to him. Otherwise, she would be in his arms and Hilde would find them between racks of fabric making love on the hardwood floor when she came in.

"We can take it as slow as you need," he said. "Just don't push me away again." He pulled her around to face him and into his arms, kissing her until she was breathless.

She leaned into his strong, hard body and rested her cheek against his chest, his jacket open, his cotton shirt warm and soft. She could hear his heart beating fast and realized she'd scared him with her disappearing act this morning.

"I'm sorry I took off this morning," she said against his chest.

He hugged her tighter. "I know you're worried about your dad. And Stacy." He sighed. "Dana, I found out that your brother Jordan got into town the day of your birthday."

She pulled back a little to look at him. "He lied about that, too?"

Hud nodded. "I'm sorry, but I think he's responsible for what happened at the well the night before last, and if he is, I'm going to have to arrest him."

She made a sound deep down in her throat as she realized that most of her family could end up in jail the way things were going. "Hud, you and I both know that if Jordan had found those bones in the well he'd have covered them with fifteen feet of dirt and never given them another thought."

Blood was thicker than water. But this was Hud and the truth was the truth.

"And don't try to make me sound so noble," she said. "I didn't tell you everything." She told him about going to see her father about his .38, then about finding Jordan searching the ranch house and finally that Jordan and her father had been arguing just before Angus Cardwell's collapse. "Is Dad's .38 the murder weapon?" she asked, her heart in her throat.

"We don't know yet. But I'm worried. I'd like you to drive out with me to talk to Stacy."

"When I stopped by her place last night on the way to your cabin," Dana said, "she wasn't there."

"Maybe she's come back. Or maybe she left something behind that will give us an idea of where she's gone. If what she told you is true, then someone was behind setting me up. I need to know who it was. And why. If she was being threatened with jail, then, Dana, I have a pretty good idea who was behind it. I just have to prove it. I need your help. Your sister might open up if we're there together."

As if on cue, Hilde came in the back door on a gust of wind. She looked surprised to see Dana at work so early and even more surprised to see Hud. She looked from one to the other, her gaze finally settling on Dana. She smiled, obviously seeing what Dana had hoped to keep a secret.

"Hello, Hud," Hilde said.

"Nice to see you again, Hilde," he said. "I just came by to steal your partner for a little while."

"Be my guest," Hilde said, giving Dana a meaningful look.

"We're just going to look for Stacy," Dana said. "It's a long story."

"I'm sure it is," Hilde said, still smiling.

Dana groaned inwardly. Her friend knew her too well. Hilde had seen the glow in her cheeks this morning, the sparkle in her eye. Hud had always been able to put it there. "Let me get my coat."

SNOW WAS PILED HIGH on each side of the highway. Beside it, the river gurgled blue-green under a thick skin of transparent ice.

"You're sure she said 'jail'?"

Dana nodded. "She looked scared, Hud. I guess that's why I believed her. She seemed to think she was in danger."

"I think she set me up to keep me away from Judge Randolph's house that night," Hud said. "It's the only thing that makes any sense."

"You think Stacy had something to do with the judge's murder?"

"Look at the evidence, Dana. The judge was murdered the same night Stacy drugged me at the bar and made sure I wasn't the one who responded to the call about shots fired at the Randolph house. Instead, my father took the call. Or at least that's the story."

"What are you saying, Hud? You can't seriously think your own father was behind it."

"Stacy was being threatened with jail, isn't that what she said? Now she seems to be running scared." Hud glanced over at Dana. "I think she's afraid because she knows the truth about that night."

"You can't believe your father killed the judge."

He sighed. "I don't know what I believe. The judge had Alzheimer's. He was about to be asked to step down from the bench. Unless he had hard evidence against Brick, then the judge wasn't really a threat."

"So then your father had no motive."

"So it would seem," Hud said as he turned off Jackrabbit Road onto Cameron Bridge Road.

"Maybe the fact that the judge was killed that night was just a coincidence," Dana said.

He wished he could believe that.

Stacy was in between husbands right now and living in the house she was awarded in the divorce settlement from Emery Chambers. The divorce that, according to Lanny, Hud had helped her get.

"It has to be about more than just splitting us up. Who would care enough to go to all that trouble?" Hud said.

"Stacy for one."

"What about Lanny?" He saw Dana shiver. "What?"

"When he heard you were back in town he was very angry."

Hud rubbed his still sore jaw. "I noticed."

He drove a few miles down the river before turning into a graveled yard in front of a large older house. There were no fresh tracks in the snow. No one had been in or out since Dana had stopped by last night.

Through the windows in the garage, Dana could see that Stacy's car was still gone.

"Let's give it a try anyway," Hud said, and opened his door.

Dana followed him up the unshoveled walk and waited while he knocked. Through the trees, he could see an open hole in the ice on the Gallatin River, the water a deep, clear green. The air smelled of fresh snow and cottonwoods.

He knocked again, then turned to see Dana bend to pick up something from the snow beside the front step. A black glove.

"It's one of the cashmere gloves my sister was wearing yesterday when she came to the house."

His mouth went dry. Stacy had come back here after the family meeting, then left again?

He reached for the doorknob. It turned in his hand, the door swinging into the empty living room. He signaled Dana to wait as he moved quickly through the house, weapon drawn. Something about the empty feel of the house made him fear he wasn't going to find Stacy. At least not alive.

Upstairs, the bedroom looked as if a bomb had gone off in it.

"It's clear," he called down to Dana.

"My God," Dana said as she saw the room, the drawers hanging open and empty, clothes hangers on the floor or cocked at an odd angle as if the clothing had been ripped from them.

She moved to the closet and touched one of the dresses that had been left behind. "She's either running scared or someone wants us to believe she is."

He nodded, having already come to the same conclusion. If Stacy was as scared as Dana had said and decided to blow town, she would have grabbed just what she needed. Or left without anything. She wouldn't have tried to take everything. Or would she? Maybe she wasn't planning to ever come back.

"Who are you calling?" Dana asked, sounding worried.

"I'm going to have some deputies search the wooded area behind the house," he said. "Just as a precaution."

Dana nodded, but he saw that she feared the same thing he did. That Stacy had been telling the truth. Her life had been in danger.

While they waited for the deputies to arrive and search the woods around the house, they searched the house again, looking for anything that would give them a clue.

They found nothing.

"Do you want me to take you home?" Hud offered.

Dana shook her head. "Please just take me back to the shop."

"Hilde's working with you all day, right?" Hud asked.

"Yes, I'll be fine. We both have work to do. And maybe Stacy will contact me."

He nodded. "I just don't want you alone. Especially now with your sister missing." His cell phone rang.

It was Roadside Café owner and former cook Leroy Perkins. "You were asking about Ginger's old roommate the other day," Leroy said. "I finally remembered her name. Zoey Skinner. I asked around. You'd be surprised how much cooks know about what's going on. The good ones anyway can cook *and* listen." He laughed. "Zoey's working at a café in West Yellowstone. The Lonesome Pine Café."

"Thanks." Hud broke the connection and looked over at Dana. "I need to go up to West Yellowstone. I'll be back before you get off work." He hesitated. "I was hoping we could have dinner together."

"Is that what you were hoping?" she asked with a smile.

"Actually, I was hoping you would come back to the cabin tonight. I could pick up some steaks… But maybe that's moving too fast for you." He gave her an innocent grin. "I can't stand having you out of my sight."

"I told you I'll be safe at the shop," she said.

"I wasn't thinking of your safety."

She met his gaze and felt that slow burn in her belly. "Dinner at your cabin sounds wonderful. I just need to go home and feed Joe."

"I'll stop off and feed Joe and then pick you up at the shop," he suggested.

She knew he just didn't want her going back to the ranch house. The thought of it did make her uncomfortable, but it was still her home—a home she was fighting to keep. "I at least need to go out to the ranch and pick up some clothes. Why don't you meet me there?"

She could see he didn't like that idea.

"I'll be waiting for you at your house," he said.

She didn't argue. She felt safe believing that no one would attack either her or Hud in broad daylight. But once it got dark, she would think again of the doll in the well and remember that she was more than likely the target. It chilled her to the bone to think of what could have happened if she hadn't gone up there with the shotgun.

"Just be careful, okay?" Hud said.

"You, too." She touched his cheek and ached to be in his arms again. Whose fool idea was it to take things slow?

As HUD PULLED into the lake house, he found his father shoveling snow.

"I don't see you for years then I see you twice in two days?" Brick said with a shake of his head as Hud got out of the patrol car.

Brick set aside the snow shovel he'd been using on the walk. "I suppose you want to talk. It's warmer inside."

Without a word, Hud followed.

"I could make some coffee," Brick said, shrugging out of his coat at the door.

"No need." Hud stood just inside, not bothering to take off his boots or his coat. He wouldn't be staying long.

Brick slumped down onto the bench by the door and worked off his boots. He seemed even smaller today in spite of all the winter clothing he wore. He also seemed stoved-up as if just getting his boots off hurt him but that he was trying hard not to let Hud see it.

"So what's on your mind?" Brick said. "If it's about the robbery again—"

"It's about Stacy Cardwell."

Brick looked up from unlacing his boots, cocking his head as if he hadn't heard right. "What about her?"

"She admitted that she helped set me up the night the judge was killed five years ago."

Brick lifted a brow. "And you believe her?" He let his boot drop to the floor with a thud as he rose and walked stocking-footed toward the kitchen.

"She said she did it so she wouldn't have to go to jail," he said, raising his voice as he spoke to his father's retreating back.

Brick didn't turn, didn't even acknowledge that he'd heard. Hud could hear him in the kitchen running water. He stood for a moment, the snow on his boots melting onto the stone entryway. "Did you hear me?"

"I heard you." Brick appeared in the kitchen doorway, an old-fashioned percolator coffeepot in his hand. "I'm going to make coffee. You might as well come on in. You can't hurt the floor." He turned his back, disappearing into the kitchen again.

"Well?" Hud said after he joined him. The kitchen was neater than it had been yesterday. He wondered if his father had cleaned it because of Hud's visit.

"Sit down," Brick said, but Hud remained standing.

"Were you the one behind coercing Stacy to set me up?" Hud demanded.

Brick turned to look at him. "Why would I do that?"

"To keep me from marrying Dana."

"Falling for Dana Cardwell was the only smart thing you ever did. Why wouldn't I want you to marry her?"

"Then you did it to get to the judge. You just wanted

me out of the way so you used me, not caring what it would do to my life."

His father frowned and turned back to the stove. The coffee began to perk, filling the small house with a rich, warm aroma that reminded Hud of all the mornings his father had gotten up to make coffee over the years, especially when Hud's mother was sick.

"Why would Stacy make up something like that?" Hud asked.

"Why does Stacy do half the things she does?" Brick turned, still frowning. "She said she did it to keep herself out of jail?" He shook his head. "I never picked her up for anything. Maybe she did something she thought she would be arrested for and someone found out about it."

"You mean, blackmail?" Hud asked. Clearly he hadn't considered that.

Brick nodded. "Hadn't thought of that, huh? Something else you probably haven't considered is who else had the power to make a threat like that stick." Brick smiled and nodded. "That's right. Judge Raymond Randolph."

Hud felt the air rush out of him. "That doesn't make any sense. Why would the judge get her to keep me out of the picture?" A thought struck him. "Unless the judge wanted to make sure you responded to the call."

His father raised a brow. "You think he staged it so I'd show up and then what? He'd kill me?" Brick shook his head. "I wouldn't put it past him. Especially since he was losing his mind. But that would mean it backfired on him if that were the case and, no matter what you think, I didn't kill the judge."

"It seems more likely that I was set up so someone could use it as a way to get to the judge," Hud said.

"I agree. But you're just barking up the wrong tree if you think it was me. No matter how strongly I felt about you not staying in law enforcement, I would never set you up to get rid of you. I'm sorry you believe I would."

"I hope that's true," Hud said, and realized he meant it. He started for the door.

"Sure you don't want some coffee? It's almost ready."

"No thanks."

"Son."

Hud stopped at the door and turned to look back at his father.

Brick stood silhouetted against the frozen lake through this front window. "Be careful. It sounds like you've got at least one killer out there. Someone who thought they'd gotten away with murder. It's easier to kill after the first time, they say." His father turned back to his coffee.

IN BETWEEN CUSTOMERS, Dana told Hilde about everything else that had happened, including Stacy's confession—and disappearance.

"I can't believe this," Hilde said. "I mean, I do believe it. I never thought Hud would ever betray you. He just isn't that kind of man."

"Why didn't I see that?" Dana said, still feeling guilty and ashamed she hadn't given the man she loved a chance to even explain.

"Because you were too close to it," her friend said. "Any woman would have reacted the same way. If I would have found my man in bed with another woman, I would have shot first and asked questions later."

Dana smiled, knowing that Hilde was just trying to make her feel better.

"Oh, darn," Hilde said.

"What is it?"

"Mrs. Randolph. She left her fabric package."

Dana laughed. "She came back to the shop again? Don't tell me. She was still looking for the perfect blue thread to match those slacks of hers."

"No," Hilde said on a sigh. "This time she bought fabric for some aprons she was making for some charity event. She said you were going to help her with it?"

Dana groaned. Had she volunteered to make aprons? "Let me run it over to her. I need to find out what I've gotten myself into this time."

"Are you sure? Didn't Hud say that you weren't to leave here alone?"

Dana shook her head at her friend. "I'm just going up the canyon as far as the Randolph house. I will be back in twenty minutes tops. And, anyway, you have bookkeeping to do. It makes more sense for me to go since you're the one with the head for figures."

Hilde laughed. "You just don't want to do this. Can't fool me." She handed her the package. "Good luck. Who knows what Kitty Randolph will talk you into before you get back."

"She always tells me how close she and my mother were and how much I look like my mother and how my mother would love that I'm working on fundraisers with her now."

"You're just a girl who can't say no," Hilde joked.

"That's probably why I agreed to have dinner at Hud's cabin tonight." She grinned at her friend on her way out.

The highway had been plowed and sanded in the worst areas so the drive to Kitty Randolph's was no problem. It felt good to get out for a while.

Dana hadn't been completely honest, though, with her friend. There was another reason she wanted to see Mrs. Randolph. She wanted to ask her about something she'd heard that morning from one of the customers.

Nancy Harper had come in to buy drapery fabric and had mentioned seeing Stacy last night.

"What time was this?" Dana had asked, trying not to sound too interested and get the gossip mill going.

"Must have been about nine," Nancy said. "She drove past. I saw her brake in front of Kitty Randolph's house." Nancy smiled. "Is your sister helping with the clinic fundraiser? I knew you were, but I was a little surprised Stacy had volunteered. She's never shown much interest in that sort of thing, not after that one she helped with. And this fundraiser is going to involve cooking and sewing."

Dana had joined Nancy in a chuckle while cringing inside at everyone's perception of her sister. "You're right, that doesn't sound much like my sister."

"Well, you know Kitty. She can be very persuasive."

"You're sure it was Stacy?" Dana had asked, convinced Nancy had to be mistaken. Stacy had helped with one fundraiser years ago while she was between husbands. By the end of the event, Stacy wasn't speaking to Kitty. The two had stayed clear of each other ever since from what Dana could tell.

"Oh, it was Stacy, all right," Nancy said. "I didn't see her get out of her car because my view was blocked by the trees. But I saw her behind the wheel and I recognized the way she drives. She really does drive too fast for road conditions." Her smile said it was too bad Stacy wasn't more like Dana.

As Dana drove past Nancy Harper's house and parked in front of the Randolph house, the only other house on the dead-end road, she wondered again why Stacy would have come here last night. If indeed she did.

The double garage doors to Kitty's house were closed and there were no visible windows so she could see if Kitty was home or not. Getting out, she walked up the freshly shoveled steps and rang the doorbell.

No answer. She rang the bell again and thought she heard a thud from inside the house. Her first thought was that the elderly woman had been hurrying to the door and fallen.

"Mrs. Randolph?" she called, and knocked on the door. She tried the knob. The door opened.

Dana had expected to see the poor woman lying on the floor writhing in pain. But she saw no one. "Hello?" she called.

Another thud. This one coming from upstairs.

"Mrs. Randolph?" she called as she climbed the stairs. "Kitty?"

Still no answer.

At the top of the stairs she heard a sound coming from down the hall. A series of small thumps. One of the doors was partially open, the sound coming from inside.

She hurried down the hall, her mind racing as she shoved the door all the way open and stepped inside.

At once, she saw that the room was the master bedroom, large and plush, done in reds and golds.

At first she didn't see Kitty Randolph on the floor in front of the closet.

Dana realized why the woman hadn't heard her calling for her. Kitty Randolph was on her hands and knees, muttering to herself as she dug in the back of the huge closet. One shoe after another came flying out to land behind the woman.

Dana stumbled back, bumping into the door as one shoe almost hit her.

Kitty Randolph froze. Her frightened expression was chilling as she turned and saw Dana.

"I'm sorry if I frightened you," Dana said, afraid she would give the elderly woman a heart attack. "I rang the bell, then tried the door when I heard a sound..." She noticed the bruise on Kitty's cheek.

The older woman's hand went to it. "I am so clumsy." She looked from Dana to the floor covered with shoes.

Dana followed her gaze. The bedroom carpet was littered with every color and kind of shoe imaginable from shoes the judge had worn sole-bare to out-of-date sandals and pumps covered with dust.

"I was just cleaning out the closet," Kitty said awkwardly, trying to get to her feet. She had a shoe box clutched under one arm. "My husband was a pack rat. Saved everything. And I'm just as bad."

Dana reached a hand out to help her, but the older woman waved it away.

As Kitty rose, Dana saw the woman pick up a high-heeled shoe from the floor, looking at it as if surprised to see it.

She tossed it back into the closet and turned her attention to Dana. "I see you brought my fabric."

Dana had forgotten all about it. Embarrassed by frightening the woman, she thrust the bag at her.

Kitty took it, studying Dana as she put the shoe box she held onto the clean surface of the vanity. "How foolish of me to leave my package at your shop. You really shouldn't have gone out of your way to bring it to me."

"It was no trouble. I wanted to see you anyway to ask you if my sister stopped by to see you last night."

The older woman frowned. "What would give you that idea?"

"Nancy Harper said she saw Stacy drive down the road toward your house."

"That woman must have no time to do anything but look out the window," Kitty Randolph said irritably. "If your sister drove down here, I didn't see her." She turned to place the fabric package next to the shoe box on the vanity. She fiddled with the lid of the shoe box for a moment. "Why would Stacy come to see me?"

"I have no idea. I'd hoped you might." A lot of people drove cars like her sister's and it had been dark out. "Nancy Harper must have been mistaken," Dana said, glancing again at the shoes on the floor. "Can I help you with these?"

"No, you have better things to do, I'm sure," Kitty said as she stepped over the shoes and took Dana's arm, turning her toward the door. "Thank you again for bringing my fabric. You really shouldn't have."

It wasn't until Dana was driving away that she remembered the high heel Kitty Randolph had thrown back into the closet. She couldn't imagine the woman wearing anything with a heel that high. Or that color, either.

But then, who knew what Kitty Randolph had been like when she was young.

At the turn back onto Highway 191, Dana dialed her friend. "Hilde?"

"Is everything all right?"

"Fine. Listen, I was just thinking. I'm so close to Bozeman I thought I'd drive down and see my dad. I called and he's doing better. They said I could see him. Unless it's so busy there that you need me?"

"Go see your dad," Hilde said without hesitation. "I can handle things here. Anyway, it's slowed down this afternoon. I was thinking that if it doesn't pick up, I might close early."

"Do," Dana said. "We've made more than our quota for the month in the past few days."

"Tell your dad hello for me."

Dana hung up. She did want to see her father, but she also hoped that Stacy had been by to see him.

But when she reached the hospital, her father was still groggy, just as he'd been that morning. She didn't bring up anything that might upset him and only stayed for a few minutes as per the nurse's instructions.

As Dana was leaving, she stopped at the nurses' station to inquire about her father's visitors.

"Your brother was here," the nurse said. "That's the only visitor he's had today."

"My brother?"

"The skinny one."

Clay. That meant that neither Jordan nor Stacy had been here.

"But there have been a lot of calls checking on his condition," the nurse added.

Dana thanked her and headed back toward the ranch.

She wanted to get a change of clothing if she was going to be staying at Hud's again tonight.

She knew she was being silly, wanting to slow things down. She loved Hud. He loved her. They'd spent too much time apart as it was. So why was she so afraid?

Because she didn't believe they could just pick up where they'd left off. They'd both changed. Didn't they need to get to know each other again—everything else that was going on aside?

And yet even as she thought it, she knew that the chemistry they shared was still there as well as the love. She knew what was holding her back. This investigation. Until Ginger Adams's killer was caught, Dana didn't feel safe. And she had no idea why.

As she drove down the road to the ranch house, she saw the tracks in the snow. Hud would have driven in to feed Joe. But there was at least another set of tire tracks. Someone else had been to the house today.

ZOEY SKINNER WAS filling salt and pepper shakers during the slow time between lunch and dinner in the large West Yellowstone café.

Hud couldn't say he remembered her. But she wasn't the kind of woman who stood out. Quite the opposite, she tended to blend into her surroundings.

The café was empty this time of the day, with it being a little too early yet for dinner.

He took a chair at a table in a far corner and glanced out the window at the walls of snow.

The town had changed over the years since the advent of snowmobiles. Where once winters were off season and most of the businesses closed and lay dormant under deep snowbanks, now the town literally buzzed with activity.

A large group of snowmobilers in their one-piece suits, heavy boots and dark-shielded helmets roared past in a cloud of blue smoke and noise.

"Coffee?"

He turned to find Zoey Skinner standing over his table, a menu tucked under her arm, a coffeepot in one hand and a cup in the other.

"Please. Cream and sugar."

Zoey was bone-thin, her arms corded from years of waiting tables, her legs webbed with blue veins although she was no more than in her early forties.

She filled the cup, produced both sugar and cream packages from her apron pocket. "Menu?"

He shook his head. "Just coffee, thanks. And if you have a moment—" he said, flashing his badge "—I'm Marshal Hudson Savage. I'd like to ask you a few questions."

She stared down at the badge, then slowly lifted her gaze to his. "This is about Ginger, isn't it?"

He nodded.

She dropped into the chair opposite his, her body suddenly limp as a rag doll's. She put the coffeepot on the table and cradled her head in her hands as she looked at him.

"I always wondered what happened to her," she said. "I heard that she'd been found in that well and I couldn't believe it."

"When was the last time you saw her?" he asked, taking out his notebook and pen.

"The night she left to get married."

"She was getting *married?*"

"Well, not right away." Zoey's face softened. "Ginger was so happy and excited."

"Who was she marrying?"

He saw her face close. "She said it was better I didn't know. Better that no one knew until they were married."

He studied the small, mousy-haired waitress. "Why was it so important to keep it a secret?"

"Ginger was afraid of jinxing it, you know? She'd been disappointed so many times before."

He didn't believe that for a minute. "Was it possible this man was married?" He saw the answer in Zoey's face. Bull's-eye. "So maybe that's why she didn't want anyone to know. Maybe he hadn't told his wife he was leaving her yet."

Zoey frowned and chewed at her lower lip. "Ginger just wanted to be loved. That's all. You know, have someone love her and take care of her." He got the feeling that Zoey not only knew who the man was but she also knew something else, something she wanted to tell him and for some reason was afraid to.

He took a shot in the dark. "This man, did he have money? He must have been older. Powerful?" The kind of man a woman like Ginger would have been attracted to.

Zoey looked away but not before he'd seen the answer in her eyes along with the fear. He felt his heart rate quicken. He was getting close. Was it possible the man was still around?

"Zoey, someone threw your best friend down a well, but when that didn't kill her, he shot her and left her there to die."

All the color drained from her face.

"Before she died, she tried to crawl out," he said.

A cry escaped Zoey's lips. She covered her mouth, her eyes wide and filled with tears.

"Ginger wanted desperately to live. Whoever threw her down that well was trying to get rid of her for good. If this man she was going to marry really loved her, then he would want you to tell me everything you know."

Zoey pulled a napkin from the container on the table and wiped at her eyes. "What about the baby?"

"Baby?"

Zoey nodded. "She was pregnant. Just a few weeks along."

That explained why there hadn't been another skeleton in the well.

Ginger hadn't been far enough along for there to be any evidence of a baby in a pile of bones at the bottom of a well.

But Hud realized it did give the father of the baby a motive for murder. "Did Ginger tell the father about the baby?" Zoey looked down. "Let me guess, he didn't want the baby."

"He *did*," Zoey protested, head coming up. "Ginger said he promised to take care of her and the baby."

"Maybe he did," Hud said solemnly. "Didn't you suspect something was wrong when you didn't hear from her again or she didn't come back for her things?"

"She took everything she wanted with her."

"Didn't she have a car?"

"She sold that."

"But didn't you think it was strange when you didn't hear from her?" he persisted.

"I just thought when things didn't work out that she was embarrassed, you know?"

He stared at Zoey, all his suspicions confirmed. "What made you think things didn't work out?"

She saw her mistake and tried to cover. "I never heard that she got married so…"

"You know things didn't work out because you knew who the man was. He's still in town, isn't he, Zoey? He never left his wife. He killed your friend and her baby and he got away with it."

Her face filled with alarm. "He wouldn't hurt her. He *loved* her." Her expression changed ever so slightly. She'd remembered something, something that made her doubt what she'd just said.

"They fought?" he guessed. "He ever hit her?" Hud was pretty sure he had, given what he suspected the man had done to Ginger at the end.

"Once. But that was just because he didn't want her wearing the engagement ring until…you know…until he was ready for them to announce it," she said. "Ginger forgot to take it off and was wearing the ring around town."

"Engagement ring?"

She nodded. "They fought about it. He wanted her to give it back so she didn't forget and wear it in public again. She refused. He hit her and tried to take it back."

Hud thought of the crime lab's report on the broken fingers of Ginger's left hand.

"What did this ring look like?" he asked, trying to keep the fear out of his voice.

"It was shaped like a diamond only it was green," she said. "He told Ginger it was an emerald, a really expensive one. It looked like it really was. And there were two diamonds, too. So don't you see? He wouldn't have given her an expensive ring like that unless he loved her, right?"

Chapter Thirteen

Dana pulled into the yard in front of the ranch house and parked, relieved to see no other vehicles. She'd worried she would come home to find Jordan searching the house again.

She wondered what he'd been up to all day since apparently he hadn't visited their father in the hospital. Why had Jordan lied about when he'd gotten into town if he hadn't been the one who'd put the doll in the well, who'd left the chocolates, who'd been trying to drive her from the ranch?

Getting out of the pickup, she walked to the porch. Someone had shoveled the steps. Hud no doubt.

Joe came around the side of the porch from his doghouse wagging his tail. He was pretty much deaf but he still seemed to know when she came home.

She rubbed his graying head and climbed the porch, digging for her keys she'd tossed in her purse after forgetting she was locking up the house now.

But as she shoved open the door and looked inside, she wondered why she'd bothered. Someone had ransacked the place.

She cursed and looked down at Joe. He seemed as perplexed as she was. Had he even barked at the intruder? She doubted it. She watched him as he followed her into the torn-up living room. He wasn't even sniffing around or acting as if a stranger had been here.

Because the person who'd torn up the house wasn't a stranger, she thought angrily. It was someone in her family, sure as hell. Jordan.

The house was a mess but nothing looked broken. It appeared he had done a frantic search not taking the time to put anything back where it had been.

She thought about calling Hud, but if she was right and Jordan had done this, his prints were already all over the house so it would prove nothing to find more of them.

Cursing under her breath, she took off her coat and went to work, putting the living room back in order. She had to pull out the vacuum since one of the plants had been turned over and there was dirt everywhere.

She promised she would fix whoever had done this as she turned on the vacuum. Over the roar of the vacuum, she didn't hear the car drive up, didn't hear someone come up the steps and tap at the door. Nor did she see her visitor peer inside to see if she was alone.

HUD DIALED NEEDLES AND PINS the minute he left the Lonesome Pine Café and Zoey.

"Hilde, I need to speak to Dana."

"Hud? Is everything all right?"

"No," he said. "Tell me she's still there."

He heard Hilde sigh and his heart dropped like a stone.

"Hud, she left earlier. She ran an errand and then went to visit her dad. But she should be at the ranch by now."

Hud groaned. Of course she would want to visit her dad again. He should have put a deputy on her. Right. Wouldn't Dana have loved having Norm Turner following her around all day? But Hud would have gladly put up with her wrath just to know she was safe right now.

"Hud, what is it?" Hilde cried. "Do you want me to try to find her?"

"No, I'm not that far away. I can get there quicker." He disconnected, his mind racing with everything he'd learned. The highway was slick with ice. He drove as fast as he could, dialing the ranch house as he did.

The phone rang and rang. Either Dana wasn't home yet or— The woman didn't even have an answering machine?

His radio squawked. He closed the cell phone and grabbed the radio. "Marshal Savage."

"It's Deputy Turner," Liza said, all business. "Angus Cardwell's .38. It doesn't match. Not even close. It wasn't the murder weapon." She sounded disappointed since she'd been so sure it was—based on Angus Cardwell's reaction to her finding the gun in his pickup.

He took in the information, his heart racing a little faster. He'd been sure it would be the gun. And after what Dana had told him about Angus's argument and heart attack, Hud had suspected Jordan Cardwell would turn out to be the person who'd used the gun. Could he be wrong about Jordan's involvement?

"But we do have a match on the prints found on both the doll and the box of chocolates," she said. "They were Jordan Cardwell's."

Jordan. He'd suspected Jordan of a lot more. What bothered Hud was the incident with the doll in the well and the box of undoctored chocolates didn't go together. One was so innocuous. The other was possibly attempted murder on Dana. At the very least, assault on an officer of the law.

"I'm on my way back from Missoula," Liza said. "Anything else you want me to do?"

"No, it's supposed to be your day off. Drive carefully." He disconnected and radioed his other deputy.

"Deputy Turner," Norm said.

"Pick up Jordan Cardwell ASAP," Hud ordered. He heard the deputy's feet hit the floor.

"On what charge, sir?"

"Let's start with assault on a marshal," Hud said. Jordan's mother and Kitty Randolph had been friends. Jordan could have had access to Kitty's ring. "Just find him and get him locked up. Let me know the minute he's behind bars."

As he disconnected, Hud thought about Kitty Randolph's emerald ring. He now knew how it had ended up with Ginger Adams in the well. He just hoped to hell he was wrong about who had killed her.

As DANA SHUT OFF the vacuum, she sensed someone watching her and turned, startled to see a shadow cross the porch.

The doorbell rang. She opened the door and blinked in surprise. "Mrs. Randolph?" The bruise on the older woman's face was darker than it had been earlier in the day. She had what appeared to be that same shoe box under one arm and her hat was askew.

Kitty Randolph smiled. "Hello, dear. I'm sorry to drop by unannounced like this." She looked past Dana. "Did I catch you at a bad time? I was hoping to talk to you. Alone, if possible?"

"Of course, come in."

"You're sure it's not a bad time?" Kitty asked, her gaze going again past Dana into the house.

"Not at all. I was just doing some cleaning myself."

The older woman turned and stuck out one leg to show off her blue slacks. "That thread you sold me was the perfect color blue, don't you think?"

Dana admired the recently hemmed slacks, telling herself this couldn't possibly be the reason Kitty had driven all the way out here. It was probably the upcoming fundraiser. Dana groaned at the thought. The fundraiser was weeks away. Was she going to find Kitty on her doorstep every day until it was over?

"Can I take your coat?" Dana asked, wondering what was in the worn-looking shoe box. Probably old apron patterns. Or recipes.

"The judge always liked me in blue," Kitty said as if she hadn't heard Dana. "That was until his tastes changed to red."

Dana smiled, remembering the red-and-gold master bedroom—and the bright red high-heeled shoe Kitty had tossed back into the closet earlier at her house.

"Would you like something to drink?" Dana asked. "I could put on some coffee. Or would you prefer tea?" She hoped Hud showed up soon, as he'd promised earlier. He might be the only way she could get rid of the woman.

"Neither, thank you. I couldn't help thinking about your visit to my house today," she said, glancing toward the kitchen again. "Sometimes I am so forgetful. You did say you're alone, didn't you?"

"Yes." Was it possible Kitty Randolph had forgotten

that Stacy had visited her last night? "Did you remember something about Stacy?"

"Stacy, interesting woman." Her twinkling blue eyes settled on Dana's face. "How could two sisters be so different? You're so much like your mother and your sister is…" She raised a disapproving brow. "She's an alley cat like your father. But then some women are born to it."

Dana frowned and almost found herself defending her sister. Instead she studied the older woman, noticing that Kitty seemed…different somehow. Oddly animated. She'd always been a soft-spoken, refined woman who'd obviously come from old wealth. She'd never heard Kitty talk like this.

"This must all be very upsetting for you," Dana said. Ginger Adams's body being found in the well had dredged up the judge's murder. Of course Kitty would be distraught.

"Yes, dear, I can't tell you how upsetting it's been." Kitty stepped over to one of the old photographs on the wall and Dana noticed with a start that it was of the old homestead up on the hillside.

"Did I ever tell you that the judge's family were well drillers?" Kitty asked.

"I didn't know that."

Kitty turned and smiled. "The judge's father drilled most every well around here. Including the one up at your family's old homestead."

THE RADIO SQUAWKED AS HUD neared Big Sky—and the Cardwell Ranch.

"I've got Jordan Cardwell here, sir," Deputy Norm Turner said. "He insists on talking to you for his one phone call."

Hud breathed a sigh of relief that Jordan was behind bars. Now at least Dana should be safe. "Put him on."

"Is this about the other night, that thing with the doll and the well?" Jordan demanded.

"You mean, where you tried to kill me?" Hud said.

"I'm telling you the same thing I told Dana, I had nothing to do with it."

"You lied about when you flew in, you lied about your relationship with Ginger Adams, and you expect me to believe you? Save your breath, your fingerprints were found on both the doll—and the box of chocolates."

"I did fly in the day before, the instant I heard about the bones in the well, and I knew Ginger," Jordan said. "I probably touched the stupid doll when I was searching for the will. And I also gave Dana the chocolates. I wanted her to think they were from you. I thought it might make her treat you a little nicer and that it would speed up the investigation so we could get on with selling the ranch."

"You are so thoughtful."

"Listen to me, I do care about my sister," Jordan said. "If I didn't put some stupid doll down in the well to scare Dana, then who did? That person doesn't seem to be behind bars in your quaint little jail."

Hud was silent for a moment, thinking this might be the first time he'd ever believed anything that had come out of Jordan Cardwell's mouth. "Did you steal a ring and give it to Ginger Adams?"

"What? Look, Ginger and I didn't last a month. As soon as she found out I didn't have any money…"

Hud pulled the list of registered .38-caliber gun owners out of his pocket as he drove. It was starting to get dark in the canyon. He had to turn on the overhead light in the SUV, taking his attention off the road in short glances as he scanned the list again.

He found the name he'd feared would be on the sheet. He hadn't even thought to look for it before. Probably because it never dawned on him to look for Judge Raymond Randolph's name. What were the chances he would have been killed with his own gun? The same gun that had killed Ginger Adams?

Hud threw down the sheet, snapped off the light and said, "Let me talk to the deputy." He told Norm to keep Jordan locked up and to get over to Kitty Randolph's and make sure she didn't go anywhere.

Then Hud tried Dana's number again, driving as fast as possible. He had to get to Dana. Every instinct told him she was in trouble.

DANA FELT A SENSE of disquiet settle over her as she stared at Kitty Randolph. "The judge's father drilled the homestead well?"

The phone rang.

"The judge knew every well his father had drilled," Kitty said proudly. "He took me to most of them when we were dating. Most women wouldn't think that very romantic nowadays. But the judge never wanted to forget where he came from. Common well drillers. But that was one reason he was so cheap. The judge was the only one in his family to go to college, you know."

The phone rang again. Mind racing, Dana barely heard it as she watched Kitty move around the room, picking up knickknacks, touching old photographs, admiring antiques that had belonged to Dana's mother's family. The older woman still had the shoe box tucked under her arm.

"Your mother, now there was a woman," Kitty said as she circled the room. "I admired her so much. Your father put her through so much and yet she never complained. She proved she could make it without him just fine. I wish I had been more like her."

Another ring. "I need to get that," Dana said, but for some reason didn't want to leave Kitty alone.

"Have I told you how much you look like your mother?"

"Yes, you've mentioned it," Dana said, thinking again about what Kitty had said about the judge's family drilling the old homestead well.

"It's funny, for a moment earlier today when I saw you standing behind me at my house, I thought you were your mother," Kitty said, then gave her head a light shake. "Sometimes I am so foolish. Your mother was such a strong woman. I admired the way she took care of *her* problems."

Dana felt a chill crawl up her spine as she recalled a comment Jordan had made about how their mother had been capable of killing Ginger Adams and dumping her down the old well.

"Is there something you wanted to tell me about my mother?" Dana asked, frightened of the answer and suddenly afraid of what was in that shoe box under the older woman's arm.

"Oh, Dana, don't be coy with me," Kitty said, her smile shifting ever so slightly. "I know you saw the shoe."

The shoe? The phone rang again. She realized it might be Hud. He'd be worried if she didn't answer it.

"I don't know what shoe you're talking about." Dana had seen a lot of shoes on the floor of Kitty's bedroom and the older woman digging in the closet as if looking for more. She wondered if the older woman wasn't getting senile as she glanced at the shoe box still curled in the crook of the woman's arm.

"The red high heel, dear, you know the one," Kitty said. "Oh, didn't your boyfriend tell you? Only one was found in the well. The other one was in the judge's closet. I'd forgotten all about it until my dear friend Rupert Milligan happened to mention that one red high heel had been found in the well. Rupert has a little crush on me." She actually blushed.

Dana felt her heart stop cold at the realization of what Kitty was saying.

The phone, she really needed to answer the phone. She started to move toward the kitchen.

"Let it ring, dear," Kitty said, and opened the shoe box.

Dana stared in shock as Kitty brought out a .38 and pointed it at her. Dana glanced toward the front door where her shotgun was leaning against the wall as the phone continued to ring.

"I wouldn't if I were you, dear," Kitty said, leveling the gun at Dana's heart. "Let's take a walk."

The phone stopped ringing. "A walk?" Dana said into the deathly silence that followed. What if Hud had been calling to say he was running late? "Mrs. Randolph—"

"Kitty. Call me Kitty, dear." The hand holding the gun was steady, the glint in the twinkling blue eyes steely. "Get your coat. It's cold out."

"I don't understand," Dana said as she carefully took her coat from the hook, afraid she understood only too well. The shotgun was within reach but it wasn't loaded.

Even if it had been, she suspected she would never be able to fire it before Kitty Randolph pulled the trigger.

"I'll explain it to you on our walk," Kitty said agreeably as she jabbed the gun into Dana's back. "We really need to get moving, though. It gets darks so early in the canyon, especially this time of year. We wouldn't want to step in a hole, now would we?" She laughed as Dana opened the door and they descended the porch steps.

Dana suspected she knew where they were headed long before Kitty motioned her up the road toward the old homestead—and the well.

"Oh, and in case you're wondering, the judge taught me how to use a gun," Kitty said. "I'm sure he regretted it since I was a much better shot than he was."

As they walked up the road, Dana saw that a vehicle had been up the hill recently. The same person who'd ransacked the house? Her mind raced. Was it possible Jordan was up here planning to pull another stunt to scare her into selling the ranch?

She couldn't believe it had been Jordan—didn't want to believe it. But right now, she would love to see any member of her family.

"Ginger was a tramp, you know," Kitty said as they walked up the road. The older woman was surprisingly spry for her age. "Your mother wasn't the least bit fazed by her. She knew your father would never have left her for a woman like Ginger Adams. For all your father's flaws, he had better taste than that."

Dana wouldn't have bet on that, she thought as she looked up at the homestead chimney. Had she seen movement up there? Twilight had turned the sky gray.

From the highway she could hear the hum of tires. Hud was on his way. He'd said he would meet her at the ranch house before she got off work. Except she'd come home early. Still he should be here soon. Unless he really had been calling to say he was running late.

"The judge, the old fool, thought he was in love with Ginger," Kitty was saying. "He thought I would give him a divorce so he could marry her. He forgot that the money was all mine. But even then, he would have left me for her and lived on nothing, he was that besotted with her. After thirty years of marriage. Can you imagine? She was just a *child*."

Dana heard the pain in the older woman's voice and looked up, surprised they had reached the old homestead in record time. No wonder, with Kitty nudging her along with the gun.

"He begged me to let him go, the stupid old fool. But I had insurance, something I knew he'd done that could get him disbarred, disgraced and leave him penniless so he wouldn't be able to support his precious Ginger and their baby." Kitty sounded as if she was crying. "We couldn't have a child, you know. But this tramp… I remember the night he brought me that red high-heeled shoe. He was sobbing like a baby. 'Look what you made me do,' he kept saying. 'Oh, God, look what you've made me do.' As if he didn't have a choice."

Dana stumbled and turned to look at Kitty, shocked by the revelation. The judge had killed Ginger Adams on his wife's orders?

"Oh, don't look so shocked," Kitty Randolph said. "Imagine what I would have done that night if I'd known he'd given her my ring? It was the only decent piece of jewelry he'd ever bought me. It never meant that much to me because I'd had to force him to buy it for our anniversary. But even if I never wore it, it was mine and he gave it to that woman. And then to hear it turned up in your well—with *her*."

Dana was too stunned to speak for a moment.

"Let's get this over with," Kitty said and jabbed Dana with the gun, prodding her toward the well opening. Kitty's voice changed, sounding almost childlike. "You don't want to get too close to the edge of the well, dear. You might fall in. It's only natural that you would be curious. Or perhaps you're distraught over the news about your mother. Sorry, dear, but after you're gone it's going to come out that your mother killed Ginger. Mary wouldn't mind, after all she's dead."

Dana balked. "You wouldn't blame my mother."

"I've given it a lot of thought," Kitty said matter-of-factly. "Your mother was afraid, living out here alone, and I lent her the judge's .38. I'd completely forgotten the gun was in the closet until the marshal called to say that Ginger had been killed with the same gun the judge was."

"No one will believe my mother killed Ginger Adams—*and* your husband."

"You are so right, dear. Your sister, the common thief, took the gun while it was in your mother's possession and killed the judge. I'll work out the details later. But when it comes out about your sister stealing fundraiser money and me having it all on video…"

"*You're* the one who forced Stacy to make it look like she and Hud had slept together."

"Oh, dear, you are so smart," Kitty said as she backed Dana toward the well. "I was quite the mastermind if I say so myself. First I hired the Kirk brothers to mow my lawn and then I planted the judge's cuff links and pocket watch in their car. I said I'd be at my sister's that night. With cell phones, no one can tell where you are. Aren't they amazing devices?"

As Kitty backed her into the darkness, Dana could feel the well coming up behind her.

"The judge was at his stupid Toastmasters. I called and told him I thought I'd left the stove on, then I waited until he was on his way home before I called those awful Kirk brothers and told them I'd left them a bonus and to stop by the house and pick it up. The door was open. It was all too easy. You should have seen the judge's face when I shot him twice in the chest."

Dana grimaced. If she'd had any doubt that Kitty would shoot her, she didn't now.

"The Kirk brothers arrived right after that," she continued. "They reacted just as I knew they would when they heard the sirens. Hud's father had been trying to get the goods on them for years. I knew he'd chase them to the ends of the earth. And he literally did. All I had to do was make it look as if the Kirks had broken into my house and then go to my sister's and wait for the terrible news."

Dana stopped moving. She could feel the well directly behind her. One more step and she would fall into it. "Why set up Hud with my sister?"

"Stacy had to do whatever I told her and I knew how badly Hud's father wanted to put those awful Kirk brothers away. He was more apt to believe they had robbed my house and killed my husband than your boyfriend." Kitty smiled, pleased with herself. "Anyway, by doing that I freed you up for my nephew."

"Your *nephew?*"

Something moved by the chimney and Dana watched

as a large dark figure came out of the shadows behind Kitty. Jordan. Let it be Jordan.

"Step back, dear," Kitty said. "Let's not make this any more painful than we have to."

As the figure grew closer, Dana saw the man's face. Not Jordan. "Lanny, be careful, she has a gun!"

Kitty began to laugh, but didn't turn as if she thought Dana was kidding. Then Dana watched in horror as Lanny made no attempt to disarm Kitty.

He leaned down to plant a kiss on the older woman's cheek. "Why would I hurt my dear auntie? Really, Dana, I can attest to how irrational you've been the last few days."

"Kitty is your aunt?"

"By marriage twice removed, but Dana you know that half the people in the canyon are related in some way, you shouldn't be surprised," Lanny said.

"Say your goodbyes, Lanny," Kitty said.

"You aren't going to let her do this," Dana said. "You and I were friends."

Lanny laughed. "Friends? But you are right about one thing, I'm not going to let her do it. I'm going to take care of you, Dana, because quite frankly I'd rather see you dead than with Hudson Savage."

He reached for her and in the twilight she saw the hard glint of anger in his eyes—the same look she'd seen at the restaurant the night of her birthday.

She dodged his grasp and felt one of the stones around the well bump against her ankle as she was forced back. She looked over her shoulder, estimating whether or not she could jump the opening. Maybe if she had a run at it, but the hole was too wide, the snow too slick around it.

She put out her hands, bracing her feet, ready to take Lanny down into the well with her if he grabbed for her again.

"You can make this easy on yourself, Dana. Or fight right up until the end." Lanny smiled. "Makes no difference to me."

"But it does to me," Hud said from out of the darkness.

Both Lanny and his aunt turned in surprise. Dana saw her chance. She dove at Lanny, slamming her palms into his chest with all her strength. He stumbled backward, colliding with his aunt Kitty, but managed to grasp Dana's sleeve and pull her down, as well.

The air exploded with a gunshot and Dana couldn't be sure who'd fired it as she fell to the ground next to Lanny.

She scrambled away from him but he grabbed her ankle and crawled, dragging her, toward the well opening. She noticed that his side bloomed dark red and she realized he'd been shot. But his grip on her ankle was strong.

She tried to latch on to anything she could reach but there was nothing to hang on to and the snow was slick and she slid across it with little effort on Lanny's part.

More gunshots and Dana saw now that Kitty was firing wildly into the darkness. Dana couldn't see Hud, wasn't even sure now that she'd heard his voice. Lanny had a death grip on her leg.

The black gaping hole of the well was so close now that she felt the cold coming up from the bottom.

This time the gunshots were louder, echoing across the hillside. Dana saw Kitty stumble, heard her cry. Out of the corner of her eye, Dana watched Kitty start to fall.

Dana kicked out at Lanny with her free leg. His grip on her ankle loosened as his aunt tripped over him, but managed to remain standing.

He let go of Dana's ankle and for an instant they were all frozen in time. Kitty was looking down at her blue slacks. One leg appeared black in the darkening light. Dana scooted out of Lanny's grasp and was getting to her feet when she heard Hud order, "Put down the gun, Mrs. Randolph."

Kitty looked up, her spine straightening, her chin going up. "I had a bad feeling when you came back to town, Hudson Savage." She smiled and Dana watched the rest play out in slow, sick motion.

Kitty dropped the gun, but Lanny grabbed it up and started to turn it on Dana. She saw the crazed look in his eyes as he gripped the gun and frantically felt for the trigger.

Hud's weapon made a huge booming sound in the deafening silence. The shot caught Lanny in the chest but he was still trying to pull the trigger as another shot exploded and he fell back, his head lolling to one side on the edge of the well.

Dana wrenched the gun from his hands and crawled back away from him and the well.

Kitty was still standing there, head up. The one leg of her slacks looked black with blood. She didn't seem to notice Lanny lying on the ground next to her.

Dana turned as Hud came out of the shadows, his weapon still pointed at Kitty. Out of the corner of her eye, she caught the movement and heard Hud yell, "No!"

Dana turned in time to see Kitty Randolph smile as she stepped back and dropped into the well.

A few seconds later Dana heard the sickening thud as Kitty hit the bottom. But by then, Hud was pulling Dana into his arms and telling her he loved her, over and over again. In the distance she could hear the wail of sirens.

Chapter Fourteen

Hud parked by the Hebgen Lake house and got out, noting that his father's vehicle was in the garage and there were no fresh tracks.

But when he knocked at the door, he got no answer. He tried the knob, not surprised when the door opened in. "Dad?" he called. The word sounded funny and he tried to remember the last time he'd said it.

As he moved through the house, it became more apparent that Brick wasn't there. Hud felt his pulse start as he reminded himself how old his father had seemed the other day, then recalled with shame and embarrassment what he'd said to Brick.

But Hud knew the panicky feeling in the pit of his stomach had more to do with what he hadn't yet said to his father.

"Dad?" he called again.

No answer. He glanced into the bedrooms. Both empty, beds made. Hud had never expected his father to keep such a neat house. Hud's mother had hated housework.

The kitchen was also empty, still smelling faintly of bacon and coffee. But as he looked out the window across the frozen white expanse of the lake, he spotted a lone figure squatting on the ice.

Hud opened the back door and followed the well-worn footprints across patches of glistening wind-crusted ice and drifted snow, his boot soles making a crunching sound as he walked toward his father.

Dressed in a heavy coat and hat, Brick Savage sat on a log stump, a short ice-fishing pole in his gloved hands. The fishing line disappeared down into the perfect hole cut in the ice at his feet.

His father looked up and smiled. "Heard the news. You solved both murders. Figured you would."

Just then the rod jerked. Brick set the hook and hauled a large rainbow trout out of the slushy water and up onto the ice. He picked up the flopping trout, unhooked it and dropped it back into the water.

Hud stood, trying to put into words everything he wanted—needed—to say to his father. Hud had been so sure that his father had set him up so he could kill Judge Raymond Randolph and frame the Kirk brothers. "Dad, I—"

"There's an extra rod," Brick said, cutting him off. He motioned to the rod resting against an adjacent stump.

"You knew I'd be showing up?" Hud asked in surprise.

His dad smiled. "I'd hoped you would."

"There's some things I need to say to you."

Brick shook his head. "Your coming here today says everything I need to hear." He reached over and picked up the short rod and handed it to his son. "If you want, we could keep a few fish and cook them up for lunch. Or if you're in a hurry—"

"No hurry. I haven't had trout in a long time," Hud

said, taking a seat across from his father. "I could stay to eat trout for lunch."

His dad nodded and Hud thought he glimpsed something he'd never seen, tears in his father's eyes. Brick dropped his head to bait his hook and when he looked up again, the tears were gone. If they were ever there.

He watched his father, thinking he might call Dana after lunch to see if she'd like trout for dinner tonight.

"I've been offered the marshal job," he said as he baited his line and dropped it into the hole.

"I'm not surprised."

"I heard you put in a good word for me," Hud said, feeling his throat tighten.

"Rupert's got a big mouth," Brick said but smiled. "The canyon's lucky to get you. Dana pleased about it?"

He nodded and hooked into a fish. "You know about Rupert and Kitty Randolph?"

"I knew he liked her. He's taking it all pretty hard. He likes to think he's smarter than most people when it comes to figuring out criminals," Brick said.

"Kitty fooled a lot of people."

"Yes, she did," Brick said.

They spent the rest of the morning fishing, talking little. Later while Brick was frying up the trout for lunch, Hud called Dana and told her he was bringing trout for dinner.

"You ask her to marry you yet?" Brick asked after he hung up and they were sitting down to eat lunch.

"I'm going to tonight," Hud said.

Without a word, his dad got up from the table and returned a few minutes later with a small velvet box. He set it beside Hud's plate and sat. "I know you bought her an engagement ring before. I couldn't afford an engagement ring for your mother so she never had one. But I was wondering if you'd like to have your grandmother's?"

Hud frowned. He'd never known either of his grandparents. His father's parents were dead before he was born and from what he'd heard, his mother's family had disowned his mother when she'd married Brick. "My grandmother...?"

"Christensen. Your grandmother on your mother's side," he said, and handed the small velvet box to Hud. "She left it to me in her will. I guess it was her way of saying she was sorry for making it so hard on your mother for marrying me." He shrugged. "Anyway, I know your mother would want you to have it."

Hud opened the small velvet box and pulled back in surprise. "It's beautiful."

Brick helped himself to the trout. "Just like Dana."

Hud studied his father. "Thank you."

"There's some money, too," Brick said. "Probably not near enough to pay off Dana's brothers and sister and keep the ranch, though."

"I doubt there is enough money in the world for that," Hud said. "Jordan won't be happy until the ranch is sold, but I'm sure he'll be disappointed when he realizes how small his share is. He would have been much better off if his mother's new will had been found. He would have gotten money for years from the ranch instead of a lump sum, and in the end come out way ahead."

"But he wants it all now," Brick said. "You think he found the new will and destroyed it?"

"Probably."

Brick handed him the plate of trout.

"I got a call from Stacy Cardwell this morning. She's

in Las Vegas. She said Kitty threatened to kill her when she stopped by the woman's place the night before she left. I guess Stacy thought she could get some traveling money out of Kitty as if blackmail went both ways," Hud said, shaking his head.

"It's a wonder Kitty didn't shoot her on the spot."

Hud remembered Dana's story about finding Kitty on her hands and knees digging in the closet. "Probably would have but she'd forgotten she still had the .38. There was a struggle, though. Dana said Kitty had a bruise on her cheek."

Brick nodded. "You could bring Stacy back to face charges."

Hud shook his head. Both Lanny and Kitty were dead. It was over.

He and Brick ate in silence for a while, and then Hud said, "I saw you with Ginger that night."

His father paused, then took a bite of fish. "I remembered after you were gone. I pulled her over that night. She'd been drinking. I thought about taking her in, made her get out of the car and go through the sobriety tests."

Hud recalled the sound of Ginger's laughter. As Hud had driven past, she'd been flirting with Brick, spinning around in that red dress and those bright red high-heeled shoes.

"I saw all her stuff in the back of her car," Brick said.

Hud wondered if the judge or Kitty had gotten rid of Ginger's belongings and her car. No one would have ever known about her death, if Warren hadn't seen her skull at the bottom of the Cardwell Ranch well.

"She told me she was leaving town," Brick was saying. "I told her to be careful. If I'd locked her up that night, she might still be alive."

DANA STOOD IN the kitchen after Hud's call, looking up the hillside. There was no old chimney or foundation anymore. It was as if there'd never been an old homestead up there. Or an old well. A backhoe operator had filled in the well. Soon after the land was cleared, it had begun to snow again, covering up the scarred earth.

Dana thought she could get used to the new view, but it would take time. She frowned at the thought, realizing she didn't have time. After everything that had happened, she had given up her fight to save the ranch. Jordan was right. All she was doing was costing them all attorneys' fees and eventually, she would lose and have to sell anyway. She'd told Jordan he could list the property with a Realtor.

She turned away from the window, turning her thoughts, as well, to more pleasant things. Hud. She smiled, just thinking about him. They'd been inseparable, making love, talking about the future. Even now she missed him and couldn't wait for him to get back.

He was bringing trout for dinner. She was glad he'd gone up to see his father. Her mother had been right about one thing. Family. It *did* matter. Her own father was out of the hospital and planning to be back playing with Uncle Harlan in the band. They'd both offered to play at the wedding. Her father had promised to cut back on his drinking but Dana wasn't holding her breath. She was just glad to still have him.

She smiled, thinking of the wedding she and Hud would have. That is, if he asked her to marry him again.

Since Kitty Randolph's death, a lot of things had

come out about the judge. Some of the things Hud had blamed on his father had been the judge's doing.

Hud had even realized that his mother's bitterness toward Brick was fueled by her family and that it had made Brick into the hard man he was when Hud was growing up.

The past few days had changed them all. At least Dana had decided she was ready to let go of all the old hurts and move on, whatever the future held.

She stopped in the middle of the kitchen as if she'd just felt a warm hand on her shoulder and it was as if she could feel her mother's presence. Wasn't this what her mother had wanted? For her to forgive and forget?

Dana smiled, the feeling warming her as she moved to the cupboard that held all her mother's cookbooks. Like her mother, she loved cookbooks, especially the old ones.

She pulled out her mother's favorite and ran her fingers over the worn cover. Maybe she would make Hud's favorite double-chocolate brownies from her mother's old recipe. She hadn't made them since Hud had left five years before.

As she opened the book, several sheets of lined paper fluttered to the floor. Stooping to pick them up, she caught sight of her mother's handwriting. Her heart leaped to her throat. Hurriedly, she unfolded the pages.

Her heart began to pound harder as she stared down at her mother's missing will.

* * * * *

YOU HAVE
JUST READ A
HARLEQUIN®
INTRIGUE®
BOOK

If you were **captivated** by

the **gripping, page-turning**

romantic suspense, be sure

to look for all six Harlequin®

Intrigue® books every month.

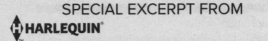
Chapter One

Hank Savage squinted into the sun glaring off the dirty
windshield of his pickup as his family ranch came into
view. He slowed the truck to a stop, resting one sun-
browned arm over the top of the steering wheel as he
took in the Cardwell Ranch.

The ranch with all its log-and-stone structures didn't
appear to have changed in the least. Nor had the two-story
house where he'd grown up. Memories flooded him of
hours spent on the back of a horse, of building forts in the
woods around the creek, of the family sitting around the
large table in the kitchen in the mornings, the sun pouring
in, the sound of laughter. He saw and felt everything he'd
given up, everything he'd run from, everything he'd lost.

"Been a while?" asked the sultry, dark-haired woman in the passenger seat.

He nodded despite the lump in his throat, shoved back his Stetson and wondered what the hell he was doing back here. This was a bad idea, probably his worst ever.

"Having second thoughts?" He'd warned her about his big family, but she'd said she could handle it. He wasn't all that sure even he could handle it. He prided himself on being fearless about most things. Give him a bull that hadn't been ridden and he wouldn't hesitate to climb right on. Same with his job as a lineman. He'd faced gale winds hanging from a pole to get the power back on, braved getting fried more times than he liked to remember.

But coming back here, facing the past? He'd never been more afraid. He knew it was just a matter of time before he saw Naomi—just as he had in his dreams, in his nightmares. She was here, right where he'd left her, waiting for him as she had been for three long years. Waiting for him to come back and make things right.

He looked over at Frankie. "You sure about this?"

She sat up straighter to gaze at the ranch and him, took a breath and let it out. "I am if you are. After all, this was your idea."

Like she had to remind him. "Then I suggest you slide over here." He patted the seat between them and she moved over, cuddling against him as he put his free arm around her. She felt small and fragile, certainly not ready for what he suspected they would be facing. For a moment, he almost changed his mind. It wasn't too late. He didn't have the right to involve her.

"It's going to be okay," she said and nuzzled his neck where his dark hair curled at his collar. "Trust me."

He pulled her closer and let his foot up off the brake. The pickup began to roll toward the ranch. It wasn't that he didn't trust Frankie. He just knew that it was only a matter of time before Naomi came to him, pleading with him to do what he should have done three years ago. He felt a shiver even though the summer day was unseasonably warm.

I'm here.

Chapter Two

"Looking out that window isn't going to make him show up any sooner," Marshal Hud Savage said to his wife.

"I can't help being excited. It's been three years." Dana Cardwell Savage knew she didn't need to tell him how long it had been. Hud had missed his oldest son as much or more than she had. But finally Hank was coming home—and bringing someone with him. "Do you think it's because he's met someone that he's coming back?"

Hud put a large hand on her shoulder. "Let's not jump to any conclusions, okay? We won't know anything until he gets here. I just don't want to see you get your hopes up."

Her hopes were already up, so there was no mitigating that. Family had always been the most important thing to her. Having her sons all fly the nest had been heartbreak, especially Hank, especially under the circumstances.

She told herself not to think about that. Nothing was going to spoil this day. Her oldest son was coming home after all this time. That had to be good news. And he was bringing someone. She hoped that meant Hank was moving on from Naomi.

"Is that his pickup?" she cried as a black truck came into view. She felt goose bumps pop up on her arms. "I think that's him."

"Try not to cry and make a fuss," her husband said even as tears blurred her eyes. "Let them at least get into the yard," he said as she rushed to the front door and threw it open. "Why do I bother?" he mumbled behind her.

Don't miss
Iron Will *by B.J. Daniels,*
available August 2019 wherever
Harlequin® books and ebooks are sold.

www.Harlequin.com

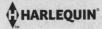

INTRIGUE

EDGE-OF-YOUR-SEAT INTRIGUE, FEARLESS ROMANCE.

Save $1.00

on the purchase of ANY

Harlequin Intrigue® book.

Available wherever books are sold, including most bookstores, supermarkets, drugstores and discount stores.

Save $1.00

on the purchase of any Harlequin Intrigue book.

Coupon valid until November 30, 2019.
Redeemable at participating outlets in the U.S. and Canada only.
Not redeemable at Barnes & Noble stores. Limit one coupon per customer.

52616453

5 65373 00076 2 (8100)0 12428

Canadian Retailers: Harlequin Enterprises Limited will pay the face value of this coupon plus 10.25¢ if submitted by customer for this product only. Any other use constitutes fraud. Coupon is nonassignable. Void if taxed, prohibited or restricted by law. Consumer must pay any government taxes. Void if copied. Inmar Promotional Services ("IPS") customers submit coupons and proof of sales to Harlequin Enterprises Limited, P.O. Box 31000, Scarborough, ON M1R 0E7, Canada. Non-IPS retailer—for reimbursement submit coupons and proof of sales directly to Harlequin Enterprises Limited, Retail Marketing Department, Bay Adelaide Centre, East Tower, 22 Adelaide Street West, 40th Floor, Toronto, Ontario M5H 4E3, Canada.

U.S. Retailers: Harlequin Enterprises Limited will pay the face value of this coupon plus 8¢ if submitted by customer for this product only. Any other use constitutes fraud. Coupon is nonassignable. Void if taxed, prohibited or restricted by law. Consumer must pay any government taxes. Void if copied. For reimbursement submit coupons and proof of sales directly to Harlequin Enterprises, Ltd 482, NCH Marketing Services, P.O. Box 880001, El Paso, TX 88588-0001, U.S.A. Cash value 1/100 cents.

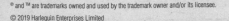

® and ™ are trademarks owned and used by the trademark owner and/or its licensee.

© 2019 Harlequin Enterprises Limited

HICOUP0719

Get 4 FREE REWARDS!

We'll send you 2 FREE Books plus 2 FREE Mystery Gifts.

Harlequin Intrigue® books feature heroes and heroines that confront and survive danger while finding themselves irresistibly drawn to one another.

FREE Value Over **$20**

Need an adrenaline rush from nail-biting tales
(and irresistible males)?

Check out **Harlequin Intrigue**®,
Harlequin® **Romantic Suspense** and
Love Inspired® **Suspense** books!

New books available every month!

CONNECT WITH US AT:

Facebook.com/groups/HarlequinConnection

 Facebook.com/HarlequinBooks

 Twitter.com/HarlequinBooks

 Instagram.com/HarlequinBooks

Pinterest.com/HarlequinBooks

ReaderService.com

**ROMANCE WHEN
YOU NEED IT**

SGENRE2018R